Other Books by Karen Baney

Prescott Pioneers Series
A Dream Unfolding
A Heart Renewed
A Life Restored
A Hope Revealed

Contemporary Romance
Nickels

Prescott Pioneers Book 2:

A Heart Renewed

By Karen Baney

Prescott Pioneers Book 2: A Heart Renewed
By Karen Baney

Publisher:
Author Services International, LLC
3317 South Higley Road
Suite 114-288
Gilbert, AZ 85297

www.karenbaney.com

Printed in the United States of America
First Printing: April 2011
Second Edition
ISBN- 978-0-9835486-2-1

To the women at Homes of Hope,
Your stories of renewed
hearts have inspired me in my own journey.

The LORD is close to the brokenhearted
and saves those who are crushed in spirit.
Psalm 34:18

Chapter 1

Star C Ranch, Texas

July 4, 1864

"You cannot be serious, Reuben!" Julia Colter shouted, not caring that she might wake her niece and nephew from their afternoon nap. Pacing back and forth across the length of the kitchen, she stopped in front of her older brother, her temper flaring almost as hot as the stove. "He is balding and fat and twice my age!"

"You will marry who I say!" Reuben thundered. "I expect you to treat Mr. Hiram Norton with the upmost respect this evening. He has shown great interest in you and the least you can do is be civil with the man."

"But, I could never love him!"

As Reuben shoved her violently up against the wall, Julia's breath left her lungs in a rush. Digging his fingers into her arms, she could feel the bruises starting to form. His brown eyes darkened with unrestrained anger as he glared down at her. She swallowed in fear, stunned by his abrupt action.

"Stop, you're hurting me," she said, trying to break free from his vice like grip.

He raised his hand as if he meant to strike her—something he had never done before. The action startled her to silence. Instead of hitting her across the face, as she thought he might, Reuben returned his hands to her upper arms squeezing even harder.

Leaning so close the heat of his breath warmed her cheeks, he said, "You have no idea what hurt is, Julia. You are an insolent little whelp. You will paste a smile on that tart little face of yours. And you will do your best to win his affections or," his voice menacing, "you will suffer my wrath, the likes of which you have yet to see."

Releasing his hold, he pushed her so hard that she tumbled to the floor in a heap. As he turned to walk away, he added in a sinister tone, "It would be best if you get used to the idea of Hiram Norton and give up fanciful notions of love, dear sister. You will not have that luxury. The sooner you come to accept that, the better it will go for you."

She sat in stunned silence as Reuben stalked to his office down the hall. Tears streaming down her face, Julia bolted to her feet, running out the front door of the ranch house to the nearby stables, still frightened by her brother's brutal behavior.

The smell of hay and horse assaulted her delicate senses as she selected a gentle mare. Throwing her saddle on the horse's back, she led her from the barn. Once under the open blue skies, she shoved one foot into the stirrup, swinging her other leg over the mare, riding astride. Nudging the mare into a full gallop, Julia fled to the one place she would always feel free—the back of a horse in the wide open pastures.

Reuben may be her guardian now, but she had only to endure a few more years of this before she would be of age and in control of her life. If only she could stop him from marrying her off before then.

At seventeen, she considered herself too young to get married, though many women her age and younger married. She wasn't ready. She didn't pine for the responsibilities marriage entailed. She liked her freedom. But, when she was ready to marry, she would marry for love and not because Reuben wished it.

Certainly, she would never marry Hiram Norton. The thirty-seven year old rancher was the exact opposite of what Julia wanted for a husband. His short stature and fading hairline made him look even older. He had a reputation for loving excess. When it came to food, his waistline showed the results of that love. There were other unsavory aspects to his reputation as well—including rumors that he frequented the saloon and brothel.

No, the man for Julia would be young and handsome. His character would be impeccable, his honor undeniable. Land, money, and wealth held no importance to her. She only cared that her dream man would be able to provide for her and their family.

As the wind tangled her long, sandy brown curls, she continued to press the horse for more speed—needing it to soothe her fear and anger. In the distance the herd of longhorns kicked up dust. The sight sparked a memory of Will, the kinder, more honorable of the Colter brothers, sending her mind racing in another direction. So many times he'd taken Julia out to the pasture, teaching her how to rope, ride, and work with the cattle. Some thought such behavior unacceptable for a lady. She was glad to learn these skills. Should her handsome young dream man end up being a rancher, he might appreciate her ability to work the ranch by his side.

Why hasn't Will written? The thought of him brought fresh tears as memories of his hasty departure flooded her mind. Not only had she buried her father, but she also lost the brother she was close to—all within a few short weeks. Almost a year ago, following her father's death, Reuben forced Will to leave the ranch when he had been deeded the house and ranch. While Will and Reuben both received half of the herd and the financial holdings, Will was left with no home or land. Unable to find anything close, he moved to the Arizona Territory, leaving Julia behind. Alone.

The only time she heard from him was in November 1863. Will wrote that he, his men, and his cattle arrived safely and set up their new home near the Granite Creek settlement in the Arizona Territory—wherever that was. No other letters came.

Despite the thirteen year age difference between Will and Julia, they adored each other. She followed him everywhere, never far from his side even when he worked with the herd. When she needed protecting, it was Will who came to her defense.

Oh, how she could use his protection now. If he were here, he would stop Reuben from forcing her to marry that awful Hiram Norton.

But, he wasn't here. He was in a distant territory, far from Texas, far from her aid. Her father left her in Reuben's care—not Will's—even though Will would have been the better choice as far as Julia was concerned.

Their father never saw the evil that clouded Reuben's heart and he knew nothing of his manipulative ways. In her father's eyes, Reuben was as good of a son as Will. If her father knew of Reuben's late nights in town or of his forceful tactics for bankrupting other ranchers and taking over their lands, he turned a blind eye. She found it hard to fathom that father could have missed such thinly concealed behavior.

As the mare started to struggle for breath, sides heaving with great effort, Julia eased up the pace. She was so torn. She had thought more than once to runaway to Arizona, but was afraid Reuben would find her and drag her back. Now he wanted her to flirt with Hiram Norton and get him to marry her. She had no desire to do what Reuben was asking. Mr. Norton may be wealthy, but he was twenty years older than her. There was something indecent in that alone. Nothing about him or his character appealed to her.

Realizing she was nearing the outer pasture, Julia turned the mare around to head back to the ranch house. She did not want to risk angering Reuben further by being unprepared for their dinner guests. *Lord, please don't make me have to marry that repulsive man. Will always said you could work things together for good. I am not seeing much good right now. Please give me the strength to make it through this evening meal.*

As she pulled the mare to a stop in front of the stables, she slid off the horse. One of the young cowboys, Bates, took the reins from her hand.

"Miss Colter, you best hurry," he said, nodding toward the lane leading to the ranch house.

A cloud of dust at the far end of the lane indicated their guests were already arriving. Julia shot a quick word of thanks to the friendly cowboy before picking up her skirts and running to the house. Reuben stood waiting with fury written on his face.

Rushing down the hall she slammed her bedroom door shut. She splashed some water on her face, wiping away the dust from her ride.

"Where have you been?" Mary's panicked voice preceded her entrance into Julia's room. Reuben's normally calm, quiet wife seemed rather anxious as she picked up the corset she laid out.

"Riding."

"Whatever for?" came the squeaky, agitated response.

Julia tore off her day dress, tossing it over a chair. As Mary came to assist her with the corset, she took her last deep breath of the evening. She hated the confining contraption. Once the stays were tightened, she lifted her arms as Mary helped settle the lovely yellow silk down over her shoulders.

"You should have been in here an hour ago," Mary lamented. "Now there is no possible way we can fashion your hair into ringlets.

The other women will think you don't care about your appearance."

They would be correct, Julia thought. "You fret, too much," she replied, brushing out her tangled curls. She would be content with twisting her unruly hair into a chignon, despite how much it fought against the pins.

"Go on. I'll finish," she instructed Mary, hoping to have a quiet moment to compose herself before entering the fray.

Mary hesitated for a brief moment before softly exiting the room. Taking as deep a breath as she could, Julia let it out in a heavy sigh. Undoubtedly, Hiram Norton was already here, waiting for her in the other room. Pasting a smile on her face, she squared her shoulders and left the solitude of her room.

"Hiram," Reuben said as Julia approached, "I do not believe you have met my sister, Julia."

It took every ounce of courage to hold her smile steady and extend her hand towards Mr. Norton's rotund frame. Taking her hand, he placed a sloppy kiss on top. "Reuben, where have you been hiding this lovely filly?"

Filly? The distasteful comment sickened her.

"Mr. Norton, a pleasure to meet you," Julia said with more decorum than she thought she possessed. As soon as his hold lifted, she discretely wiped the back of her hand on her dress.

"Miss Colter, you are absolutely stunning," he replied, allowing his lustful gaze to rove over her neckline, down her curvy figure, making overtly inappropriate stops along the way.

She fought to tamp down her mounting abhorrence. As the guests were seated around the table, she eagerly helped Mary set out the food.

Still irritated by Mr. Norton's uncouth comment, she decided to fight back as she took her seat. "Mr. Norton, my brother tells me you have been very successful with your ranch, despite the Union's blockade. Tell me, how do you do it?"

Reuben's eyes narrowed slightly, letting her know he caught her barely hidden sarcasm.

"My lovely Miss Colter, such matters are too complicated for your simple mind to understand."

Another mark against Mr. Norton—condescension towards women, she thought, keeping the sweet smile firmly in place. Lobing a spoonful of potatoes on her plate she waited for him to continue.

"However, I shall endeavor to enlighten you," he said with an air of superiority, snatching the potatoes from her hand. "While the Union may have blockaded our route to drive cattle to the New Orleans market, they have made no such effort to stop us from driving to points north or west. It seems that as long as we aren't supplying the Confederate Army, they care little where we sell our cattle. We have simply changed our route north to the railways in Missouri. While I don't care for the Union and their imposing ways, a profit is a profit. And I have made significant gains by being one of the first Texans to sell to eastern markets by way of Missouri."

"If a large profit is to your liking, why not drive the cattle west towards the California market where prices are more than triple that of the eastern markets?"

Reuben shifted in his chair uncomfortably. His darkening eyes warned her to hold her tongue. She knew she should have heeded the warning, but she preferred being forthright. Let Mr. Norton find that out now.

Mr. Norton laughed off her question, causing her to dislike him even more. "You are a spirited little woman, I will give you that. But your comment shows your youth and your naivety."

Taking not one, but two large pork chops from the platter she handed him, he said, "While the prices west are much higher, so is the cost to drive the cattle such a great distance. The length of time it takes to drive the cattle to California is almost three times as long as the northern route. It is also much more dangerous. There are many more Indians and cattle thieves westward. It would simply not be profitable to drive the herd west."

His snooty tone grated on her nerves. When she opened her mouth to speak, Reuben interrupted. "Perhaps, dear sister, you should leave the business matters to men. I'm sure you would be much more interested in knowing how Mrs. Withers' new baby is faring."

Mrs. Withers quickly picked up the conversation, monopolizing both Julia and Mary's time. While Julia was surprised Reuben even knew the woman had a child, she was thankful for the opportunity to ignore Mr. Norton.

As the conversation continued, she felt something brush against her knee then move away. She kept her focus on Mrs. Withers' overlong description of her young son and on eating the meal, until she felt the unmistakable presence of a man's hand move above her knee. She stole a glance and confirmed Mr. Norton's hand rested most inappropriately on her thigh. Angling her legs further away from him as discreetly as possible, her stomach churned. When Mr. Norton pressed closer, she thought she might lose her dinner. The man appeared to have no limits.

Standing abruptly, she said, "If you'll excuse me. I'm not feeling quite myself." Without waiting for a reply she hurried to her room.

Reuben scowled after his sister. Her behavior had been completely unacceptable, despite his attempt earlier in the day to reason with her. This silly idea of marrying for love must have worked its way into her thinking from the stories their father told of their mother. No one married for love.

He certainly hadn't. While Mary was pleasant looking enough and easy to control, he did not love his wife. He had married her to increase his social standing among the area ranchers—something his father never seemed to care about. Her father had been one of the wealthier men in the area and he was easy to win over. In fact, Reuben thought, most everyone he met was easy to manipulate—except Will and Julia.

It didn't matter. Will was gone and out of the picture. He was no longer a nuisance, even though it was Will's fault that he was in such a financial mess. When he left with half the herd and half the financial holdings, Reuben was unable to pay debts to some very powerful men—a situation he was desperately trying to resolve.

The last bite of his pork chop churned in his stomach as fear gained a foothold. He needed Hiram's money from the marriage arrangement to Julia. It was his only hope of turning things around.

As his guests finished the meal, Reuben stood. "Gentlemen, shall we retire to the front porch for some refreshments and cigars?"

The men eagerly nodded, obviously wanting to be away from the women as quickly as he did. As Hiram stood, Reuben pulled him aside. Speaking loud enough for the others to hear, he said, "We'll join you in a moment. Hiram and I have a few business matters to discuss."

Leading Hiram back towards his office, Reuben hoped Hiram would still be amiable to the agreement they discussed several days ago at the saloon, despite Julia's less than enthusiastic attitude this evening.

Before he offered a seat, Hiram took one, starting the conversation on his terms. "Julia is quite lovely. You've been holding out on me. When you asked for such a large sum, I assumed she must be dreadful to look at."

"So you are pleased?"

"To a point. While she'll keep me entertained, she needs to learn to control her tongue, especially in front of guests. I'm surprised you haven't dealt with this already."

Reuben frowned. If only Hiram knew what he was up against. With any luck, he wouldn't find out until after his wedding day. "Well, Father has only been gone a short time. He doted on her, so it will take some time to teach her to properly respect a man."

"Ah, there's the catch. I'll have to train her myself then." Hiram laughed. "It will be a fun challenge—breaking her. Too bad you didn't have more time to do the job yourself. You could get a much higher price for her, as beautiful as she is."

The price he was asking was enough. Normally prone to greediness, when it came to selling his sister's hand in marriage, he felt it prudent not to get too greedy. He was running out of time and needed to pay his debts soon. Once that pressure slackened, he could focus his energy on rebuilding his wealth.

A brief hint of remorse came over Reuben. Had he stooped so low that he was selling his sister for money? But, it was not as if he were selling her to a brothel. No, he was just selling her to a wealthy rancher. She would live in luxury. What could be bad about that?

He knew living with Hiram Norton would not be pleasant. The man had a reputation for being ruthless to his business associates, to his women, and even to his mother. He had no limits. He made Reuben look like a saint. Julia would undoubtedly be miserable married to him until she learned her place.

Chiding himself, he refocused his attention back to what Hiram was saying. He needed this man's money, not a sudden case of conscience.

"After we have our cigars," Hiram was saying, "then, I will take Julia for a walk. See if I still fancy her. When I return, we will announce our engagement. It will be short. No longer than a month."

Reuben held back a gasp. He hadn't expected Norton to want a short engagement. "You know what the townsfolk will say with such a quick wedding. They will think my sister has been compromised."

Pulling a large stack of bills from his coat pocket, Hiram slammed it down on the desk. "I don't think you will care too much what is said about your sister's reputation. Who knows, what they say may end up being true anyway."

The dark look on Hiram's face sent shivers down Reuben's spine. Ruthless seemed a rather inadequate word to describe the man before him. He had to make sure Julia did not ruin this deal, for he did not want the added pressure of Norton's anger.

Mary knocked on Julia's door not more than ten minutes after she left the meal. Her voice was timid when she spoke. "The men have retired to the front porch for cigars. Reuben requested that you return to the parlor with the women."

Sighing, Julia did as instructed. She listened to the gossip of the rancher's wives and wished her friend Caroline Larson was in attendance, so she might actually be able to enjoy the evening. The Larsons owned a ranch to the east of the Star C and they had been longtime family friends. Before father passed away last year, the Larsons were always invited for every social gathering—sometimes they were the only guests. Since then, Reuben saw little use for Mr. Larson's moral ways and only included them on rare occasions to pacify her or his wife.

Not paying attention to the boring conversation, Julia missed seeing the men return from the outdoors. Mr. Norton's hand on her forearm jolted her from her thoughts. "Miss Colter, I was hoping you might take a walk with me."

"And who will be acting as chaperone?" she replied coyly, not wanting to be alone in his presence.

Mr. Norton laughed, a sound she was beginning to detest. "Silly girl, I am much too old for a chaperone. I assure you, your reputation will be safe with me. I simply want to stroll for a few moments with a beautiful woman on my arm."

She thought a stroll might be too much for the man. He was sweating profusely and seemed to have difficulty walking the distance to the door, as his breath came in short, heavy bursts. She looked to Mary for support. She smiled and nodded her approval, oblivious to Mr. Norton's reprehensible behavior. As Reuben stood next to Mary, his eyes narrowed with a silent warning. Heeding the unspoken message, she stood and accepted Mr. Norton's arm.

Outside, the air barely cooled in the waning sunlight. Julia grew warm in a matter of seconds. She wished she thought to grab her fan when a sour odor wafted from the man at her side. Averting her face, she tried to catch an untainted breath of air. Unsuccessful, she decided parting her lips to breathe through her mouth might be preferable.

Nearing the stables, Mr. Norton stopped abruptly, turning towards her. The quick motion—seemingly impossible coming from the man who seemed to struggle walking much of a distance— frightened her. Sucking in air quickly through her mouth, a slight tickle lingered in the back of her throat, almost bringing on a cough.

When he spoke, his voice took on a sinister edge. Even in the dimming light she could see the contempt in his eyes. "Miss Colter, while I admire your feisty spirit," he said as he grabbed her wrists. "It would serve you not to embarrass me again, especially by questioning my business practices in a room full of my peers. I can make your life most unbearable if you cross me." Without warning he pulled her close and crushed his mouth down on hers as his hands took great liberty in exploring her body.

The shock of his action took a moment to register. Once it did, Julia brought her booted heel down hard on the top center of his foot, just as Will showed her. He dropped his hold instantly, crying out in pain. As he limped toward her, she ran for the front of the house to put some distance between them. She stumbled on a rock, giving Mr.

Norton time to catch up. He grabbed her bruised upper arms with surprising strength.

"Do not ever do that again," he said in a hostile tone. "Do you not know that Reuben has promised you to me? Make no mistake, *Miss* Colter, I am a powerful man. If you want to live a decent, peaceful life under my roof, you best lose some of your haughtiness. Or, I will take whatever measures necessary to force it out of you."

She blinked, trying to absorb all that he said. Was he saying that Reuben already agreed to her marrying this loathsome man? An ominous chill swept over her as he continued his intense stare. Her heart beat rapidly within her chest as her panic rose. She could not— would not—marry this dreadful man!

Dropping his hold on her, Mr. Norton extended his arm and placed her hand in the crook. "Smile," he commanded as he limped to open the front door.

Though her smile came insincerely, his seemed quite pleased. He crossed the room slowly, still favoring his injured foot, before stopping in front of Reuben and Mary. "Reuben, it gives me great pleasure to announce that Julia has eagerly agreed to accept my offer of marriage. She was so delighted that she agreed to a short engagement. We will be married in a month." His fingernails dug into her arm daring her to speak otherwise.

The smirk on Reuben's face told her this had been their plan all along. Such a public announcement, even though it was completely false, would be difficult to break. *Lord, help me. I cannot marry that man.*

Chapter 2

Larson Ranch, Texas

August 4, 1864

Adam Larson glanced up, watching the approaching rider pull to an abrupt stop in front of the ranch house. A smile twitched at the corner of his mouth as he watched her dismount from riding astride in a dress. To the best of his knowledge, only one woman in the area dared to bend the rules of proper society in such a way. As Caroline's squeal floated across the distance from the house to the corral, his suspicions were confirmed. The rider was indeed Julia Colter.

Leading the young gelding through a series of training exercises, he wondered again about Julia's decision to marry Hiram Norton. He heard the news, not from Caroline as he expected, but rather from one of the neighboring ranchers who witnessed the strange announcement. It made no sense. She was far too spirited to be tied down to someone so controlling. And she was half his age. There were plenty of eligible men much closer to her age—including his older brother Georgie. Even Adam himself would be considered a good match.

The thought startled him. To think of him married to Julia. She was nice enough to look at. But, he knew her far too well. She was audacious, unconventional, and mischievous. Too much of a tomboy for most men, though she might make a fine wife for a rancher—if he needed help with herd and didn't care if or when supper was ready.

Any man that married her would be in for a lifetime of trouble.

As Julia and Caroline took a seat on the front porch, he waved. Though he struggled to think of the young girl he knew for years as a woman, he did have eyes. It was hard not to notice Julia's shapely figure. She was most definitely a woman now. No doubt that's what

Hiram Norton saw in her.

Yet, what could she possibly see in Hiram? Adam heard the rumors about Hiram's shady business dealings. He personally witnessed the man leaving the saloon in the clutches of a soiled dove on more than one visit to town. Surely Julia knew of his unsavory reputation. He could not envision her marrying such a man.

Snorting, the gelding drew Adam's attention back to the training, though his mind didn't stay there long.

The Larson and Colter families had been friends as long as Adam could remember. Many Sunday afternoons and holidays passed with the two families enjoying each other's company. Since the Colter brothers were already grown men when he was a young lad, Adam spent most of his time cajoling Caroline and Julia into his boyish pursuits—not too difficult a task, given Julia's adventurous personality and the fact that Will taught her many manly skills. Caroline didn't stand a chance against the two of them.

Once, at the age of thirteen, Julia challenged him to a roping contest after school in the playground. At fifteen, his confidence soared. He planned to embarrass her for brashness. Instead, he left the schoolyard that day embarrassed at being trounced by a girl—a younger girl nonetheless. When she finally caught up with him, he saw the innocence in her eyes and easily forgave her. She hadn't intended to wound his male ego in the slightest. She was just being her usual competitive and flamboyant self.

Still, he sensed things began to change after that. He focused more of his time and energy towards helping his pa build up their horse breeding business. He spent less and less time hanging out with Julia and his sister. The friendship, while not ending, took a different shape—one involving much less contact as the years rolled by. Frowning, he tried to remember the last time he spoke to Julia other than in passing at church. Had her birthday in January really been the last time their family visited the Star C? That was nearly eight months ago.

"You seem a bit distracted, son," Pa commented, placing a strong hand on his shoulder. His pa turned his head to follow Adam's line of sight. "Julia's visiting."

Adam nodded. "Why do you suppose she wants to marry Hiram?" he asked, even though it wasn't his concern, but also knowing his pa would give him a straight answer.

Pa laughed, his eyes sparkling. "I don't think any man understands the heart of a woman."

After Adam took the gelding around in another circle, his pa spoke again, more seriously. "Wondered a bit myself if Reuben isn't pressuring her into such a union. Certainly seems far different from the Julia we know." Pa's voice faded to a mutter, only deepening Adam's apprehension on Julia's behalf.

"Caroline, what am I going to do? The wedding is just over a week away and I still have no idea how to get out of this." Julia voiced her fears, her throat constricting in panic. "I cannot marry that wretched man. I never agreed to his offer." Having previously shared the details of her awful, unwanted engagement with her dear friend, she hoped they would have come up with a way out by now. They hadn't.

"Let me think for a minute," Caroline said, tilting her head to one side.

Julia paced under the shade of the Larson's porch while Caroline remained seated, her boots giving sound to the agitation wound so deeply in her soul. As her friend tapped her finger rapidly against her temple, Julia knew she was thinking through the situation. *Please Lord, provide me a way out of this.* The familiar prayer echoed through her mind as she walked back across the length of the porch.

For weeks, she prayed, begging God for a resolution to this situation that would not involve her becoming Hiram's wife. For weeks, her prayer went unanswered. She endured Hiram's forceful kisses with each of his visits and she wearied of the feel of his hands on her body. Bile crept up her throat as she recalled his last visit to the ranch when he tried to take advantage of her, before she managed to free herself. Sharing a bed with this man for the rest of her life—she shuddered at the thought—would be completely unbearable.

Wringing her hands, she walked the length of the porch again.

At last, Caroline shot to her feet. "I've got it!" Excited green eyes looked in her direction as the sun reflected off of her golden blonde hair.

Julia's anxious posture remained, though her feet stilled. "What?" she asked, hopeful.

"Well, since the engagement was very publicly announced, I think the only way out of this is a very public denouncement."

Julia nodded.

"And it will do you no good to appeal to Reuben or that nasty Mr. Norton privately."

It hadn't. She tried several times, only becoming more discouraged with each attempt.

"The only way to ensure there is an end to this charade is to end it—very publicly."

"How?" The dim light of hope flickered a little brighter.

"What you need to do is break off the engagement on Sunday morning following the service at the church in front of everyone."

"At church?" Julia shrieked, picturing herself forever shunned after such a display.

Caroline held up her hand, stopping her from further protests. "Hear me out. Mr. Norton will, of course, be there and insist you sit next to him. Throughout the service, you should appear distracted, maybe even distraught. Then, as the two of you are leaving the church, you break down in tears and accuse him of being with another woman."

"But, that's a lie." Did the path to freedom have to involve dishonesty?

"Julia, do you want to escape this or not?"

At her nod Caroline continued, "Then you tell him that you cannot marry someone who would bed another woman even before his wedding vows have been uttered. Don't give him a chance to respond and make it very clear that you will not marry him ever. Then, don't get in the carriage. Instead, take my brother's horse and ride off. Once you're gone, I'll reinforce that you will never marry such a man."

As she considered the idea, her friend anticipated her reservations. "I know that you don't know for *certain* that Mr. Norton has given himself to another woman. But everyone will believe you—especially given his reputation." Taking her hands,

Caroline gave them firm squeeze. "This will work. I know it."

Julia bit her lip as she remembered his stern warning the night of their engagement. She feared how Mr. Norton might treat her should this plan fail. Trying to mask her despair, she asked, "Won't Adam be mad if I steal his horse?"

Caroline rolled her eyes. "You're not stealing it. You will be distraught and looking for transportation. It will be a matter of convenience that his horse is the one you will *borrow*. I'll send him over to fetch it later in the afternoon. You can relay any messages to me through him to let me know how you are faring."

Julia folded her arms around her waist. "If this fails…"

"We'll pray for success," Caroline reassured her with great optimism. "I can't imagine that God wants you with that man any more than you want to be with him."

After several silent seconds passed, she looked at Caroline out of the corner of her eye as hope took deeper root. "I hope I never cross you. Your mind is quite devious." She laughed nervously.

"These are desperate circumstances. I want to see you wed the man of your dreams and not be forced into a dreadful lifelong marriage."

Hugging her friend, Julia smiled for the first time in weeks. Just maybe this would turn out alright.

Adam waited impatiently as Georgie pulled the wagon to a stop in front of the house a few hours after Julia left. Eager to see if a letter arrived for him, he led the gelding back to the stables. The minutes of brushing down the animal seemed like hours as he thought of what news might await him. If he received the news he hoped for, his dream would begin to take shape, even though it meant leaving the loving home of his family.

The last year had been difficult on the Texas cattle industry. The primary market for his father's cattle was in New Orleans, which was being blockaded by Union troops, forcing prices down to an unsustainable level. With falling prices and the added strain of finding new markets, the Larson's horse breeding business also suffered. Many ranchers were pulling up and moving to the west or northwest, leaving less of a demand for Larson's quality horses. So, the family ranch suffered losses in both areas.

For the past several months, these losses gave Adam pause as he considered his future. At nineteen years old, it was time for him to determine what path he would take—whether it involved continuing to work at his father's side with the horses or striking out on his own. Each option held significant risks and rewards, which he weighed cautiously. Finally, he sent a letter inquiring about an opportunity—one that would allow him to be independent, yet have some safety in knowing he would not be alone.

Once he finished caring for his horse, it was all he could do to walk calmly into the house and ask Mama if Georgie brought him a letter from town. When she handed it over with a confused look, he knew she read the return address. Giving her a quick kiss on the cheek, he sprinted to his room closing the door behind him. Plopping down on his bed, Adam tore open the much anticipated letter from Will Colter.

June 3, 1864

Dear Mr. Adam Larson,

I was pleased to receive your letter inquiring about the possibility of starting horse breeding operations at Colter Ranch. I had been thinking on the idea before receiving your recent letter—although as mail goes in the West, nothing seems to be recent.

While you were just barely eighteen when I left Texas last year, your father mentioned more than once that you have a natural talent with horses and that you have been, as you confirmed in your letter, the primary breeder and trainer for the past few years. I know well the quality of horseflesh produced from Larson's stables, as Jackson, the stallion I brought from Texas, is still the best animal I have ever owned.

With so many settlers and ranchers arriving in the Prescott area, that is what they call the nearby town, and with the cavalry stationed at Fort Whipple, there is a great need here for quality horses. I have already begun plans for building a larger barn and have made arrangements to purchase a few additional studs, hoping to position Colter Ranch in such a way as to meet that need.

Please consider this my formal request to employ you as the breeder and trainer at Colter Ranch. I realize that you may need time to make arrangements and say goodbye to your family. I also realize that the mail is incredibly slow here. Would it be possible for you to leave Texas by September? If you follow the same route that I did, you should be here by early November at the latest. Perhaps you could send me a brief letter in reply letting me know your plans, although you may very well arrive before it does.

I am looking forward to your arrival.

Sincerely,

William Colter

Adam could not believe his eyes. Will Colter hired him! He was moving to the Arizona Territory!

There was much to do in the next few weeks to get ready. He would need to purchase supplies for the trip. He would also need to speak with his father. Folding the letter neatly, Adam stood and went to find his parents.

After a quick peek in the kitchen to confirm his mother was there, he went in search of his father. George Larson was in the stables having just finished rubbing down the mare he rode that morning. A pang of nostalgia hit as he watched his pa. Both father and son were roughly the same height and build, short but well-muscled. Pa ran his hands through his golden blonde hair—the same hair Adam sported. When he cleared his throat, his pa looked up. Sometimes when he looked at his father, it was almost as if he was looking at himself in the future. *Will I start to show signs of gray hair at that age?*

"Pa, I have some news." Adam hesitated, suddenly very nervous. "But, I want to tell you and Ma together."

"Of course, son. Why don't you go in and see if your Ma has some coffee on. I'm almost finished here."

Adam did as requested. His mother's questioning look did not help his nervousness, but he was relieved his father didn't make him wait too long before joining them.

"Now, why don't you tell us what this is all about?" Ma asked as she handed each of them a cup of black coffee.

Taking the seat across from his parents, Adam took a quick sip of the beverage, considering how he might explain his plan, his dream, and the move it would entail.

"Pa, Ma, you know how much I love you and Georgie, and Caroline, and the girls…" He smiled at his own reference to his three youngest sisters as his parents nodded. "And you know how you've always encouraged me to find my own dream."

Ma's green eyes misted with unshed tears. Pa nodded again, fidgeting with his untouched coffee.

"I have made the decision to move to the Arizona Territory," he blurted out, mentally kicking himself for his lack of finesse and the whimper it caused to escape from his mother's lips.

"A while ago, I sent Will Colter a letter asking about setting up horse breeding and training operations on his ranch. I received his answer this afternoon and he said that he wants to hire me."

The pride in his father's eyes was almost too much. Glancing away, Adam continued, "I know it is a long way from home, but I need to be able to make my own way. Be my own man."

"Son, you have our blessing," his father said softly, reaching across the table to grasp his hand in an uncharacteristic move.

A few of the tears escaped the brim of his mother's eyes as she asked, "When will you leave?"

"The first of September. Maybe a little earlier if I can gather everything I need by then."

"So, soon?" Her voice caught.

Adam nodded.

"Now dear, it will be just fine," Pa said turning to his wife. "Adam is a fine young man and he will make us proud… Already has."

"But, I will miss you so."

"I know, Ma. I will miss you both… All of you… But, I believe this is the direction I am to take."

"Son, I know you have prayed about your future for some time, and we have as well." His pa stood, moving to his side. "We will miss you greatly, but you're right, I believe this is God's calling for your life. And God willing, someday travel between our two homes will be easier and we will get to see you again."

Moisture collected in the corner of Adam's eyes as his pa pulled him into a giant bear hug. Blinking quickly, he regained control. It was going to be harder than he thought to leave his family.

That evening following supper, Pa broached the subject to the entire family. "Adam has something he wants to tell us."

Clearing his throat of a sudden lump, Adam took a deep breath. "I'm moving to the Arizona Territory to work with the horses at Will Colter's ranch."

Nine year old Helen jumped up from her chair without asking permission to leave her seat. Launching herself into his arms, she cried, "I don't want you to go!"

Bethie, just a year older than Helen, stayed in her seat, but echoed her sister's complaint. Fiery red-headed Missy flashed blue eyes of shock his direction—for once speechless.

"When will you leave?" Caroline asked. Her normally jubilant smile vanished.

"First of September."

"So soon?" the fourteen year old Missy asked. "Can't you wait until the first of the year?"

Adam smiled. "Then I suppose at the first of the year you'll be asking me to stay just until summer."

Missy's wild mass of red curls bounced as she nodded her head. Oh, how he would miss the girls—his sweet, adorable, sometimes troublesome sisters.

Georgie, four years his senior, normally rather well composed, seemed caught off guard by the announcement as well. "Didn't figure you'd ever leave Larson Ranch," he said, shaking his head.

Adam shrugged.

"We certainly wish you well. Will's lucky to have you," Georgie added.

Another glance around the table and Adam knew just how deeply his family loved him. Not an eye was clear—each shaded with at least a hint of moisture, though some cried unashamed. As his gaze moved back towards the patriarch of this brood, his pa stood.

"When you leave, son, I want you to take one of the best studs and one of the best mares with you." Adam's jaw dropped. His father could not be serious.

"It is the least we can do to get you started on your own. And you deserve the best, because you have always given us your best. Our horse business will sorely miss your talent, as we will miss you." His father stopped abruptly and went to embrace his son for the second time that day. When he pulled back, Adam saw the moisture in his pa's eyes.

It was going to be very hard to leave his family behind.

Chapter 3

On Sunday morning, Julia woke from a fitful sleep. The dream had been so real—too real. She saw herself standing at the front of the church, screaming hysterically at Hiram, accusing him of all manner of lies. Then she left, riding from town on a pure white horse, glowing in the sunlight. Instead of being free, like Caroline's plan, she had been dragged to the ground with heavy chains weighing her down. Hiram chased after her and forced her to wed him that day. As her dream took her in shackles to his ranch house, to his bed chamber, she blessedly woke, spared from the dreadful scene.

As she washed for the day, her hands shook uncontrollably, making it difficult to pin the stylish ringlets into place. Eventually she gave up, asking for Mary's assistance. Despite her anxiety, she would go through with Caroline's plan. She had to. *Lord, please give me the strength.* She prayed while securing her hat to her head.

Reuben pulled the wagon around front and helped Julia into the back like every Sunday morning. Patting her lap, her niece, Elizabeth snuggled close. Eddie, her nephew, took his customary place at her side, while Reuben and Mary shared the front seat.

On the ride in, she rehearsed the scene in her mind. She reminded herself to pay close attention to which horse Adam Larson rode so she did not take the wrong one. She thought she would recognize his horse, but wanted to be sure she did.

As Reuben pulled the wagon to a stop in front of the church, Julia's stomach lurched. At breakfast, she ate just a few bites of toast. Regardless, she thought she might dump that little bit out on the steps of the church as agitated as she was.

Before she managed to step out of the wagon, Hiram Norton arrived to assist her. His possessive hold around her waist lingered as he helped her down from the wagon. Offering his arm to her, she obediently slipped her hand in the crook. Her throat constricted even more as he led her up the steps. She tried to smile, thinking it must have looked rather strained. Caroline would probably say that was perfect for the coming theatrics. To Julia, it was the reflection of her nerves and no acting was involved. As Hiram ushered her to his pew, away from the other Colters, she longed to be free from his presence—forever.

During the service, she did not have to pretend to be distraught, for she truly was. What if she fainted before she could go through with this? What if Hiram chased her down and declared her to be insane? What if he smoothly talked his way around the pending scene? Before she knew it, the time was upon her as the last refrain of the last hymn echoed in the small church.

Julia's heart pounded so loudly in her chest she was certain Hiram could hear it. Standing, she allowed him to escort her from the pew. When he stopped just before reaching the doorway, she stifled a groan, her fear rising. She was hoping to wait until they were outside.

"My dear, you look unwell. Is everything alright?" Hiram asked, appearing genuine.

She knew this was her chance, even if they were not quite outside yet. She fought past the constricting of her throat. "No!" she shouted. Her voice reverberated loudly throughout the church. All conversation stopped and everyone looked at her, so she plowed forward. Taking her hand from his, she slapped his face—something she had wanted to do for some time now.

"Everything is not alright. I cannot believe you slept with that woman! Have you no regard for me that you would do such a thing?"

Further words caught in her throat when she saw Reuben's face go brilliant red with anger. Hiram, on the other hand, appeared genuinely shocked. She had to seal this now before she lost all courage.

"I cannot marry you. I cannot marry a man with no regard for the sanctity of marriage. It is over, Hiram. I never want to see you again!" she screamed at full volume while stepping away from his reach. Turning on her heel, she ran out the front of the church, down the steps and headlong into Adam Larson as he untied his horse from the hitching post. *Thank you, Lord.*

The stunned look on his face etched in her mind as she grabbed the reins from his hand and mounted the horse. Forcing the mare into a hard gallop for effect, Julia refused to glance over her shoulder. As soon as she was out of sight, she dropped the mare to a gentle lope.

She had to breathe. Her hands were shaking, her heart pounding in her ears. She felt lightheaded as spots danced before her eyes. *I will not swoon. I cannot swoon.*

Sliding off the mare, she rested her forehead against the saddle, closing her eyes. The smell of horseflesh and leather helped calm her nerves. For a moment she thought she might be sick, but the feeling soon passed. Climbing back into the saddle, she pointed the mare toward home.

Once at the ranch house, she knew she should care for the mare, but tied her to the front hitching post instead. That would certainly appear the more flighty and distraught action. As she walked down the hall to her room, she unpinned her hat. Throwing it to the floor, she fell face down onto the bed and sobbed. *Lord, forgive me for the deception. Please, let this be done.* Whether it was the emotion draining from her or the lack of sleep from the night before, Julia fell fast asleep.

Reuben clenched his fist at his side, utterly mortified by Julia's ill-fated outburst. Heat rose to his face in proportion to the volume of her voice. Stupefied, he watched numbly, helpless to steer this runaway scene from destruction.

Hiram's face was pale. It was obvious, as he watched Julia bolt from the building, that he never expected such a scene. Neither had Reuben.

Rallying from his horror, he grabbed Mary's elbow. "Come on," he grunted tersely, eager to be out the doors of the church. A slight whimper escaped his wife's lips as she grabbed a hand from each child, dragging them along at the fast pace he set. Hopefully, he could get out of the churchyard before Hiram came to his senses.

"Get in," he commanded his shocked family, not bothering to assist them. Climbing up to the seat, he waited just long enough for Mary to pull herself up before slapping the horses into motion headed for home.

Julia had gone too far, he thought, his jaw tightening as he ground his teeth. She had cost him everything. There was no possibility of her marrying Hiram now. Worse yet, Hiram had already paid for her hand, adding to his overwhelming debts. Hiram was not a man he wanted to be indebted to.

As fear fueled his anger, he considered his options. He was a smart man. Savvy. Capable of overcoming insurmountable obstacles. Perhaps Jamison would be amiable to paying for the pleasure of marrying Julia. Or Alcart.

Mentally scrolling through the list of his associates, another thought occurred to him. He could not leave Julia's behavior unanswered. She was far too obstinate for any of the men he had in mind. No matter who he chose, they would want a submissive, complaisant wife regardless of her beauty. He had to get her under control. Teach her a lesson. And fast.

No doubt Hiram would show up on his doorstep soon looking for the money he already paid. Unfortunately, he already used some of it to stall his creditors. They were greatly displeased by the amount of time it was taking him to pay back his debts. He could ask for no more time than the few weeks he had left. He needed money now or he would lose everything.

Letting his anger burn, he pulled the wagon to an abrupt stop in front of the house. Leaping down, he strode into the house—steps full of fury—straight for her room. It was time for her first lesson to begin.

Thud. Julia woke a short time later to the sound of Reuben crashing through her door. As she turned over, her brother picked her up and threw her against the wall, knocking the air from her lungs. As she struggled to take a breath, Reuben squeezed his hold on her arms.

"Do you have any idea what your outburst just cost me?" His voice boomed with unrestrained rage.

"Reuben, I—"

The force of the blow to her face startled her so much that it took a minute to register that he hit her. How could he? He was supposed to protect her, not harm her. She tried to move her hand to touch her cheek but he held her pinned against the wall. She felt her face grow warm as a welt formed around her eye.

"Hiram has pulled out of our arrangement. Months of work for nothing! And the money..." He growled. She could feel his hot breath on her face. "You could not be content to simply marry a wealthy man for the betterment of your family."

"I did not agree to—"

Reuben grabbed her by the throat and clamped his strong hands tight limiting the amount of air she could intake. Clawing at his hands she tried to loosen his hold to no avail. She could not breathe. Looking into his dark brown eyes she silently begged for mercy. There was none. His fierce eyes held only a look of pure evil. He was going to kill her.

"Reuben!" Mary screamed from the hallway. He loosened his grip just enough for some air to make it down her throat, expanding her lungs.

The sound of front door slamming echoed down the hall. Julia struggled to take another breath. Even through the blur in her vision, she recognized Adam Larson standing in the hallway. When he cleared his throat to announce his presence, Reuben slowly loosened his fingers from her neck. Leaning close to her ear, he whispered so only she could hear, "There are ways to cause you pain that are not visible to others. Make no mistake, you will pay for this."

Turning on his heel, he pushed Adam aside as he stormed from her bedroom. Mary followed him, not even offering to help. Perhaps she was afraid of suffering the same fate.

As soon as she was free, Julia crumpled to the floor, her shaky legs no longer able to hold her weight. Ragged gulps of air failed to soothe the burning in her throat. Rolling over to all fours, she fought to catch her breath as her eyes refused to focus clearly on anything before her.

"Are you alright, Miss Colter?" a soft male voice sounded from somewhere above her.

Her head hurt. As a gentle hand lay on her shoulder, she remembered Adam was there.

"Let me help you sit up," he said, tenderly lifting her to her feet.

She felt dizzy and her vision blurred as she tried to stand on her own, her breath still short and insufficient.

"Sit on the bed." He continued to speak in soft tones, much as she had seen him do with his horses.

Just how much had he witnessed? What would he tell Caroline?

As her breathing started to return to normal, her vision cleared in one eye. The other felt swollen and raw.

Adam kneeled on the floor in front of her holding her hands. Concern wrinkled his face. "Are you hurt? Do you need to see the doctor?"

She tried to speak, but her throat burned too much. She shook her head. The motion caused her dizziness to return.

"Can you walk a little, perhaps outside for a bit of fresh air?"

When she nodded, he put his arm around her shoulders and helped her stand. After a few steps, she moved away from him, able to continue on her own. As they walked toward the front door, she heard Mary in the kitchen.

Mary popped her head out. "Just so you know, he's gone to the saloon." The words dripped with blame.

Ignoring her, Julia continued to the front porch and took a seat in her favorite rocking chair, hugging her arms close around her body. Adam stood across from her, leaning against the rail with his arms crossed over his chest. When he made eye contact, she averted her gaze. Several moments passed before either spoke. Then they spoke at the same time.

"He's never…"

"I think you should…"

Adam nodded for her to continue.

"He's never done that before," Julia croaked. It hurt to talk. She bowed her head. Staring at her clasped hands, the tears flooded down her swollen cheek. She was scared. She never thought Reuben was capable of harming his own sister and she just provoked him to a new level. If she believed his threat, and she did, he would seek vengeance. She couldn't imagine in what way.

"Julia… Miss Colter. I think… I know it is not my place to… I think you should come stay with our family for a few days. I don't think it is safe to leave you here."

34

She still could not look Adam in the eye.

"What he did was wrong. No man should ever treat a woman that way, no matter how angry he was. And most certainly not your brother, your guardian. Please, come with me. Ma won't mind."

In truth, Julia wanted nothing more than to get away from Reuben's control. Any sense of safety and trust she once had in him fled the moment he choked her. But she was also terrified of what he would do to the Larson's if he found her there. Or what he would do to her.

She shook her head. "I can't go. Thank you for your help, but I'm sure your folks are worried about what is keeping you so long."

She stood and moved toward the door.

Gently touching her arm, Adam said, "If you change your mind anytime, day or night, you hop on a horse and get on over to our place—anytime, Julia." His voice was firm and sincere.

Then he turned and untied both the horse she borrowed and the one he rode over. Taking both sets of reins he mounted the first horse and led the other one home.

Julia went inside and grabbed a cup of water, avoiding Mary's gaze. When she finished choking down the liquid, she sought the solace of her room. Kneeling before her bed she rested the side of her face without the swollen lump on the quilt her mother made for her. *Papa, why did you leave me to Reuben's care? He wants nothing for my good and only wants to use me.* Touching her fingers to the mark on her face, she winced at how much it hurt. What good had this morning's drama done if it ended like this? Was it better to suffer Reuben's wrath than a lifetime of marriage to that despicable Hiram Norton?

"I'm going over to the Colter's after dinner," Caroline stated as she passed the potatoes to Missy.

Adam stiffened at the determined set of his sister's chin. She would go—he had no doubt—even if it might put herself in danger.

"She wasn't at church today," Caroline added as a frown darkened her green eyes. "That is not like her. Something is wrong."

Guilt gnawed at Adam's gut. He knew exactly what was wrong. She probably still had a horrible bruise on her face from last week's encounter with Reuben's fury. He told no one what he witnessed— not even Pa or Ma. Not Caroline. Several times during the week, as he prepared for his trip west, he considered riding to the Star C and bringing her back. Ma would take care of her and Pa would not let Reuben near the place after seeing her battered face.

"That'd be fine," Pa conceded, not knowing his daughter could get mixed up in Reuben's awful behavior.

Adam couldn't let her go by herself. But, he didn't feel he could tell her or his parents why. "I'll go with you," he offered, hoping no explanation would be needed.

Caroline frowned at him. He glanced away to keep her from reading him like she always did.

"Good," she said when he refused to look back at her. "I would not mind the company. Now hurry up and eat," she said.

Once he finished, he went out to the stables and saddled two horses.

They rode in silence to the Star C, contrary to Caroline's earlier comment. Adam wondered what kind of reception they might receive. Would Reuben throw him out on sight because of what he witnessed last week? Should he insist on seeing Julia anyway?

As they stopped in front of the house, Reuben came outside. "What do you want?" he asked glaring at Adam.

"I came to see my friend," Caroline said. "When she missed church this morning, I was worried she was still overcome with grief from her broken engagement. I thought she could use a good cry."

At first, Adam thought Reuben was going to send them both packing. But, as Reuben stepped aside, he let out a silent sigh of relief.

As soon as Caroline saw Julia, her eyes went wide and a gasp fell from her lips. Adam followed his sister's gaze. The deep purple bruise on Julia's face would not have been easily hidden. Was that the same one from last week?

Before Adam could stop his sister, she cried out, "What happened to your face?"

Reuben answered quickly, "She fell off her horse last week in her haste to leave the church, isn't that right, Julia?" Even though he directed the question to Julia, he stared Adam down, challenging him to say differently.

"Yes, it was really quite silly." She agreed, avoiding eye contact with both of them.

"Come, let's sit out here and visit for a while," Caroline said.

As Caroline took a seat in the nearby rocking chair, Reuben turned and went inside, slamming the door behind him.

Julia flinched before sitting in the same rocking chair she sat in last week when Adam begged her to leave. Seeing the aftermath made him feel worse for not trying harder. While he remained within earshot, he sat at the opposite end of the porch to give the girls the appearance of privacy. He pulled out a small piece of wood and his knife from his pocket. Whittling away, he listened intently.

"What *really* happened, Julia?"

"It is as Reuben said."

"No it's not. I can see it in your eyes."

"Please, let it be, Caroline. I don't want to risk making him angry again."

"Who? Mr. Norton?"

Julia made no movement or sound.

"Reuben?"

Still no sound.

"I knew it. Is this because of what happened at church last Sunday?"

Adam glanced over and saw tears welling in Julia's frightened eyes.

"Please, I can't talk about it."

"Can't or won't?" Leave it to his sister to be so subtle.

"Won't. Can't. Does it make any difference? I don't want to relive that day." Julia glanced in Adam's direction and he caught her gaze. What was that look? Was she pleading with him to get her away from here? He didn't understand and she looked away before he could make sense of it.

"I am free of Hiram, but I am afraid I made an enemy of my brother in the process. I will say no more. Just pray for me. Don't come back here for a while...especially not alone."

The fear in Julia's voice was evident. Caroline picked up on it too. "You're scaring me. If you're in danger, I want you to come

37

with us. We can protect you."

"Just go."

Caroline looked confused and hurt and motherly all at the same time. She was fiercely loyal to her friend and would not want to leave if she thought Julia was in danger.

Standing, Adam took charge, "Caroline, we best be going." Giving her a gentle tap, he pointed to the horses. After Caroline was out of earshot, he whispered to Julia, "Remember what I said last week. Don't hesitate to take us up on our offer."

Then he mounted his horse. Touching the brim of his hat, he locked gazes with her. "Miss Colter," he said nodding. She waved as they turned to leave. Lord, Adam prayed, please let her have the good sense to leave before it is too late.

Chapter 4

Star C Ranch, Texas

August 30, 1864

More than two weeks passed since Caroline and Adam visited her. Julia felt like a prisoner in her own home. While she avoided Reuben as much as possible, she still had to endure meals three times a day with him. Then, this morning at breakfast, he asked to speak to her in his office.

Her hand shook as she reached for the door knob. She opened the door and stepped into the room that had once been her father's office. The large walnut desk still sat in the same place. Only, instead of her kindly father sitting on the other side welcoming her with a grin, it was her brother instilling fear. He looked up and pointed to the chair across from the desk. At least the large piece of furniture sat between them and she would have time to flee, should he become violent again.

Once she took the offered chair, he began, "I am extremely disappointed in your behavior of late. Breaking the engagement with Hiram Norton was a foolish mistake. But, given your age, I am willing to overlook the error in your judgment. I have taken it upon myself to see you wed to a wealthy man, so you will have all that you need."

Julia swallowed, not trusting him one bit. Reuben never looked out for anyone's interest besides his own. He'd already proven that point the first day he hit her.

"Therefore, I expect you to be on your best behavior this evening when Mr. Lewis Jamison joins us for dinner this evening. He is a suitable match. He has wealth enough to lavish you with gifts. You will live a life of ease as his wife."

"Have I no say in the matter?" she asked frowning. "Have you already offered my hand this time as well?"

Fire shot from Reuben's golden brown eyes. "If I say you will wed, then you shall wed. I have not forgotten, nor forgiven your foolishness. Do not dare to cross me a second time!" he shouted, slamming his fist down on the desk.

She wanted to speak out against the whole notion of him arranging her marriage. But, even though the physical scars healed, she remained afraid of her brother. Seeing compliance would serve better, she changed her approach. "I will do as you ask, brother. I will treat Mr. Jamison kindly at dinner this evening." *But, I will not marry him.*

Mr. Jamison was not quite as old as Hiram—he was perhaps a year or two younger. Unlike Hiram, Mr. Jamison was at least pleasant looking. At first, Julia thought she would completely abhor the man, given his association with Reuben. However, throughout the evening meal he seemed rather attentive. He asked her questions to draw her out. She did her best to answer with the minimal amount of information, enough to satisfy Reuben, but not enough to really encourage Mr. Jamison.

Following the meal, Mr. Jamison asked Julia to join him for a walk. While she was more than ready to have him leave but one look from Reuben told her she better agree. Taking his offered arm, she followed him outside.

As soon as they were alone, Mr. Jamison turned toward her. "You are quite attractive, Julia."

She blushed at the inappropriate comment and the familiarity, maintaining an air of indifference.

At her continued silence, he pressed further. "I think I shall like bedding you very much."

The nerve! She raised her hand to slap him, but he caught her wrist.

"Yes, a woman with much spirit definitely needs broken. I shall very much enjoy the challenge."

He pinned her arms behind her back and kissed her hard on the mouth. His possessiveness repulsed her. When he restrained her against the wall and took liberties with his hands, she had enough.

She would not be molested by this two-faced man. Bringing her foot down hard on his, she made contact. He let out a yelp of pain. Making sure he got the message, she kicked him hard in the shin. While he was distracted, she turned and ran inside the house to her room.

Julia heard the muffled sound of a heated exchange between Reuben and Mr. Jamison. Then horse hoof beats thudded down the drive. At first she thought Reuben would confront her immediately and she almost wished he had, preferring not to prolong the anticipation of his punishment—however severe it might prove to be. He never came. Instead, the sound of another horse riding fast away from the ranch faded in the distance. Then, all was calm. Sneaking a peek out her door, she heard no sounds. Reuben was gone.

Sighing in relief, Julia donned her nightdress. Somehow she managed to dodge that situation. Hopefully tomorrow morning she would not have to pay. When she finished brushing her hair, she turned down the lantern and went to sleep.

"I wouldn't marry that shrew if she were the last woman on earth!" Jamison shouted. "You have taught her nothing about the ways of men. Deal's off."

Reuben swallowed hard, trying to rein in his anger before he alienated Jamison more. "Look, she's been coddled far too much by her father. It's going to take some time to undo that."

"Do you suppose she'll go along for a while then make a spectacle of me like she did Hiram Norton? I will not stand for that," Jamison said as he untied his horse from the hitching post.

Desperate, Reuben tried to think of something to say to change the course of this conversation. "You thought she was beautiful, didn't you?" he asked in a diplomatic tone. "Why don't you take her to the preacher tonight? There's no need to wait a month or more."

"Ha! You'd like that wouldn't you. Pawn your headstrong sister off on me—laughing all the way to pay your creditors. What kind of fool do you take me for?"

Panic rose. How did Jamison know why he needed the money?

Were his creditors so angry that they had been talking?

"Don't look so surprised. Whenever any man comes looking for a piece of my fortune, I do some careful digging. I think it's quite important to understand a man's motivation. Let me know just exactly what his frame of mind is."

As Jamison mounted his horse, Reuben knew he lost this battle.

"Make no mistake, Colter, I never enter into a business arrangement that is not more profitable for me than my associate. In your case, you really have nothing to offer." Kicking his horse's side, Jamison took off down the lane.

Rage overtook Reuben as he pounded his fist into the outside wall of the ranch house. The rough wood chewed his knuckles, leaving a bloody mess behind—just like Julia had done to his last hope for keeping the ranch.

Anger and fear mixed in his heart, a lethal combination. He would punish Julia. But first, he had to figure out how—how to break her, to mold her into what a man like him would want.

Storming towards the stable, he selected a docile mount. If only his sister could take a lesson from this beast. Once saddled, he took off towards town.

Stopping in front of the saloon, he dismounted and tossed the reins over the hitching post out front. Shoving the doors open with the force of his anger still brewing, he made his way to the bar. He was in no mood to deal with the poor wretches gathered around the poker tables.

A scowl in the bartender's direction was all that was needed for a glass of whiskey to appear. Tossing his head back, he let the liquid burn down his throat in one gulp. Slamming the empty glass down on the table, he waited but a few seconds for it to be refilled. The second round found a similar fate. By the third whiskey, he calmed just enough to savor its affects.

"Sumthin' ailin' ya, hon?" Jasmine's silvery voice whispered in his ear. "Cuz, ya know I can make most anythin' better."

As she slid her hand over his chest, Reuben tensed. Normally, he'd welcome her advances, but not tonight. "I'm not in the mood."

"Hmm. Sumthin' shore is wrong," she said, shaking her head. "Is it what that spitfire sister of yourn done to Mr. Jamison that got you all in a hissy?"

Grabbing her hand, he spun in his seat to face the soiled dove. Through gritted teeth, he asked, "How'd you know about that?"

"I had the pleasure of relieving Mr. Jamison's frustrations for him." She nodded her head to where a much more sedate Jamison sat, engaged in a game of chance.

How many other people already knew? Downing the rest of his whiskey, he nodded for more. Downing it in a flash, he tapped his fingers agitatedly, waiting for more.

"Hon, that ain't gonna solve nuthin' with yourn prissy sister," Jasmine cooed, placing her hand on his arm to keep him from chugging the next drink. "What you need to do is tame that prissy gal."

Rolling his eyes, Reuben's patience was wearing thin. He already knew that's what he needed to do. He just wasn't sure how. "How do you propose I do such a thing?"

Jasmine's crooked yellow teeth were unveiled with a smile. "Hon, ya done it more than once here. Ain't no different way to be taming a wild woman."

His heart beat faster as the meaning behind her words sunk in. "Leave me," he ordered as he considered her idea. The men he sought to pair Julia with wouldn't care much about her state, as long as she was submissive.

Downing the rest of his drink, he stumbled to the door and pulled himself up on his horse, with one goal in mind. Surely this would be the thing that would save him.

"Julia! You w-w-wench."

Julia shot upright in bed at the sound of her brother's drunken slur. The door to her room flew open with such force the window rattled in its frame. Reuben came toward her. She could not see much in the dark, as very little moonlight shown through the window.

"You wench. That is twice you have cost me." He smacked her hard across the face before holding her down. "I told you not to cross me again."

"Reuben, don't!" She protested what expected to be another brutal beating.

"Oh, don't worry, *dear* sister. I am not going to kill you. I am going to teach you a lesson—that there are some things far worse than death."

He began undressing himself. What was he doing?

She started to move, and he slammed her back on the bed, before he pressed her deeper against the bed with the full weight of his body.

Terrified, she started thrashing, trying to get him off. But he was much too strong for her. He hit her across the face again. When she inhaled a deep breath to scream, he clamped one hand down over her mouth. With his other hand, he tore at her nightdress. She tried to fight him, but he overpowered her.

No. Don't do this. Please don't do this. She pleaded inwardly, unable to scream out for help.

And then he did what no brother should ever do to his sister. He took away the gift meant for her husband. He ruined her.

When the deed was done, he laughed with pure evil emanating from his voice. "I told you there were ways to bring you pain not visible to others, but you did not listen. Perhaps you will comply like a good little girl when I bring the next suitor around."

Then he stood. Grabbing his pile of clothes, he walked out her door, closing it behind him as if nothing had happened.

Julia stiffened her body, willing her mind not to dwell on... She had to remain strong—just for a little while longer. She listened for the soft click of Reuben's door closing. Then she waited for the house to be still. The welt on her face heated, throbbing as it grew in size.

She wanted to die. What he had done to her...

She fought against the sudden, overwhelming urge to wash herself over and over—to cleanse her body from the worst betrayal.

Instead, her mind took over. She had to leave.

Her heart beat so fast she thought it might leap from her chest and land on the floor that she wanted to sink into, swallowed into oblivion, ever to forget her brother's heinous act.

Silence. Then Reuben's snoring filtered through the house.

Julia jumped up from the bed. Not knowing what else to do, she removed the carpet bag from under her bed and filled it with a few personal items and two serviceable dresses. Donning her split skirt and blouse, she moved swiftly and quietly.

She would need money and a place to go.

Stepping into Reuben's office, she lit a lamp but kept it burning low. She rooted through his desk until she found a stack of bills. She took what she thought she needed and no more. Surely her inheritance would more than cover anything she took.

Don't think about what just happened. Keep moving. Run.

As she moved papers on Reuben's desk, she came across a stack of letters. Her hand stilled as she read her name on the outside. They were addressed to her—from Will. He had written. Reuben kept them from her.

She thought for a brief moment to take them, but a creaking sound brought her up short. She quickly extinguished the lamp. Not moving, she waited several minutes.

When she heard Reuben's snoring again and no further sounds, she grabbed her bag and made her way out the front door. She hoped the cowboys on night watch would not hear or see her. She needed to escape. As quietly as possible, she saddled one of the fastest mares in the complete dark, thankful for her years of experience. She led the horse several yards from the house before she mounted. Holding the carpet bag in one hand and the reins in the other she rode as hard as she could to the Larson's—it was the only place she thought she might be safe.

Adam woke with a start, reaching for his gun. He listened. There. Horse hooves pounding closer. He made his way to the front door, noting that no one else woke to the sound. Slowly cracking the door open, he pointed the rifle towards the noise. The tiny sliver of moon offered almost no light, making it very difficult to see who rode into the ranch.

A horse whinnied as the rider pulled it to a stop in front of the house. Whoever it was, they weren't wasting time heading to the house. *Click, click, click.* Came the sound of light footfalls—almost feminine, onto the front porch.

As the figure reached up to knock on the door, Adam suddenly realized who it was. "Julia!" he whispered loudly.

She jumped, backing away, as skittish as an unbroken horse.

"It's me. Adam," he said, opening the door wide.

She must have moved toward the sound of his voice, for the next thing he knew, she collapsed into his arms crying over and over again, "Help me, help me, help me."

For several minutes, he held her close, stroking her loose hair. Whispering words of comfort, he worried over what dreadful thing must have happened to cause her to leave at this time of night and in such a hurry.

A dim light fell over his shoulder and he glanced back seeing Caroline standing at the edge of the kitchen. Placing his arm around Julia, he led her to a chair. As he tried to coax her to sit, she held on tightly to him, burying her face in his chest. Not wanting to rush her, he stood still.

When Caroline finally peeled the distraught Julia from his arms, he saw it. A huge lump on her face. Reuben hit her again, Adam thought, clenching his jaw. Anger boiled to the surface. He would ride out there tomorrow and set Reuben straight.

"There, there," Caroline said. "You are safe now." She nodded toward the door.

Adam took that as his cue to leave. He went outside, tripping over something. Reaching down, he scooped up her carpet bag and set it inside the door. Untying her mare from the post, he took the horse into the stable and began taking off the gear. While he rubbed down the horse, he thought of many ways to connect his fist with Reuben's jaw. The man has no conscience. Who beats their sister? Or any woman for that matter?

After Adam left the room, Julia gathered her wits, desperate to explain why she was there. "He raped me, Caroline. I had to leave."

Caroline's brows furrowed so deeply, she thought her eyebrows might touch. "Who did?"

Silence.

"Who?"

"Reuben." The name came forcefully from her throat with a guttural groan.

Anger flashed across Caroline's features. "We have to get you out of here. If he would resort to such unthinkable behavior, then staying with us is not going to keep you safe."

She nodded in agreement.

Caroline tapped her finger against her temple as she often did when thinking through a problem. "Adam will take you with him. But he will have to leave tonight instead of the first of September. I don't know if he has everything he needs, but I think it would be best if you both rode on horseback anyway." She dipped a towel in some cool water and handed it to Julia.

Julia blinked, confused. She took the cool cloth and pressed it to her swollen face. "What are you talking about?"

"I just assumed you knew."

"Knew what?"

"Adam is leaving to go work for your brother."

Julia tensed.

"Not Reuben. Will. He is going to the Arizona Territory to work for Will."

When did this happen?

"Anyway, he was going to leave the first of September. But now, I think he should leave with you tonight. You will be safe with him."

"It's not appropriate for two young unmarried people to travel together," she reminded her friend.

Caroline thought for another moment. "Of course it is. If you are Julia Larson."

Chapter 5

Had his sister gone completely mad? Adam stopped short when he heard Caroline say something about Julia Larson. What was she talking about?

As he stepped back into the kitchen, Caroline said, "You will travel as Adam's sister, Julia Larson. He can take you to Will and you won't have to return here. You will be safe."

The fear in Julia's eyes was obvious. So was the doubt. Having only heard part of his sister's plan, he asked, "Caroline, what are you talking about?"

"Stay here," she said to Julia, before pushing him outside into the darkness of the night. "She can't stay here. It is not safe for her. Reuben wounded her terribly—worse than you can even imagine—and I'm afraid he would only come and take her away and inflict worse pain on her should she stay here."

"I agree. But, what were you saying about taking her to Will?"

"You were planning on leaving soon anyway. I think you should leave tonight."

Adam staved off a moan of frustration. Keeping his voice even he said, "I'm not quite ready. I need a few more days."

Caroline laid her hand on her brother's arm. "Julia does not have a few more days. She needs to leave now—before daylight. And wagon travel is not going to be fast enough. You will have to travel by horseback. I also think you should change up your route. Go northwest up to Kansas and join a wagon train there. That way, if Reuben does send men after her, he won't expect either of you to be traveling in that direction. He will assume you have followed the same route as Will."

"I haven't said goodbye to Ma and Pa." The words were out before he could take them back.

Caroline sighed. "I know I'm asking a lot. Please believe me when I say Julia's very life could be at stake. I will handle our family. Please, if not for Julia—please, do this for me."

His heart broke. Of course he would do this for Julia. He was an honorable man and she needed protection. He would not hesitate to help anyone in such a situation, much less a lifelong friend. It was just not the way he planned to leave home, in the middle of the night, with just two horses and whatever they could fit in their saddlebags. And without saying goodbye.

"Go," he said. "Get some food together for us, while I gather my things."

He quickly grabbed a few of the items he planned to take. Other than a change of clothes or two, he packed his Bible, the letter from Will, his revolver, and knife. He already told Pa which two horses he planned on taking, so he readied them for the journey. By the time he was finished, Caroline had packed them several days' worth of food. He secured Julia's carpet bag behind her saddle on the mare. He would ride the stallion.

Adam gave Caroline instructions on what to do with the horse from Star C. At dawn, she was to let the horse out in full gear to wander back to the ranch.

Not wanting to leave without saying his goodbyes, he took a quick minute to pen a note to his family.

> *Dear Pa and Ma,*
>
> *This is not how I envisioned leaving you. Certainly not without saying goodbye and giving you my love. As Caroline will explain, it was necessary for the safety and well-being of a friend. Know that I love you and will miss you as I start this new life. I take with me the faith you instilled in me, as well as the many lessons you've taught me. I could not have asked for a better family.*
>
> *Your loving son,*
>
> *Adam*

The shock of what just happened wore off and reality started setting in. Julia felt the steady movement of the horse beneath her. A trot was as fast as Adam would let them go on his prize horses. In the darkness of night, she could barely make out Adam or his horse in front of her.

She could not breathe.

Her brother ruined her. How could he do that? Did he have no morals at all? What kind of monster was he?

She wanted to throw herself in a river and scrub every inch of her body, washing away any hint of the horror of the past few hours.

Bile rose to the back of her throat. She was going to be sick.

Yanking back on the reins, she pulled her mare to an abrupt stop. She was too dizzy to dismount properly, so she swung both legs to one side and slid off the horse. She could not breathe. She could still feel the weight of Reuben's body on hers.

"Oh, God!" she cried.

Falling to her knees, Julia bent in half with her face to the ground. When she lifted her head, she felt sick. Then she lost the contents of her stomach. There, crouching on the ground she wanted to cry out to God—to ask him how he could allow such evil to befall her. But she had no words. No feeling.

She felt dead inside.

Dropping her head into her hands she sobbed.

Adam turned his head to the side when he thought he heard a noise. He caught the sound of Julia's horse stopping. He turned around to find her. She was crumpled on the ground next to her horse. He heard the unmistakable sound of her retching.

I did not even think to see if she was injured before we left. Stupid. She could be in need of a doctor and here we are fleeing to the middle of nowhere.

Locating her canteen, he dropped to his knees next to her. She began to sob uncontrollably. *What exactly did Reuben do to her?* He started to wonder. Not certain of what to do, he placed his hand on her shoulder.

As he handed her some water, he spoke softly, like he would when he was trying to calm a frightened horse. "Here. Take a few sips."

She drank a few sips between sobs, but still her body shook. His fingers brushed hers when she handed him the canteen. Her hands were like ice!

What should he do? They needed to get moving, but she could not ride her horse like this. *Lord, give me wisdom.*

Taking her in his arms, Adam gently rocked her back and forth. He whispered words of comfort in soft tones. When she started to calm, he continued the motion, waiting patiently.

After a few more minutes, he said, "We must press on. Can you ride?"

No answer.

"Julia?"

Only soft, steady breathing answered. She had fallen asleep.

Now what? After trying to rouse her unsuccessfully, Adam decided he would have to carry her in his arms on the same horse, tethering the other horse behind. It was either that or slump her over on her stomach on her horse. Thinking of how humiliating it would be should she wake up, he decided against it. She had been through too much already.

Standing, he tried to figure out how he was going to hold Julia, mount the horse, and grab the reins for both without dropping her. He picked her up. When she unconsciously placed her arms around his neck, he was relieved. That should help. Balancing her in his arms, he held the reins for both horses in one hand and the horn of his saddle in the other. Placing one foot in the stirrup, he pushed up. The first try he did not push up with enough force to clear the horse's flank. On the second try he was successful. Getting settled in the saddle, he readjusted her so she would be as comfortable as possible. She still clung to him as he started the horse out at a walk. He knew better than to try to press for anything faster in this challenging situation, despite the urgency to cover as much distance as possible.

The further they rode into the night, the more her closeness stirred him. Her hair smelled like vanilla as it rested between her face and his chest. A few tendrils caught by the wind tickled the side of his neck. Her side pressed against his torso forever altering his view of this childhood friend. He no longer struggled with seeing her as woman instead of a little girl.

He would do whatever was necessary to protect Julia Colter and see her safely to the Arizona Territory.

"Papa! Papa, wake up."

His little girl's voice invaded Reuben's slumber. Slowly opening his eyes, he squinted at the light shining in through the window.

"Papa! Auntie Julia is gone!" little Elizabeth cried.

Shooting upright in his bed, he grabbed his daughter by the shoulders and shook her. "What do you mean Julia is gone?"

Elizabeth dissolved into tears, failing to give him the answers he needed. He shouted at her to leave his room then grabbed his trousers and a shirt, dressing hastily. His head pounded with his swift movements, causing him to slow his pace.

"Mary!" he hollered for his wife as he approached the kitchen. "Where is Julia?"

"How am I supposed to know? She's your sister."

Getting nowhere, he ran to Julia's room. A flash from his drunken stupor the night before danced across his vision. A brief pang of regret threatened near the surface. He was sorry it took such extreme measures to temper his sister.

Elizabeth's words came back to him, reminding him that Julia was gone. He searched through her things, noting an empty space in her dresser and the missing carpet bag.

Bursting out of her room, he stormed to his office. Pacing back and forth, he tried to decide what to do. If she left after he fell asleep, she would have nearly half a day head start. And where would she have gone? To the Larsons? To Will?

Rubbing his palm against his pounding head, he knew he had to send someone out looking for her. He had to get her back. Rushing out to the bunkhouse, he found his foreman and instructed him to send someone trustworthy to speak with him for a special assignment.

Half an hour later, Bates appeared in the doorway of his office.

"Please take a seat," Reuben said, unable to hide his tenseness.

Bates did as instructed.

"It seems my foolish sister has run off in the middle of the night. I suspect she may have headed to Larson's ranch. I need you to ride out and bring her back."

"Yes, sir," Bates said, rising.

Gideon Bates mounted his steed, still puzzled over why Colter would choose him to go after his missing sister. In the year he worked on the Star C, he spoke to him only once—and that was to secure his employment away from Will Colter. Other than that brief conversation, he had no contact with Reuben.

Nevertheless, he had been sent to fetch his boss's sister.

He had seen Julia Colter in the pastures. Not the typical female. Sure to be a thorn in any man's side. He could understand Reuben's frustrations with her.

When he arrived at Larson's ranch, the place seemed deserted. He dismounted and headed toward the barn but didn't find anyone.

Ambling toward the ranch house, Gideon paused. Odd that the youngest Larson boy wasn't working with the horses. He thought the young man practically ran the horse side of the business. Reaching up his hand, he rapped on the door twice.

A young blonde woman answered the door. "May I help you?" she asked.

"Ah, yes, Miss…?"

"Larson. Caroline Larson."

"Miss Larson," he nodded. The defiance written in her stance told him he might have a better chance using a heap of sugar with this one. "Might you have a moment?"

"Certainly, Mr…?"

"Bates. From the Star C."

A brief shadow passed across her features before she offered him a seat on the front porch. "What brings you here, Mr. Bates?"

"Well, seems Miss Colter has wandered off. Mr. Reuben is mighty worried. You wouldn't happen to know where I could find her?"

Miss Caroline Larson folded her arms across her chest and stood. The defensive posture contradicted her words. "I have no idea where Julia is. I haven't enjoyed her company since before Reuben started trying to marry her off to the most unsuitable of suitors."

"I see," Gideon said, rubbing his hand across his jaw. "Any idea where she might have headed?"

"No. None at all."

He stood. "Well, I guess I best try the place up the road. Seems I've taken enough of your time."

She eyed him warily as he mounted his horse. He started to turn to leave, when he noticed the fresh tracks headed north up the road—the opposite direction of town and the most likely destination for anyone traveling from their ranch. He paused, turning his face back towards her.

"Noticed your brother ain't training any horses today."

"Papa sent him out on an errand," she replied too quickly.

She knew something. He was sure of it. He was also sure he wouldn't get much more from her. Whatever she knew she was holding on to something fierce. No matter.

Turing the horse back to the Star C, Gideon covered the ground quickly. After tying his horse to the rail, he sought out Colter in his office.

"Didn't find her at Larson's," Bates said. "But, I did find that the younger son was gone. And there were some tracks headed north from their property."

"Adam is gone?" Reuben failed to hide his surprise at this announcement. He never thought Larson would be bold enough to help her flee.

"Yup."

Reuben remained silent for a few moments, gathering his

thoughts. If Julia fled with Larson headed north, it was clear they were planning a permanent move. But where? And why north? Nothing readily came to mind. Heading west would have made much more sense. He would have assumed they were headed to Will.

Reaching into his desk drawer, he pulled out the stack of cash, stopping short. The stash was much smaller than last night. His blood boiled. That shrew! She stole his money!

When he pounded his fist down on the top of the desk, Bates flinched. He was ruined. Completely and utterly ruined. With most of his financial resources drained and with Julia gone, he would be a dead man. Norton or one of his creditors was sure to take payment with blood if he failed to produce it in currency.

His one last hope would be if he could find Julia in time.

"Bates, I want you to take this," he said holding out far too much of his precious money. "Find her and bring her back. If you do, I will make it worth your while." He lied. He had nothing left with which to pay the man, though he played poker enough to have developed a strong and believable façade.

Bates nodded his agreement as he took the offered money.

As Bates left his office, Reuben hoped he would find Julia soon. He was running out of time.

Chapter 6

Colter Ranch, Arizona Territory

September 9, 1864

Hannah stretched as the first rays of light streamed through her bedroom window. As she moved, Will draped his arm over her waist and slid her toward him. She felt his breath tickle the nape of her neck.

"Good morning, Mrs. Colter."

In the week since their wedding, he greeted her the same way every morning. She smiled as he kissed her neck. Smelling bacon frying, Hannah tried to get up, but Will held her in place.

"I need to get up and start your breakfast."

"Mmm. You smell good."

"Will, I mean it."

"Let Rosa see to it. I want to keep you here a bit longer."

Swatting at his hands, she remained firm. "I don't want Rosa to cook us breakfast. I want to do that. It's my kitchen."

Releasing his hold on her slowly, he sighed. "I don't see why you're upset about it. Rosa gets paid to cook and clean for everyone on the ranch."

Hannah continued the conversation as she readied herself for the day. "Because, this is my house. If I'm not cooking and cleaning and caring for my husband, then what do you suggest I do?"

Will stood behind her now. He pulled her close again, turning her to face him. The look in his eyes said trouble. As he wiggled his eyebrows, he said, "Make babies?"

"William Colter!" She squealed before pushing him away. "I'm serious."

He grinned mischievously. "So was I."

Putting her hands on her hips in exasperation, she frowned. *Does he really not understand what it is like to have another woman*

57

working in my kitchen?

"Don't give me that look. Okay," he said throwing his arms in the air in mock surrender. "I understand you want to cook and care for me. And I appreciate it. I just don't want you burdened with cooking for all the ranch hands. That's why we have Rosa."

"Did you forget that I've spent the last four months working at the boardinghouse cooking for large numbers of men? Cleaning their rooms and doing their laundry? I think I can handle it."

"It's not about your ability to handle it," he said as he took her hands in his. Looking down into her eyes, he continued, "As I expand the ranch and hire more cowboys, neither one of you will be able to handle everything on your own."

Hannah tilted her head to the side, still somewhat irritated that he didn't understand her.

"Look, this house is your domain. Rosa works for both of us. Talk to her and work things out however you want." Winking, he continued, "Then, when you make me the proud papa of a herd of children and have your hands full, you'll still have help."

At the mention of children, Hannah looked away. That was still a difficult subject for her. Especially since it was well over two years into her first marriage before she conceived. Then she lost her first and only child just a few months into the pregnancy, shortly after her first husband died in a tragic accident. She had a lot of doubt and fear about her ability to bear Will any children.

Looking back into his eyes, she sighed. She saw the look of concern on his face. This was not a conversation for so early in the morning. Standing on her toes, she stretched up to give him a quick peck on the lips.

"I am sure Rosa and I will work everything out," she said walking from their bedroom into the main part of the ranch house.

"Good morning, Rosa."

Rosa nodded as she placed huge portions of food on two plates. *She must be used to serving only men. That is twice the food I could ever eat in one sitting.* Smiling, Hannah took a seat across from Will at the table.

A knock came from the front door. Will stood to open it. "Ben," Will greeted his foreman. "Have breakfast with us."

Up until this point, Hannah had Will all to herself in the

mornings. She wondered what prompted the unusual visit as she stood to serve Ben some breakfast before Rosa took the rest of the food to the bunkhouse for the ranch hands.

Setting the smaller portion she dished up at her place, she slid the other plate across the table to Ben.

As soon as Will finished grace, Ben started the conversation. "Have you given any thought to driving some of the herd to California?"

Will swallowed a bite of eggs. "Probably should already be headed that way. It's getting kinda late in the year for a drive."

"Yer accident set us back a bit but, we can be ready in a week. Already been layin' in supplies. Just need to figure out who all is goin', how many head ya want to sell, and if we need to hire more men."

Will nodded. "Best not to wait much longer. We'll take a thousand head. The rest we'll need to keep for the army contract and the contracts in town. We'll definitely have to take Snake, unless you've found someone else who can cook on the trail."

"We?" Ben questioned. "I hope ya ain't thinking of goin'."

Hannah took new interest in the discussion. Surely her husband of a week would not be leaving her side already?

Eyes darting away from hers, Will said, "I think I should go. It's my cattle."

"Yer married now. Got a whole different set of responsibilities." Ben held Will's gaze, not giving him much of an option.

Trying to hide her smile behind her hand, she stifled a giggle by taking another bite of food. Leave it to Ben to find a way to scold Will and act fatherly without making him mad and without reminding him that he still wasn't fully healed from his accident.

"I suppose you're right."

"I figured I'd take Snake to cook and Covington to wrangle. I'll need 'bout seven or eight men for two shifts of four. That won't leave ya more'n two or three to help out here. Don't sound like that'll be enough."

"Why don't you take Jed, Hawk, Pedro, Raul, and Whitten. And the two new men, Foster and Webb," Will said. "That'll leave me, Owens, Diego, and Miguel. We can corral half of the herd one day while we take out the other half. Then switch them out the next day."

"Sounds mostly good. I'd rather have at least one more with me. What ya gonna do 'bout night guard?"

Hannah listened as the conversation bounced back and forth between her husband and Ben. The confidence Will projected amazed her. He seemed more than capable of running such a large operation.

Eventually, Will settled for accompanying Ben to Prescott for the day to see if they could hire two more men. One would go on the drive and the other would stay behind to stand guard at night when all the cattle were in the corral.

With plans in place, the two men left. Hannah stood, taking the dishes to the wash basin. Filling it with warm water from the reservoir, she let the dishes soak, anticipating Rosa would be bringing the rest over from the bunkhouse shortly.

Moving over to where two crates stood stacked one on top of another, Hannah resolved to unpack the rest of her things. The top crate already had the lid pried off. Lifting the lid, she leaned it against the bottom crate.

Now she remembered why she had been putting this off. There were too many painful memories tied up in the items in this crate that she packed over a year ago before she and Drew left Cincinnati.

A towel and apron were wedged into the corner of the crate. Pulling them out, she set them aside. The first item of significance was her mother's china. The beautiful floral patterned dishes had been passed down from her grandmother to her mother, then to Hannah at the tender age of twelve after her mother's passed. She had used the dishes daily in Cincinnati in the home she shared with Drew.

A lone tear dropped onto the first dish in the stack as memories of her first love invaded her thoughts. She had been very much in love with Drew. When he died unexpectedly in an avalanche just before they arrived in Prescott, she thought she would not be able to live without him. Yet, over time her heart healed and she met Will, whom she loved and adored.

It was so confusing to be full of joy with her new husband, while still—in moments like these—filled with grief for her first. Yes, she understood why she put off this chore of unpacking.

Squaring her shoulders, Hannah determined not to let herself grow melancholy. Quickly unwrapping each of the dishes, she set them in a pile to wash with the other dishes for the morning.

She found a few other personal mementos in that first crate, including a photograph of her and Drew. What should she even do with such a thing now? She didn't want to throw it away. Yet, she could not set it on her dresser and have her new husband look at it day after day. Laying the photograph aside, she decided to deal with it later.

Looking around the room, she contemplated whether she should worry about the other crate now or not. Opting to wait until later, she searched for a place to display some of her knick knacks.

While Will seemed to think the ranch house was small, Hannah thought it quaint. He had big plans to build a large board structure, instead of the log cabin they now occupied. The kitchen had room enough for two people to move about. The kitchen, dining area, and living room were all one large open space. The fireplace in the living room stood opposite the kitchen on the other end of the room. There were two bedrooms along one side of the house.

Walking toward the fireplace, she placed the items in her hand on the mantle. Going back to the table, she picked up the picture of her and Drew. Then she headed for her bedroom. Pulling out the bottom drawer of the dresser, she lifted her undergarments and placed the picture face down in the back of the drawer. She moved the undergarments back over top. Perhaps one day she would be ready to part with the picture. Just not today.

Making her way back to the kitchen, she decided to go ahead and clean the dishes, since Rosa never appeared with the ones from the bunkhouse. She must have washed them over there instead or perhaps in her little shack.

Later that morning, she found Rosa working on the laundry. Picking up the wet items from the basket, Hannah shook them out and hung them on the line. At first, Rosa looked at her warily, though she softened when she saw Hannah was there to help.

"Rosa, I was thinking that we could work together completing the domestic chores here. I mean, there is no reason for you to carry the entire weight by yourself."

"Si, señora. I help."

Hannah was not sure exactly what the young woman meant. She

knew *si* was *yes* and *señora* was *missus*. But she was not convinced she was getting through.

"I would like both of us to cook the meals. On laundry days, we will both do laundry. On cleaning days, I will clean the ranch house and you will clean the bunkhouse."

With fear in her eyes, Rosa asked, "No less money?"

"No less money," she quickly reassured the half-Mexican half-Apache woman. "You will be paid the same. We will help each other."

"Si, señora," Rosa answered with a big smile.

As Rosa continued to wash, Hannah hung items on the line to dry. Looking out over the lake, she breathed deeply of the pine-fragranced air. She still could not believe she lived on this beautiful piece of property, flanked by white granite mountains, dotted with tall pines, and nestled in a grass covered valley. The afternoon grew as hot as the hottest summer days back in Ohio, yet it was September. By nightfall, she would be wishing for a light wrap. The weather here was so perfect.

When it came time to start supper preparations, she outlined the planned meal. They would have fried potatoes, beef steaks, beans, and pecan pie. The pie would be a special treat. Before she moved out to the ranch on her wedding day, she gathered a large basket of pecans. She saved them to make pies over the next few weeks. If the portions they used on the ranch were smaller than what she was used to at the boardinghouse, the pecans may last longer than she first thought.

From what she learned in her first week on the ranch, Will had some thirteen men that worked for him. A few of them, like Ben Shepherd, worked for his father back in Texas and made the journey west with Will. Most of the men were hired on just prior to the trip, although she thought he mentioned that two of the four Mexican men joined the group in Santa Fe. Peter Foster and Amos Webb were hired just prior to her wedding. They were the only ones to join since Will arrived in Prescott.

She smiled as she thought back to her first morning on the ranch. Will instructed all of the cowboys to line up to officially meet her. He told them they were to address her as Mrs. Colter at all times. As he introduced each man, she greeted them as she would any man,

Mr. Shepherd, Mr. Convington. After a few snickers, Will whispered in her ear that it was not necessary to be so formal with them. Several went by their last names, except for the two youngest, Jed and Hawk. Oh, and there was Snake. And the Mexicans went by their first names as well. She felt odd at first when she addressed the men thusly, but she gradually became accustomed to it, though she had very little interaction with them since the first day.

The trip to Prescott proved more productive than Will hoped. He and Ben were able to find three more men. One he would keep on permanently, if he worked out. His name was Warren Cahill. Seems he had worked on a ranch prior to seeking his fortune in mining. Said he found mining to be a whole lot more work than ranching. Will would send Cahill with Ben on the drive.

The other man that would head out on the drive with Ben was Simon Palmer. Though he had no experience with cattle, he was good with horses. Will decided Palmer would be the wrangler for this drive, freeing up Covington to ride with the herd.

The third man he hired was Ian Flanagan. Obviously Irish, from the name and his speech, he looked as solid as a tree. He had a sister with him who was taking a job in town for the time being. He said he'd be more than happy to work as the night guard until Will's men returned from the drive. Then he said he'd be looking for work in town.

Dismounting Jackson, his favorite horse, Will had to admit Ben was right this morning. He had been foolish to think he should go on the drive to California. He was tired just from the half day in town and his headache had returned. No doubt he still was not fully himself after the accident.

About six weeks ago he had been riding out on the eastern edge of his property when Jackson spooked. He was thrown from the horse. Normally, that wouldn't have caused him much more than a bruised hind end and bruised ego. Unfortunately, when he landed on the ground, he hit his head hard on a rock. It was two weeks before he woke up. When he had, he struggled to remember a few things at first. Eventually, most everything came back to him.

Everything except his ability to read. It was so odd. He was still able to manage the ledgers and calculate sums and distances— anything mathematical. At least he thought he retained those skills. Maybe he should have Hannah double check the ledgers just to be certain. But when it came to reading words on a page, like in his Bible, he just could not make sense of the words, not even old familiar passages.

And he missed it.

He missed being able to read his Bible on his own. Before the wedding, Jed and Hawk took turns reading scripture to him in the morning. Since Hannah was now at his side, she took over that role. In the evening, she insisted they spend an hour working on his reading skills. She seemed to think he was improving, but Will disagreed, still frustrated over having lost the ability.

Besides not being fully healthy, he would have been miserable if he left Hannah to go on the drive. In the week since their wedding, he wanted to spend more and more time at home. He even took himself off of the rotation for herding the cattle, something he thought he would never do. Though, he would have to help out again when the men left on the drive.

When he stopped working with the cattle, he started working on building up the horse breeding and training business. While he knew a little about training horses, he certainly did not know as much as Adam Larson. Hopefully the young man was on his way west. He had not received any returned correspondence from Larson to the offer he made back in June. Despite having regular mail service within the territory, communication outside of the territory seemed very slow.

There was no rule anywhere that said as a rancher you had to work the cattle. Many ranchers back in Texas rarely worked with the cattle, at least when they neared forty or so years of age. Not that Will was close to that. He just turned thirty last month. But, some of the ranchers he knew focused more on the business side of running a ranch, while some preferred working with the cattle.

Will had a keen mind and many plans for Colter Ranch. His contracts with Fort Whipple and many businesses in Prescott meant he no longer had to drive the entire herd to distant markets. As each new hotel or restaurant opened in town, he successfully negotiated contracts to supply beef. He even built a smoke house and small slaughter house for preparing orders. Snake handled most of the butchering and smoking.

This coming year, in addition to starting the horse business, he was also going to start growing his own horse feed. He detested farming and hoped to hire someone from one of the many incoming wagon trains who would be able to manage it. If things went well, he would even grow extra and supply feed for the local livery or perhaps the fort.

Hearing the supper bell, Will set aside the bridle he was mending and made his way to the ranch house. As he entered, he gave Hannah a quick kiss on the cheek. "Hello, beautiful."

She smiled at the compliment, but continued dishing up two plates so Rosa could take the remaining food out to the bunkhouse. Taking a seat across from him, she bowed her head, waiting for him to say grace. When he finished, he dug into his meal. This was so good.

"Did you work things out with Rosa?"

"Yes. It was so strange. At first she thought I wanted to cut her pay. But when I explained she would be paid the same, she was fine with whatever terms I set."

"Good." He paused to finish chewing a bite of steak. "Would you mind this evening if we went over the ledgers instead of working on the reading lesson?"

"I thought you were fine with the ledgers." Concerned tinged her voice.

"I think I am, but it wouldn't hurt to have you check my work for the last few weeks. It makes no sense to me why I would be able to do that but struggle with words."

"Remember that Dr. Murphy said head injuries often have unusual outcomes. I'm just thankful that you have no other lingering issues."

Will nodded. How could he tell her it made him feel stupid to no longer be able to read?

As he finished his last bite of food, Hannah stood. Eyes sparkling with excitement, she said, "I have a surprise for you... Pecan pie."

"Mmm. You spoil me."

Once the table was cleared and Hannah finished the dishes, Will retrieved the ledgers and laid them out on the table. When she sat down and started reviewing the numbers, her eyes went wide.

"What is it?" Will asked, worried that he overestimated his ability with numbers.

"It just that... That is a lot of money."

Leaning over her shoulder, he looked at the tally. "No that is what it should be. It all adds up, right?"

"The calculations are correct. I'm just used to the meager earnings of a doctor. This has a few more digits than I expected." She laughed nervously.

Letting out the breath he was holding, Will explained, "That is more than what we made my last year at the Star C with twice as many cattle. The Lord has been good to us."

"Very good, indeed."

Chapter 7

Cimarron Crossing, Kansas

September 13, 1864

They made it. Finally. Cimarron Crossing.

Adam sighed as he dismounted his stallion, relieved to see a wagon train camped just outside of the small settlement. Their arrival could not have been timed better.

These last two weeks were the most challenging thing he experienced in his young life. The first few days of the journey he set as fast of a pace as he could without injuring the horses. Even though they camped at night, he could not shake the feeling they were being followed. He forced himself to stay alert to keep watch throughout the night. On the third night, exhaustion pulled him under and he slept. Little good that sleep did him. After two weeks of travel, he was physically and emotionally drained.

The trip to Cimarron Crossing took longer than expected. They ran out of food after a week. It probably would have been sooner, but Julia barely ate anything he put in front of her. Then part way through the second week, he shot some quail. They ate well that night and the next morning. That was three days ago. Neither had a bite of food since.

He was emotionally drained as well. Being around Julia in her dark state of mind was difficult. He never would have thought the jubilant jovial Julia would have retreated so far. She was deep within herself—not speaking—and barely even going through the motions.

One minute, his heart broke for her. Then the next, his anger flared at Reuben for whatever he did to her. It must have been something even more terrible than he could imagine since it drove away the adventurous, happy girl he once knew.

Right now, her emotional state was the least of his worries. Adam had to get them to Santa Fe. He had very little money, so it was unlikely he could purchase passage for the rest of the way. The only option he could think of was to find them some work in exchange for transportation, food, and shelter. Leaving the silent Julia with the horses, he set out to do just that.

Approaching a group of men standing by one of the campfires near the wagon train, he prayed for wisdom. He had to get them something soon and it had to be with this group. He had no way to provide for them until the next wagon train came along.

"Excuse me," he said to the group of men. "Would any of you know where my sister and I might find work? We need to continue on to Santa Fe as soon as possible."

One short man spit a stream of tobacco juice at his boot. "I know where your sister might find work—especially if she's pretty. Not so sure about you though." He slapped his hand down on his leg as he bent over laughing, causing the hole-ridden hat on his head to tumble to the ground. His friends joined in with a similar response.

Moving away from the uncouth crowd, he sought out the wagon master instead. Perhaps he would be more willing to help.

After a brief conversation, the wagon train master suggested that he check with the freighters. They were the ones usually looking to take on folks mid-trip—as long as Adam didn't need to go any farther than Santa Fe. Once they got to Santa Fe, he would figure out how to get them the rest of the way to the Arizona Territory.

Hope renewed, he made his way to where the freighters camped. The first ten freighters he asked laughed in his face. Who wanted to take on a brother and sister team and provide from their limited supplies for them?

He was about to give up when he met Chauncey Jones. The man was young, not more than four or so years older than Adam. He was built like a large oak tree, all sturdy immovable muscle.

"My name is Adam Larson." He started his now well-rehearsed speech. "My sister and I are in need of transportation, food, and shelter for the trip to Santa Fe. Julia is an excellent cook and would also care for any laundry needs. I am experienced with livestock and capable of driving a wagon."

"Chauncey Jones is the name, and you're in luck."

Adam's jaw almost went slack when Chauncey replied affirmatively.

"We lost a man on the way here. I need a driver. Be happy to have someone other than Smitts do the cooking. Gettin' tired of the charred mess he calls food. Can your sister make something a mite tastier?"

"Yes, she can."

"Great. She can ride with you in the freight wagon you'll be driving. Won't be payin' no wages. Just your services in exchange for food and transportation. I'll provide a tent for camping at night, as well as food for ya both."

"One tent?" Adam cringed inwardly. How could he possibly share a tent with her? If only he could hold on to the image of her when she was thirteen. That would certainly help keep his confusing feelings away.

"Well, it's all I got. Sides, with you being brother and sister there ain't no reason why you can't be sharing a tent. I ain't got no bedrolls so you'll either have to do without or rustle up some on your own."

"We have bedrolls. I also have two horses I would like to keep. Is there any way we can throw in food and water for them as well?"

Chauncey rubbed his hand across the stubble of his chin and thought for a moment. "Tell ya what. Since I ain't got to pay wages for the man that we lost, I'll go ahead and throw in the feed for the horses, too."

Thank you, Lord, for providing. "Thank you, Mr. Jones."

"Aw, just call me Chauncey. No need to be so formal."

Adam finalized the arrangements and went to get Julia and the horses. She was staring off into the distance. A deep sadness and pain hung over her like dark storm clouds. She had retreated into her prison of despair and pain. He wished he could help her carry that burden.

Shaking his head to clear his mind, he approached her. "I found us a way to Santa Fe."

She turned her head to look at him, her dull eyes squinting against the sun.

He took a seat next to her. "I found a freighter looking to hire us for the rest of the journey to Santa Fe. In exchange for your cooking and cleaning skills, and my driving skills, he is providing us with the use of a tent, food, and water."

"*A* tent?" she asked her voice low and lifeless.

He was so surprised that she finally spoke that he took a moment to respond. "Yes, I'm sorry there is only one. I know it's not ideal, but we will come up with some sort of divider for privacy. Given that everyone thinks we are brother and sister, we will have to make do with that. I saw how full the wagons were packed with freight. There will not be enough room for either of us to sleep there."

"Very well."

Really? I thought she would put up more of a fight? I'm not even remotely fine with the idea.

Standing, he helped her gather up her things. Then they made their way to Chauncey's wagons. He introduced Julia to him. When Chauncey asked if she would be able to make supper for them that evening, she nodded and asked where the cooking supplies were kept. He showed her. Quietly, Julia started preparing the meal.

As the aroma wafted about the wagons, Adam's stomach growled. He was more than ready for some sort of food. When she handed him a plate, it was all he could do to remind himself to eat slowly.

Unfortunately, she needed no such encouragement. He watched as she took a few nibbles of food before setting it aside. She was going to get sick if she didn't start eating.

"Julia," he said nodding his head towards her plate. He was going to say more, but she shot him an angry look. Then picking up her plate she slowly ate the rest of her food. When she finished, she jumped up and started cleaning, avoiding eye contact with him for the rest of the evening.

After the sun set, many of the freight drivers, or teamsters as they were called, set up crates to play cards and drink whiskey. Exhaustion already pulled at Adam, so he set up the tent. When he unrolled it, he found the previous driver's bedroll, so he took one of those blankets and rigged up a divider down the middle of the tent. Julia was sitting nearby staring at the toe of her boot as if it were the most interesting thing she had ever seen.

"I have the tent set up. I would like to retire, if you don't mind." Then leaning closer so only she could hear, he added, "I have a divider up as well."

She nodded before getting her bedroll.

Julia entered the tent. She should be upset that she had to share a tent with an unmarried man who was not related to her. She should be concerned about what would happen to her reputation should someone find out that she was not really Adam's sister. But she didn't care. She was already ruined. What more could society say to her?

Laying out her bedroll on one side of the divider, she heard Adam doing the same on the other side. At least the divider was not see-through.

"Good night, Julia," he said before what sounded like rolling over on his side.

She knew she treated him poorly since they left Texas. She had been short with him—when she didn't ignore him completely. She was grateful for his help, but found it impossible to move beyond what Reuben did to her. It consumed her thoughts to the point that she had nothing left to give to Adam, not even politeness or common courtesy. A little nudge of guilt infiltrated her thoughts. Perhaps she should make some effort to be pleasant to him even though she felt dead inside.

Clearing her throat, she responded stiffly, "Good night, Adam."

She could not close her eyes or try to sleep. Every time she tried, she saw Reuben's face inches from hers. She felt the weight of his body on her, crushing the air from her lungs. She felt him ruin her.

It made her sick. It scared her. What if he found her? Would he subject her to such torture again? A sob escaped her lips before she could stop it.

Rolling onto her side, she cried.

How could God let this happen? She thought he loved her? She thought he protected his children? It would have been better to kill her that night than to allow her to suffer day after day remembering what Reuben did to her.

The bitterness took firmer hold of her heart.

The sounds around camp eventually died down as all of the teamsters retired. Still Julia was awake. She turned her head into her blanket to hide the sound of her sobs. She would never be... Be what? Be a wife? Be a mother? Be pure again?

Slowly, exhaustion won and she slept.

Again, Adam thought he heard Julia sobbing. The thin blanket acting as a divider between them was not enough to muffle the distinct sound. He could tell she was trying to disguise it, but she couldn't. His heart ached for her. He wanted so much to pull back the divider and just hold her in his arms, to rock her back and forth like he had that first night. *Lord, I can't comfort her, but you can. Wrap her in your love. Comfort her in her pain.*

Gideon Bates stood, stretching his sore back. This vantage point would let him see a wagon train coming into town and follow its movements without being detected.

After getting his orders from Reuben, he delayed leaving Texas for a few days to gather information about where Larson might be. He had no desire to take off north based solely on the tracks heading out that way from Larson's ranch.

What he discovered convinced him the delay had been a wise decision. Turns out Larson was supposed to be leaving—just not on the night that he did, but rather a few days later—to take a job with Will Colter in the Arizona Territory. Very suspicious that he should leave in a hurry without the provisions he had been stocking. Only thing that made sense was that he had Julia Colter with him.

Learning the connection Larson had with Will Colter proved to be valuable. It provided the basis for the plan Gideon set into motion. Instead of trying to chase their tracks on a roundabout route and risk not catching up with them, he decided to head straight for Santa Fe. They had to pass through here to get to the Arizona Territory. They would be traveling with a wagon train—for he was positive Larson wasn't stupid enough to travel alone for long.

When they came, he would be waiting. Then maybe he could get some of that back pay from Reuben. It never set well with him, doing hard work and not seeing pay for months on end. That had never been his agreement with Reuben. He was supposed to get paid monthly. If he played his cards right in his present situation, he would get enough to make up for it.

Nine days later, the freight wagons arrived at Fort Union, New Mexico. The trip between Cimarron Crossing and Fort Union was not an easy one, not that Adam had any previous experience to compare it to. When they ran out of water yesterday morning, he was glad to know they would press on to Fort Union with as few stops as possible. The first thing each man did was refill the water barrels, drink their fill, and water the animals.

Once camp was made, Julia approached him. Hand on her hip, and fire in her eyes, she asked, "Does Will know we're coming?"

The question caught him off guard, as did the manner in which it was delivered. "He is aware that I am coming," Adam answered trying to keep the irritation from his tone. "Though, I never confirmed my departure since we left in a hurry."

"Perhaps," she said, dropping her hand to her side as she softened her tone, "I will write to him and post it from here before we leave."

"I will do the same, since I should have already sent him some word."

She nodded curtly and left.

Adam blew out a frustrated sigh. He understood that she was hurting, but he was tired of being the object of her wrath. The whole way from Cimarron Crossing to Fort Union had been tense. He tried to set her at ease and anticipate her needs. No matter what he did, she still looked on him with anger in her eyes.

Within minutes, Julia returned with a few sheets of paper. Thrusting them in his direction, she held out a pencil with her other hand. Obviously, she expected him to write his letter first. Taking the offered items, he turned without a word. Once he found a place to sit, he began composing the letter, debating just how much he should say surrounding his untimely departure.

Dear Mr. Colter,

I apologize for the delay in returning your correspondence. An urgent matter required my immediate attention. However, I wanted to let you know that I am already on my way and hope this arrives before I do.

Adam stopped. Should he mention that Julia was with him? Would she say something? To be safe, he added a quick sentence that she was with him—nothing about the reason behind it—then signed his name.

When Adam returned her pencil, Julia composed a brief note to Will. She stared at the blank page for several minutes wondering how to begin. Most of what she wanted to say, she did not think she could say even in person much less a letter. Deciding to stick to the facts and keep it brief, she wrote:

Dearest Will,

I am on my way to the Arizona Territory. The situation in Texas has changed for the worse and I find myself in need of a new home. I am hoping that you will welcome me once I arrive. Fear not for my safety on this trip, as Adam Larson has taken it upon himself to see I arrive unharmed.

Your sister,

Julia Colter

She snorted as she wrote the word "unharmed." She was harmed, before she even left. And she doubted whether she would ever be anything else again. Sealing the letter, she stood and delivered it to an officer who agreed to take it with the military mail. Now, at least Will has a chance to get a warning of her arrival.

Chapter 8

Two days later, the freight wagon train arrived at their destination. When Adam said his farewells to Chauncey, he was surprised when he handed him several paper bills. He said that both he and his sister did such fine work that he felt he owed them at least a little bit of money. Stunned, Adam thanked him before leaving.

Now that they were back down to two horses, saddle bags, and bedrolls, Adam was thinking through how to get them the rest of the way to the Arizona Territory. He really needed a wagon and a team of oxen. They also needed a tent, of which they would not be sharing. He would sleep in the tent and Julia would sleep in the wagon. They needed food, water barrels, and more. From what Chauncey said, they were probably another month or so out from Prescott.

He and Julia made their way from the plaza where Chauncey was selling his wares to the western edge of town. There he found a wagon train that had been waiting for Indian activity to settle down before departing for points west. Speaking with the wagon master, Adam discovered they were going to roll out in two days. He had to get started now if he was going to secure the necessary supplies.

He had no money, save for the few bills from Chauncey. Certainly not enough for the supplies he and Julia would need for the rest of the trip. He would have to sell one of the horses. There was no other way. It broke his heart because they were going to be his contribution for his new job on Colter Ranch and they were a gift from his pa.

Adam walked over to the mare and began taking off the gear.

"What are you doing?" Julia snapped out of her daze long enough to pay attention to what he was doing, her voice sharp with accusation.

Adam sighed inwardly. He was growing weary of her short tone. "I am selling the mare."

Her jaw dropped. "Whatever for?"

"Because, we have to have supplies, a team, and a wagon to get to your brother's ranch. We can't just ride the horses with no food and water the rest of the way. We need money. Unless you have some buried treasure, I am going to have to sell the mare."

Julia's look softened. "Wait."

She dug around in her saddle bag, finally pulling out a large stack of money.

"Where did you get this?"

"I took it from Reuben's desk before I left."

"You *stole* it?"

"I did not! My father left me an inheritance which Reuben was supposed to manage for me until I became of age. I knew I would need money to run. This is significantly less than what my inheritance should be, so I did not *steal* anything." She defiantly crossed her arms to emphasize her point, her curls bobbing from the sudden jerking of her head.

"Okay," he conceded, flipping through the stack. There was more than enough to cover their expenses. A smile twitched at the edge of his mouth. He would not have to sell the mare after all. *Thank you, Lord, for providing for us in this unexpected way.*

Ready to purchase supplies, he started to walk away from camp. Pausing, he asked, "Would you like to come with me?"

She uncrossed her arms and both her stance and her tone of voice softened. "I would like that."

"Come on, sis," he teased, offering her his arm.

They made their way back to the plaza area and purchased water barrels, feed for the horses, and a few other items. Adam was pleased that they found someone selling a six yoke of oxen and wagon at a fair price. In one afternoon he purchased all of the supplies they needed to travel the rest of the way to Colter Ranch.

As Adam was loading the last of the supplies into the wagon,

Julia recognized a familiar face headed her direction. Her heart pounded furiously in her chest and her palms grew sweaty. It could not be. No, she was certain it was Jethro Pace, only he had one arm. What was he doing in Santa Fe?

She knew he worked on the Star C, but in her panicked state she could not remember when he left. Was it with Will? Or was it after? Could Reuben have sent him here to fetch her back?

As he grew closer, his face lit up.

"Adam Larson!" Jethro Pace called out as he stepped towards them.

Adam looked up, confused. His scrunched eyebrows and forehead gave her the impression that he was trying to place the man who called out his name.

Suddenly his face lit with recognition. "Jethro Pace, from the Star C. What are you doing here?"

"I might ask you and Miss Colter the same," Jethro said, vigorously shaking Adam's hand with his only hand.

Chauncey had just arrived at the tail end of the conversation to help Adam with the items he purchased from him. "Miss Colter? You mean Miss Larson?"

Jethro hesitated. Julia shot him a pleading look. Her stomach plummeted to the ground as she envisioned her and Adam's subterfuge dissolving before her eyes.

"Mrs. Larson?" Jethro asked with a confused expression puckering his tan face.

This was going to be a disaster. "Jethro Pace," Julia interrupted. "How did you get to Santa Fe?"

"Well, I was headed west with yer bro—"

"Really? You came with Will Colter?" she cut him off before he could finish the word. "Why didn't you continue on?"

Jethro looked even more confused. "Ah, um... I took some nasty shots when we ran into Indians. My arm was infected so the doctor here in town had to take it off. Saved my life he did. But Will had to move on. Can't complain though, he left me with enough money to settle here."

"That was very generous of Mr. Colter," Julia commented, nervously fidgeting with the edge of her sleeve.

"Who is Mr. Colter?" Chauncey asked, hefting a crate into the back of the waiting wagon.

Adam responded before anyone else could get a word in edgewise. "He is a good friend of the Larsons. We grew up on neighboring ranches and our fathers were close friends. I am on my way to his new ranch in the Arizona Territory to start breeding and training horses for Mr. Colter."

"I see. Well, that's the last of your things, Mr. Larson, Miss Larson. It was a pleasure working with you." Chauncey tipped his hat to Julia, then turned and left.

"It was good to see you again, Jethro. Can we pass on anything to Will for you?" Julia asked trying to end the awkward conversation quickly.

"Ah, just tell him I said thanks for all he done. Mr. Larson. Mrs. Larson," Jethro said before leaving.

She nearly collapsed from nerves as she waved to Jethro Pace's retreating back. *Mrs. Larson, indeed.* She breathed a huge sigh of relief when Adam helped her into the wagon and drove them out to the west end of town. That was close.

Mrs. Larson? Gideon Bates fisted his hand in frustration from his hidden perch behind one of the freight wagons.

He had been prepared for anything—except that. Larson had a lot of nerve marrying the poor girl in the dead of night and then taking off with her. Somehow that piece of information never made it to his ears before now. Maybe that was why she rejected all the men Reuben paraded before her. She already had a beau and plans to leave with him.

Now what should he do? If he tried to take her back to Reuben, Larson would definitely follow to collect his wife—and it would be kidnapping then. Gideon had done some things he wasn't proud of in his life, but he never broke the law.

No. Taking her back to Reuben was out of the question now. He would want to marry her off to some other man and she couldn't be married off, cause she already was. Reuben would not be too happy about that.

If he went back to Reuben empty handed, he was sure to lose his job. Even though he'd been working for him just over a year, he learned enough about him to understand that he would see this present situation as a failure on Gideon's part. Reuben wasn't one to reason in a normal fashion.

"Mighty fine quandary," he whispered as he led his horse from the town square. He'd have to give it some thought for a few days.

Mrs. Larson? For some reason, when Jethro Pace called Julia that, Adam's heart started racing and a weird fluttery feeling settled in his stomach. What was wrong with him? This was Julia, a long-time friend of his family. Why would he be reacting this way?

"That was close," she said with a nervous laugh.

He cleared his throat. "Yes, it was."

Too close, he thought, as he tried to get his emotions under control.

Once back at the wagon train circle, his emotions started to settle. Then he helped Julia down from the wagon. When he touched her hand, lightening shot through him, stirring up the confusing feelings all over again. As soon as she was safely to the ground, he quickly released his hold. Why was he suddenly so nervous around her?

Shaking off the unsettling feelings, he left her to start supper while he went to find the wagon master. He found the short stocky man as the last touches of light faded from the sky. He spoke briefly with him to see if he and Julia could join the wagon train west. The wagon master agreed before assigning them a place.

With business settled, his mind returned to the jumbled emotions sparked from this afternoon. Slowly walking back to camp he tried to understand what was happening. He was acting like a fool—getting all flummoxed around his childhood friend. This was Julia Colter—the girl who beat him in a roping contest. The girl that could ride as well as any man. The one that would prank him in school as often as she could.

The woman who wormed her way into his heart these last

weeks, despite her curt words and melancholy.

As he turned the corner around the end of their wagon, he caught a glimpse of her in the firelight. She was standing over the skillet, finishing supper. The light from the fire highlighted her shapely silhouette. Adam thought he had never seen such a lovely woman. He gazed at her as if it were the first time he had truly seen her. Her sandy brown curls trailed down her back, gathered together by a dark ribbon. Her smile could brighten a gloomy room, though she wasn't smiling now—hadn't in a very long time. And those blue, mischievous eyes.

A sigh escaped his lips unguarded.

Adam shook himself from the thoughts that both warmed him and scared him all at the same time. Clearing his throat, he let her know he was back.

Watching her prepare a meal seemed surreal. Prior to this trip, he'd never seen her cook and assumed she didn't know how, with all of the time she spent outdoors. Surprisingly she was a good cook. He took a seat just as she handed him some supper.

"Is everything settled?" she asked, her voice bordering on pleasant.

Swallowing a bite of food, Adam replied, "Yes. We leave the morning after tomorrow."

"How long do you think it will take?"

"The wagon master said we should arrive by the first of November, maybe a little earlier if we do not run into bad weather or danger."

"Good." Having finished her meal, she sat there for a minute before continuing. "Adam... I, um... I..." she stammered. He waited. "I'm sorry that I have not thanked you for rescuing me."

"Julia—"

"No, let me finish. I know you sacrificed a great deal to get me out of Texas in a hurry. You were not able to say goodbye to your family or plan your departure as you wished. Instead, you took compassion on a friend in danger and you did everything you could to get me out of that danger. You have kept me safe. You have kept me sane. And I have done nothing but snap at you and make myself difficult to live with. You saved my life. You may not understand all that has happened, but you did save my life. And for that, I am grateful."

When she turned and looked into his eyes, Adam was never more thankful that they now had separate sleeping arrangements. The look of gratitude nearly undid him.

Later, during the middle of the night, he woke with a start. He listened to see if he heard Julia crying in the wagon. Complete silence. Then he realized that it was the silence that caused him to stir. He had become so used to the sound of her crying that when it was missing it seemed off. *Thank you, Lord, for giving her rest. Please keep mending her wounded heart.*

Two weeks later, well into the Arizona Territory, Julia realized the nightmares had stopped. Despite traipsing across the wilderness, she felt safe for the first time in over a year. Ever since her father died, she was on edge at the Star C—even before Reuben became violent towards her. But now she felt safe on the trail with Adam.

During the day in the silence, she had too much time to think. She was still angry that God would allow this tragedy to befall her. If God was so loving, why would he allow her to be raped, to be ruined? Why would he stand by and quietly watch as Reuben beat her? Was that how a loving God acted? Especially since He had the power to stop all of it. What kind of twisted being would refuse to use their power to help someone in trouble?

Then, she thought of a verse she remembered from childhood. *In this world you will have trouble. Or something like that. Seems like an excuse for the all-powerful God to do nothing.* Well, if she was going to be left on her own, she would just rely on herself—and maybe Adam.

Growing weary of her own thoughts, she started a conversation with Adam to distract herself. "Tell me why you brought your horses all the way out here." Out of the corner of her eye, she thought she saw him sit a little straighter in the springboard seat of the wagon.

His green eyes lit with excitement as he responded, "Well, when I told my pa and ma about my plans to move to Will's ranch to work with the horses, Pa told me he thought I earned the pick of the horses as payment for the years of training I put in at home. He told me I could pick any two I wanted. So, I picked one good stud and one good mare, both known for the quality of their offspring. I was glad he let me take them."

"Why?"

"When I first got the idea to strike out on my own, I really wanted to start my own horse breeding and training business. I thought about going west, but the most important thing was that it would be my own. I started discussing the idea with Pa and he suggested it might be better to start working for someone else or even partner with them, so the expense wouldn't be so great in the beginning. When Caroline mentioned that Will had made it to the Arizona Territory, I got the idea to write and see if he would be interested in working with me. If I was in a better position, I would have asked to be a partner. But as of right now, I only have two horses and my skills."

She nodded.

"It was several months before I had any kind of reply. In truth, I wrote one letter and he sent one in return. But, I trust Will and am sure the final arrangements will be beneficial to both of us. He even said he started the buildings and purchased a few horses specifically for breeding."

"Sounds like a dream come true," Julia said trying to keep the sadness over her situation from her voice.

"Not quite. I hope the experience I gain and the wages I earn will eventually let me run my own place. This is a good start."

She was quiet for several minutes. In danger of returning to her heavy thoughts, she started the conversation again. "I thought that all this time Will never wrote to me."

"You had no letters? I thought you were close."

"We were—are. But, I only received his first letter stating that he made it safely to his new home. I wrote to him all the time, almost weekly at first. But, when I never received any response month after month, I thought maybe he forgot me." Looking off to the distant flatlands, she continued. "Then, the night I left, when I was going through Reuben's desk for the money, I came across a stack of letters from Will addressed to me. Reuben had them this whole time and he kept them from me—and he had opened them."

"I'm sorry. That was wrong."

"I know it was. All I can think is that Reuben has been doing his best this last year to manipulate me and get me to do his bidding."

"Do you have the letters?"

"No. I was too frightened to leave any indication of where I was going. I knew Reuben would notice them missing. But, I'm glad to know that Will wrote. Judging by the stack, he wrote a lot."

Adam reached over and gave her hand a squeeze. The action propelled her to get out some of her pent up thoughts.

"Did you know Reuben tried to force me to marry Mr. Norton?" she asked.

Shaking his head, he replied, "I only knew that you were engaged, not any details about how it came to pass."

"On more than one occasion, I told Reuben I was too young to marry. At first he suggested names, or invited various associates over for supper. He would seat me next to the men and try to force me to talk to them. With Hiram, something was different. Reuben arranged a dinner party where Hiram was scheduled to be one of the guests. That morning, Reuben and I got into an argument."

Julia paused as tears began pooling in her eyes. "I remember telling him that Hiram was too old, more than twice my age, and that I was not interested. That is the first time Reuben hit me. He slammed me up against the wall and warned me that I should listen. But, I was too stubborn. I didn't want to marry that lecherous man."

Adam's voice was soft when he spoke. "Julia, you did nothing wrong. I think it is perfectly acceptable for a woman to choose her husband and not be forced into a horrible situation."

She snorted in disgust. "Too bad Reuben didn't see it your way. That night, without ever asking me for my hand, Hiram and Reuben very publicly announced my engagement. Hiram pressed for a quick wedding, undoubtedly because he was concerned that I would run. I thought about it then. But, Caroline and I came up with the idea of the scene at the church. I needed a public denouncement that could not be refuted. Otherwise, I would only be buying myself a few weeks or months. Of course, you saw the outcome of that day."

Looking down at her hands she grew silent. A part of her wanted to confess everything, but she knew it was not appropriate. She had shared too much already.

Growing nervous, she laughed off the seriousness of what she shared. "I don't know why I'm telling you all of this."

Adam reached across the seat and put his arm around her shoulders. The comforting action brought a new wave of tears. He sat there silently, letting her cry it out. When her tears subsided, Julia straightened in the seat.

"Thank you, Adam."

"You are very welcome."

Gideon Bates watched Julia Colter—er, Larson—from across the circle where he camped with his new employer. For now, he was working as a teamster for one of the freighters hauling goods from Santa Fe to Prescott.

Not deciding is sometimes as good of a plan as deciding something, he thought. Other than a brief note to Reuben to let him know he had caught up to Adam Larson and Julia, Gideon hadn't determined his next move. He was still pondering what would be best for him. He wasn't entirely certain he could trust Reuben to pay him if he did return with Julia.

But Larson didn't need to know that. So for now, he would just watch. See if the answer to his quandary didn't present itself.

Chapter 9

Colter Ranch, Arizona Territory

October 10, 1864

"Boss, got two letters for ya," Owens said as he entered the stables after making deliveries in town.

Will had just returned from riding with the herd for the day. He set his saddle in its designated spot and walked over to take the letters from Owens. Turning both letters over, he noticed one had additional writing on the outside. He concentrated, but the words danced on the envelopes like meaningless symbols. Shoving them in his pocket, he continued removing the bridle and blanket from Jackson.

While he suspected one of the letters was from Adam Larson, he had no idea who might have written the other. His sister Julia had yet to send him a letter. As time went on, he grew more concerned about the lack of correspondence from her. Over the last few weeks he was not able to shake the sense of foreboding whenever he thought of her. Something was wrong. It didn't make sense that she wouldn't write at all in over a year. They had been far too close.

Laying the brush aside, Will led Jackson into his stall. Once he fed and watered the horse, he left the stables to find Hannah. He did not want to wait until after supper to find out the contents of the letters. Peeking in the kitchen, he did not see her. Walking back outside, he found her sitting on a blanket near the lake working on her mending. It was a lovely day, warm enough to soak up the sun, as Hannah was doing now.

When his shadow fell across the blanket, she looked up. She set aside her mending and moved to get up.

"Stay, I'll join you," Will said, pulling the letters from his pocket. He handed them to her with a heavy sigh. He was growing tired of not being able to read. "These came today. Would you please read them for me?"

"Of course. It looks like there is one from Adam Larson and one from Jethro Pace. Which would you like me to start with?"

"Which one has the writing on the outside and what does it say?"

"The one from Mr. Pace. It says, 'Saw Adam and Julia Larson. They should arrive soon.'"

"What!" He jerked the letter from Hannah's hand. His jaw tightened as he stared at the writing. It was still jumbled to him, but that couldn't be what it said.

When he looked up from the letter to Hannah's face, shocked eyes greeted him. He handed the letter back. "Are you sure it says 'Adam and Julia Larson'?"

"Yes, I'm certain. Do you want me to read the rest or not?"

At his nod, she opened the letter and read:

Dear Boss,

I just wanted to thank ye for yer help in Santa Fe. After you and the boys left, I met me a fine señorita and got married. She helps me with the thangs that are too difficult one handed. I am working on Alexander Morrow's ranch. He said he met ya.

Thanks for taking good care of me and leaving me more than a fair sum.

Regards,

Pace

Will was glad to hear his former hand was settled and able to work in Santa Fe. It was just the note on the outside that bothered him. What did he mean by Adam and Julia Larson? Julia didn't marry him did she? She was too young to get married. He frowned at the thought.

"What's wrong? Isn't the news from Mr. Pace good?" Hannah asked.

"Yes, the news from Pace is good," he said, expelling his breath in a rush. "Please read the other letter." Maybe something in Adam's letter would shed some light on the situation.

"It is from Adam Larson. Isn't he the young man you said would be coming to help with the horses?"

"Yes."

"He says: 'I apologize for the delay in returning your correspondence. An urgent matter required my immediate attention. However, I wanted to let you know that I am already on my way and hope this arrives before I do. Julia is with me.'"

Will's frown etched deeper. "Does it say anything else? Is that it?"

"That's all. He just signed his name at the end."

Will stood and paced back and forth with his hands fisted at his side. "What does he mean Julia is with him!"

His mind conjured all kinds of reasons for the two cryptic letters.

"And Pace's letter, what did he say on the back again?"

Turning the letter over, Hannah confirmed, "Adam and Julia Larson." She paused a moment. "Oh. You don't think they got married do you?"

"She's seventeen! She's too young to get married. What was she thinking? I can't imagine Reuben would have agreed to such a thing." Then again, maybe Reuben did not know. Maybe Julia and Adam ran away together.

"But, we don't know for certain. Neither letter says anything conclusive. Perhaps Mr. Pace was mistaken. He obviously wrote his note in a hurry."

Still pacing, Will shook his head. "Explain to me under what circumstances the young Adam Larson would be referring to my sister by her first name?"

"There are a number of reasonable explanations. First, the letter seemed hurried. It seemed rather short for a response about working at the ranch. Didn't you tell me your two families were rather close? Wouldn't that be reason enough?"

"That is still no reason to be so familiar with my sister!" He knew that was what really bothered him—the thought of Larson being, well, familiar with Julia.

"Will, please sit. You are making me nervous."

He stopped pacing and took a deep breath. Slowly, he lowered to the ground, sitting across from her. Looking directly into her eyes, he aired his concerns. "I'm just worried. Julia is so young. I don't want to see her get hurt."

Hannah took his hands in hers. "Your *sister* is coming. That is a good thing, no matter who else she might bring with her. And Mr. Larson is coming to help with the horses and expand your business. Won't it be nice to see them again?"

"You're right... But, I can't shake the feeling that something bad has happened. I can't explain it. If he has done anything to hurt her or coerce her into marriage, there is no telling what I'll do."

"All will be well." She rested her hand on his cheek. He hoped she was right.

Two weeks later, a plume of dust signaled riders coming in from the south late in the afternoon. Other than the sleeping Mr. Flanagan, Hannah and Rosa were alone at the ranch. The rest of the men, including Will, were out in the field with the grazing cattle.

Hannah debated whether or not to wake Mr. Flanagan. He was certain to be tired after guarding the cattle last night. Yet, she felt uneasy about the approaching riders.

Motioning Rosa to follow her into the ranch house, she quickly located the extra rifle Will left with her. She loaded the gun, just in case. As she cracked the door open to peer out, she saw a wagon's canvas cover reflecting the bright sunlight.

Then it suddenly dawned on her. The boys were back from California!

Throwing the door open, she propped the rifle on the porch and waited for the men to come into clearer view. Sure enough, Ben Shepherd was riding in the front of the group.

A bleary-eyed Ian Flanagan emerged from the bunkhouse, pulling his suspenders over his loose cotton shirt.

"It's alright, Mr. Flanagan!" she yelled across the yard. He nodded, but stood watch until Ben stopped near the corral.

She walked the short distance as Ben dismounted. "Welcome home, Ben!"

"Mrs. Colter," he greeted with weary eyes. "Glad to set sights on this place again."

"When did you last eat? Should Rosa and I get some food ready?" she asked, though it was mid-afternoon.

"Ma'am, we'll be fine 'til supper. Mostly we'd like to take a dip in the lake and get cleaned up, after we see to the horses and wagon."

She smiled. "You might want to send one of the boys out to the pastures. Let Will know you're back. I know he'll be eager to catch up with you."

Ben motioned Hawk over, one of the few men that still appeared to have some energy left. After a brief conversation, Hawk mounted his horse again and rode off towards where the cattle were grazing for the day.

Hannah excused herself. Hurrying back to the ranch house, she and Rosa started a few pots of coffee. Half an hour later, she heard a horse riding in from the pasture. When she looked out the window, only Will had returned. The rest of the men must be staying out until supper, as usual.

She was trying to remember how many mouths they would have to feed when Will entered.

"Can you fix up something nice for the boys tonight. There's nothing like a good home cooked meal after being on the trail for almost two months."

Reaching for the coffee pot, she raised it in question. At his nod, she filled a mug for him. "Rosa and I are already planning something special."

"Ben will be joining us in here tonight. I'll want to talk to him about the drive."

She nodded.

"Good news so far is that we didn't lose any men. Was glad to hear it."

When a brief cloud of emotion masked his face, Hannah wondered how many men her husband had lost over the years.

"Anyway, I'll leave you be," he said, giving her a quick peck on the cheek before draining the last of his coffee and heading back outside.

The next morning, Hannah hurried to get breakfast on the table. Today Will was taking her into Prescott to visit Betty Lancaster. The last time she saw her friend was on her wedding day, almost two months ago. She missed the older woman's companionship. During Hannah's time at the boardinghouse, the two often talked for hours each day as they prepared meals, washed the never-ending stack of laundry, or cleaned the bunkhouses. She tried to talk with Rosa but, it was not the same. While Rosa could get by speaking English, she never seemed comfortable doing so.

Cracking the last egg in the mixing bowl, Hannah whisked the eggs together until they were smooth before pouring them into the hot skillet. She started stirring to scramble the eggs when a wave of nausea hit her. She hoped it would pass. But, after another minute, she felt the bile rise. Tossing the spoon aside, she ran for the front door. Rounding the corner of the ranch house, she lost the contents of her stomach. Bracing herself with one arm against the house, she took several deep breaths.

Running from the barn, Will dropped a pail of milk next to the front door. He hurried to her side, concern written on his face. "Are you alright?"

"I'll be fine. I just need a minute."

"Are you sure?"

"Go, have your breakfast. I'll be in soon." The thought of food made her feel ill again.

He hesitated a moment before he picked up the milk pail and went inside. As soon as the door shut, she heaved again.

Having gone through this before, she was now fairly certain she was with child. She missed her last monthly and it seemed she was about to miss her next. When she was carrying her first husband's child, she had been ill for weeks sometime around her sixth to eighth week. If she figured correctly she was about six weeks along. That would put the baby due sometime in June.

They were going to have a child!

Her excitement quickly died when she remembered the fate of her first child. What if she lost this one, too? She would be crushed. So would Will. Maybe she should wait to tell him until she was further along—more likely to see the babe to term. No, that was not fair to Will. He would want to know.

Taking another deep breath of pine-scented air, Hannah squared her shoulders and entered the house. When she inhaled the fragrance of the cooked eggs, she felt queasy again. Once across the threshold, she made no move towards the table. She closed her eyes and willed herself not to be sick again, afraid of worrying Will more. Other than a dry piece of bread, she didn't think she could stomach much food this morning.

"You're not well. I can see it on your face," he said. Taking her arm, he led her to a chair. "Maybe we should postpone our trip to town."

"No!" She had been looking forward to this for days. "I will be fine in a bit. I'll just eat a piece of toast then we can be on our way."

Dark golden brown eyes pierced her gaze. The worry on his face broke her heart as she held his gaze, unwavering. She *would* be going to town today, despite the morning sickness. Tearing off the corner of a piece of toast, Hannah nibbled slowly. As she swallowed, she smiled at him, careful not to look at the food on his plate, lest her stomach chose to rebel again.

When he emptied his plate, he stood and retrieved the Bible. He set it before her, as was their morning routine. She barely had eaten half of the toast, but pushed the remainder aside. Flipping through the pages, she found the marker in Matthew where she had been reading from the Sermon on the Mount.

"Therefore, I tell you, do not worry," she started reading aloud. "Who of you by worrying can add a single hour to his life?"

Hannah paused. Even after all this time, here she was, still learning how to give up her worries. Amazing how God would put them here in these verses on the day she realizes she is with child.

She continued through the end of the chapter before closing the Good Book.

Will stared at her, worry and fear crossing his face. Perhaps he struggled with the message of giving his worries to God, too. Slowly, the worry faded from his features, turning to calm surrender. With a sigh, he stood.

"How soon will you be ready to go?"

Hannah's face lit up with a big grin. "I'm ready now. Rosa already agreed to take care of the dishes."

"Let me get the wagon ready and I will be around to pick you up in a few minutes," he said as he moved toward the front door.

She desperately needed this time with Betty and was grateful he didn't stop her from going.

A few minutes later when she heard the wagon pull up, she went outside. Will helped her up to the seat before joining her.

"You're starting to look better," Will said as the wagon neared the top of the first hill out of the valley where their home stood.

Hannah smiled as she turned toward him. "Yes, the fresh air is doing me wonders."

The day was perfect as were many days in the Arizona Territory. While Hannah brought a shawl with her, she probably wouldn't use it until the return trip this evening. The sun was warm and the sky was deep azure blue. She loved her new home.

"When do you suppose Julia and Mr. Larson will arrive?" She carefully phrased the question to keep from implying the two were married.

"Probably within the week."

Ah, he's back to his short answers, she marveled. When they first met, she had thought his short answers were a lack of interest. Over time she came to learn that it usually met he was either nervous or preoccupied. She figured it was the latter, given his sister was a touchy topic of late.

As the silence stretched, she struggled whether or not to tell him her news. *What if I lose the child?*

Do not worry.

No matter how much she worried, God was still in control. He would care for her and this child. Letting this truth settle over her heart, she decided to share the joyful news with her husband.

"I don't want you to worry about me being sick this morning. It's a good thing."

Will looked at her with one eyebrow arched. "How is that a good thing?"

"Well, I'm sick because I'm with child. We're going to have a baby!"

Chapter 10

Did she just say what I thought she said?

Will stopped the wagon, his heart pounding fiercely within his chest. He turned to look Hannah in the eyes.

"We're what?"

"We're going to have a baby, probably sometime towards the end of June." Her face flushed with excitement and her eyes gleamed.

"A baby…" Will echoed.

He was going to be a papa! Joy bubbled up from within. He hugged Hannah to him in a tight embrace before thinking that it might be bad for the baby to squeeze her so tight.

Releasing his hold, he said in awe, "I'm going to be a father!"

Her face glowed with overwhelming joy.

Moving closer, he lowered his lips to hers, showing her just how happy he was with the news. When he pulled away, she was breathless and her blush went a deeper shade. She was so beautiful, this mother of his children.

Clearing his throat, Will reached for the reins and set the wagon in motion again. She scooted closer to him on the seat, looping her hand through the crook of his arm.

"How long does the sickness last?" he asked.

"Oh, I don't know that there is any set time of when that goes away. I know the last time I was with child, I was sick for several weeks. Working with Drew, I learned it can be different each time."

Will hoped it would not last long. It would be so hard to watch her suffer and not be able to help. "Last time, were you ill all the time, or just in the morning?"

"Mostly in the morning. Then by the afternoon or evening I was ravenous."

"Well, if you feel you need to rest more, please have Rosa pick up the extra work. I don't want you overdoing it."

"I'll be fine." She smiled up at him.

As they topped the last hill before descending into town, Will beamed, his heart overflowing. He was going to be a father. He secretly hoped it would be a son, but as soon as the thought came, he realized he would love a daughter just as much. He would need to get started making a crib soon. What else does one do to prepare for a baby, he wondered as he pulled the wagon to a stop in front of Lancaster's Boardinghouse.

Setting the brake, he looped the reins around it. After jumping down from the wagon, he walked around to the other side with a hop in his step. Instead of holding out his hand to help Hannah down, he put his hands on her waist and gently lowered her to the ground. Giving her a kiss on the cheek, he sent her inside to visit with Betty while he saw to other business.

Hannah entered the dining hall. Not much had changed since she left a few months ago to marry Will. The main room still housed the three tables with long benches on both sides—enough room for about ten men at each table. The savory smell of the midday meal drew her to the kitchen. Thankful that her stomach settled on the drive in.

The older, somewhat plump woman hunched over the stove stirring a pot of stew. Betty's silver and black streaked hair was pulled back tightly at the base of her neck. She hummed one of her favorite hymns as she added a dash of salt to the bubbling pot.

"Please tell me you aren't working by yourself and that you've hired some help," Hannah said, announcing her presence.

"Hannah, dear!" Betty said, turning in surprise before engulfing her in a warm embrace. "Let me look at you. You are positively glowing! Marriage must agree with you."

After greeting her friend, she continued, "In all seriousness, haven't you hired any help yet?"

"Well, there are still so few women here. And most of them are too busy with their own families to take on a job. I'm hoping the next wagon train will bring someone."

The dark circles under Betty's eyes did not match her happy tone. There was no doubt that her friend was exhausted and working much too hard.

"Has Paul been helping?"

"Oh, yes, dear. He barely even goes out to do his mining anymore. Only once every ten days so he can legally keep it. He's out hanging the laundry now."

"Maybe I should send Rosa to help out for a while?" If Betty continued to work this hard, she was sure to get sick.

"Oh, no. I am sure there is far too much work on the ranch for you alone."

Perhaps Betty was right, she thought, subconsciously placing her hand over her abdomen where her child grew. It would be too much to handle alone especially as time went on.

"So, how is that husband of yours treating you?" Betty asked, changing the subject.

Hannah sighed. "He's wonderful. I think the most difficult adjustment has been getting used to what it takes to run a ranch. They were stretched pretty thin while most of the men were driving the cattle to California. I'm so glad they are back now."

"Ben stopped by on his way through town yesterday." Betty's expression softened as she let out a gentle sigh.

"Ben?" Hannah asked, quirking an eyebrow.

Betty's face flushed as she ignored the question. Taking a seat across from Hannah at the small table in the kitchen, she said, "You were telling me about Will."

Shrugging, Hannah decided to let the subject lie for now. "Will has a horse trainer coming from his hometown in Texas—Mr. Larson. He should be arriving soon. We just received word that Will's sister, Julia, will be with him."

"So, his sister is coming? Tell me about her."

She only knew a few things about Julia. "Will says she is only seventeen, thirteen years younger than him. He speaks very fondly of her and I hear their closeness in his tone of voice. He loves his sister dearly and would do anything to protect her. I'm afraid we know very little about what prompted her to head west. Will seems to think something happened with their eldest brother Reuben. It'll be nice to meet her when she arrives."

A noise from the dining hall brought Betty to her feet. It was Mr. Boggs, one of the miners who boarded there. He had been elected to the territorial legislature earlier this fall, probably because of his outgoing nature.

"Mrs. Lancaster, I thought you might like to know we have a wagon train headed our way. They are less than an hour away." Nodding toward Hannah, he said, "Mrs. An— , I mean Mrs. Colter, nice to see you again. Is Will about town today?"

"Yes. He was going to meet with Mr. Vincent from the La Paz Express at the Juniper House. Then I think he was planning on visiting Gray & Company's store."

"Ladies, I shall be off then," he said, bowing in mock formality. Hannah giggled at the silly gesture.

Standing, Betty moved towards the stove. "An hour will put them here right around lunch time. I best get more food started."

Remembering how full the dining hall gets when a wagon train arrives, Hannah stood. "What can I do to help?"

After Betty discussed what additional food items they would need to prepare, both women set about their tasks. It was just like all those months ago, working and talking alongside each other.

"Dear, I am so glad that you are happy with Will."

She thought back to their short romance. "I guess I knew a good thing when I saw it."

Both women laughed at this, knowing full well it had been a difficult decision for her to let go of mourning her first husband.

Nervously, Will looked around the lobby of the Juniper House, the hotel that opened earlier in the year. Though he corresponded with Mr. Vincent about the possibility of selling him horses for the new pony express line, the La Paz Express, he had no idea what the owner looked like.

This opportunity was a good one. Since the line ran from Prescott to La Paz, Mr. Vincent would need quality horses to make the run across the three hundred some miles of desert. From Mr. Vincent's returned correspondence, he learned there was also a second line from La Paz to Los Angeles, finally opening up communication outside of the Arizona Territory.

A thin, short gentleman dressed in a fine black suit caught his attention.

"Will Colter," he said, holding out his hand to the man he hoped was Mr. Vincent.

"Albert Vincent," the gentleman responded, craning his head up to make eye contact with him. A smile played on his lips. "Shall we find a place to discuss business?"

At Will's nod, Mr. Vincent led him from the lobby to a table in the dining room. After a man came by and filled two coffee cups, Mr. Vincent started the conversation.

"I must admit, I was surprised to receive your letter stating that you were breeding and training horses here in the territory."

"Pleasantly surprised, I hope?"

"Most definitely. The cost of shipping quality horses from California is astronomical—especially to the more interior locations, such as Prescott. Between that and the toll roads, it's a wonder I can make any profit on the La Paz Express line," Mr. Vincent said, lifting the steaming coffee to his lips.

"From what I was told, you have a need for a large number of horses. Is that still the case?"

"Yes. Right now, I need a few here in Prescott rather urgently. Then there are several way stations on down the line that could use a few more horses. The Apaches are doing what they can to keep the mail from making it between Prescott and La Paz. Just last week they decimated all of the horses at one of the more remote way stations. I've already shuffled horses between other stations to cover that part of the line for now but I could use some more."

Over the next hour, Will and Mr. Vincent finalized the arrangements.

Mr. Vincent had the livery owner, Craig Roundtree, join the tail end of their discussion. "Craig will handle purchasing the horses for Prescott and the stations between here and Wickenburg based on the instructions I've left him. The rest of the line, I'll be supplying from California for the time being. If I'm pleased with the quality of horseflesh, Mr. Colter, we'll be in touch."

With that, Mr. Vincent stood and held out his hand. Will shook it, satisfied with sealing the deal verbally for now.

"Craig will show you the livery and pass on any additional information that may be helpful. Good day, Mr. Colter."

"This way," Craig Roundtree motioned as they stepped onto the busy street. "Leland Frye is the rider I work with. He'll want to give a test run to any horse prior to finalizing the sale. He's usually in town every other Wednesday and Thursday before he heads out on the next run."

After arranging a date and time to bring by one of the horses, Will took his leave. He had the buyers. Now all he had to do was build up his breeding and training business with Adam.

If he still hired Larson. That would all depend on what the real situation was with his sister. The Adam Larson he knew was an honest young man, extremely gifted with horses. Yet, since receiving the letter from him and the one from Pace, Will wondered how well he really knew him.

You already offered him the job. The little voice in his head reminded him. It was right. He had offered Larson the job and he wouldn't be on his way here without having accepted the offer. It was only right to stand by the agreement. Didn't mean he had to be happy about it.

As Will walked down Montezuma Street towards Gray & Company's store, he heard the unmistakable sound of a wagon train rolling into town. When he turned towards the sound, he saw Mr. Boggs heading towards him.

"Will, there you are! I saw your wife was here and she mentioned you might be at Gray's."

Will shook the miner-turned-politician's hand. "How are you, John?"

"Doing well. I was wondering if anyone had invited you and Mrs. Colter to the governor's ball next week, on the eighth? Governor Goodwin wanted to make sure all of the area ranchers and their families were included."

"This is the first I have heard of it, but I'm sure Hannah would be upset if I declined."

"Excellent. We'll see you at the Governor's mansion then around six in the evening on the eighth then."

Seeing the wagon train settlers had stopped at the town plaza,

Will decided to visit Gray & Company later. Knowing Hannah, she was probably helping Betty cook and planning to serve. He was almost to the dining hall, when one particular wagon caught his attention. A young man was untying two of the most magnificent horses Will had ever seen. Then the young woman with him stepped out from the shadow of the wagon, sandy brown curls bouncing with each step.

"Julia!" Will yelled from across the plaza before he fully realized it was his sister. Covering the distance quickly, any thoughts of anger over the situation fled. He swallowed her in his giant big brother bear hug, lifting her feet from the ground. "You're here!"

"Will. Oh, I've missed you," she said. Her excited words did not match the stiffening of her body as he set her down. Something seemed odd about her reaction. "Let me look at you."

Her eyes traveled the length of his body, before she said, "Still tall and tan, huh?" She giggled.

He grinned. He wanted so much to pepper her with a thousand questions, but held back, knowing there would be plenty of time for that later. Remembering that Larson was supposed to be with her, he turned and looked around.

"Will, it's good to see you," Adam said, extending his hand.

Will frowned and shook the young man's hand, squeezing his hand tight. "Tell me, Larson, what exactly is going on between you and my sister?"

Chapter 11

"William Edward Colter! What kind of question is that?" Julia scolded, taking in the bone-crushing grip he had on Adam's hand. She was surprised he wasn't grimacing from the pain.

"It's a reasonable question, given the letter we received from Pace, stating that 'Adam and Julia Larson' were on their way." Will's ire was evident. "How do you explain that?"

Julia forgot how much he looked like Reuben, especially when he was angry. The darkness in his eyes brought the memory of Reuben's abuse to the forefront of her mind. Shivering against the images, she took a deep breath and turned her focus on what Adam was saying.

"Did you receive our letters?"

"I received one from you, wherein you simply said that Julia was with you. Not Miss Colter."

"Didn't you receive my letter?" she asked, trying hard to push away the fearsome memories.

At the curt shake of his head, she began to understand what he was thinking. *He thinks Adam married me. He has no idea why I am here.*

Sighing, she looked up to make eye contact. His golden brown eyes were still dark. Swallowing the lump in her throat, she said, "Please listen. Things with Reuben were... I had to leave... It wasn't safe for me to stay any longer..." Her voice caught as the emotion trapped her again.

Another deep breath and she continued, "I really do not want to go into all the details now, but please believe me when I tell you that Adam has been a perfect gentleman. We have travelled west under the pretense of being siblings. When we ran into Jethro Pace, we were in the company of a friend that thought we were related and he heard our friend call me *Miss* Larson. I'm certain that is where the confusion lies. Adam has done nothing wrong. He saved my life and protected me."

Will eyed the young man warily, acting as if he did not fully believe her story. Crossing his arms, he stood rigidly straight. She had seen this maneuver more than once. He was much like their rooster when he puffed his chest out before staking his claim. He meant to be intimidating.

And Adam fell for it.

"If there had been any other way to see to Miss Colter's safety, I would have made every effort. Unfortunately, the circumstances required a hasty departure and I thought the guise was the best way to protect her reputation."

Will grunted. No one said anything for several uncomfortable minutes.

Finally, Will uncrossed his arms and his expression softened. "Let's go get some dinner. Hannah has been waiting to meet you."

"Hannah?" Julia asked as he offered his arm. Adam prudently said nothing and fell in step behind them. Making their way across the beautiful green plaza, she guessed their destination was the cluster of log buildings that had a line out the front door. As they neared the line, delicious aromas wafted from inside.

"My wife." Will answered her earlier question. "Hannah is my wife."

I never thought you would be married. Will had never taken interest in any of the women in Texas and she thought he might stay single forever. This bit of news definitely changed things. What if Hannah didn't want her living with them?

"How long have you been married?"

"Two months."

Julia smiled. This was the Will she remembered. Straight and to the point, especially when he was preoccupied. Nevertheless, she would drag as much information from him as possible before meeting this woman.

"What is she like? How did you meet her?" *Will she like me?*

"I met her right here, at Lancaster's Boardinghouse. Well, no that's not exactly true. I first met her at Fort Whipple, though we weren't properly introduced. Then, she came to work for Betty— that's Mrs. Lancaster, the owner of the boardinghouse. I supply beef for Lancaster's. But the day I met her, I was in town for a meeting.

She was serving up dinner here at the dining hall."

"What is she like?" Julia asked again as the threesome entered the very same dining hall.

"See for yourself," he answered grinning sheepishly as he waved to a beautiful woman.

She, presumably Hannah, had the most interesting shade of blonde hair with touches of red. She was short—near Julia's height, but maybe shorter. She was carrying armloads of food to the diners, as if she had done the very same thing hundreds of times. She probably had, since she used to work here.

"I see Betty put you to work," Will teased his wife as he took a seat.

She smiled back. "I'll come sit with you in a minute after I get a few more people served."

Julia watched her brother as he followed Hannah's every movement. He was obviously smitten with his wife. Then she took the seat across from Will. Adam sat next to her, leaving the seat next to Will open. She resisted the urge to squeeze Adam's hand. He was still tense from the initial encounter with Will, judging by his ramrod straight posture. This was probably not the reception he imagined when he planned to work for her brother.

As she looked around the dining hall, her eyes snagged on a familiar face. Her stomach plummeted to her feet and she squinted. "Bates," she whispered in shock. Had he followed her all the way from the Star C? Had Reuben sent him to fetch her back?

Panic rose. Her breath came in staccato bursts. Blood drained from her face and lightheadedness threatened the last ounce of her control. She could not go back. She would not go back. He could not make her. *Please God!* Her heart cried out.

Gentle fingers curled around her clammy hand resting in her lap, snapping her out of her spiraling thoughts. Green eyes met hers as she focused on Adam. "It's okay," he mouthed, then gave a nod towards where Bates sat, letting her know he recognized the cowboy, too.

Leaning near her ear, he whispered. "I won't let him take you back. I promise." He squeezed her hand but did not release it.

Blinking rapidly, Julia tried to keep the tears from forming. She trusted Adam. He kept her safe this long. He wouldn't fail her now—

she hoped.

Glancing back at Will, she was relieved to see he missed the entire exchange, as his gaze was firmly glued to his wife as she approached the table.

His wife returned from the kitchen with four cups and a pot of coffee. She filled them and set one before each of them, placing the last for herself next to Will. Then, she bustled back to the kitchen one last time, returning with four plates of food.

As she set the plates in front of Julia and Adam, she said, "Betty says this one is on the house. First time I've ever seen her do that."

Once Hannah was seated next to him, Will made the introductions. He carefully watched Adam throughout the meal, still trying to decide if he could trust him. Even though he hadn't married his sister, he had traveled with her all the way here without a chaperone. That thought wasn't sitting very well.

"Julia, it's so good to finally meet you," Hannah said, warmly smiling at his sister. "I've been rather nervous about it. But, I like you already."

As Julia replied, Will studied her. Again he felt like something was off. She wasn't herself. She would not make direct eye contact with him, although she did with Hannah. The dark circles under her bright blue eyes added several years to her appearance. She was only seventeen, but she looked old, haggard, defeated. *Defeated, where did that idea come from?* Yet it fit.

When a man sat on the other side of Julia, Will noticed her visibly stiffen and scoot a little closer to Adam. What would prompt her to react in such a way? This was his buoyant and outgoing kid sister. She was nervous, almost skittish, like the horse he once saw that had been grossly mistreated. He would never forget the pure look of terror in the animal's eyes whenever anyone approached. Now, he recognized that same look in Julia's eyes when she glanced at him. Something terrible had happened.

As they finished the meal, Hannah suggested Julia help her and Betty wash dishes. That left Will alone with Adam. Judging by the way the young man shifted in his seat, he was concerned. *Well, Will, how are you going to handle this? Make him sweat or offer an olive branch?*

Swallowing his earlier indignation, he said, "I'm sorry if I put you on edge."

He paused, gathering his thoughts. Perhaps business first would ease their tensions.

"I have purchased a few studs and mares and we have built out the stables. I think you'll be pleased with the facilities."

"Thank you. I've been looking forward to this for months. I'm sorry about not being clearer in my letter regarding Julia—Miss Colter."

"No need to be formal. I realize our families are close and that you have never called her Miss Colter. Please don't let my misunderstanding change that."

Adam shifted again. He looked at the table a moment before saying, "I brought two of the Larson's finest with me, one stud and one mare."

"You didn't have to do that."

"They were a gift from my father—a reward for the years I spent helping him breed and train horses. They are a fine pair. I wanted to bring something to the arrangement, and though I do not have money to contribute, this is the least I can do."

Will was humbled by his generosity. If he asked, he would let him keep the pair entirely for himself, yet it seemed that was not what Adam wanted to do. Conviction pierced his conscience. Here he had been standoffish and accusatory, when Adam had done more than his end of the agreement. All he was supposed to do was show up. Instead, he brought both his sister and horses.

Picking at a loose sliver on the tabletop, Will responded, "It seems you have done a great deal more than was required. And I'm not just talking about the horses. It sounds like your departure was rather hasty on account of Julia."

Adam cleared his throat. "Yes, I left unprepared and earlier than intended." He paused, as if carefully weighing what he should say.

"And in the dead of night. I don't know what happened to cause Julia to ride out to our house in the middle of the night. What I do know, I will not say. I believe it is best for her to tell. But, trust me, there was no mistaking the fear in her eyes nor the real sense of urgency to flee to safety. It was Caroline's suggestion that I head west that night and take Julia with me, without even saying goodbye to my family." The sorrow of missed goodbyes was evident in his voice.

Will took in what Adam said and wondered, yet again, what really happened to Julia. "Thank you, for putting her safety before your own family. It speaks greatly of your character. Forgive me for judging you otherwise."

"I think I might have acted the same way, should I find Caroline in a similar situation. I might even have decked the fellow that showed up on my doorstep unexplained."

Will laughed. "Yes, well, had I not received the letter from you a few weeks ago, I think my initial reaction would have shocked you—when you woke up." Slapping Adam on the back, he hoped the teasing would repair the earlier strain.

"Listen, there's something else you should know," Adam said. Will tensed again. "Julia spotted Gideon Bates here in the dining hall."

"Now? Today?" Though the answer was obvious, Will couldn't help asking the questions. If Bates was here…

"Yes. Before Mrs. Colter joined us for dinner. Julia was petrified. I think she's afraid he is here to take her back."

Rubbing his chin, Will considered the situation. "That's not going to happen. But, it does make me question how and why he left the Star C—and why he ended up at the same destination. Too much of a coincidence."

"Agreed. I didn't see him on the wagon train west. I would have recognized him immediately."

"Thanks for letting me know," Will said, wondering how he missed seeing Julia's reaction. He would have to do a little digging. See what Bates was up to and why he was here.

He didn't exactly trust the man. He initially hired him last year just weeks before his planned departure. Only Bates decided Reuben's offer of more money was enough to turn Will down—even though he already agreed to go. That was all he knew of Gideon Bates.

He would definitely have to find out more. In the meantime, he would make sure Julia wasn't alone. Best not to give Bates an opportunity if he was here to take her back.

Standing, Will and Adam walked outside towards Adam's wagon.

It was Adam that broached the subject of returning to the ranch. "When should we head out?"

"It is getting rather late in the day and I still have some unfinished business here in town. I thought I might set the ladies up with a hotel room for the evening. Perhaps you and I can camp under the stars, or see if Betty has any bunks left."

"Camping under the stars would be just fine with me."

"I have a feeling that Hannah is going to want to help Betty with supper preparations, so we will eat here. I'm going to head over to the hotel to see if they have any rooms left. The livery is right over there." Will pointed to it. "You may want to board the horses there tonight. Just tell them you work for me and that I will settle the account in the morning."

At Adam's nod, Will walked over to the Juniper House. He was able to reserve a room for Hannah and Julia to share. He would much rather be sharing it with Hannah, especially having learned she carried his child. Was that really this morning? It seemed like days ago now. But, he did not want to leave Julia alone with Adam when he could provide for her, nor did he want to spend money on two hotel rooms.

As Will walked her and Julia to their hotel room, Hannah longed to have a few minutes alone with him. They barely had a minute to celebrate or even talk about her pregnancy. When she envisioned how this evening would unfold, she saw them together back at the ranch talking into the night about plans to get ready for the baby.

Instead, she settled for a quick kiss in the hallway with whispered promises of talking later.

Closing the door behind Will, Hannah took off her boots and stretched out on the bed. Patting the spot next to her, she encouraged

Julia to relax as well. While it was somewhat awkward to be sharing the room with her husband's sister, she hoped to make the situation more comfortable by getting to know her better.

Although she already knew the answer, she opened with a safe topic. "Tell me, have you known the Larson family long?"

"Oh, yes. My whole life really. Adam's younger sister, Caroline, is my best friend. We are only months apart in age and have been inseparable most of our lives."

"I remember Will telling me Adam worked with horses for years, but he seems so young. Do you know how hold he is?"

"He's nineteen. For as long as I can remember, he would talk on and on about horses. Every paper he wrote in school had something to do with horses. By the time he was thirteen, George, that's his pa, involved him in most of the training. Within a year or so he was the primary trainer. He has a natural talent with them."

"I guess that's why Will spoke so highly of him."

"So how did you end up here and married to my brother?" Julia asked.

Hannah sighed. Although it was just over a year ago, it seemed like decades since she left Ohio. "Well, I was married to a doctor back in Ohio. When his brother robbed a bank, the town turned on us and it became necessary for us to move. Drew, my husband, felt we should move to the Arizona Territory. The journey was rather long, four months or more. We reached the San Francisco Mountains in January during a terrible snow storm. After being stranded for several days, the storm finally lifted. Drew was on the mountain looking for firewood when he was caught up in an avalanche..." Hannah's voice choked on the last words. After taking a minute to compose herself, she continued. "He died on that mountain, only two weeks out from our new home."

Julia's brow wrinkled. "I'm sorry to have brought up a painful memory."

"Ah, well, it is part of my life. Nothing that can change. Even though I loved Drew dearly and I did not want him to die, I would not change what has happened. It has all led me to here and now. If I have learned nothing else from the pain, I have learned to trust God through it. He has been faithful to provide for me, bringing friends to walk alongside me, and bringing me a new husband that loves me deeply."

Julia was silent for several minutes. She looked like she was waging an internal battle. "Why would you trust God when he had the power to save your husband but stood by and let him die?"

Hannah knew that this question really had nothing to do with Drew and everything with Julia struggling to reconcile the pain in her own life. She had seen the pain in Julia's eyes, even though she tried to mask it. *Lord, please give me wisdom and the words to say that will help start some healing in Julia.*

"The Bible is very clear that, even as Christians, we will not be free from pain. Jesus even said himself that in the world there would be trouble. But he also told us to take heart because he has overcome the world. Also, the Bible says that the purpose of our trials is to purify our faith. It says that our faith is of more worth than gold.

"So, even though I do not like the pain, I know that God is using this in my life to strengthen my faith. It is not my place to question why God chooses one path for us versus another. It is through these experiences that my real faith was born, where I really had to rely on God and trust that he wants the best for me—though it took me some time walking through the pain to really understand all of this."

Julia picked at lint on her dress, before looking away. Tears started rolling down her cheeks. "Reuben beat me when I refused to marry who he wanted me to."

Hannah sensed there was more—a deeper wound. But, Julia said no more. After waiting several minutes, she squeezed her new sister's hand. "You are safe now."

Chapter 12

Julia wanted to say more, to confess all that happened. Yet, she just met her brother's wife a few hours ago. How could she pour out her soul?

By mutual silence they must have agreed it was time to retire. Both readied for bed and Hannah turned down the light. Within minutes, Julia heard her soft breathing and wished she could fall asleep so quickly. Instead, she lay there wide awake. What would she tell them about why she left? Certainly, the fact that Reuben beat her was reason enough to leave. Should she tell Will the full awful truth? Could she? Did it even matter?

Hannah's words rolled through her mind. *Did she really mean that God let me be raped by my brother to somehow prove my faith?* That seemed completely heartless.

But, Hannah said that her faith was worth more than gold and that it was through the pain that her faith was really born.

Rage mounted. *I do not believe it, God! I cannot believe you would willingly allow this to happen to me. And for what? To prove my faith? I have lost all faith in you because of this. I cannot trust you any more than I trust Reuben!*

Rolling over on her side the tears began to fall again. A part of her wanted to trust God and to rely on him to save her. But, God had let this happen. This should never happen to anyone, especially if God was a loving God.

I love you still, Julia.

Where had that come from? That was not possible. She pushed the thought from her mind and gave into the sorrow.

When her sobs subsided, she closed her eyes to sleep. But, she could not. The memories from that night returned—poignant—as if she were reliving it over again. She could not force the image of Reuben's face from her mind. She felt the weight of his body on hers, trapping her.

Would this nightmare never leave her? Was it not bad enough to have lived through it once, why did she have to relive it over and over again?

How blessed it had been the last month, not having been visited by this ghost nightly. Why had it returned suddenly? Was it because Will looked so much like Reuben? Was it from the discussion with Hannah or from the appearance of Bates? Maybe it was from her anxiety over how much to explain to Will and Hannah.

The turmoil assaulted her continually until she fell into a fitful slumber.

The next morning, Julia woke early, groggy and still exhausted. Rolling out of bed, she glanced over at Hannah, still sleeping peacefully.

She poured some water from the pitcher on the dresser into the basin before splashing it on her face. Blotting it dry with the towel, Julia tried to force the inner pandemonium down. Emotionally, she was drained. She did not have the energy to deal with the questions that would come today and hoped to put them off as long as possible. She secured her unruly curls into a loose chignon at the base of her neck.

Opening the door she stepped into the narrow hallway. She pulled the door shut behind her, cringing at the creaking sound. Hopefully Hannah was not a light sleeper.

She made her way downstairs into the lobby. Looking at the clock on the wall, it was barely past six, but she needed fresh air. Perhaps that would calm her nerves. She nodded to the man at the front desk, before walking out the front doors.

The fragrance of pine infused her lungs as she breathed deeply. The little town of Prescott was still fast asleep. From the walkway in front of the Juniper House, Julia looked around. Down one street, there was a store and several saloons. Nearby on another street there was a large sign that said *Arizona Miner*, which she assumed was the newspaper. Along that same street, there was a sign for the Livery and La Paz Express. The street opposite the one with the saloons was where Lancaster's Boardinghouse stood. The green grass and tall pines of the town plaza acted as a barrier between the opposing businesses. A few tents from the wagon train were scattered about the plaza. She recognized one as Adam's tent.

If only all men were as honorable as Adam, Julia thought. Ironically, if that were true, she probably never would have gotten to know just how honorable he was. Even in the midst of an unusual situation, such as sharing the tent, he acted in her best interest and in a way that made her feel safe.

Safe. That was the feeling missing last night. She had not felt safe again. Yet, isn't that the reason she was here—to be safe? To escape physical harm? Perhaps once she was settled on the ranch, the feeling would return.

As Julia considered walking towards the plaza, Adam emerged from the tent. Why had she not noticed before how handsome he was? As quickly as the thought came, she chastised herself for it. No man would want her—she had been ruined. She would never marry. Impatiently, she brushed at the tear sliding down her face. Would she never stop crying?

Staying in the shadows, she watched as Adam drew water from the town well. He poured some for a drink and then splashed the rest on his face, much as she had done moments ago. She was glad he was going to be at the ranch.

Other people started to move about the plaza to start their day. Julia was not sure how long she stood there before realizing it had been for quite a while. Her foot was numb and she tapped it on the ground to get some feeling back. She took a tentative step towards the plaza as pins and needles pricked their way up her foot. She noticed a bench outside the back door of Lancaster's facing the plaza and she made her way towards it. The savory aroma of bacon frying wafted through the air as she got closer. When she was about to take a seat on the bench, a man came rushing out the door with two empty buckets in hand. She thought it was Betty's son, though she could not remember his name.

"Miss Colter," he greeted before taking the buckets to fill them from the well in the plaza.

For some reason, after all those months being referred to as Miss Larson, her own name felt foreign. Then again, she did not feel comfortable in her own skin no matter what name she used. Growing weary of the constant battle in her mind, she stood and knocked on the back door. As she suspected, Betty was quick to answer.

"What brings you here so early?" Betty asked.

"I thought I might help you with breakfast this morning since I rose earlier than expected."

"That would be wonderful, dear. Come on in."

Julia noticed yesterday the older woman's frequent use of the term "dear" and thought it endearing. She had a way about her that made you feel like you were part of her family, although no blood connection was present. Betty was probably almost old enough to be her grandmother at least that was the impression her silver and black streaked hair gave. Betty quickly put her to work setting out baskets of freshly baked biscuits.

Noise began filtering in from the dining hall. When Betty asked her to take mugs and coffee out to the waiting customers, Julia started to comply. She froze in the doorway from the kitchen when she realized the room was full of thirty or so men. Nervous, her hands began to shake. She was angered at her own reaction. Never before had she been afraid of men. Was this another side effect from the trauma she suffered? She willed her feet to move forward, but they remained firmly planted in the kitchen.

"It's okay, dear, they are harmless."

As Julia finally summoned the nerve to step over the threshold, she looked up. Her lungs refused to fill with air as she noticed Will entering the dining hall with Hannah. In the shadowed light he looked like Reuben's twin, except a little bit taller. Unexplained fear gripped her and the shaking of her hands grew so bad she dropped both the mugs and the full pot of coffee. As the tin mugs clattered to the floor, everyone turned and looked in her direction. Her hands grew clammy and she started to feel lightheaded. Knowing she might swoon if she did not move, she quickly crouched to the floor to pick up the mugs.

"Here, let me help you with that," Adam said as he reached for the now emptied coffee pot.

"Oh, dear, are you alright?" Betty asked as she stood behind Julia.

Adam handed Betty the coffee pot. "It looks like we'll need another batch of coffee."

Julia stood with the last of the mugs from the floor. Adam led her back into the kitchen and took the mugs from her still trembling hands. After setting them on the counter, he started to usher her out the back door when Will entered the kitchen.

"Are you alright?" he asked.

She could not look at him nor answer for the lump wedged firmly in her throat. Adam pointed to the bench outside the door and she sat. She heard him exchange a few words with Will before he joined her on the bench.

"You look like you have seen a ghost," Adam spoke in soothing tones. "Tell me what has you so frightened."

"He looks so much like... Reuben." Her entire body trembled and the tears flowed again.

Adam said nothing. He simply took her in his arms, resting her head on his shoulder. He rocked her back and forth, much like he had the first night on the trail, murmuring comforting sounds.

When the sobs and fears subsided, Julia pulled away. The bottom of her skirt was stained with coffee.

In the distance, Hannah retched as Will stood by her side. Seeing him tenderly rubbing his wife's back, holding her as she was sick—Julia felt no fear. She saw him as the kind big brother she adored.

What would it be like to live with them? Would she constantly see a reminder of Reuben or would she be able to see this tender side of Will? Could she separate the one from the other?

Looking back at Adam, she saw something in his shining green eyes before he masked it. The look was something deeper than concern. "I find myself again in your debt, Adam Larson."

He smiled at her, not really acknowledging the statement. Anytime she mentioned her gratitude, he seemed to get shy.

As he stood, he asked, "Would you like to go in for some breakfast?"

The lump returned to her throat as she thought of the crowded room full of men. He must have sensed her anxiety.

"Stay. I will go get you something and bring it out here... That is, if you're warm enough?"

She nodded and Adam entered through the back door. She glanced over to where Hannah and Will were earlier, but they were gone. They were probably inside eating their meal. She could hear muffled words coming from the kitchen again. It sounded like Adam speaking with Betty. Just a minute passed before he returned balancing two plates and mugs of coffee. Seeing his hands were full, she stood to close the door behind him. They both took a seat on the bench with Julia taking the offered food and drink.

Adam bowed his head, and she followed his example. Old habits were hard to break.

"Lord, we thank you for this beautiful morning, the cool weather, and your grace which sustains us. Please calm Julia's fears and help her to trust that you will protect her. We thank you for keeping us safe and allowing us to reach our destination. Bless this food to our bodies. Amen."

But, you are wrong, Adam, I cannot trust him to protect me, for he has already failed to do so. Her anger threatened to resurrect as she picked at the food on her plate. Seeing the concern on Adam's face, she made an attempt to chew and swallow the food before her.

"Will says we will leave this morning soon after breakfast. We boarded the horses at the livery last night, so I'll go pick them up. He also said Hannah was going to the store this morning to pick out some fabrics and that you were welcome to join her."

Julia nodded. She had little time to pack, having left in such a hurry. While she was able to pick up a few things along the way, it would be good to purchase material and sewing supplies for a new dress.

By the time she finished pretending to eat, Hannah joined them and the two women walked across the plaza to the building labeled "Gray & Company."

As they entered the store, Julia's eyes took a second to adjust to the dimmer light. They were greeted by a friendly shopkeeper.

"Mrs. Colter, a pleasure to see you. I heard that husband of yours finally let you come into town."

"Mr. Young. Good to see you again. This is Will's sister, Miss Julia Colter. She has just arrived from Texas."

Mr. Young greeted Julia then pointed out the sewing supplies and fabrics when Hannah inquired. Julia found a lovely dark green calico print that would go perfectly with her fair complexion and blue eyes. She asked Mr. Young to cut off the amount needed while she looked around for some lace. Seeing none, she decided a simple dress would be fine. Hannah asked for small quantities of some white cotton fabrics. Julia thought the amount too small for undergarments and assumed she was shopping for some other purpose.

As Julia reached into her reticule to pay for her purchases from what little money she had left, Hannah shook her head and told Mr. Young to place everything on Will's account.

Leaving the store, Hannah said, "Keep the rest of what you have for something special. Will would be upset if you didn't let him provide for you."

Will and Adam were waiting outside the store with the wagon. Adam finished tethering the horses to the back of their wagon—well his wagon now—before helping Julia up to the wagon as he had done countless times over the past months. She watched as Will lifted Hannah by the waist and deposited her on the seat of his wagon. Her brother treated her almost like she was one of those fragile porcelain dolls she had once seen in the window of the shops back home.

Texas was no longer her home, she remembered as Will led the way out of town. Colter Ranch in the Arizona Territory was now her new home.

Chapter 13

Awed by the scene before her as the wagon topped the hill, Julia studied the valley below. On the western border, unusual grayish-white mountains burst forth from the grass covered valley floor. A beautiful deep blue lake sparkled with touches of silver reflecting the bright sun. Next to the lake, a quaint log cabin welcomed her home. A large barn and corral, the bunkhouse, and several other buildings stood nearby.

To the north, the massive herd of cattle grazed between tall pine and juniper trees. Not all of them were longhorns, she marveled. It looked like Will had several Herefords in mix. She could make out six men on horseback on different sides of the herd. As the wagons neared the bottom of the valley, another man on horseback rode toward Will's wagon.

"We were a mite worried, Boss, when you didn't return last night."

Julia would recognize that voice anywhere. It belonged to Ben Shepherd, her father's foreman who came with Will from Texas.

"I see we have some company." Ben rode his horse toward her wagon. "Miss Colter, Mr. Larson, good to see you made it here safely."

"How have you been? Has Will been giving you as much trouble as always?" she teased.

Ben laughed—that deep bellied laugh that she loved. "Would not have it any other way, Miss Julia," he answered with the familiar name he used—when she wasn't in trouble.

Grinning she fired back, "Some things never change."

As the wagons finished the descent to the bottom of the valley, Will stopped his near the ranch house. Adam followed suit, coming around the side to help Julia down.

Feet on the ground, she stretched, trying to work out the kinks in sore muscles. Then, turning in a full circle with arms stretched wide and head tilted back, she breathed deeply of the fresh crisp air. This place was even more stunning from the valley floor than it had been from the top of the hill.

"Ben, will you help us get these things unloaded while Adam shows the horses their new home?" Will asked.

Ben dismounted his black mare and tied her to the hitching post in front of the ranch house. There was not much to unload of Julia's things, just a carpet bag containing a few items. All that was left in their wagon was a few of Adam's personal items and the small amount of food remaining from their long trip. Grabbing the crate with food items, Ben carried it into the house and set it on the table.

As Julia followed behind him, she saw a young Mexican woman busily preparing the midday meal. The aroma was enticing and she suddenly realized just how hungry she was.

"Rosa, this is Will's sister, Julia," Hannah introduced.

"Buenos Dias," Rosa said, her accent slightly different from what Julia was used to from the Mexicans in Texas. She also noticed the woman's high angular cheek bones, which made her look part native.

Then Hannah showed her around the house. "This will be your room," she said, indicating one of the two bedrooms off of the main open room which served as kitchen, dining, and living areas.

Entering the small bedroom, Julia was immediately drawn to the handcrafted dresser. Running her hand along the smooth top, she smiled. She opened each of the drawers, noting how effortlessly they glided shut. No doubt Will's craftsmanship. A smaller matching table rested next to the bed.

She turned as Will brought her carpet bag into the room. Setting it on the bed he said, "I didn't see anything else that looked like it was yours. Is this all you brought?"

"There was no time to bring more," she answered softly, begging the memories to stay buried.

He paused for a moment, twisting that same old tan cowboy hat around in his hands. "Julia, I just want you to know how glad I am that you are here. So is Hannah. Despite whatever happened to bring you to our doorstep, I hope you will feel at home here."

Stepping closer, he spread his arms out, meaning to hug her. Panic choked her breath and she moved away from the almost-embrace. Coming up short, he gave her a puzzled look, obviously confused by her reaction. Though he made no further attempt to touch her, she could see the hurt written on his face.

"I'll leave you to your unpacking, then," he stated as he backed out the door.

Staring at the empty doorway, her anger and fear battled. She wished she could feel comfortable enough to let him hug her. It's not that she feared Will would ever harm her or become violent with her. He just looked so much like Reuben, it was hard to put it from her mind.

Sighing, she opened the carpet bag and removed the few items she brought from home. This was going to be harder than she thought.

Will frowned as he entered the kitchen, perplexed by Julia's odd reaction to his hug. He made eye contact with Hannah and saw a question reflected there. "I'm going out to see if Ben and Snake want to join us for dinner."

"I'll walk with you," Hannah said.

Once they were outside warmed by the sun, Will started, "Please tell me, was that fear in Julia's face this morning when I entered the dining hall?"

At Hannah's nod, he continued, "I don't understand what's going on with her. Yesterday when I greeted her with a hug, she stiffened. Then, well, you saw what happened this morning. Now I wanted to give her a hug and she backed away."

Letting out a long frustrated sigh, he paused by the corral. "This is not the same jubilant, adventurous sister that I left in Texas."

"Last night she told me that Reuben beat her."

Will stopped abruptly and turned to face Hannah as his heart broke at the news. "What else did she say?"

"She didn't elaborate. But, I sensed there was something more…" She broke eye contact. "Sinister, perhaps? I'm not sure."

Anger and guilt assailed him. Anger at Reuben for whatever he did to Julia. Anger and guilt, directed toward himself, for not bringing her with him last fall. He should have, even though it was against his father's last wishes. He knew what kind of man Reuben was, but he did not want to believe he was so corrupt that he would lash out against Julia.

"Will," Hannah said as she laid her hand on his arm. "This was not your fault."

He did not agree with his wife, but kept the thought to himself. "But, why is she frightened of me?"

"Honestly, I have no idea. What I do know is that we have to give her time and as much space as she needs. Be gentle and calm around her, always reassuring."

Will nodded in agreement. "I'll do my best."

Hannah reached up and gave him a kiss on the cheek before returning to the ranch house.

Even if he had done nothing to cause Julia to fear him, it still hurt. They had been so close growing up. How could anything that Reuben did cause her to react this way towards him? He loved her. He had always been kind to her. They talked so easily back in Texas.

Kicking the toe of his boot on the corral post, he tried to push his feelings aside for now. She only just arrived and would need some time to settle in. Then maybe things would get back to normal.

As Adam approached, Will nodded toward the bunkhouse. "There's a bunk available for you."

Grabbing his things from the wagon, Adam followed him. Carefully opening the door, to keep from disturbing the night shift, Will showed him an empty bunk.

"Once you're settled, come back up to the house for dinner," he whispered. "It should be ready shortly."

Adam nodded.

Walking back outside, he headed toward the slaughter house. The door was closed, a good indication that Snake was preparing some of the beef for the smoker. When he was not slaughtering, he usually left the door propped open to allow fresh air in. Then Will opened the door and told Snake dinner was ready. Snake waved it off and said to leave a plate for him. He would be up after he got this batch in the smoker.

By the time Will made his way back to the ranch house, Ben and Adam were already seated at the table. Julia sat next to Hannah's chair, across from Adam. As soon as he seated himself, Hannah set out the food.

Once grace was said, Will started the conversation. "Hannah, I forgot to tell you in the rush of yesterday that Mr. Boggs invited us to the Governor's Ball on Thursday."

Looking around the table, he added, "I would like for all of you to attend." Will knew Ben would be somewhat uncomfortable. He never seemed to like the big parties before.

"Will Bet—, I mean Mrs. Lancaster, be attending?" Ben asked. His question was met with discretely covered shocked looks on both Will and Hannah's faces.

Hannah recovered quickly. "I'm sure Betty and her son will be there."

"Adam, I want you there to meet as many of the townsmen as possible. It'll be good for them to get to know you since you'll be working with several of them."

"Certainly," Adam replied.

Will remembered the letter he picked up this morning from the postmaster and handed it to Hannah. "I must be getting old, forgetting so many things today," he said winking at his wife. "Who is it from?"

Julia looked at him, for the first time since arriving, confusion creasing her brow. Adam had a strange look on his face as well. He figured he better explain why he would be handing correspondence off to his wife.

"A few months ago I was thrown from my horse—you remember Jackson," he said looking at Julia. She nodded. "When I landed, I hit my head and was unconscious for several weeks. When I finally woke, my memory was fuzzy for the first several days. Everything eventually came back—except my ability to read." He hated admitting it, but knew there was no use pretending things were different.

Hannah jumped in, "But we are working on that. Until he fully recovers, Will has asked me to read to him."

"And Hannah graciously agreed."

His wife smiled softly at him before breaking the seal. She quickly scanned the letter, probably determining if it should be read privately later. When her eyes went to the bottom of the page, she set

125

the letter aside. Turning to Julia, she said, "It's from you. I guess we know that wagon travel can be faster than the mail around here."

Will laughed at the irony of receiving the letter from his sister the day she arrived. "Anything in there that we don't already know?"

Julia shook her head as Hannah said, "No, nothing new."

Snake entered through the front door and Hannah rose to get his plate and a mug of black coffee. He smiled a toothy grin when he saw Julia. The men were bound to notice her. She was a woman—beautiful or not, there weren't many women in the area. Will tried to temper his protective instincts as Hannah set the plate in front of Snake.

"Who is this lovely lady, Boss?" Snake said, taking a sip of his coffee.

"Julia, meet Daniel Raulings, although we call him Snake. Snake, this is my sister, Miss Julia Colter."

"You're a mite finer to look at than yer big brother," Snake said in his usual cantankerous way. "Pleased to meet you Miss Colter."

"Mr. Raulings," Julia acknowledged, barely making eye contact. Again, odd behavior from his sister.

As Snake shoveled the food into his mouth, he winked at Julia and asked, "She always this shy, Boss?"

Normally he would have teased right alongside Snake, but for some reason his directness set Will on edge.

"You don't have to worry Miss. I don't bite. Ha, get it—snake bite." He laughed at his own joke.

Julia stood abruptly. "Please excuse me," she said before rushing out the front door.

Snake's jaw went slack. "I'm sorry, boss. Didn't mean to offend. Just being my usual ornery self."

Will started to stand, perturbed at Snake and confused by Julia. He stopped when Hannah placed her hand on his arm.

When she spoke, she looked directly at Snake, "No harm done, Snake. Julia has had a long journey and is undoubtedly trying to adjust to her new surroundings. I'm certain no offense was taken."

She stood. "If you'll excuse me gentlemen, I would like some fresh air. Please leave your things on the table. Rosa and I will clear them away later."

All four men rose to their feet amidst murmurs of "Thank you,

Mrs. Colter."

Hannah gently latched the front door behind her. She scanned the area and found Julia standing by the horse corral, gently rubbing a mare's muzzle.

Leaning against the rail next to her, Hannah said, "You know Snake is harmless. He feels terrible and thinks he offended you."

Julia nodded.

As the mare grew tired of the attention, she snorted and trotted away. Julia's gaze followed her around the corral. "When he said I was shy—I have been called many things in my life, and shy has never been one of them. Growing up, I was unconventional. Will taught me how to rope and ride. I would rather be out in the field or in the stables than cooking over a stove. And all because it was a great adventure, something new to learn and discover. My father was the same way, full of 'spunk' as he put it."

Her voice grew distant journeying back to another place and another time. "Father let me be free, until I was fourteen. Then he started insisting that I stay in the house more, learning to cook and clean. It wasn't that I didn't know how to do those things, for I did. I just wanted to be free and for me that meant being a cowboy. So, from the age of fourteen until the day Father died, I tried to be a proper lady. I learned to be a charming hostess when called upon.

"Then he died and he left me to..." Her voice cracked. Clearing her throat she continued, "To Reuben's care."

Julia turned so abruptly it almost startled Hannah. Holding her gaze steady, she frowned. "If he had any idea what would happen, I doubt very much that he would have left me with Reuben."

"What happened?" Hannah asked, wondering if she was ready to say.

Julia turned and looked back out at the horses in the corral. "I know I should be telling Will all of this, but I can't. I...he..." She sighed, the burden of the situation weighing heavily. "I told you last night that he beat me, but there is more. Something terrible. Evil. I...cannot bring myself to speak of it."

Hannah placed her hand on her shoulder. As she did, Julia sought refuge in Hannah's open arms. She held her as she cried for several minutes until Julia hiccupped and pulled away, wiping her eyes with her handkerchief.

"This," she said, waving her hand by her red-rimmed eyes, "is all I can manage these days. I have lost my desire for adventure, that love of life. All I do is cry, night and day."

Hannah could feel her pain, although it was not entirely the same. "When Drew died, I thought I would never stop crying. The grief and loss would hit me at the oddest times and months later. Even after I met your brother, I still grieved for Drew. But, this too will pass."

"I don't feel like it ever will."

"Give it time, Julia. When I worked with Drew, I saw flesh wounds that took months to heal, while other wounds took but a few days. Your wounds are deep, and they will take time to heal. Do not put pressure on yourself to be somewhere other than where you are. Will and I will love you no matter what."

Turning to go back to the ranch house, Hannah said, "If you ever want to talk to me or Will, please do so. We are here for you."

Reuben's stomach dropped to the floor as he re-read the letter for the third time. *She married Larson.* Three simple words that would be his death sentence—the end of everything he held dear.

He was going to lose the ranch.

Crumpling the letter in his hand, he tossed it on the floor, letting out a wail of anger and desperation. His shoulders dropped in defeat.

Maybe he could pack his things and start over somewhere else. He had a little money left. Not much. But it would get him someplace where no one would know him. Slowly, he could work his way back. He still had his most valuable asset—his wit and charm.

Yes! That's what he would do.

Leaving the comfort of his office, he headed down the hall to his bedroom. The house was quiet, as the children were napping. No sounds came from the kitchen, so he hurriedly grabbed his carpet bag and stuffed several changes of clothes into it. On his way back to his office, he confirmed that Mary was outside hanging the laundry. Taking the last of his money, he shoved it in the bag.

Walking out the front door, he made his way to the stables and saddled the best horse he owned. Who knows, he might need to sell it later for some cash.

Once the horse was readied, he led it from the barn, wondering if he should have at least left Mary a note to let her know he would not be returning.

A click of a gun cocking snapped his attention to two men on horseback.

"Going somewhere, Reuben?" Hiram Norton sneered.

At the nod of his head, Hiram's companion dismounted and walked towards Reuben, gun leveled at his chest.

"Hope you weren't thinking of running off," Hiram said, steely look in his eyes. "You still owe me a good sum of money for that shrew sister of yours. And you've put me off long enough. It's time to pay up."

"What did you have in mind?" Reuben asked, trying to buy some time to figure some way out of this.

"Only thing you have left is land and blood. Think I might just take both."

Chapter 14

The first few days at Colter Ranch passed quickly for Adam. While he bunked with the cowboys, he spent very little time with the men, except for meals and an hour or so in the evening. Breakfast and supper were served at the long table in the main room of the bunkhouse, with all the men vying for seconds. While the cowboys were sent to the field with packed lunches or jerky and bread, Adam ate the midday meal in the ranch house with Will, Hannah, Julia, Ben, and Snake. If any of the other boys were in for the day, they would join the group.

The stables were better than he hoped—for such a remote place in the wilderness. Well, they were fairly close to Prescott, but other than the town and the fort, there was no one for miles. Adam was pleased with the choices Will made for the building, the corrals, and the equipment. It was evident he spared no expense on equipment or horses.

At least three horses were four to five years and would need broken soon. Another handful were two to three years. They were at the perfect age as far as Adam was concerned. Young enough that they would learn to trust him long before he put a saddle on their backs. Three of the mares were foaling. Will told him he bred them in the summer so they should foal early next year. Several of the horses should already be ready for sale according to Will. He just wanted to make sure they met Adam's expectations.

With so many horses requiring his attention there was so much work to be done. Back home, his pa never had more than two or three at a given age since Adam was the only one working them. There would be no time for him to ease into his responsibilities.

Taking the training bridle down, he took it with him as he led Percy from his stall. Percy was a jet black colt sired by one of the studs Will purchased. Both the sire and the colt were solid animals. Yesterday, he spent time getting Percy used to the bridle. Today, he would continue the training. Once in the corral, he placed the bridle over Percy's head. The horse handled it well, just a flick of his ears to let him know he was at least thinking about what was going on. Speaking in soft tones, he led Percy through a series of exercises walking him in circles and lines.

While he worked, he thought of Julia, as he often had since arriving at the ranch. After having spent so much time with her on the trail west, seeing her only at dinner seemed like nothing. He wondered how she was doing and if she told Hannah and Will what really caused her to leave Texas.

He flinched as he remembered the day she took his horse and he witnessed Reuben beat her. He prayed for her every day, wanting God to free her from her misery. Yet, he could tell during those brief encounters over dinner that she was still struggling. She was so quiet, so distant.

Percy snorted bringing his attention back to the horse. He finished the circle and Percy was waiting for the next instruction. Zigzagging back and forth through the corral, he led him through the next series. Once Percy completed the steps, Adam removed the bridle and let him run free for several minutes. When he gave the signal, Percy stopped and approached him. This horse was a fast learner.

As he finished brushing down Percy and returning him to the stall, Hannah rang the supper bell. Adam wished, probably for the fifth time that day, that he could have supper at the main house. But, growing up on the ranch, he knew the protocol. The main house was for family only. Will was breaking those same unwritten rules by even allowing them to eat there midday.

Washing up outside the bunkhouse, he paused before jumping into the fray. Sometimes he found it difficult to go from the serenity of working with the horses all day to the noise and activity of the bunkhouse. He opened the door to see Rosa already setting out the heaping plates of food.

"Hey, Adam, you better take a seat quick," Jed said. "Before cranky old Whitten here decides to take all the food."

Whitten jabbed the younger man in the ribs with his elbow. "Least I'm not some young pup still being weaned."

"I'd rather be a young pup than a cranky old man!" Jed shot

back.

Hawk whispered so only Adam could hear, "Careful of the gravy. Saw Pedro hanging around it."

Adam nodded, biting the inside of his cheek, trying not to smile. Pedro, one of the Mexican cowboys that worked the night shift, was known for his practical jokes with jalapeños. It was funny, as long as it was not your mouth on fire. Last night Adam warned Hawk when he figured out which dish contained the surprise pepper, so it seemed Hawk was returning the favor.

The friendly banter continued around the table until all the food was gone. Many of the boys were younger than he was. Covington, Jed, and Hawk were all younger. Owens was Adam's age and Whitten was just a year older than him. Then there was Snake. He must have been close to Will's thirty years. Ben, of course, was old enough to be their father, maybe even grandfather. The Mexicans were less forthcoming about their ages, but Adam put them all between twenty and twenty-four.

When Rosa came around to gather up the dishes, Diego jumped to his feet to help. Adam smiled at the thought of a romance budding on the ranch, though he longed for it to be him and Julia. The thought sobered him, but he knew it was true. He came to care for her deeply during their time on the trail.

Someone asked him a question, jarring him from his thoughts. "Pardon?"

"Heard you are going to that fancy Governor's Ball tomorrow. Guess horse trainers are higher up than us cowboys," Owens stated, looking none too pleased.

While what Owens said was true to some extent, Adam tried to think of how to diffuse the situation. "Will wants me there to meet some potential customers. Nothing more." *You hope there is more. You hope to dance with Julia.*

"On a first name basis with the boss, too, I see."

"Will's family and mine have been friends and neighbors my entire life. So, yes, we're on a first name basis."

Owens harrumphed, but let it lie after a stern look from Ben.

The four Mexicans gathered up their things. After thanking Rosa for their packed lunch, they headed out the door to start their turn with the cattle. That was another difference between the ranching in Texas and here. Back home, they often corralled the cattle at night and had one or maybe two men on watch. But to send four out to the field? When he questioned Will about it earlier, he said it was not safe to do otherwise. From Jed, he learned that the Apache were a constant threat and cattle thieves seemed particularly active in the territory.

Snake, Cahill, Webb, Whitten, and Owens pulled out their deck of cards. Owens jabbed a giant wad of tobacco in his cheek.

"Deal you in Larson?" Snake asked.

Adam shook his head.

"Another goody-goody church going man," Owens said, sending a stream of tobacco juice near Adam's feet.

Ben looked up from the book he was reading. That was usually all the warning any of them needed to straighten up. But Owens failed to heed the silent warning.

"Too good for us Larson?"

Adam sighed inwardly. He had no idea what he had done to get on this man's bad side, but that's where he was. "No. Just not interested in poker."

When Adam turned to join Jed and Hawk in whatever they were discussing, he heard the scrape of a chair before the impact of Owens's weight knocked him face down to the floor. Trying to free himself, Adam kicked at the man's shins. Before he could make any further attempt, Ben lifted Owens off his feet. Dragging him by the shirt collar, Ben threw him outside.

"Don't know what's gotten into you but you go cool off on your own, before I make you," Ben said before slamming the door shut. He took a deep breath and returned to his chair picking up where he left off in his book.

Adam stood and brushed the dust from his pants. Jed and Hawk were looking at him wide-eyed while the card players went on without Owens.

"What was that all about," Jed asked as Adam took a seat on the floor next to him.

"Wish I knew."

The next morning, as Adam was working in the corral, a rider came down the road toward the ranch house. Dropping his hold on the bridle, he walked into the barn where Will was working on some piece of furniture.

"Got a rider from town," he said before returning to the corral.

Within minutes, the rider was close enough for Adam to get a clearer view.

Standing straighter, he tightened his jaw. "Bates," he forced the name through gritted teeth, just as Will stepped from the barn.

"What are you doing here?" Will thundered as Bates dismounted.

"A good day to you too." Bates' sarcastic tone belied the friendly words. Tossing the reins over the edge of the corral, he used it as a temporary hitching post.

Adam quickly removed the bridle from the horse he was working with. Then he moved around to the other side of the corral, letting the horse run free for the time being.

"I've come to inquire about employment," Bates said, changing to a more amiable tone.

"Mighty long way to come looking for a job," Will said, folding his arms across his chest.

"Well, I didn't initially set out with that in mind. But, things change."

"I know you were on our wagon train," Adam said.

Will said, "So, let's start with why you left Texas."

For the next half hour, all three men stood there with defensive postures. They listened as Bates told about Reuben hiring him to bring Julia back and how he met up with them in Santa Fe instead of chasing them down on the trail.

"But, after I heard that man in Santa Fe say you married Miss Colter," Bates said, looking at Adam, "I knew it wouldn't be smart to force her to go back. Might not be one for always walking the straight and narrow, but I ain't too fond of outright breaking the law either."

"Married? Who said we were married?"

"When you were loading your wagon, that man addressed Miss Colter as Mrs. Larson."

Thank God Bates had misunderstood. Who knows what he'd

have done with Julia then. And maybe it would be better to play along for a while.

Apparently, Will thought so. "So you gave up your mission for Reuben when you learned Julia was with Adam?"

"Yeah. When I found out they were married, I figured there was no chance Reuben would pay me for returning her. Honestly, I wasn't too sure he would pay me if she hadn't been married."

"Why's that?" Adam asked.

Bates snorted. "He still owed all of his hands two months back pay. We hadn't seen a penny from him for a while. Then, all the sudden when Miss Colter—I mean Mrs. Larson—took off, he had a stack of cash. He happily handed over some of it to send me off to fetch her."

Will eyed Bates warily. Adam guessed he was weighing the truth of the story.

Getting an idea, he asked, "So, if you're not such a bad guy, why did you agree to go after Julia when she was running from Reuben. Surely you knew about the abuse?"

Bates' head jerked towards him in genuine surprise. "Abuse? Are you suggesting Reuben handled her roughly?"

"Not suggesting it. Witnessed it myself. After she broke off the engagement with Hiram Norton. He was strangling her. Not sure if he wouldn't have killed her if I hadn't shown up."

Now both Will and Bates looked at him, disbelief on their faces. Though he hated for Will to hear the details in this way, he was glad he said it, because it showed that Bates had no idea what happened to cause Julia to leave.

"I just thought she was a rebellious young lady. Never thought she might have good reason to take off," Bates muttered.

Silence settled over the group for several minutes.

Finally, Will spoke. "Why'd you come here, Bates? Last time I hired you, you broke our agreement for more money."

"Guess I came here 'cause I know you to be an honest man. Good to your word. And you're right. What I did was wrong. I don't blame you for being leery." Looking down at the ground, Bates kicked a small rock with the toe of his boot.

"Not so sure I trust you enough to hire you. What's to keep you from taking Julia back even now?" Will asked.

"She's married."

Adam shook his head. Will mimicked his movement before saying, "No, she's not."

Gideon Bates couldn't believe his ears. Here he'd come all this way for such wrong reasons. Turns out the one right thing he did—not taking a married woman from her husband—was all based on a misunderstanding.

Yet, he could see in Will Colter's eyes the complete distrust. *I'm sure he thinks this piece of information will change my mind.* But, he made up his mind already. Even if there was some reasonable way to return Miss Colter to Reuben he wouldn't do it. He had no desire to make that long trip again.

Knowing what he knew now, he certainly would not take her back to an abusive brother. No, he'd watched his little sister suffer too much at his drunken father's hands. He wouldn't knowingly put any woman in that kind of a situation.

Will and Larson were still staring at him. Probably waiting for him to say something. Better give it a shot.

"Look, no matter what you've said or what I've done in the past, I ain't here to take Miss Colter back to Texas. I firmly gave up that idea in Santa Fe. And what you've said now—well, I think she's with the brother that will treat her best." Hopefully they would see he meant the words.

After several more minutes of silence he figured it'd be a slim chance in Hades for him to get a job here.

"Well," he said, "I appreciate your time. Sorry to have wasted so much of it."

Taking the reins of his horse in hand, he started to mount. "Best be on my way."

"Wait!" Will said, stopping him.

As Gideon turned, Will continued, "I've been looking for another man for the night shift. If you want it, the job is yours."

Smiling, Gideon accepted the offer. "Glad to have it."

"Just make sure you don't abuse my trust. I'm not prone to

giving third chances," Will said, glaring at him.

Swallowing hard, Gideon heard the message loud and clear. Might be a good time for sticking to the straight and narrow.

After Will had Adam show Bates to the bunkhouse, he went in to talk to Julia. Kicking himself, he wondered why on earth he consented to give Bates a second chance. Wasn't the best idea he had. Especially since it would probably send Julia into a fit.

But something about his story and his demeanor made him think Bates might have changed.

Regardless, he would talk to Ben later about keeping close tabs on him. The idea to put him on the night shift was brilliant. He'd be out in the field with Pedro and the other Mexicans. He would have no opportunity to sneak anything by Will at night. During the day between him, Ben, and Adam, there was no chance of Bates getting within ten feet of Julia.

Slowly, he opened the ranch house door, apprehension filling him.

Julia and Hannah were both in the kitchen baking.

"How are my ladies?" he asked, getting their attention.

"Just fine," Hannah smiled. Oh, that look melted his heart every time. "What brings you in at this time of day?"

"Can we sit for a minute?" he asked. "All three of us."

Julia quietly took a seat at the table while Hannah poured some coffee and brought it to the table. As soon as she sat down, he started his explanation, hoping it would be received well.

"We had a visitor this morning."

He paused. There was really no way to ease into this.

"Gideon Bates came looking for work."

At Julia's gasp, Hannah took her hand.

"He explained why he was following you and why he never took you back to the Star C."

"And you believe him?" she shrieked.

"I do."

The look of betrayal she shot him seared his heart like a hot branding iron on a young calf's rump.

"I hired him for the night shift," he added.

"How could you!" she screamed, standing so fast that her chair threatened to tumble.

"Calm down!" he shouted back.

"I will not calm down. He's one of Reuben's men. He was following me to take me back. You even just said it! Why would you think hiring him was a good idea?" Julia accused.

Hannah's expression wasn't much better. Confused. Wary.

"Look, he had plenty of opportunity to drag you back if he had wanted to. But, along the way he realized it wasn't the right thing to do." Well, maybe he only fully realized that just this morning. But that wouldn't help his argument. "You don't have to worry about anything. You'll be safe. He'll be out in the fields at night. Pedro will keep close watch on him. The rest of the time, me, Ben, and Adam will be around. You have nothing to fear."

Disgust overwhelmed Julia's face. "I can't believe you would do this to me!"

When she stormed into her room, he stood to follow her.

Hannah stopped him. "Give her some time, Will. She's hurt and confused and just not able to deal with any more surprises right now."

Grunting, Will turned and headed back to the barn without a word. He didn't have to justify his decisions to his sister. He was trying to help her see that things would be fine.

When was the happy Julia going to return?

Chapter 15

Julia returned to the solitude of her room while Hannah bustled about the kitchen with Rosa, cleaning up from dinner. A morning full of anxiety over Will's hiring of Bates only added to her tension about the upcoming evening. They would be leaving shortly to make the trip into Prescott to attend the Governor's Ball, which meant a large crowd of mostly men.

Prior to the incident, as she was now referring to Reuben's actions, Julia had not been afraid of men. Perhaps she had just been naïve before. But, she had not been afraid. Now, things were different. If her own brother could act in such a way, how could she possibly trust any man? Tonight she'd be surrounded by them.

Piling curls on top of her head in a fashionable manner, she held back a sigh. The only benefit of having naturally curly hair is that it looked stunning for special occasions. The rest of the time it was a constant nuisance. She was wearing the best of her three outfits, not having time to finish her new dress yet. The dress was more serviceable than anything, although in comparison to some of the clothing she had seen in the West, some might consider it pretty. It was nothing like the fine silk gowns she wore for formal dinners back in Texas. But the navy blue color made her eyes stand out. For someone so afraid of men, she was putting a lot of effort into her appearance.

As she entered the living room, Will greeted her, dressed in one of his nicer shirts but still wearing trousers and that hat! Julia rolled her eyes just thinking about that tan hat. The thing was tan more because of years of dust than because of its original color. A dark brown would have been a more prudent color, at least she recalled their father mentioning it—many times. Will got it nearly eight years ago and still had not replaced it. She wondered if he ever would.

Hannah was also ready and waiting on Julia. Her dress was a brown calico Julia had not seen before, although she doubted it was brand new. It looked a little snug about her midsection, but otherwise had a very flattering silhouette.

"Ben has the wagon out front. Shall we go?" Will asked, offering his arm to his wife.

Stomach fluttering, Julia nodded. Tonight was going to be a long night if she failed to calm her anxiousness.

When she stepped through the doorway, the first sight that greeted her was a stunningly handsome Adam Larson. He wore a white crisp shirt with a western style tie, much like the one her father used to wear, and wool trousers. He had taken the time to slick his golden blonde hair, parting it to one side. He cleaned up nicely. His green eyes sparkled as she approached the wagon. Her stomach tightened more.

"You look lovely, Julia," Adam said as he helped her into the back of the wagon since there was little more than enough room for Will and Hannah on the seat.

"You look pretty dashing yourself." Her lips revealed her thoughts before she could stop herself.

Embarrassed, she ducked her head as she took a seat on the blanket spread out in the back of the wagon. She arranged her skirts around her outstretched legs to ensure modesty. Adam took the seat next to her, while Ben rode his horse. At Will's command, the horses moved forward to take them into town.

Will and Hannah chatted in hushed tones amongst themselves. She felt Adam's gaze more than once, but decided to focus on the road behind them instead. She could not believe she had flirted with Adam Larson!

What she said was true, though. He did look dashing. She glanced over at the same moment he did.

"How are you settling in, Julia?" he asked.

"Fine, I guess."

His voice took on a disappointed tone as he said, "I haven't seen much of you since we arrived. I guess I got used to being around you all the time."

Julia felt the same way. After those months on the trail where she was with Adam all day, she missed him. She could change that, though. With Rosa and Hannah doing the cooking, they really didn't need her help all of the time. Maybe she could spend some time helping him train the horses.

"I guess you are pretty busy with the horses," she ventured.

"Yes. I was not prepared for the number that need training. I'm afraid I am not doing as thorough of a job as I would like. There aren't enough hours of daylight. Some days, I even light some torches around the corral so I can continue working with them."

"I could help you... I mean... There's not enough work to keep three women busy so I could help a few days a week. That is if you would like help."

"I would love your help. I know what a good horsewoman you are." The tenderness in Adam's voice sent her heart beating.

Don't get your hopes up. Adam will never want a ruined woman. For just one night she wished the accusing voice would be still. She was weary of its taunting about something she had no control over. She could not stop Reuben. She had not been strong enough.

The downward spiral started and tears burned in her eyes. Turning her head away from Adam's view, she willed the tears to stay away. She would not cry. Not tonight. No matter how scared she was of what awaited her at the party, she would forget about her messy life—if only for this one night.

Squaring her shoulders, she turned back toward Adam. Voice shaky, but growing stronger with each word, she said, "Then it's settled. I will help you with the horses starting Monday."

Adam's grin answered for him.

Once in town, Will looked for a place to park the wagon. The Governor's Mansion was on Granite Street, but there was no place nearby to leave the wagon. He did not want to leave it on Montezuma near the saloons, so he decided to pull back onto Granite to drop off the ladies. He finally ended up parking the wagon across town by Lancaster's.

Walking back up the slight slope to Granite Street, Will smiled, excited about the evening. In addition to dancing with his beautiful wife, he was also looking forward to the business contacts that would be made this evening. It was a unique opportunity that he would try to make the most of. Hannah waited for him outside so he hurried to join her.

The Governor's Mansion was a log structure, most definitely the largest building in Prescott other than the hotel. The building could fit three or four of his ranch houses inside with a little room to spare. He heard the construction of the mansion was done under armed guard, not for fear of someone stealing something, but rather to offer protection against the Apaches. Now, several other buildings started to spring up along the street, proving that Prescott was getting safer. The inside was massive. The living area, which had been converted to a ballroom this evening, was in the center of the building. Several rooms lined three of the four walls, the fourth wall being the entrance he was standing in now.

"Governor Goodwin," Will greeted, shaking the man's hand. "William Colter, and this is my wife, Hannah."

"Mr. Colter, pleased to meet you," the governor said. Recognition dawned on his face when he turned to greet Hannah, "And a pleasure to see you again Mrs. Colter."

At first Will was taken aback, until he recalled that Hannah and her first husband had traveled to the territory with the governor and his party.

Moving further into the room, he led Hannah over to greet Betty and Paul.

"Betty," Hannah said, hugging her friend, then nodded a greeting to her son, Paul.

"You are glowing again, dear. I suspect it is not just your handsome husband that's causing it."

Will and Hannah both blushed.

"We'll talk later," Hannah said.

As the music stared he led her to the dance floor. Taking her in his arms, he looked down. His breath caught. She was so beautiful— and she did have a strange enchanting glow about her this evening.

"You're stunning," he whispered.

"Thank you my handsome husband." She smiled up at him and his heart did a little flip. "I think Betty knows our secret."

"Well, I don't suppose we can keep the baby hidden forever," he teased.

Hannah tilted her head back in laughter. "No, I don't think we can for much longer."

When the song finished, no matter how much he wanted to be in his wife's presence, he led her over to the side. "I need to speak with a few people. But save a few more dances for me?"

"Of course."

"And don't overexert yourself." Concern clouded his eyes.

"The two of us will be fine, Will. Dancing is good for expectant mothers." Shooing him away, she said, "Now go be about your business."

After introducing himself and Julia to the Governor, Adam escorted her directly to the dance floor. She seemed rather nervous, but he hoped she would let herself have a good time tonight and forget about the past months, if only for a few hours.

When he put his hand on the small of her back, he could not help but notice how perfectly it fit there. He smiled down at her—not too far down, as he was only a few inches taller than her—nothing like the height difference between Will and Hannah. When she looked up at him, his breath caught and whatever he was about to say was lost. Those beautiful blue eyes. He could stare into them all night.

Julia turned her head looking at the other dancers, breaking the spell. While the proper distance apart, she was still close enough he caught the faint scent of vanilla. He let his eyes travel over the features of her face which seemed like a good idea, until he came to her lips. The desire to kiss her seemed almost overwhelming.

He needed to distract himself.

Clearing his throat, he asked, "Are you enjoying the ball?" *Silly, this was the first dance.*

"Hmm?" she asked turning her gaze back to him.

The question seemed stupid the first time so he decided not to repeat it. "Thank you for volunteering to help with the horses." There. Gratitude. That should be better.

"Of course. Is that Ben dancing with Betty?"

Adam looked to the couple she nodded towards. "I believe it is and he's grinning ear to ear. Have you ever seen him smile?"

Julia laughed—a sweet sound that caused his heart to warm. "I have. Only it's rare and never quite so dramatic."

He laughed at her observation.

When the song ended, he started to pull away so he could go speak with the men Will wanted him to meet, but Julia's grip tightened.

"Please, don't leave yet," she pleaded. The laughter was gone from her eyes and fear had taken up residence. Was she afraid of dancing with these strangers?

He did not want to leave her side, but Will expected him to mingle. The inner conflict lasted only a second before he agreed to the dance. "Yes, Miss Colter, you may have this dance," he teased. "Then I must take my leave for a while. But I hope you will save me a dance or two later."

Her grip on his hand tightened and instead of smiling like he hoped, she tensed. She attempted to tease, but it came out strained, "If you must."

"Julia," he said. She would not make eye contact. "Julia, look at me."

When she finally made eye contact, he said, "You are safe here. It is just a dance. Meet some people and have a good time, like you did at those parties your father held."

She looked like she struggled for control. Moisture gathered in the corner of her eyes, but did not spill over. He thought himself a fool for mentioning anything to do with Texas. Of course those would be painful memories for her. He could not leave her in this state of mind. When the song ended, he escorted her outside.

The air was brisk. The temperature dropped rapidly as the sun went down. She shivered and he wished he had a jacket to give her, but he didn't. Walking to the far end of the front porch of the mansion, he put his arm around her. She felt like she belonged there.

Sighing, Julia spoke first. "Thank you. I don't know what came over me. I know I cannot monopolize your time this evening. It's just that… You put me at ease," she said softly.

"Will you be alright?"

Taking a deep breath she let it out slowly then turned to face him. The moonlight highlighted one side of her face, leaving the other in shadow and giving her a mysterious appeal. Adam again resisted the urge to kiss her. He knew she was still too fragile and that any such action would only damage their friendship. He would be patient.

"Yes, I'll be alright. We can go back now."

Just before they re-entered the mansion, she stopped. "Adam?"

"Yes?"

"Thank you for being my rock."

He smiled at her. Maybe there was hope.

"Major, it was good to see you again," Hannah said as the officer from Fort Whipple finished the dance.

"May I have this dance, lovely lady?"

Hannah turned to see her husband posing the question. Letting out a tired sigh, she answered, "If you don't mind, I'd love to take a break."

Will took her hand and led her to the refreshment table. Leaning close to her ear, he said, "Seems Betty has been with the same dance partner most of the evening."

"Oh, I hadn't noticed," she said, still sipping the punch. "Who?"

Wiggling his eyebrows, he replied, "Ben."

"Really?" She noticed they danced together a few times. With the long string of men asking to dance with her, she had been more focused on talking with them rather than what was happening elsewhere.

Will grinned. "I think it's sweet. Care for some fresh air?"

At her nod, he escorted her to the front porch. The cool air was refreshing after seemingly hours of dancing. Hannah moved to stand by the railing, with him following close behind. Wrapping his arms around her, he rested his bony chin on the top of her head.

"Mrs. Colter, you are positively breathtaking this evening," he said, his voice husky. "You even smell good, too."

She giggled at his teasing. "Yes, but my feet feel like the size of watermelons."

"But, do they taste as good?"

"William!" She swatted at his arm, as she turned to face him. Before she could say anything further, he kissed her. She threw her arms around his neck as he deepened the kiss.

"Nope," he said pulling back. "You don't taste like watermelon."

She sighed. He certainly was in a playful mood. "How much longer were you planning on staying?"

"I had been hoping for one more dance, especially since I'm leaving you with Betty and Julia tonight."

She was about to agree, but yawned instead. Resting her head on his chest, she said, "Would you settle for a dance out here. Then take me home?"

He wrapped his arms around her and swayed to the music, not really dancing. Hannah breathed deeply of his scent. She wished they would have taken a room at the hotel. But, with so many guests in town for the ball, it was already booked. Betty offered to have Hannah and Julia to stay with her in her private quarters. Will, Ben, and Adam would bunk at the boardinghouse. It seemed strange to be apart from her husband, even if it was only for one night. As they continued to sway to the music, she felt her eyelids getting heavy.

"Unless you want to carry me down the hill, I suggest we leave soon."

"Very well. Let me find Betty and let her know we're leaving and to keep an eye on Julia."

A minute later, Will returned to escort her to Lancaster's. He seemed more pensive since returning.

"Do you think Julia had a good time?" he asked.

"I think so, why?"

"She just didn't seem herself, especially early in the evening. It was as if she were frightened to be here. That is not the same Julia I remember."

"How so?"

"Growing up, she loved parties. She would spend hours getting ready. Then when the guests started arriving, she was energized by it. Her face would light up and she wanted to talk to as many people as she could. But, tonight she was not herself. She seemed shy, wanting to hang back. The only time she seemed normal was when she danced with Adam."

Hannah heard the concern in his voice. "And which bothers you more? Her not being herself or her dancing with Adam?"

Will sighed. "I'm not bothered by her dancing with Adam. He's a good man. I have no concerns with him. I am, however, very concerned about the different person Julia is." He paused before asking, "Has she said anything more to you about what happened?"

Hannah, while having told Will most of what Julia said, had not mentioned that Julia was having trouble dealing with how much he and Reuben looked alike. She didn't want to add to his worry, especially over his looks, for there was nothing he could do about that.

"No she has said nothing further."

They arrived at the back entrance to the private quarters of Lancaster's. "Come in for some coffee?" Hannah asked.

Will pulled her to him. "I want to come in, but not for coffee," he said before kissing her deeply. If he kept the kiss going much longer, it was a good possibility that Betty and Julia would have no place to stay for the night.

Hannah put her hand on his chest and pushed him away. "Good night, dear husband."

As he closed the door behind her, she could hear the frustration in his voice, though it was muffled by the door. "Good night, Hannah."

Adam made his way to where Julia was dancing with the Secretary of the Territory, pleased at his good fortune that the song just ended.

"Miss Colter, a pleasure meeting you. What a fine dancer you are," the secretary acknowledged, before turning Julia over to him.

"Adam," she breathed his name with a rush of relief. "I have danced about all I can take. Would you be so kind as to escort me back to the boardinghouse?"

Maybe not quite as good fortune as he thought. "Certainly," he replied, careful to keep the disappointment from his voice.

They made their way to Lancaster's in silence. Adam sensed her relief to be away from the crowd. He wanted to ask her how long she would continue living in the past, but knew if he did so, he would break the trust between them. She was still living in fear, even after travelling all the way here to a safe place. There was nothing for her to fear here, yet she did. He wanted so much to shake her and wake her up to that fact.

But, as he learned tonight, she saw him as her rock. No matter how much he wanted to push her to leave the past behind, he wouldn't take away the security she felt with him.

As they neared Lancaster's, Adam heard voices inside, likely Betty and Hannah catching up. He wanted to stop and take Julia in his arms—and kiss her. Dancing with her had been incredible, serving only to intensify his feelings.

Instead, he turned to face her, saying, "I enjoyed your company this evening."

"Thank you for keeping me safe," she said before walking through the door.

As it closed and obscured her form, he wondered how long he might have to wait before she might be ready to consider him as a suitor. *Lord, give me patience.*

Chapter 16

Tennessee

November 9, 1864

The air grew colder as the sun set, sending a chill through his navy blue wool overcoat. As Sergeant Thomas Anderson wove his way between the trees of the dense western Tennessee forest, he searched for a place to stop. While the dispatch he carried was important, it was not so urgent that he needed to ride through the night, for a change.

Spotting an old dilapidated cabin ahead, Thomas reined in his horse. He tied his mount to a tree then quietly walked the distance to the structure. There was no light coming from the cabin. Turning his ear toward it, he listened intently for several minutes. No sounds either. Taking his time, he approached the cabin keeping out of the view of the window and door. Once near the window, he carefully peered through it. Not seeing anyone inside, he rounded the corner and entered through the door. The place was deserted.

He walked back to his mount and led the horse into the cabin. It would be a tight fit, but it would be safer than leaving the horse tied outside in plain view, announcing his presence to any rebels in the area. Once both man and animal were settled, he dug through the saddle bags for some feed for his horse. As she happily chomped away, he opened some of his rations. Leaning against the sturdiest wall of the drafty cabin, he chewed the food slowly. He found doing so made the meal seem bigger to his empty stomach.

Since becoming a dispatch rider, Thomas learned how to stretch his limited food supplies. Even though he should have this dispatch delivered to the general in two days, he would eat sparingly just in case he ran into any rebels or needed to take a longer, safer route from his original plan. It was a routine he was now well familiar with.

Thomas thought back to how he ended up working for Colonel Woods in the First Brigade of the XVI Corps. The journey was bizarre and twisted—far too strange to be called destiny.

Just over a year ago at his trial for an attempted bank robbery, the judge, who had been a friend of his father's, gave Thomas the option to either serve his jail time or enlist in the Union Army. The choice was unprecedented. Not wanting to go jail, Thomas enlisted in one of the regiments from Ohio. After serving with them from November 1863 to January 1864, their forces had been significantly reduced and he was transferred to the 89th Indiana Regiment as an infantry man.

The 89th Indiana Regiment was part of the XVI Corps led by Major General Andrew Jackson Smith. Smith and his corps were ordered to Louisiana in early March to participate in the Red River Campaign. After several skirmishes with the Confederate forces, all dismal failures, Smith's commanding officer reorganized the campaign.

One day towards the end of March, everything changed.

Smoke clouded his vision as he crawled along on his stomach. Easing his head over the embankment, he took aim and fired. The bullet connected with a rebel's leg, sending him to the ground. Ducking down again, Thomas hurried to reload the rifle through the muzzle.

"Watch out!" Mixford yelled at the approaching rider.

The crack of a rifle echoed as Thomas looked up at the rider. Blood spewed from his chest staining the copper tube slung over his abdomen.

"Help!" the dispatcher cried weakly as he fell from his horse, landing on the ground with a thud next to Thomas.

He kneeled down taking in the man's graying skin color.

"Take this," the dying man said, placing his shaky hand over the copper message tube. "To Major General Smith."

As coughing racked the man's body, Thomas stared in shock.

"Come on, Tommy boy," Mixford said, slapping his back. "You

heard the man. You gotta ride it down the line."

Numbly, Thomas lifted the copper tube from the man as the life faded from his eyes. Looking around, he noticed the dispatcher's horse just a few feet away. Strapping the message tube to his body, he dropped his rifle and grabbed the man's lighter carbine and pistol and any ammunition he had on him. Running towards the horse, he jumped up and kicked the horse into motion in the same instant.

Quickly the noise of rifle fire and cannon blasts faded to the background. All he could hear was the heavy breath of the horse beneath him, sides heaving from the strenuous pace. A four foot fence loomed before him. Squeezing the horse's sides, he urged her forward. Leaping effortlessly over the obstacle, the horse clearly understood his intent.

Blood racing through his veins, he pressed on, clearing several more obstacles. When the enemy line pressed close, he leaned over the side of the horse. Crossing his right hand with a pistol over to balance on his left arm, he fired off a few shots in defense. As the space between Union and Confederate lines widened, Thomas returned the pistol to his side.

Ahead a captain waved for him to stop. In that moment, the foolishness of his action sank in. He pulled to a stop as the captain of the guard said, "Ladies fair lose their hearts on a night such as this."

Blinking, Thomas realized the cryptic phrase was some sort of passcode. Scrounging his mind, he tried to think if the dying dispatcher said anything that would have been helpful. Thinking of nothing, he stalled.

"Yes, um... I suppose you are looking for some sort of response."

Crossing his arms, the captain of the guard repeated the words.

Playing forgetful, Thomas took off his forage cap and rubbed his forehead. "Um... was that the one that had something to do with pirates?" He muttered to himself. "No. No." He shook his head. "That's supposed to be a reference to a book. I know it," he stumbled to silence, as a frown formed on the captain's face.

A few minutes passed quietly as the captain scrutinized him. "Who's the dispatch for?" the captain asked.

"Major General Smith, sir."

"From?"

Thomas cringed inwardly as his mouth suddenly became dry. Not only was he going to hang for abandoning his post, he was going to be shot by this man for stealing a dispatch. Why did he always seem to get into these impossible situations?

Only, the situation hadn't turned out to be impossible, Thomas thought, swallowing the last bite of his tasteless rations. His horse snorted, signaling she had finished her meal as well. Standing, he removed the feed bag from the mare.

That day in March set his life on a new course. Thomas decided to come clean to the captain, explaining in detail what happened to lead him to pick up the missive. He offered to let the captain verify the authenticity of the communiqué. Leaving him under armed guard, the captain went to discuss the situation with Major General Smith. In a few minutes, he returned, letting Thomas deliver the message instead of shooting him.

Major General Smith was rather nonchalant about the whole affair, until he read the dispatch. It had been pivotal that he receive the message before sundown as it contained orders for the men to march to a new line by morning. If not for Thomas's swift action, that battle could have turned out much differently. The Major General recognized that fact. He instructed the captain of the guard to send word back to Thomas's commanding officer that he was being transferred to the brigade's command to become a dispatcher for Colonel Woods.

Thomas could not believe his fortune. Things never turned out that way for him. At least they hadn't growing up. They hadn't when he was hanging around with the Rogers gang, either.

Yet, here he was, going on his eighth month as a dispatch rider for Colonel Woods and occasionally for Major General Smith.

Strange job, dispatch riding was. When he was not out on a run, the colonel often sent him on special assignments to gather information about enemy activities. Last week, he and two other scouts pinpointed the Confederate General Hook's position, heading for Franklin, Tennessee. After Thomas reported back to Colonel

Woods, Woods sent a report via Thomas to Major General Smith. Major General Smith then sent Thomas with the same report to Major General George Thomas at headquarters in Nashville. When Major General Thomas finished reading the report, he composed a new report and Sergeant Anderson was sent to deliver it to General Grant—the current dispatch secured safely across his chest this very moment.

Stretching out on the floor of the cabin, Thomas pulled his wool blanket around him to ward off the chill. He wondered what General Grant might think of a former failed bank robber being entrusted with a critical communication. Would he be shocked?

While completely trustworthy since entering the war, he had been a different man prior. He was young and made many foolish choices, the biggest one—getting involved with Ed and Sam Rogers. But, he had been so angry after his father died. He was just fourteen then. When his older brother, Drew, left for medical school, Thomas was forced to live with his Uncle Peter, who vacillated between being too controlling and not caring at all, depending on his mood. He certainly never cared enough to keep him completely out of trouble. Over time it seemed as if Uncle Peter preferred the nights Thomas stayed away from home. It was one less responsibility he had to deal with.

Thomas's downward spiral did not seem like a dangerous or bad path when he started. In school, he joined the Rogers' when they bullied other kids. It made him feel powerful and in control, something he never felt at home. Then, as the three of them grew older, they grew bolder. They would steal petty items from the mercantile, the very one his father had owned and his brother had sold. He had been so angry with Drew when he sold it.

Two years after Drew left, he discovered alcohol and he enjoyed it. He and the Rogers would spend time well into the night at the saloon drinking and gambling. He had a keen mind and quickly became an expert poker player. He earned enough money to support his drinking and kept it hidden from Uncle Peter. By the time he was eighteen, Thomas planned to make a career out of gambling.

Then, Drew returned home. At first Thomas was going to live with the Rogers, but after Drew married, he convinced Thomas to live with them. The six months he lived there proved contentious and ended in the two never speaking again.

Well, at least not until after Thomas tried to rob the bank and was in jail. As it turned out, his actions caused Drew and his wife no small amount of hardship. Drew was a doctor and from the day of the failed bank robbery until the day they left Cincinnati, he had but a handful of patients—and all because of what Thomas did. It was just weeks before Drew and Hannah left that Drew paid Thomas a visit in jail. He started to feel some remorse for his actions, but hardened his heart when Drew showed up. He felt Drew was holier than him and had come to gloat. Many times Thomas thought back to that conversation and knew that was not the case at all. Drew told him they were moving to La Paz in the Arizona Territory and that if Thomas ever got his life together, he would be welcomed.

Who has their life forever changed by someone—forced to move from his home—and, then offers to welcome that person back, forgiving everything? *I guess Drew would.*

For the past month, Thomas toyed with the idea of actually taking Drew up on his offer once he was finished in the army. Would Drew really welcome him back as he said? If he did, would his wife, Hannah? Guilt stabbed him in his chest. What must it have been like for his sister-in-law to leave her home because of him? Would she hate him?

Well, he was not sure what he would really do once the war was over. Right now, it did not look like it would be ending soon. Rolling onto his side, he closed his eyes. Pushing the familiar guilt away, he fell asleep.

The next morning just before dawn, Thomas startled awake. Quietly, but swiftly, he jumped to his feet while pulling his pistol from its sheath. He grabbed his carbine with his other hand. His horse's ears' twitching indicated that he was no longer alone. Flattening himself against the wall, he moved to peer out the door.

Rebels!

He counted three of them walking toward the cabin. His heart started pounding. He would have merely seconds to plan his escape before they were upon him. Having slept with the copper message tube strapped to his chest, as he usually did, he would just need to get his horse and his blanket. Leaving either would be unwise.

Crouching down to the ground, he slid the wool blanket towards himself. Once he had a firm grip on it, he mounted his horse, securing the blanket under one leg. He would stow it properly later, if he made it out of this. Slowly turning his horse toward the door, he ducked his head to clear the opening as he dug his heels into the mare's flank. Hunched over the mare's back, horse and rider burst forth from the cabin.

The action had the intended effect. He surprised the three rebels. He shot the closest one in the arm, keeping him from shooting back. Then he shot the second in the leg, before charging the third. Once upon the third man, he used the butt of his now empty pistol to knock the man to the ground unconscious.

Digging his heels into the mare's flank again, Thomas pushed the mare into a full gallop. He rode at the fast pace for a good thirty minutes before stopping to rest his horse and secure his blanket. That had been close.

After a quick break, he mounted his horse and continued on at a gentler pace, now certain he was alone and the rebels had not followed him. He rode through dinner and continued on until suppertime when his stomach would allow him to wait no more. Seeing a farmhouse off in the distance, he debated whether or not to stop. One never knew which side these folks were on. Choosing to make your presence known to someone sympathetic to the enemy could prove deadly. Deciding the morning's encounter was enough for one day, Thomas rode past the farmhouse and found a place to stop in the forest for the night.

The routine of feeding his horse and feeding himself was familiar. He was glad he chanced bringing his blanket, for the air was colder tonight than the previous. Sleep came fitfully, perhaps from dwelling too much on his past. Several hours before dawn, he finally gave up and decided to press on.

Mid-afternoon he arrived at Grant's camp. Giving the appropriate signal to the captain of the guard, he was escorted to the General's tent. General Grant was much quieter and less imposing than he thought. He softly asked for the correspondence. He instructed Thomas to see the captain of the guard for rations and a place to stay for the evening. Then he was to return to the General in the morning.

Following the captain of the guard, he stopped short,

recognizing his old friend, Mixford, from the 89th Regiment. The man simply went by his last name, too low ranking to matter and too informal to care for giving his first name. The two had served together through the march from Tennessee to Louisiana and then during the Red River Campaign.

"Mixford, how are you?" Thomas asked.

"Tommy, is that you? Them rebels ain't got ya yet? Hee, hee."

"Naw, I'm too fast for them."

"More like your guardian angel is lookin' out fer ya!"

Thomas had shared some of his past with Mixford, at least the part about his strange sentencing for the robbery. When his friend heard the details, he insisted it was Providence and not fate or luck that spared him from jail.

"When we heard that ya were transferred to the Brigade, I wasn't t'all surprised, Tommy," Mixford said. "Providence must got something special planned fer ya, the way he keeps ya outta trouble."

"I wouldn't say he keeps me out of trouble. I have the scars to prove it." And scars he did have—many visible reminders of near misses with death. He had been shot on four occasions. Although most were flesh wounds and healed quickly, they still left a mark.

"Ah, but yer still here and sassy as ever, I see."

They spent the next hour swapping tales over the fire before the long trip caught up with Thomas. Knowing his day would start early and likely involve a return trip to Nashville, he took his leave.

What if someone is really looking out for me? His last thought for the night faded as sleep settled around him.

Chapter 17

Colter Ranch

November 15, 1864

Agitated. Confused. Edgy. Cooped up.

Argh!

Julia had to get out of this ranch house. Working the horses with Adam, as she had earlier in the week, would not help soothe her anxiety.

She had to ride—far from her thoughts and jumbled feelings.

As if spending days looking at Will and being reminded of her other brother wasn't bad enough, now she had to deal with the strange—dare she call them romantic—feelings she was having towards Adam. Something about the time they spent dancing at the Governor's Ball made her see him in a different light.

She would talk to Hannah, but she seemed consumed these last few days with planning for her baby. Will and Hannah finally told her they were expecting a son or daughter sometime around June.

If she couldn't talk to Hannah about Adam, and she couldn't talk to Adam for obvious reasons, who could she talk to? Certainly not God. He got her into this mess to begin with.

What good would it do anyway? You're ruined, remember? There's no chance of a courtship or marriage with any man, much less Adam.

That was it. Storming back to her room, Julia donned her tan split skirt and white shirt. Plopping her black cowboy hat down on her head, she walked at a brisk pace out the front door without a word to Hannah or Rosa.

Carefully checking the stables to make sure Will was not there, she picked a chestnut mare and saddled her.

"Planning on riding somewhere, Miss Colter?" Jed said as he entered the stables to select his mount for the day.

"Um, yes. I was planning on riding out to the herd," she confessed without thinking that he might tell Will.

The shocked look on his face gave her the gumption to do just that. She would show these cowboys what she was made of. She was not some timid mousy domestic woman. She was pureblooded cowgirl and had the skills to prove it.

Finishing with the saddle, she found a length of rope perfect for lassoing should the need arise. She curled the rope into loops and hung it from the horn of the saddle. As she led the horse outside, she nearly collided with Adam. Her heart flipped when his face brightened, adding more fuel to her out-of-control emotions.

"Morning, Julia," he greeted in his usual calm voice.

"Morning," she answered as she mounted the horse.

Without so much as another word, she kicked the horse into a full gallop. Her hair streamed out behind her, tickled by the wind. As the mare's breath grew heavy, she eased up some, getting her bearing. The herd was still off in the distance, but she wasn't ready to be seen just yet. Veering the horse eastward, she decided she would circle around the far way.

The sound of horse hooves beating the ground began to work out some of her frustration. She was one with the horse, her motion reflected in the long strides of the mare. She contemplated continuing on out of sight, but chose to pull up instead.

Slowing to a lope, Julia battled in her mind. She was tired of the memories of Reuben. She hated not just what he did to her—she hated him. She wanted him to suffer like he had made her suffer—day after day, relentless, daunting. She hoped he would go straight to hell and burn forever.

Realizing she clenched the reins so hard they were leaving a dent in her skin, she loosened her grip. Taking a deep breath, she turned her face towards the sun. Closing her eyes, she soaked in its warmth.

She despised being so angry, carrying this bitterness. Moving here was supposed to make her feel safe. She was supposed to be able to forget. Yet, the only time she found any solace was in the rare moments where she was around Adam.

Now, that peaceful respite was being invaded by these confusing thoughts. He looked so handsome at the dance. His eyes were bright, alive. The way he looked at her sent pleasant little tingles up and down her arms. She meant it when she called him her rock. He was. Steady. Immovable. Safe.

Out of the corner of her eye she caught a movement, distracting her from her endless cycle of emotions. A young calf, probably nine months or so old, was hiding behind a tall juniper tree. Julia grabbed the rope and formed a lasso. One, two, three twirls of the loop over her head before gently floating the loop around the calf's neck. Pulling the loop closed, but not too tight, she nudged her horse near the calf. Speaking in calming tones, she encouraged the young animal to follow her lead back to the herd.

Once near the herd, the cowboys rode over to see what she was doing. They all sat atop their mounts with slack jaws, as if they had never seen anyone handle such a routine task. When the calf was near enough to the herd, she dismounted and removed the lasso from the calf, slapping it on the rump. The calf quickly disappeared from sight, swallowed by the herd. She smiled, a real heart-felt smile, at her accomplishment.

When she turned back toward her mount, she noticed the men still staring at her. Covington dismounted and was about to offer to help her back on her horse when she saw to the matter herself. Looking down at him, she smiled.

"Where did you learn to do that?" he asked, dumbstruck.

She briefly wondered whether he meant mounting her horse without assistance or roping cattle. She assumed he was referring to the latter.

"Will taught me."

The men glanced at each other, whispering with incredulous looks.

Hawk, one of the youngest men, spoke up next, "Did you lasso that calf yourself?"

"Certainly," she said. Forming another loop she demonstrated her skill on a steer. Only this time she rode over and removed the rope instead of closing the loop.

Covington, already back on his horse, commented, "She's better than Owens. Takes him a good two or three tries!"

The men laughed it up, especially since Owens was not within earshot. Julia knew she had won their respect.

After a few more minutes, the men broke up and rode among the herd. She decided she would stay in the field despite the growling of her stomach. It felt good to be in control of something.

"Have you seen Julia?" Hannah asked as soon as Will stepped through the ranch house door for dinner.

"No, why?"

"She left right after you did this morning without saying where she was going and I haven't seen her since. I'm worried."

Will frowned. That was unlike Julia to not at least mention where she would be. "Perhaps she was working the horses with Adam."

Just then Adam walked in for the meal. "Who, Julia?" At their nods, he added, "I haven't seen her since she saddled the chestnut mare this morning. She left without a word."

Will's blood burned and he clenched his jaw. What could she be thinking, taking off for a ride on her own in this dangerous territory? Had she no sense at all? She could be in danger in need of help even now.

Ben was in town with Snake today making deliveries. That left only Adam and Will to go searching for her. Despite his hunger, Will knew if someone was in danger, every second would count.

"Larson, you're with me," he said. Turning to look at Hannah, "We'll eat after we find her."

Will saddled Jackson, his most trusted stallion and Adam saddled one of the mares. Once they were ready to go, Will had half a plan on where to ride. They would ride out to the herd first to see if anyone had seen her. Motioning for Adam to follow, he took off in that direction.

As they neared the herd, he saw her. She was there chatting away with Hawk and Jed as if she hadn't a care in the world. Will's anger rose when he noticed her hair was loose, certainly not becoming a proper woman. Pulling to an abrupt stop next to Julia's mount got her attention.

"What do you think you are doing?" Will thundered, failing to check his anger.

Fear crossed her features briefly before turning to sass. "What does it look like I'm doing? I'm riding and helping with the herd." She jutted her chin forward in defiance.

"What... Why... What made you think that would be acceptable especially since you told no one where you were going?" Will stammered. Had she no concern for her own safety?

"I needed to ride."

"Do you have any idea of the dangers out here? It is not like back in Texas where you can ride out to the far fields and not worry. If you had ridden away from the herd, you could have encountered Indians or cattle thieves! You are going back to the ranch house, now!"

"I suppose you will confine me to the house now."

She was intentionally goading him. Through gritted teeth, he replied, "Back to the ranch, now."

When she did not turn her mount towards home, he upped the ante. "Your choice, Julia. Head back now, or let me carry you back in front of all these fine gentlemen." Perhaps drawing her attention to the crowd would serve as motivation.

She jutted her chin even higher then turned the mount toward the ranch house at a canter. He nodded for Adam to follow her.

Speaking to the cowboys, who suddenly seemed nervous, he said, "In the future, if Miss Colter takes it upon herself to join you with the herd, I hope you'll point her back to the ranch house. Escort her if necessary."

He turned and rode back, not relishing the confrontation that would be awaiting him.

Julia was furious. What right did Will have to humiliate her in front of the hands? How could he? Jumping down from the horse, she took it into the stables and began to unbuckle the saddle. Adam was at her side in minutes.

"I'll take care of that. Why don't you go on up and have dinner? I know Mrs. Colter has been worried sick."

Snorting, she mumbled, "I'll bet she has."

Adam frowned at her comment and finished caring for her horse.

Having no other choice, she stormed into the house. Within seconds, Will was back and looked none too happy. Hannah said nothing as she dished up four plates of now cold food.

When Will spoke, his voice sizzled with angry tension. "What in blaze's name has gotten into you? Why would you just take off like that?"

Since he remained standing, Julia decided to remain standing to keep him from intimidating her by standing over her. "I needed to get out... To clear my mind... Riding was the only way to do that."

When he gave her a skeptical look, she continued, "Don't give me that look. You understand exactly what I'm talking about. You're the same way too. When you have so much going on inside you don't know what to do with it, you ride. You know it's the same for me." She hoped the dagger would pierce him to the heart, for she knew she was right.

"That is not the point. Riding, in itself is not an issue. It is riding so far out, unescorted and without letting any of us know where you are going. That kind of stuff will get you killed out here!"

Adam entered the room, but stayed near the door.

"Death would be better than this burden I carry!" The words were out before she could retract them.

When Will raised his hands in frustration, she flinched and crouched down afraid he was going to hit her. His expression was confused.

It was Adam who spoke next. "Tell them, Julia." Then he turned and walked out the door to give them privacy.

Julia's anger evaporated at the instruction. Adam was right. She needed to talk this out, not ride it out. She needed to tell Hannah and Will. Taking a seat at the table, she folded her hands in her lap and stared at the plate of food before her. When Will took a seat, she gathered her courage to tell them all that happened.

"After Father died and Will left," she said directing her attention to neither Will nor Hannah, but the fireplace on the far wall instead, "Reuben changed for the worse. He was determined to marry me off to a wealthy rancher. The suitor he chose was Hiram Norton, a man more than twice my age. The first encounter I had with Hiram left me sick to my stomach. He was far too familiar with me. Then, when I tried to confront Reuben, he and Hiram turned the discussion into an announcement of my engagement to Hiram. Neither had ever discussed it with me. But the announcement was very public and difficult to break.

"The week before the wedding, I went to Caroline, Adam's sister," she said for Hannah's benefit. "We came up with a plan, which I executed the following Sunday. I publicly announced that I thought Hiram was unfaithful and I made a dramatic exit, taking Adam's horse.

"Once back at the ranch, Reuben..." Her voice broke. "He slammed me against the wall, choked me, and threatened me. If it hadn't been for Adam coming to collect his horse, I don't know what might have happened."

Julia heard Hannah's gasp. She ventured a look at Will and saw anger on his face—just like Reuben—only not quite as vicious. Looking over at Hannah, she saw tears streaming down her face. Hannah reached over and squeezed her hand.

She did not want to, but she knew she had to tell them everything.

"Then, several weeks after the broken engagement, Reuben arranged another suitor. This time it was Lewis Jamison. He told me if I knew what was good for me that I should comply with his wishes. When Mr. Jamison escorted me on a walk, he refused to keep his hands to himself. He spoke to me in a lewd manner. I got away from him and ran into the house and refused to come out.

"At first, I thought Reuben would pound down the door and harm me again. When several hours passed and the house grew still, I thought I was safe, so I readied myself for bed.

"Then, in the middle of the night, Reuben burst into my room. He was drunk and very angry. He reminded me that there were ways he could hurt me that no one could see." Tears streamed down her face as she choked on the last words. "Then he pinned me to the bed and raped me."

"I waited for the house to be silent. Then I packed some things and took some money and rode out to the Larson's. I didn't know what else to do. After telling Caroline everything, she convinced

Adam to bring me here."

Several minutes passed as Will tried to take in all that his sister said. The word "raped" hung in the air between them like a boulder suspended by too fragile a rope. Any anger he had towards Julia was now turned on himself. He should have brought her when he came west. He knew better than to leave her with Reuben.

His stomach rolled. How could Reuben do such a thing to his own sister?

It was Hannah who spoke first. "I am so sorry Julia." She stood and wrapped her arms around his weeping sister. "It was not your fault that this happened."

No, it's my fault. I should have found a way. I'm sorry.

Will watched, detached from the scene before him as overwhelming guilt hemmed him in. Julia buried her face against Hannah's shoulder and sobbed. Hannah rocked her back and forth whispering words of comfort and love. Just like Mama would have done if she'd been here.

When her crying slowed, Will stood and walked over to the chair she was sitting on. He kneeled before Julia and took her hands in his. Tears ran down his own face, as he said, "Forgive me. Forgive me for not being there to protect you."

He searched her eyes. The bitterness and fear he saw reflected scared him more than her secret.

Chapter 18

After walking out the front door of the ranch house, Adam took Will's tethered horse to the stables, the heated argument from the ranch house still ringing in his ears. Julia said she would rather die than carry this burden. He was certain now that there was something more sinister than just a physical beating that took place on the night they fled. *Lord, please give her the courage to tell Will and Hannah the truth, all of it, and let them be a comfort to her.*

Once in the stables, Adam removed the saddle from Jackson. Taking his time, he brushed the horse. He longed to see Julia leave her hurt behind. He knew as long as she carried this with her, she would be miserable and unable to love. He hoped that someday, soon, she would be able to open her heart to him.

Since the Governor's Ball, she only helped him with the horses once. Other than that, he saw very little of her. But, she was constantly in his thoughts. Her eyes had sparkled with life when they danced and she never looked more beautiful than she did that night. Walking her to the boardinghouse and leaving her at the door had been torture for him. He wanted nothing more than to take her in his arms and kiss her. He felt a tug on his heart. It was changing to fit hers. He wanted to make her his wife, to love her and protect her forever.

But, he made no move to share his feelings with Julia. She was not ready. The hurt and bitterness eating away at her heart would stand between them until she was ready to let it all go. Until he saw some of sign of her heart healing, he would say nothing to her and focus instead on the friendship between them. Forking some hay into Jackson's stall, he hoped his resolve was strong enough.

Leading one of the young fillies from her stall, he spoke in soft, soothing tones. He gently placed the bridle over the horse's head and began the various training exercises that were so familiar to him. His stomach growled and he wished he would have thought to grab a plate of food before leaving the ranch house earlier.

As he made another circle with the filly, Will approached the corral with a plate in his hand. Adam removed the bridle and let the filly trot around while he took the offered food and moved to the outside of the corral. Will propped one foot on the bottom rung and said nothing as Adam ate. He stared at the filly, though it was obvious he was not really seeing the horse.

After several minutes, he finally spoke. "Did you know?"

He wasn't sure exactly what Will was referring to, so he decided sharing what he knew might answer Will's question. "I knew that Reuben beat her. Even witnessed such an attack when I went to retrieve my horse. I encouraged Julia to leave that day, but she didn't want to. I don't know what happened the night we left. She told Caroline and Caroline was concerned enough to convince me to leave right then."

Will was silent for some time. The change in emotions on his face showed he was fighting a battle within himself. When he spoke, Adam did not know what to expect. "She has been hurt very badly by Reuben, both emotionally and physically. I just want to let you know..." Will choked on the words. "...how much I appreciate you being there to rescue her when I couldn't."

When Will turned to face him, hand held out for a handshake, Adam noticed the moisture in Will's eyes. He took the proffered hand. "I would do anything for her."

"I know you would." Will's haunted look concerned Adam. "Give her time."

At Adam's raised eyebrow, Will continued, "I know you care deeply for her. Anyone with eyes can see that. But, the pain she is dealing with from Reuben's hand is more tragic than I could have imagined. She is going to need some time to work through it. Pray for her, Adam, please."

He nodded at the pleading in Will's face. He would do exactly that, every day, as he had been since Julia first showed up on his doorstep.

The next several days, Will wrestled with what his sister told him, blaming himself for not being there to protect her. He should have brought her with him to the Arizona Territory. At the very least, he should have not let her stay with Reuben. What she faced at his hand was horrific. Days later, he could barely wrap his mind around it.

Since the day she told him and Hannah what happened, meal times were strained. He was stuck in his own thoughts and he sensed Julia was too. She had grown quiet. Hannah told him that she would barely speak with her when they cooked meals or washed laundry. She said she heard Julia crying herself to sleep nightly. Hannah tried to talk to her several times, but Julia closed up, unwilling to discuss the subject further.

Hannah told him she felt completely helpless—not knowing how to help Julia through this. He admitted to feeling the same way. As much as he wanted to, he could not undo what Reuben did. He could not repair Julia's brokenness. The only thing he could do was pray. Even that didn't seem to be enough.

As Will finished saddling Jackson, Adam led his saddled chestnut mare out of the stables. They were headed to Prescott for a meeting with Craig Roundtree and Leland Frye. The mare Adam was riding was one of the horses Will hoped to sell to the La Paz Express. It was one of his fastest and a solid example of the quality of animal they could expect from Colter Ranch.

Mounting his horse, Will nudged him forward into a gentle canter. Realizing he forgot to make sure his revolver was loaded, he checked it now. It was. He chastised himself to get his mind on the task at hand. Riding without thinking was something he could not afford to do. There was still a great threat of Apache attacks and they spotted signs of cattle thieves in the area again. He needed to remain vigilant.

As much as he tried to stop his mind from wandering, he could not. Over and over his mind accused him of failing his sister. Julia told them at first she feared she might have been with child, but discovered soon enough that she was not. *Lord, thank you for letting that be the case.* He would not have been able to live with himself if that had happened.

Pushing the thoughts aside for the moment, he scanned the town of Prescott as they arrived at the top of the hill, looking for changes. A new building advertised a doctor in residence. He would make a point to introduce himself before leaving. Perhaps he should bring Hannah in for an examination, just to be safe. He acknowledged he was concerned about her pregnancy because he witnessed the loss of her first baby from her first marriage. He did not want to go through it knowing it was *his* child.

Forcing himself to smile, he tied Jackson to the hitching post in front of the livery. Adam followed suit. Entering the livery, Will waited a moment for his eyes to adjust to the dimness, a sharp contrast from the bright, unrelenting Arizona sun. Craig was seated behind the small desk off to the right of the entrance.

"Will, pleased to see you again," he said as he stood and offered his hand.

Will shook his hand and introduced Adam. "This is the trainer I told you about, Adam Larson. Don't let his youth fool you. The young man has several years' experience training horses and was vital in making his father's business in Texas successful."

Adam smiled at the praise and shook Craig's hand. "We brought a mare for you to inspect. I'm sure you will be pleased with the quality."

Will was pleased with Adam's confidence. He would do well in this business.

"Let me track down Leland. He'll want to give her a test run."

Adam and Will did not have to wait long for Craig and Leland to join them out front.

Letting out a low whistle, Leland said, "That is one fine looking horse."

"Is she fast?" Craig asked.

"Fast as the wind. Smart too," Adam answered.

"Would you care to take her for a run?" Will asked, knowing that as soon as Frye rode her, the sale would be guaranteed.

"Absolutely, let me fetch my saddle," Leland replied with a huge grin.

Adam finished removing his saddle just as Leland returned. Leland took his time looking the mare over before saddling her. Will knew he was looking for any signs of blemish or mistreatment. Even though it was tempting to be offended that the man didn't trust him,

Will knew that wasn't why he examined the horse carefully. He would have done the same, especially given the important role she would play in riding the mail route between Prescott and La Paz. Once Leland finished his examination, he saddled the horse.

Giving the command, he trotted the horse around the town square to get familiar with her. Then, after getting Will's permission, he took off in a full gallop up the hill on the road towards Colter Ranch. Will heard the rapid beat of horse hooves for a minute before the distance covered was too great to carry the sound back to their ears. Craig was smiling—a good sign. Ten minutes later, Leland Frye rode at breakneck speed back into town, reining the mare in hard. Stopping in front of them, he dismounted with practiced ease.

"She's perfect. Great speed, solid handling, and she quickly adapted to my riding. Exactly the kind of animal we need," Leland said, somewhat breathless from the ride.

"Craig, would you care to ride her?" Adam asked.

"Naw. Leland is far pickier than I. If he says she's perfect, then we'll take her."

The four men returned to the office to hammer out the details. Craig purchased the mare and discussed the need to have several more horses of similar quality sent to the way stations along the trail. The La Paz Express would be ready to purchase more as soon as Will could return with them. Adam and Will agreed to return in a few weeks with the animals.

Leaving his horse and the extra horse Adam brought, anticipating the sale would be successful, Will and Adam headed across the square to Lancaster's in time for dinner.

"Will Colter," Betty exclaimed as she entered from the kitchen. "What brings you and Adam to town today?"

"We were just over at Craig Roundtree's to sell him one of the mares for the express line. How have you been?" Will asked.

"Fantastic! We've hired some help." Her broad smile telling more than her words. Just then a young Chinese woman entered the room. "Yu, come here. I'd like you to meet Will Colter and Adam Larson."

The young woman's jet black hair was pulled back in a braid. Her simple cotton clothing was different from what Betty and Hannah wore. When Betty introduced her as Peng Yu, she smiled then bowed. Not sure what was the appropriate response, he nodded. The young woman returned to kitchen.

"Peng Yu and her husband, Peng Liang, arrived last week from California. They were looking to open a laundry, but Paul convinced them to work for us. I'm glad they agreed. I've been in desperate need of help since you went and took Hannah away," Betty teased.

"You introduced her as Yu." Will was confused by the couple having the same first name.

"Oh, their custom is that their first names are like our last names. She would be Mrs. Peng and Yu is like our first name. It took me by surprise too."

"Glad to see you have help. Where are they staying?"

"Paul finished a small shack for them. It is simple, really, just a room about the size of our private living quarters. I am so happy with the couple. They are such hard workers and always have a pleasant disposition."

"No trouble from any of the boarders?" Will asked, knowing there were some who hated the Chinese.

"You know me, Will, I don't tolerate bigotry. If any of them so much as hints at having a problem, they can go down to Cal's boardinghouse and suffer through that goo he tries to pass off as food." Her momentary frown turned back to a smile as she started towards the kitchen. "Well, let me stop talking your ear off and get you two some food."

When Betty returned with two plates of food, Will remembered Hannah's request. "Betty, would you and Paul be able to join us for Thanksgiving dinner?"

"Oh, I think that would be wonderful! We never really get to take a break, but with the Peng's here, I think we should be able to get away for the afternoon."

"Hannah will be glad to hear it."

Will and Adam finished their meal in silence before saying their farewells to Betty. Adam had a few purchases to make at Gray & Company, so Will decided this would be the perfect opportunity to go meet the doctor.

Stepping up on the boardwalk lining the front of the building, Will hardly believed that in a few short weeks, the doctor already had a building up. The saw mill must be churning out boards quicker than he thought. He reminded himself to talk to George Lount, one of the mill owners, the next time he was in town about placing an order for the new ranch house he hoped to start on in March if the weather held. With the baby on the way and with Julia living with them now, he wanted to at least get started on the house so it might be ready by summer.

As he opened the door, he looked around the clinic. There were some finishing touches needed. The walls were still bare wood, although the smell of paint wafted to the parlor. There were two rooms and a hallway off of the parlor. Peeking in, one room looked like an exam room, complete with a cabinet full of small viles. The other was unfurnished. Seeing a man bent over a bucket of paint, Will approached the unfurnished room.

Clearing his throat, Will said, "Are you the new doctor?"

The young man rose and turned. "Yes, Dr. Hank Armstrong." Leaning around Will to look towards the lobby, he asked, "Is there an emergency?"

Will shook his head as the man wiped his paint stained hands on a cloth. "No. I was in town and saw the sign. Thought I would introduce myself. I'm Will Colter, a rancher from nearby."

"Pleased to meet you Mr. Colter."

"Please call me Will. Guessing by the state of your clinic you just recently arrived?"

"Yes, from California. I've been here just under two weeks. The town council was kind enough to get a jump start on the building though."

"California, huh?" Seemed like they got as many folks coming from California as they did anywhere else. "What brings you east?"

Dr. Armstrong laughed. "I know, it sounds unusual with all the folks moving to California that someone would leave there. I saw the advertisement in the San Francisco newspaper that the new territorial capital was looking for a doctor. It sounded like a grand adventure. San Francisco has numerous doctors, some which try their hand at gold mining and go back to the trade when their dreams of getting rich fail. The place was starting to get a little too crowded for me."

"Well, we're glad to have you here. And your timing is perfect." Will hesitated, not exactly sure if it was appropriate to mention Hannah's condition. The man was a doctor, so it shouldn't matter.

"My wife, Hannah, is expecting our first child." Will beamed. He couldn't help himself. Anytime he thought of their child he got this silly, bubbly feeling.

"Congratulations, Mr. Colter. Do you know how far along she is?"

"Two months, she thinks." He hesitated again. He wanted to mention his concerns.

His face must have given him away, because Dr. Armstrong asked, "Do you or your wife have some concerns?"

"Yes, I mean… Hannah lost her first child from her first marriage. She was around four months then."

"You're concerned she might have difficulties this time?" At Will's nod, Dr. Armstrong continued, "Well, each pregnancy for each woman is different. If she hasn't had any symptoms, then there is no need for alarm. Perhaps you could bring her to the clinic for an examination soon? Set any fears aside."

"Thank you, Doctor. I'll do that."

Will turned to leave, but stopped at the doorway. "Do you have plans for Thanksgiving, Dr. Armstrong?"

"No, not yet."

"Please, join us at the ranch. We would love to have you."

"I would be delighted. How do I get there?"

Will smiled. "Just see Paul Lancaster. He and his mother will be there as well. Perhaps the three of you can ride out together?"

"That would be wonderful. I look forward to meeting Mrs. Colter in a few days then."

The two men shook hands before Will stepped out on the boardwalk and headed directly for his stallion. Hopefully Hannah would not mind him inviting the new doctor.

Chapter 19

Taking Annabel from the stall, Adam placed the bridle over the palomino's head. The five year old mare was one of the finer animals Will purchased. With his guidance, she was learning quickly. Though the man Will bought her from said she was saddle trained, Adam had his doubts.

Once in the corral, he walked backwards as he led her around so he could observe her movements. She seemed comfortable around him—at ease—willing to take his lead.

A throat clearing behind him brought him up short. Turning, he stopped just before walking into Julia. She was dressed in her tan split skirt with a white shirt. Her dark cowboy hat hid the mass of curly hair, except for what was held together with a ribbon at the back of her head. Blue eyes flashed with mischief.

That was the Julia he remembered. That look—the same look she gave him in school whenever she played a prank on him—made him wonder now just what trouble she was scheming in her head.

Slowly, a playful smile stretched across his face. "Morning, Julia."

"What's that look for?"

A chuckle escaped his lips. "Just remembering how much trouble you caused me in school."

"I never caused you trouble, Adam Larson," she shot back, placing her hands on her hips. Tilting her chin up in defiance she added, "I just executed your sister's ideas to perfection."

His chuckle turned to a deep bellied laugh, as he relished the hint of a smile on her face—perhaps the first since they left Texas. "I suppose it was Caroline's idea to put that frog in my lunch pail?"

A giggle—light and free, like Julia used to be—floated across the air. "Yes, it was your sister's idea." The light in her eyes brightened. "As was the snake, the rotten apple, the bees—"

"That was not funny. I got stung. Three times. And my hand

hurt for days afterward." Adam sighed. "I was mad at you for a while after that stunt. I couldn't work with the horses."

"You recovered just fine," Julia replied, crossing her arms in mock defense.

"Yes, yes, I did."

Both stood there for several more seconds, leaving Adam to wonder just what prompted her initial look of mischief. He didn't have to wait too long to find out.

"So, shall we saddle up Annabel?" she asked.

The smile faded from his lips. "I was planning to do just that in a few minutes. I was going to take her out, though not anywhere near the herd just yet."

"Good, I'll get my things."

As she turned back towards the stable, Adam grabbed her arm. "Wait a minute. You are not taking her. *I* am."

Fiery blue eyes flashed on him. "Why not? You know I'm capable of handling her. I've ridden much greener horses before."

A frown crammed his eyebrows together. "It's not a question of your capabilities. I have no idea how Annabel is going to react."

"So, let me take her."

"No."

Julia walked along Annabel's side, placing her hand along the mare's back. Making a full circle, she came up behind Adam. "Please, Adam," she pleaded. "I need to do something useful. I know the risks if she's not ready. I can handle it. If she throws me—"

"If she throws you, Will is going to have my hide." *And if you get seriously hurt, I wouldn't forgive myself.*

Voice soft, she tilted her head down, and looked up only with her eyes. "Please."

Adam's heart stopped for a beat or two. She could not have any idea how that look affected him. He'd seen Caroline use the same look on her beaus and, until now, he never understood why they foolishly did whatever she asked.

"Fine." He capitulated against his better judgment.

Her face lit with a big smile. "Thanks, Adam."

She ran into the stable and returned with a blanket and her saddle. Laying the saddle on the ground, she strode to Annabel with the blanket.

"Go slow," he cautioned. "Let her get used to the feel of the blanket."

She shot him an "I know" look over her shoulder. His stomach tightened. Maybe he should change his mind.

As she gently laid the blanket over Annabel's back, she spoke in soft encouraging tones, just like he would have done. Smoothing the blanket out with her hands, she continued to speak quietly. Taking the reins from Adam's hand, she walked Annabel around the corral for several minutes, with only the blanket on.

"Think she's ready for the saddle?"

Adam nodded, before grabbing her saddle. Realizing how much lighter it was than his own, he thought having her ride Annabel first might not be such a bad idea.

Gently he set the saddle on the horse's back, talking to her softly as he cinched the straps. Once the saddle was in place, he gently stroked her mane. Then taking the reins back from Julia, he walked Annabel around the corral for nearly an hour before he was willing to let Julia mount the horse.

"Ready?" he asked.

"Yup." Before he could offer to assist her up, she already mounted the horse.

Annabel pranced at first, nickering. She was most definitely not saddle trained. Adam's jaw clenched as he considered whether he should have Julia dismount. Just when he was about to ask, Annabel settled.

"I'm going to walk her around for a few minutes before I give you the reins."

At Julia's nod, he started.

Annabel grew more comfortable with the situation, adjusting to Julia's weight on her back. Finally, he handed over the reins, moving outside of the corral to minimize the number of distractions.

As Julia led the mare in a slow walk around the corral, he remained tense, stiffening at the slightest abnormal movement from Annabel. He was never this tense around horses. Certainly wouldn't be if he had been riding. He kept reminding himself that Julia is a good horsewoman—as good as they come. She was doing fine. He had nothing to worry about.

Another half hour passed before Julia kicked Annabel into a

trot, still inside the corral. The two seemed to be doing well, both enjoying the anticipated freedom of a long ride. Adam relaxed some.

"Do you want me to take her out in the field?" Julia asked as she passed his stationary post outside the corral.

"No. I think you are the first rider she's ever had. Don't want to push her too far the first time."

"Okay," she replied, slowing her to walk again. "She's doing good, but you're right. Probably not quite ready for the—"

The dinner bell rang, cutting off Julia's statement. Annabel lifted her hooves high in the air in an agitated manner as the sound of the bell echoed across the valley.

Adam jumped up on the side of the corral post, ready to climb over. "Hold her tight!"

Then he watched helplessly as Annabel reared up. The air *wooshed* from his lungs as Julia fought to stay on the horse's back. The second time Annabel reared she caught Julia off balance. Without a sound, she tumbled over Annabel's hind quarters to the ground, narrowly missing the corral post with her head. With a loud groan, she landed hard on her backside.

Annabel stopped, thankfully, near the entrance far from Julia's still form. Adam leaped over the corral post to her side.

Just as he made it to her, she started to sit up with a deep moan, followed by a huge gulp of air.

"Are you alright?" he asked, running his fingers along her arms and legs to check for broken bones. She swatted at his hands.

"I'm fine," she snapped. As she stood, slowly, she added, "Nothing more than a bruised ego." Brushing the dirt from her skirt, she let out a tiny whimper as she tried to stand fully straight, resting her hand on her back side.

"You don't look fine," he argued.

With a twisted frown, she replied, "I'm fine. Just a little bruised. Wasn't the first time I've fallen off a horse, you know."

Adam considered his options as she took a few tentative steps favoring her right leg. He could carry her inside. Tell Hannah and Will what happened before fetching the doctor.

As he came close to do just that, she scowled. "What do you think you're doing?"

"I was going to help you inside."

Back straightening, with an edge to her voice, she said, "I'm fine. Just take care of Annabel."

Limping her way to the stable, she leaned on the stable wall as she made her way back outside. He watched as she slowly walked towards the ranch house. Will ran toward her, obviously displeased that she was injured. Adam turned away, not wanting to witness the ensuing argument. Instead, he removed the saddle from Annabel and returned her to her stall.

"William! Put me down!" Julia screamed, pounding her hand down on his shoulder.

"I will not!" her brother shouted, as he carried her into the house.

Hannah jumped up from her seat at the table. "What happened?"

"Julia is hurt."

"I am fine," she corrected. "Just a little bruised."

"From what?" Hannah asked.

Julia bit her tongue as Will laid her down on her bed, thankfully out of the eyesight of Snake who was already waiting at the table for dinner.

"From what?" Will echoed.

"From falling off a horse," she replied softly.

"What on earth!" Will shouted. "Were you riding that unbroken mare?"

She looked away, knowing Will would speak his mind regardless.

"Look at me! Were you?" he asked again, shaking her shoulders.

"She's not completely unbroken."

Will threw his arms up in the air in defeat. "You try my patience. Why on earth were you riding her? And what was Adam thinking to let you?"

"Will," Hannah said, softly. "Please, give us a minute."

A grumble followed Will as he stormed from the room.

Julia sighed. "I'm fine. Really. It wasn't the first time I've been thrown. Won't be the last."

Hannah smiled. "No, I don't suppose it will. Let me take a look."

Laying back, she let Hannah double check her for signs of anything broken. She could already feel the bruise forming on her back side. No doubt she'd be sore for several days from this one.

But, oh, it had been worth it! Annabel was a smart animal. Graceful when she wasn't afraid. She calmed quickly. If only Julia had paid closer attention to the time and had dismounted before the bell rang. No one would be hovering over her now, or stewing angrily in the next room. She could hear Will barking at Adam even through the wall.

"I don't see anything serious," Hannah said. "Just some nasty bruising."

"Good. Can we go eat now?"

At Hannah's nod, Julia righted her appearance, remembering to toss aside her hat before returning to the dining room. As she sat down she winched. Maybe she would volunteer for dishes duty so she wouldn't have to sit for too long.

Will narrowed his eyes at her. Adam stared at his plate, guilt written all over his face. Snake looked like he was ready to slither away from the tension in the room. Hannah bowed her head. Ben smirked.

A slight shuffle of a foot under the table sounded before Will dropped his head and offered grace. When his head snapped up, he looked even less pleased than before.

She was tired of this. Tired of Will being cross at her for things he taught her how to do. He should not be the least surprised by her behavior, especially when he encouraged it all those years back home.

"Will, calm down," she said.

"I will not calm down. You could have been seriously injured!"

"But, I wasn't. If it had been Adam riding that horse, he could have been just as seriously injured. It's those risks we take to train the horses. Those don't change if it is a man or a woman on the back of the horse."

Will slammed his fist down on the table, maintaining a rigid posture until Hannah gently laid her hand over his closed fist. Slowly he pulled in his anger, though his words still came out harsh. "Adam knows better than to let you get on such a green horse."

Adam's head dropped lower as he pushed his food around on his plate.

"How dare you blame Adam for this! You share more of the responsibility for this than he does!"

"How so?"

"You're the one who let me follow you everywhere on the Star C. You taught me to rope. You taught me to shoot. You taught me to ride a green horse. You taught me ranching! And now you sit there, willing to blame others because I'm not some sweet prim and proper domesticated housebound sister. What did you expect?"

Will dropped his gaze to his food.

She wanted an answer, not some silent washing over of the topic. "What did you expect, Will?"

When he looked her in the eye, she swallowed hard. "I never expected it would turn out like this. Have some common sense, Julia. Stop putting yourself in danger."

She parted her lips to lash out.

"Let it go. Let us eat in peace." The warning in his eyes did more to still her tongue than his words did.

Silence filled the room, except for the clank of utensils touching plates. Julia concentrated on her meal, hoping it would pass quickly, eager to hide away the rest of the day. Away from Will. Away from his perfect wife. Away from the reminder of what drove her here in the first place.

Chapter 20

Colter Ranch

November 24, 1864

Thanksgiving Day started early for the women of Colter Ranch. Being a stickler for her family's tradition, Hannah begged Will to hunt for a wild turkey yesterday. Unfortunately, he and Ben returned with an elk instead. She tried not to show her disappointment when they returned, but she was disappointed. She grew up serving turkey for the holiday and it just did not seem like Thanksgiving without it. At least they would still have mashed potatoes and gravy, even if there would be no turkey and dressing.

Peeling yet another potato, Hannah smiled at the thought of the celebration planned for the afternoon. She was excited that Betty and Paul would be joining them. She was also looking forward to meeting Dr. Armstrong. When Will told her he had invited the new doctor, she reassured him that she was pleased. As far as she was concerned, the more people at their gathering the better. On the farm where she grew up, her parents always hosted a big feast. Her aunt and uncle would come, along with several neighbors. She treasured the time spent with family and friends and this year would be no different.

Handing off the peeled potato to Julia, Hannah smiled at her sister-in-law. Julia did not return the smile, as she had not with any of the smiles Hannah offered since her arrival, save the very first.

She was concerned for her. She thought Julia's confession would open the door for healing. Instead, she seemed more distant and withdrawn, almost as if she was reliving it all over again. Hannah prayed for her daily, asking God to heal the young woman's broken heart and restore her faith. She had obviously suffered—was suffering still. Only God could heal all of her wounds.

Rosa hummed as she prepared the elk roast. As usual, Hannah

encouraged her Mexican cook to go easy on the spices. Her stomach wasn't as strong as Rosa's, although she found she was in the minority there. Will and most of the men seemed to prefer the spicy seasonings Rosa used.

Once the last potato was peeled and in the boiling pot, she dumped the peelings in the waste pail. She rubbed her sore back. Being with child still seemed a little unusual, especially since she was barely showing yet. Every night, Will would try to get her to lay still so he could determine if he could see the baby start to bulge and each night he swore she looked a little bigger than the night before. She smiled thinking about it. He was so happy about becoming a father, probably because he had such a good example, from the stories he told her.

Strange, how both Will and Reuben could have experienced the love of their father, an honorable, kind man, yet they turned out so differently. From the way Will described his father, he followed in his footsteps. He was a man of God seeking to live a life worthy of his Savior. His kindness and gentleness had been one of the things that attracted Hannah. His spirit was genuine. His protectiveness over those he loved was unparalleled in her experience. She was humbled, knowing God cared for her enough to bring her such a wonderful man.

A sudden wave of exhaustion hit her. Odd how at times she felt more energized by the baby, while other times she felt like it was sucking away all of her energy. She planned an elaborate meal for the day, but right now all she wanted to do was go lie down.

Julia looked over and must have seen how tired she was. "Why don't you go lay down and Rosa and I will finish here?"

Hannah thanked her and did as she suggested. Closing the door behind her, she heard Will's voice as he entered the ranch house. Just as she curled up on the bed, he came in the room. Too tired to open her eyes, she just laid there.

"Julia said you looked worn out. Are you alright?" Concern flooded his voice.

"I'm fine. Just tired."

He sat down on the edge of the bed and pushed her loose hair back from her face. She opened her eyes to his worried face. She smiled, hoping it looked more energetic than she felt. He searched her eyes for several minutes. Then he kissed her forehead.

"Get some rest," he said, closing the door behind him.

Julia struggled to pull herself together for the day. She was not looking forward to having the house full of people, not because she minded the work of preparing for the day. Rather, she did not feel like herself. She was still uncomfortable around everyone. She knew telling Hannah and Will had been the right thing, but the peace she hoped would come still eluded her. That was what she craved more than anything. Peace.

The past few weeks she decided to stop asking why. She could not change what happened to her as much as she wanted to. Asking why only churned the emotions like a tornado inside her. She felt worse each time she asked God why. She could not hold a grudge against Him anymore either. She knew better. But, not holding a grudge, and being on speaking terms with God were two entirely different matters.

Then there was Adam. Since the day she fell off Annabel, she avoided him. She had never seen him so tense and worried about her before as he was when she was working with the horse. There was something more. More than friendly concern. More than fear of her being harmed. She did not want to name the look he gave her, for it would only add to her sorrow of being a ruined woman.

As if all these worries weren't enough, Julia worried over her relationship with Will. He seemed subdued since she told him her secret, at least when she wasn't doing something that provoked him to anger. Hannah told her he felt it was his fault. As ridiculous as his blaming himself was, Julia could not bring herself to tell him that. Daily she was reminded how much he looked like Reuben. She could not stand to talk to him more than was necessary to get through the day, much less to assuage his guilt. She knew she should. She just could not.

Once she finished rolling out the pie dough, she carefully pressed it into the pie plate. One of the cowboys went down by the creek earlier in the week and picked pecans for the ladies. They had more than enough for the four pies she was planning on baking today—well, that Hannah planned to bake. After the crusts were prepared, she set about mixing up the filling. Hannah's recipe was the best, so that was what she used. The sweet filling highlighted the natural pecan flavor like no other pecan pie she remembered.

When the last pie was in the oven, she took a break, walking outside for some fresh air. Despite the late November date, the days were still rather pleasant, not requiring much more than a shawl. The nights were a different story. Once the sun was down, the temperature would drop by as much as thirty degrees. Most nights were below freezing. When she asked if it snowed here, Hannah assured her it did, though most of the time the snow would melt off during the sunshine the next day.

She breathed deeply, picking up the fragrance of pine and juniper. While she liked Texas, she liked the Arizona Territory as much. The rolling hills and unique granite mountains spoke to her in a way nature had not before. Just gazing at the pine tree dotted mountains brought a smile to her face—a rare occurrence. This seemed to be the only time she found any measure of peace.

A noise along the road drew her attention. A wagon drove down the road, likely their guests arriving. She did not want to act as hostess, so she went in the ranch house to check on Hannah. Cracking the door open, she stopped short at Hannah's crying.

"What is it?" she asked.

The fear in Hannah's eyes was evident. "I'm spotting. I'm afraid I'm going to lose the baby."

"Stay here," Julia said.

Running for the stables, she frantically tried to find Will. As she rounded the corner, she walked straight into Adam as he walked out of Percy's stall. He put his arms around her to steady her. When she tensed, he quickly dropped his hold. It was too late to stop the flood of confusing emotions Julia felt rising to the surface. She stared at him mutely for several seconds before remembering what she was doing in the stables in the first place.

"What is it?" Adam asked.

Trying to forget how close he was, she cleared her throat. "Have you seen Will?"

"He's putting one of the horses—"

"Julia." Will said as he closed the stall next to them.

"Come quick. Something is wrong with Hannah."

His face went pale seconds before his feet moved into action. She tried to keep up, but Will's long legs moved too fast. As they neared the ranch house, the wagon carrying their guests pulled to a stop. But, Will was already inside, leaving Julia to decide what to do.

Remembering one of their guests was the new doctor, Julia asked, "Dr. Armstrong, did you bring your medical bag with you? Mrs. Colter needs to…um…see you."

Jumping down from the wagon seat, Dr. Armstrong reached over the side and grabbed the bag, answer enough for her. She did not wait for their other guests to disembark. Instead she ushered the doctor to Hannah's room.

"Dr. Armstrong is here," she said as she opened the door.

Will had an inconsolable Hannah in his arms.

"Mrs. Colter, what seems to be the concern?" the doctor asked calmly.

Between hiccups, Hannah managed to explain that she had some spotting in the morning and had been tired all day. When she woke from her nap and was still spotting, she grew concerned that she might lose the child.

"Miss… er… I am sorry," Dr. Armstrong directed his attention to Julia, "I did not catch your name."

"Miss Julia Colter."

"Miss Colter, would you be able to assist Mrs. Colter, while I conduct an examination?"

Her mouth went dry, so she nodded instead.

Will spoke up. "I can help with whatever is needed." His pale face and the fear in his eyes said differently.

The doctor must have thought better of Will's suggestion for he said, "Mr. Colter, I understand your concern. The examination won't be but a few minutes. However, I think it best that you wait outside."

Julia saw the look that passed between Will and Hannah before he turned and closed the door behind him.

Dr. Armstrong explained what he was going to do and stepped out of the room for a minute to allow Hannah to get ready for the examination. Julia helped her, and tried to comfort her, despite being rather anxious herself. When Dr. Armstrong returned, he completed the examination quickly.

"Everything looks normal. I know this might not sound comforting, but some women tend to spot especially in the earlier months. This doesn't mean you will lose the child. Many who experience similar symptoms have delivered very healthy babies."

Hannah nodded numbly and Julia wondered if she truly believed what the doctor was saying.

Dr. Armstrong continued, "Please rest for the remainder of the day and perhaps for another day or two. When you feel your energy returning, then you are cleared to move around more. If you have more severe symptoms, such as pain or increased bleeding, come see me, or send someone for me right away. Otherwise, let's see if this does not pass in a few days with some rest."

Julia watched as Hannah dabbed at her tears. Hoarsely, she responded, "Thank you, doctor."

Dr. Armstrong left the room to talk to Will.

"I'm sure everything will be fine." Julia tried to sound encouraging. When she opened the door to leave, Will was there waiting. She stepped aside to allow him to enter then shut the door behind her. When she looked up, she met the questioning gazes of their dinner guests.

Taking a deep breath to calm her nerves, Julia reminded herself that these were good friends of Hannah and Will. Pasting a smile on her face, Julia welcomed Betty and Paul to the ranch.

"Hannah is feeling a bit under the weather."

Betty's eyes filled with concern, so Julia rushed to add, "But, the doctor believes she will be back to normal with a day or two of rest. I'm so sorry she won't be joining us for the holiday meal."

She wasn't sure what to do next. The cowboys would be coming up to the house soon for the meal. Will was still in the room with Hannah. She had three guests who were looking to her for direction. Inwardly she fought against the desire to flee.

Drawing from the social graces she learned when her father was still alive, Julia offered the three guests a seat at the table. Adam entered followed by Ben, Jed, and Hawk. She greeted each by name and assigned them a seat at the table, ignoring their questioning looks. Rosa gathered the dishes from the ranch house and set the table before getting the remaining dishes from the bunkhouse. When she returned, Diego was carrying the large stack for her, trailed by Pedro, Raul, and Miguel. Covington and Whitten bounded in just seconds later, followed by Owens, Foster, Webb, and Cahill. Bates volunteered to stand watch with Snake while the others enjoyed the holiday meal.

Once everyone was introduced and seated, Julia retreated to the kitchen to help Rosa with the finishing touches. Not realizing she was followed, she jumped when Adam spoke.

"Can I help?"

Julia could not imagine Adam helping with the meal. For someone who didn't care much for cooking herself, she became somewhat defensive when he asked. "We're fine. Please go, sit. Get to know our guests."

The cloud veiling her eyes sent him scurrying back to the table. She followed behind with bowls loaded with mashed potatoes, gravy, elk steaks, and more. It took both her and Rosa several trips to set all of the food on the table. By the time the last item was delivered, Will entered from his room and took his seat at the head of the table.

Will apologized to his guests for joining them late and thanked Julia for taking charge. As soon as grace was finished, the conversation started.

Dr. Armstrong said, "This is a lovely meal."

Julia looked down. Not wanting attention drawn to herself, she hurriedly redirected the conversation. "Dr. Armstrong, where do you hail from?"

"Most recently San Francisco. While it was a vibrant and growing city, I found it much too crowded for my taste."

"Betty, how is the boardinghouse?"

"Oh, dear, it's such a treat to be away from the work today," Betty said. She recounted stories of the latest politics, big mine discoveries, and other events from town. More than once, Ben asked her questions, engaging. If Julia didn't know better, she might think Ben Shepherd was sweet on Betty.

By the time Betty finished talking, everyone seemed to be full, pushing their plates away.

When Will started to stand, Betty stopped him. "I'll fix a plate and take it in to Hannah."

"I'm sure she'll appreciate it."

Julia quickly stood to collect the plates, frightened of being left in charge of entertaining their guests. Covington suggested the men go play a round of horseshoes. The men agreed and made their way to the area by the bunkhouse to set up for the game.

She breathed a huge sigh of relief. She and Rosa gathered the rest of the dishes. When she went to grab the bucket to bring in more water she found it missing. She was certain she left it next to the wash basin earlier that morning. When she opened the front door to see if she absentmindedly left it outside, Adam walked up to the house with the missing bucket, now full.

"Where do you want this?" he asked.

"In the large pot on the stove," she answered, touched that he would think to help by fetching water.

After he filled the pot, he returned the bucket to its assigned place. He stood there for a few minutes, just watching her and Rosa.

"Julia," he started but was interrupted by Betty bustling into the kitchen.

"How is Hannah?" Julia asked, hoping Adam would take his leave.

"Oh, she's fine. Just tired. Nothing to worry about, as I told her," Betty responded.

Adam was still standing by the wash basin, shifting from foot to foot. Betty looked over to him, but directed her words to Julia, "Dear, why don't you take a walk by the lake and enjoy some fresh air. I'll help Rosa with this then check on Hannah a little later."

One thing Julia learned about Betty—she seemed to have a knack for taking over a kitchen. Wanting to get away for a few minutes by herself, she agreed and hoped Will would not be upset that their guest was washing the dishes. Adam was still lingering in the kitchen, so she pretended to ignore him and walked toward the front door. He followed.

Chapter 21

"Mind if I join you?" Adam asked.

Julia wanted to be alone with her thoughts. She wasn't in the mood for his company. But, she didn't want to be rude either. Reluctantly, she nodded for him to join her. He held the front door open for her and assisted her with her shawl. Turning the corner by the house, she set a brisk pace to the lake, still hoping he might decide to leave her alone.

Walking along the shore of the lake, she thought about leaving the ranch. She was so tense here. She couldn't seem to forget what happened—what Reuben did to her—as long as she stayed. Will and Hannah acted strange around her. They didn't seem to know what to do or what to say around her anymore. She didn't know how to act around them either.

It was time for a change of scenery.

"I want to leave the ranch," she said bluntly.

Adam took two steps in front of Julia and stopped. Turning to look her in the eye, he asked, "Why do you want to leave? Where do you want to go?" He sounded frustrated, almost discouraged.

"Ever since I told Hannah and Will about what happened back in Texas, things have been awkward. I can't stay."

She grew quiet. Just how much could she tell Adam? Throwing some measure of caution aside, she continued, "Every time I look at Will, I see Reuben and remember the awful things he did to me. Those feelings of terror overwhelm me every time I sit down to a meal, or sit in the same room with him. I can't keep reliving this every day."

"But, what about Hannah? Doesn't she need your help?"

"I'll wait a few days, but if it looks like she's on the mend, then I'll need your help."

When he nodded, she went on. "Will you take me into Prescott in a few days? I want to find out if the mercantile or hotel is hiring."

Adam seemed to consider her words before replying. When he spoke, he looked across the lake, not making eye contact. "I will take you, but only if Will agrees."

"You can't tell him. I don't want him to know I am thinking of leaving, especially if I can't find a way to make this work."

"What you're asking is—"

"I will tell him you are taking me to town to do some shopping. Will might be upset, but I'll convince him he needs to stay for Hannah's sake and that I'll be safe with you."

He was silent.

"Please do this for me."

When he started walking again, she wondered if he might say no. Keeping pace with him this time, she hoped he would agree. He stuffed his hands in his pockets and slowed his pace. From months of traveling with him, she read his action as a sign that he carefully considered his options. By the time they were halfway around the lake, he had yet to respond. Her hope fell, believing he would refuse to help her.

Then he spoke. "What you are asking is difficult because I work for your brother. While you may be eager to leave the ranch, I am not. It's important for the horse training business that Will and I trust each other. By taking you to town now, but hiding the motivation, I risk damaging that trust. Once lost, it's difficult to rebuild."

"But..." When she opened her mouth to defend her request, he stopped and turned to look at her again. Her rebuttal died and she waited for him to continue.

Sighing, Adam said, "Don't ask me to lie to Will. I will take you, but I will not lie about it. I'm also concerned for your relationship with your brother. You may want to get as far away from him as possible now, but there will come a time when you may want to or need to return to the ranch. Just tell him the truth now. There's no need to hide it from him."

Julia thought about the wisdom of what he said. She didn't have to tell Will she was leaving because she could not look at him. But, she could tell him she wanted to get a job in town. "I'll talk to him and Hannah about moving."

"Then, when you're ready, I'll take you."

Several days after Thanksgiving, Julia was relieved that Hannah felt better. She decided she would discuss her plans with them in the evening and have Adam take her to town the next day. As she set the table she rehearsed in her mind what she would say to them in a few short minutes.

Will came in from a long day in the fields. He looked tired and traces of worry still settled in the slouching corners of his eyes. She started to reconsider her plan at the sight of him, but decided to move forward despite how he looked. She tried to smile at him, but it came off more strained than genuine. Hannah brought in the last of the food and the three took their seats.

As soon as grace was said, Julia gathered her courage. "Hannah, Will, I'm planning on moving to town."

Will's face contorted in a frown, reminding her again of Reuben. "What do you mean you're moving to town? What about Hannah? What if—"

"Will," Hannah interrupted. She placed her hand on his arm. "Let Julia finish."

He made no further comment, so Julia explained, "I have asked Adam, if you approve, to take me to town to see if I can find work at the mercantile or hotel. If I'm able to find a job to support myself, I would like to move out in a week or so."

Will's frown lessened, but the edge to his voice hinted at his concern. "You don't have to do this. You're welcome here. Haven't I made that clear? I can provide for you until you marry. There's no need to move into town."

The condemning voice in her head stabbed her heart again with accusations that she would never wed. *Doesn't Will understand that no man would want me?* Tears pooled in the corner of her eyes. She took a deep breath to regain control.

"I will never marry," she whispered.

"That's nonsense."

"Is it? What man wants a ruined woman? Would you?" She accused him.

His silence was the only answer she needed.

"No, you would not. Nor would any man. So, since marriage is not possible for me, don't you think it's wise that I learn some means of supporting myself? You can't take care of me forever."

Will laid his fork down and stared into her eyes. She felt as if he were scouring her soul to see if what she said was true. Uncomfortable, Julia looked away.

"You are welcome to stay here. I can provide for you as long as you need it."

Anger bubbled up again. He did not understand what she was saying. "With or without your blessing, I am getting a job in town and moving out." Her appetite gone, she threw down her fork and ran out the door.

She stopped on the porch, waiting for her tears to subside. She listened to Will and Hannah's muffled conversation through the closed door.

Hannah spoke first. "You have to let her choose her own way. If she doesn't want to stay here, I don't think you should force her."

"But, what does she mean no one will marry her? You've seen the way Adam looks at her. It's only a matter of time before…"

She couldn't make out the rest of what Will was saying as he lowered his voice. Confused, she tried to make sense of what he said about Adam. Just how did Adam look at her? Weren't they friends? Fear gripped her heart when she considered that he might have different feelings, maybe romantic feelings for her. She could not marry because of what Reuben had done. Not Adam. Not anyone. She would have to tell him her secret. She couldn't bear to lose his friendship.

Nearly a half hour went by and Julia stayed frozen on the front porch. She heard the discussion die down from inside several minutes ago. The door barely creaked open. She glanced to see Will stepping onto the porch.

"I would prefer you stay here, where I can take care of you and keep you safe. Where you can help Hannah. She does need the help, even if she tries not to show it."

"But she has Rosa."

"Yes, but even then, there's much work to be done. If she starts to feel ill again I think the doctor will limit her activities. Then she will need your help. And it's not just the cooking, cleaning, and laundry. She needs your friendship. She is scared of losing the baby. I am scared of losing the baby. We both need you here, Julia."

Confusion filled her heart. She was unprepared for this argument. She was certain with Hannah feeling better, neither would be able to use this as an excuse for her to stay. She didn't want to leave if Hannah truly needed her help, yet she was not sure she could stay.

"If Hannah continues to be in good health, would you approve my moving out after Christmas?"

He seemed to consider her suggestion, but she did not want to take any chances.

"Please let me do this. I need to support myself. I need to get away for a while. If I leave after Christmas that gives us a few more weeks to make sure Hannah is in good health. It also gives me time to prepare for the move. If she needs me to return later, closer to when the baby is due, I'll come back. I just need to do this. Please understand."

Will remained quiet for a moment, likely deep in thought, as was his way. When he spoke, Julia could tell he still wasn't pleased with the idea. "I don't want you to go, but I won't force you to stay. If this is what you really want, then I'll take you to town."

"I've already asked Adam. He can see me safely there tomorrow."

In the fading light, she saw a frown pass over his face. But he offered no objection to Adam taking her. She waited several more minutes, thinking he still might object.

Will turned toward the ranch house door. After opening it, he said, "Please remind Adam to take his pistol and a rifle tomorrow."

When he closed the door, she let out a long breath, relieved he consented—even if it was indirectly. Stepping off the porch, she went to find Adam. Not finding him in the stables or corral, she walked over to the bunkhouse and knocked on the door.

"Miss Colter." Owens opened the door. "What brings you to our humble abode?" Leaning against the door frame, he crossed one leg over the other in a rather casual pose.

Julia resisted the urge to roll her eyes. The man put her on edge. "I'm looking for Adam."

"I'd be happy to help with whatever you need."

Tapping her foot impatiently, she repeated, "I need to speak with Adam."

Chapter 22

Adam heard the exchange between Owens and Julia at the door of the bunkhouse. He stood and reached the door, just as Owens became a little too mouthy for his taste.

"If you are looking for a handsome gentleman to take you for a stroll, I would be happy to oblige," Owens said. Adam wanted to wipe the smirk from the cocky cowboy's face.

His pulse quickened at the comment as he started to understand where Owens's animosity came from. He pushed his way past him, nearly tripping as Owens deliberately uncrossed his legs sticking his foot out as Adam crossed the threshold. Side stepping quickly was the only thing that saved him from tumbling into Julia. Once he regained his balance, he offered her his arm.

"What brings you over here," he said in a low voice moving them quickly away from Owens's hearing.

"Will has agreed for you to take me into town tomorrow to look for a job."

Adam kept his concern to himself. When he suggested Julia tell Will the truth about wanting to leave, he never expected Will to agree to it. Now he wavered between talking her out of moving for his own sake and letting her go without a word. He feared once she was gone, she might not come back. That thought grieved him deeply.

"So, what time would you like to leave?" he asked, allowing her to determine the schedule.

"I would like to be there first thing in the morning when the store opens, so they won't be too busy."

They finalized the plans for the morning. Then, Adam walked her back to the ranch house.

As he neared the bunkhouse, he heard laughter floating across the air. The men seemed in a jovial mood, which did not match his own. He veered towards the solitude of the stables. He did not bother to light a lantern, as he was content to stand in the little light from the moon. Standing in front of Percy's stall, he reached his hand over the top of the stall gate and rubbed the young horse's nose.

What would he do when she left? He would barely see her—only when he was in town on business. She would have a job and might not even be able to take time to visit with him.

He was so sure that God was preparing her to be his wife. How could that happen if she moved away? When would he see her again? How could he know when she healed and might be ready to love him?

It all seemed so unfair. To love her so completely, but to have to let her go.

Patience. All things work together for the good for those who love the Lord. Wisdom in the form of his mother's voice penetrated his heart. So often she said those very same words to him growing up.

He would wait. What other choice did he have?

The next morning, Julia donned the new green calico dress she finished days ago. It was the nicest dress she had and she wanted to make a good impression on her prospective employers. Looking in the mirror she took extra care pinning her hair into place. She wished she had a more stylish hat to wear instead of the serviceable bonnet. Certainly, it was better than her cowboy hat. Sighing, she placed the bonnet atop her head, tying the rather large ribbon beneath her chin.

When she exited the ranch house, Adam waited with the wagon. While she would have preferred to ride a horse astride, she thought it might be a bit scandalous and suggested the wagon instead, not wanting to give any potential employers any reason not to hire her. Adam seemed rather pensive, not making eye contact or smiling as he usually did. He helped her into the wagon and turned it up the road towards town.

They were over halfway to town before Adam said a word. "You don't have to do this."

"Yes, I do."

He glanced at her and parted his lips, but no sound came forth. She thought Adam might explain his comment or try to talk her out of leaving. Instead, he closed his mouth and said nothing further until they topped the last hill overlooking Prescott.

His voice was devoid of emotion when he spoke. "Where would you like to go first?"

"Gray & Company."

He pulled the wagon past the row of saloons on Montezuma Street, stopping in front of Gray & Company's mercantile. She could tell by the set of his jaw that he was not pleased with her choice. She supposed she would rather not live next to a saloon either, but if it got her away from the painful memories, she would.

After Adam helped her down, he leaned against the wagon and crossed his arms. He nodded for her to go in without him. Seeing his obvious disapproval made her more nervous. She squared her shoulders and lifted her chin, entering the store with a purpose.

Mr. Young looked up from the catalog he was perusing when she entered the store. "Miss Colter, what brings you to our store at such an early hour?"

Julia smiled despite her nervousness. "I came to inquire about a position with the store."

"Who is your friend?" Mr. Young asked, nodding toward where Adam stood outside. "Why doesn't he just ask for himself?"

"I am inquiring on my own behalf, Mr. Young."

"I thought you were living on your brother's ranch."

The question seemed nosy and she fought to remain polite. "I am currently living on Colter Ranch, but would like to move to town."

"And why would you want to do that?"

Growing more irritated, she tapped her foot. "Because I would like to support myself."

Mr. Young considered the matter for a moment. "I'm sorry, but we don't need any help at this time."

Couldn't he have told her that at first, rather than asking so many invasive questions? Julia turned to leave but stopped short when Mr. Young spoke again.

"A word of advice, Miss Colter. Some people might not take too kindly to such an independent woman, especially knowing her brother is a well-to-do rancher in the area, more than capable of providing for her needs."

Julia glared at him. "Good day, Mr. Young."

He muttered something under his breath as she stormed out of the mercantile.

Deciding the short walk to the hotel would help her work off her anger, Julia nodded to Adam and took off down the street. She paid little attention to the stares coming from half drunken men looking through the saloon windows. Adam was at her side in two strides.

"I take it there was nothing available?" he asked positioning himself between the saloons and her.

"Humph." Striding with purpose, they were at the Juniper House in a minute. She reached for the door handle, but Adam grasped it first. Holding the door for her, he motioned for her to walk through. Taking a deep breath, she pasted a half-hearted smile on her face.

"I'll wait here," he said, indicating a chair in the hotel lobby.

Julia looked around the room trying to determine how she might ask about a job. Seeing no one in the room, other than Adam and the man behind the front desk, she decided he would have to do.

As she approached the front desk, the man smiled and greeted her. "Good morning, ma'am. How may I help you?" She saw him glance at her left hand and back over her shoulder at Adam. He was probably trying to make sense of the unlikely couple.

"My name is Miss Julia Colter, and I was wondering if I might speak to the manager?"

"Is something not to your liking, Miss Colter? If so, I will be more than pleased to correct the situation."

"No, it is not that. I…um…was hoping to inquire if there were any positions available at the hotel."

"Ah, I see. Well, in that case, I will see if Mr. Barnard will see you." He started to turn, but paused. "By the way, my name is Mr. Albert Hamilton and I am pleased to meet you Miss Julia Colter." He smiled broadly before taking his leave.

Julia stood there, hoping that Mr. Barnard would see her. She hoped to convince him she was qualified for any number of jobs. If he did not hire her, she was not sure where else she could work. Betty had all the help she needed at her boardinghouse—not that she wanted to work under the frequent attention of such a large group of men, recalling her nervousness the one time she tried to help.

Very little time passed before Mr. Hamilton returned. "Mr. Barnard will see you. This way." He motioned for her to step around to the side of the counter.

She followed him until he stopped to open the door. Mr. Hamilton motioned for her to enter the room then closed the door behind her.

"Miss Colter," the man seated behind a large mahogany desk said. "Pleased to meet you. Please take a seat," he added pointing to one of the chairs across from the desk. "Mr. Hamilton said you were asking about working at the hotel. What qualifications do you have?"

Julia quickly took a seat. "I am trained in the social graces as well as domestic chores." She had not expected the question, so she kept her answer brief.

"Well, I doubt that you are trained in gourmet cooking," he said. She shook her head. "I already have sufficient staff to clean rooms as well as in the kitchen."

"Oh." Perhaps he would not have a need for her services after all.

Mr. Barnard propped his elbows on his desk and formed a tent with his lengthy fingers. As he looked her up and down, Julia tried not to squirm under the scrutiny. He bobbed the index finger of his right hand against the complementary finger of his left hand, keeping them formed in a tent. She wondered if he even realized he was doing so.

"I think you are in luck, Miss Colter. How would you like to work the front desk?"

"First," she started, making direct eye contact, "I want to be clear that I cannot start until after Christmas." When Mr. Barnard nodded, she continued, "Second, what does such a job entail?"

"Well, you would greet the customers each and every time they entered or left the hotel. Then you would manage reservations, assign guests to rooms, collect payment for their visit, and show them to their rooms. You would have to be well versed in all of the key features of our establishment. In addition, you would have some oversight of the cleaning and kitchen staff acting as an intermediary between them and me."

"What would Mr. Hamilton do, then?" She wondered aloud.

Mr. Barnard chuckled. "Mr. Hamilton would oversee your duties. Once you are fully trained, he would watch the desk after dark, for your safety, of course. During the primary business hours he would assist me with other matters."

"What about living arrangements?"

"There is one small room left back near the offices for staff. You may have that as part of the arrangement."

"There are no concerns with me waiting until after Christmas to start?"

"I want you here on the Monday after Christmas. If you can be here by eight then the job is yours."

Dumbfounded, she could barely speak.

"Thank you, Mr. Barnard," she managed as she stood.

Mr. Barnard stood and showed her to the door. "Tell Mr. Hamilton to give you a quick tour, Miss Colter. We shall see you soon."

Her head spun as Mr. Hamilton showed her around. She hoped she would remember where everything was in a few weeks. When Mr. Hamilton finished the tour, she joined Adam in the lobby. Her smile confirmed she would be working there.

Chapter 23

Nashville, Tennessee

December 14, 1864

Sergeant Thomas Anderson stood before Major General Thomas with a dispatch from Major General Smith. The day prior, Smith instructed him to report the status of their fortification attempts along the southwestern edge of Nashville to Smith's commanding officer, Major General Thomas.

Once Major General Thomas completed reading the dispatch he instructed Sergeant Anderson to wait for his response. Having heard a rumor this morning, he wondered if the major general before him was planning any action against Hook's army. The rumor was that General Grant was so displeased with Major General Thomas's inaction that he ordered Major General Logan to go to Nashville to assume command.

The major general motioned Thomas forward and handed him the dispatch. As Thomas was leaving, he saw a line of the other corps commanders' dispatchers waiting to give their report.

Quickly finding his horse, he rode back to Major General Smith in the dimming light of the setting sun. He pulled to a stop in front of the major general's quarters, giving the appropriate signals. Smith smiled a greeting as Thomas entered.

"Did you arrive before the others?" Smith questioned.

Thomas smiled at the major general's enthusiasm. "Yes, sir."

"See, that is why I ordered you to be reassigned as my dispatcher. You have a fine reputation for being the fastest."

"Thank you, sir," Thomas replied, glad for the praise. He pulled the missive he carried from the copper tube and handed it to Smith.

"Odd," Smith commented taking the paper from Thomas. "He normally sends no lengthy reply."

Thomas knew Smith was not speaking directly to him so he

stood there waiting for his next assignment. Having worked closely with Smith for the past month, he anticipated the major general would send him off with a reply.

"Captain!" Smith shouted for the captain of the guard.

The captain entered and standing at attention, replied, "Sir?"

"Gather the colonels immediately," Smith commanded. As the captain left the tent, Smith whispered to himself. "Didn't give us much notice did he?"

"Sir?" Thomas inquired confused by the major general's behavior.

"Huh? Oh, Sergeant, you may wait outside, but stay nearby. I will need your services again after I meet with the colonels."

Thomas exited Smith's quarters and waited at a small campfire nearby. He opened his rations, eating slowly—a hard habit to break even when he was at camp. The colonels of the brigades of the XVI Corps arrived in short order. He was close enough to the major general's tent to overhear part of the conversation, but not close enough for it to be clear. The colonels seemed as displeased as Smith had been.

"Sergeant Anderson, the major general is requesting you," the captain of the guard informed him.

As he stepped back into the tent, Thomas barely announced his presence when Smith started in.

"Sergeant, I need you to run this dispatch up to Major General Thomas in quick order. Wait for his confirmation, then report back here."

He did as instructed and made the trip back to headquarters for the second time that evening, now in the cover of darkness. He delivered the message to Major General Thomas whose reply was simply a verbal acknowledgement with no further instructions.

Jumping back on his mare, he rode down the line to Smith's quarters. Once he delivered the message, Smith instructed him to ready his gear and to report back at three in the morning. That was only a few hours away.

Yawning, Thomas handed his horse off to the captain of the guard for care. He made his way to his tent. Once there, he checked his pistol and carbine, ensuring he was ready for the morning. Curling up on the ground, he pulled his blanket around him and fell fast asleep.

The night captain of the guard woke him shortly before three in the morning, giving Thomas just enough time to make his way to Smith's quarters. Smith instructed him to wait nearby and be ready at a moment's notice—meaning drink some coffee.

Despite the fatigue begging him to sit and rest, he remained standing as he sipped his coffee. Over the last twenty-four hours he must have ridden up and down the line half a dozen times. Something was definitely afoot in their current campaign moving them most likely towards a confrontation with the rebels.

Shortly after sunrise, Smith called him in. Giving him dispatches for each of the colonels commanding the brigades, Smith instructed Thomas to ride the lines, yet again.

Thomas mounted his horse. Dense fog still hung in the air, forcing him to ride at a slower pace, requiring his attention to remain sharp. It took him nearly a half hour to cover the short distance down the line to the farthest colonel. With each message he received verbal acknowledgement of the orders before riding on to the next. An hour later he reported back to Smith that all brigades were ready for battle. Smith again, instructed him to remain nearby.

While he loved the excitement and adventure of riding in a battle, he despised the waiting game. He sensed the anticipation building around him, yet he could not be involved. Shortly after eight in the morning, the fog lifted enough for the battle to begin.

The loud thunder of cannon fire preceded the low whistle of the cannon balls flying through the air. Another loud, but muffled sound indicated the weapon made contact with the intended target. Over and over again the same pattern repeated. Even though he was far from the front lines, he imagined the scene of men shouting accompanied by rifle shots, smoke and ash filling the air.

It was afternoon before Thomas was called into Smith's tent for further instruction. Smith sent him with a dispatch to Major General Thomas.

Eager to be part of the action, he mounted his horse and urged her to a gallop. As he rode down the line, he kept his body leaning low, using his mare for cover from rifle fire. Ash and smoke made visibility difficult. He nearly missed instructing the mare to jump one of the fences along the route, having lost track of where he was along the line. He squinted hoping to better identify his position. When he rode through here last night, he was well within the Union camp. Something seemed off.

Slowing his horse's pace, Thomas glanced at the men on the east side of the line. Through the thick polluted air, he was not able to distinguish the uniforms to determine if they were Confederate or Union. Deciding to move to a more sure position, he pointed the mare in a slightly westward direction. That should position him deeper into Union troops.

Thomas was relieved to see one of the captains of the guard for another corps. He was more confident of his position in the line and, for the remainder of the ride, he should be safe—well as safe as riding the line in the middle of a battle can be.

Suddenly the noise of the cannons ceased. Thomas marveled how the onset of cannon fire was so noticeable. But, it became less so when in the midst of the battle until they sounded no more.

He pressed on to Major General Thomas's position. He delivered the message then waited for instruction. The major general wrote a hasty reply and blotted the ink, too impatient to let it dry fully. He instructed Thomas to deliver orders to Smith to move their position to cut the Confederate's line in half.

The ride back to Smith's camp was quieter, with no cannon fire, only the occasional pop and whistle of rifle fire.

Thomas's body jerked to one side seconds before he felt the heat in his right arm. Keeping his grip on the reins, he glanced down. Blood drenched the right sleeve of his uniform just below the singe marks. Hoping he was just grazed, he kicked the horse for more speed. He started to feel a bit dizzy and his field of vision narrowed to a few feet in front of his mare's head. Willing his eyes to stay open, he concentrated on what he could see. He was there, in Smith's camp and he was fairly sure the captain of the guard was giving a signal. He tried to remember what he was supposed to do next as fire shot up his arm and into his shoulder. Just before running into the captain, he yanked back on the reins, coming to an abrupt stop. The action served to unseat him from his horse.

Falling to the ground, Thomas tried to keep his focus. Once on the ground, he sat up and gave the return signal to the captain of the guard. Ignoring both the man's concern for his wellbeing and the pain fighting for his attention, he stood to his feet. The world was spinning and tilting, causing his stomach to lurch. A scene of another dispatcher flashed before his eyes. That man had died and Thomas was the one who picked up the dispatch. Shaking the image from his mind, he walked into the tent and handed the missive to Smith.

When Smith saw his arm, he yelled for the captain of the guard. He heard something about keeping this man from bleeding all over his desk. Thomas was confused, but followed the captain as he left the tent, certain it was not entirely by his own power.

The captain led him to another tent where the moans of the injured intermingled with smell of rotting flesh. The acrid smell of blood—his own blood—was too much to consider.

Closing his eyes, he thought of home and warm summer days and how a fresh breeze tickled his face. He tried to focus on the memory of the sweet cinnamon aroma of Hannah's fresh baked apple pie and Drew's laughing smile when he forgot some of his concerns.

He had to stay conscious. He felt something being lifted from his back. His left hand immediately went up to his chest feeling for the leather strap attached to the copper tube. It was gone! He has to get the message to the major general. He tried to sit up. He must complete his mission. Or had he already?

Someone pushed him down onto a cot. When he tried to sit up again, strong hands held him down. Cold air hit his chest. He opened his eyes and glanced down seeing only his long johns covering his chest. The pounding in his head prompted him to close his eyes against his will.

Thomas screamed in pain as someone put pressure on his right arm. He felt like he was floating on a lake or down the Ohio River. He was cold.

Someone jabbed his arm and he gritted his teeth. It felt like they were cutting his flesh. The pain was too great and a blanket of warmth enveloped his body. *I don't want to die.*

Sometime later, Thomas woke. He felt terrible. His right arm was stiff and burning with pain. He lifted his head slightly which sent a wave of dizziness over him. Glancing down at his right arm, he was relieved to see it in tact and wrapped in bandages. The dizziness was too much, so he laid his head back down.

Again Thomas woke, this time to voices. When he tried to sit up, one voice called him Sergeant Anderson and instructed him to lay still. He complied. The same voice, while distant, was talking to him. He focused in on the words.

"Sergeant, you took a pretty nasty hit to your arm, but we got the bullet out. You need to rest."

"But I have to get the message to Major General Smith."

"You already delivered the message, Sergeant. Thanks to you we cut the rebel's line in half and they are retreating as we speak. You did your job, now rest."

Thomas took their word for it. Closing his eyes, he succumbed.

Chapter 24

Colter Ranch

December 26, 1864

The sun barely tinged the sky light pink when Julia fastened her carpet bag closed. Turning down the oil lamp, she left the small bedroom at the ranch house for the last time. She was both nervous and excited about what the day held. Entering the living area, she took a deep breath. Both Hannah and Will were up, ready to wish her farewell.

Yesterday, Christmas Day, had been strained when Will tried to convince her to abandon the idea of moving. But, she remained steadfast. Hannah was back in good health. The daily reminder of her past life continued to propel her forward to her new life in town. There was too much pain to stay.

"I made some bread and packed some of Snake's delicious jerky for you," Hannah said, handing her a small bundle. As soon as it was transferred to her hand, Hannah wrapped her in a hug. "I will miss you, sister. Please come back to visit on a day off soon."

When Julia pulled back from the embrace, she saw the moisture in Hannah's eyes as she choked back her own tears. In the short time she lived on Colter Ranch, Hannah made her feel at home. She was becoming a good friend. Julia would miss her, too. She would say as much, if it weren't for the large lump clogging her throat.

Will cleared his throat. "I wish you'd reconsider." At the shake of her head, he stopped short. Instead, he leaned down to hug her. She stiffened and reminded herself this was Will.

When he stepped back, he said, "Well, when you miss riding, come back and we'll go out for the day."

Julia nodded as Adam knocked on the door. She followed him out to the waiting wagon, handing him her small bag. He helped her up to the seat then joined her. She gave a final wave to Hannah and

Will standing in the doorway, illuminated by the oil lamp burning on the table inside.

Swallowing back her tears, she willed herself not to cry. She was a strong woman. This was the best option for her to support herself. She needed the independence. The job at the Juniper House would provide that in a safe, respectable place.

They covered the distance to town quickly, albeit in silence. Other than a brief greeting this morning, Adam said nothing. She sensed he had something on his mind, yet he kept to himself.

Pulling the wagon up to the hotel, he set the brake. Then he came around and assisted her down, his hand lingering on hers for just a moment. She looked into his sad eyes wondering what would cause such concern. He leaned over the side of the wagon to retrieve her lone bag. When he handed it to her, he stopped and stared at her.

"Julia," he said, taking her empty hand, standing very close. "I…" He stopped abruptly, as if changing his mind.

She stood there for a moment, unable to move. Her heart beat wildly, anticipating what he was going to say. Suddenly, Adam reached up and tucked a stray strand of her hair under her bonnet, before trailing his fingers down the side of her face, leaving warmth behind. She didn't know which was more disconcerting, his action or her reaction.

Taking a step back, he offered his arm and she took it. Just before opening the door of the hotel, he stopped and turned toward her again.

"I hope you find what you are looking for," he said. "Know that you will be missed greatly."

She heard the unsaid message—that *he* would miss her. Growing uncomfortable with his strange behavior, she tried to make the moment less serious.

"I'll be right here in Prescott. It's not like I'm half the country away. Come visit when you're in town," she said with a smile.

"I will do that."

Still, he made no move to leave. His gaze was intense. Julia, cognizant of the time, reached for the door at the same time he did. His fingers covered hers. He let them linger for a moment. She pulled her hand away, allowing him to open the door for her.

"Goodbye, Adam," she said trying not to show how much his

touch affected her.

"Goodbye, Julia," he whispered. The click of the door latching behind her added a finality to his words.

Squaring her shoulders and taking a deep breath, she turned and walked into the Juniper House, to her new life. Mr. Hamilton was waiting at the front desk, as she expected.

"Miss Colter, welcome to the Juniper House. I trust your trip was pleasant?"

"Yes, Mr. Hamilton, it was."

"I'm pleased to hear it. May I?" Mr. Hamilton asked gesturing towards her bag. She handed it over and followed behind him as he led her down a narrow, nondescript corridor.

"This," he said, "is the employee quarters." Stopping in front of the door at the end of the hall, he opened it. "This is your private room. Please take a few minutes to get settled. Then join me at front desk for the grand tour."

Mr. Hamilton stepped from the room closing the door behind him. Julia looked around the small quarters. There was a bed in the center of the room, a stand next to the bed, a small chest of drawers along one wall and a small table with a chair on the opposite wall. The room was barely large enough for her to move around all of the furniture.

She stowed her clothing in the chest of drawers. Placing her Bible on the night stand next to the oil lamp, she sat on the edge of the bed. She supposed she would not be spending much time here. Standing, she slid the empty carpet bag under the bed. She noticed a few hooks along the wall behind the door, so she took off her bonnet and hung it there, along with her shawl.

She checked her appearance in the mirror hanging above the dresser. She looked tired with dark half-moons resting under her eyes. Standing straighter, she lifted her head slightly hoping to project more confidence than she felt. Closing the door behind her, Julia made her way down the hall and back to the front desk.

Mr. Hamilton smiled as she approached. He led her through the lobby, explaining the layout of the hotel. "Down this wing is the restaurant and kitchen. Most of our guests take their breakfast and dinner here. While the chef tries to keep the menu consistent, it's often dependent on supplies and whether or not fresh game is readily available. We do have a steady supply of beef from a local rancher, your brother, I believe."

Waving his hand towards the dining room, he continued, "If we are busy in the restaurant, you may be required to assist with taking orders or delivering food."

Weaving through the empty tables, Mr. Hamilton led her back to the kitchen. "This is the chef's domain." Julia heard muttering coming from the back pantry area. Mr. Hamilton seemed a bit nervous and turned her around the other way. "You can meet Chef later."

Walking back through the dining room to the front lobby, he led her down another wing. "These are the guest rooms on the first floor. We have additional guest rooms on the second floor, with the stairs at the end of the hall."

Opening one of the rooms with the key he picked up from the front desk, he motioned for her to enter. Once inside, he left the door open. "All of the rooms are laid out similarly. Each room has a window along the outside wall, then a dresser, bed, night stand, mirror, and wash stand. At the end of each floor we have a washroom and other facilities are available outside. Not quite the luxury of some hotels in, well, less primitive places, but we have the best accommodations available in the young capital."

"Will I have to clean the rooms?"

"Goodness, no," Mr. Hamilton replied. "We have a young woman who cleans the rooms and handles all of the laundry. You are not expected to help with any of those sorts of chores."

He led her from the room and locked it. Then he led her down the hall, pointing out the washroom he mentioned earlier. Next, he took her upstairs to show her that the rooms were identical to the downstairs. Once the tour was complete, he led her back to the lobby.

"Mr. Barnard is quite particular about greeting each and every guest by name. When anyone enters the building, if you have not yet learned their names, introduce yourself and ask how you may help them. If you encounter a situation you are unsure of, my office is across the hall from Mr. Barnard's. Just ask and I will be happy to assist you."

Pointing to the ledger on the front desk, he continued, "This is the guest book and ledger. We keep track of reservations and guests here. If someone comes to rent a room and they have not reserved a room, just look here and choose a room that is empty. There," he said, opening a cabinet door under the desk, "is where all of the room keys are kept. We have a second copy in Mr. Barnard's office should the need arise."

Mr. Hamilton paused, tapping his finger on his chin as if he was trying to recall something. "Oh, yes. You will work from eight until six or seven each day. You will have a break in the early afternoon for dinner and then you may eat supper after the end of your shift. Food is provided in the restaurant and you may have anything the chef is preparing for the day. However, we expect that you will eat in the kitchen out of the sight of our guests. You are expected to have eaten breakfast prior to arriving at the front desk in the morning."

Julia hoped she would remember the long list of instructions. It seemed daunting. Her concern must have shown.

"Do not fret, Miss Colter. Just be your charming self and you shall be fine. I'll be in my office if you need my assistance." He paused before taking his leave. "Oh, I almost forgot, you will get one day off per week to do as you wish. And, if any, um, uncouth individuals enter the premises, please seek my assistance immediately."

At Julia's nod, he turned and left.

She was still mentally reviewing the list of duties when a young gentleman entered the lobby from the guest wing. Remembering what Mr. Hamilton said, she smiled.

"Good morning, sir. How might I assist you this morning?"

"And who might you be?" he asked, grinning broadly, dark eyes sparkling in amusement.

"Miss Julia Colter. And you, sir?"

"Mr. Maxwell Brighton. A pleasure to meet you, Miss Colter," he said. Taking her hand, he placed a kiss on top.

She was taken aback by the gentlemanly gesture. She had not expected social graces to apply to her position. She might discuss what to expect with Mr. Hamilton later.

"How may I assist you?" She repeated not certain what she should do next.

"I have several gentlemen joining me this evening for a business discussion. I wondered if you might be able to reserve a private table for four at six."

"It would be my pleasure to see to the details, Mr. Brighton. Are there any special requests?" she asked, improvising—wanting to make sure she covered everything.

"That will be all," he said turning toward the door.

"I hope your day is pleasant, Mr. Brighton."

"Ah, you have already made it so, Miss Colter."

Julia blushed as the suave young man left. She jotted a note down to ask Mr. Hamilton what she should do to see to the dinner reservations.

Several more men entered the lobby and stopped short upon seeing her. She started to wonder if this was the best place for her. If every man gave her such intense scrutiny, she was not certain she would like it. Each of the gentlemen changed their course from the dining room to the front desk, smiling at her.

"Gentlemen, good morning. Can I assist you with anything?"

One of the men jabbed his companion in the ribs. "I think I have lost my heart," he said. "Might you help me find it?"

Her face heated. "Hardly. I am but a humble hotel clerk," she said, drawing from her years of verbal sparring with two older brothers and a ranch full of cowboys. "And most certainly not Cupid."

He chuckled at her response. She hoped he would leave it at that.

The man he jabbed earlier returned the favor. "Hobbs, it looks as if the lady has put you in your place. Perhaps you will weigh your words more carefully in the future?"

"Ah, indeed she has." His gold eyes crinkled with silent laughter. "Miss?"

"Miss Colter. And you are?"

"Mr. Hobbs. This is my associate, Mr. Franklin. The other fellow over there is Mr. Hardy."

"Pleased to meet you gentlemen," Julia said, mentally rehearsing their names. Mr. Hobbs had the gold eyes. That would be how she would remember his name. Mr. Franklin was a bit rotund and had a bit of a curl in his beard. Mr. Hardy looked tired. She was sure she would remember their names.

Mr. Hardy asked, "Have you seen Mr. Brighton this morning?"

"Yes, Mr. Hardy," she said reinforcing his name in her mind. "He left a moment ago."

"Did he mention joining us for breakfast?" Mr. Franklin asked, looking as if he was ready for the meal to commence.

"I'm sorry. He made no mention of it."

Mr. Franklin turned toward the dining room, followed by Mr. Hardy. Mr. Hobbs lingered.

"I hope I did not offend you earlier, Miss Colter. I tend to speak before I think things through. I suppose it's a shortcoming of my youth—at least that's what Mr. Franklin would say."

"Not at all, Mr. Hobbs," she replied smiling.

"Thank you, Miss Colter, for your assistance."

Mr. Hobbs took his leave, presumably joining his companions. Julia breathed a sigh of relief. She wondered if all their guests would be so attentive and if she had the gumption to deal with them.

She had been gone two days. That was it. Adam already missed her.

Dismounting Annabel, he led her into the stall and began rubbing her down. A smile twitched the corner of his lips. This is the horse that threw Julia. He just returned from riding her around the lake a few times and she seemed much more comfortable now.

Thinking of Julia and Annabel started an idea forming in his mind. Her birthday was only a few weeks away. That might be his next chance to see her. The smile on his face grew to an outright grin. He would make her a little wood carving of the chestnut mare that she rode out to the herd not so long ago. It was the perfect gift. She would love it.

Rushing through the rest of Annabel's care, he finished in record time. Closing the stall behind him, he went to Will's workbench area to see if he could find a small scrap of wood that might work.

Bent over a small piece of furniture, Will looked up at his approach.

"Evening. What do you think?" Will asked, stepping back so Adam could get a better look at the small bassinette.

"For the baby?" he asked. "It's nice. I think Mrs. Colter will love it."

"Still have to smooth out the rough edges. Then put the finishing touches on it."

"Mind if I take a look at the scrap pile?"

"You still whittling?"

"Yes. Keeps my hands busy when my mind is working hard," he said with a little laugh.

Will smiled before turning his attention back to his craft.

Adam sorted through the pile looking for something suitable. Finding just the right piece, he began to envision what it would look like. A galloping horse mid-stride, legs stretched out full. Julia sitting on top hunched forward with her long hair flowing behind in the wind. As he blinked, the image faded, replaced with the reality of a small, ugly piece of bare wood. It was perfect.

Stuffing the piece in his pocket, he started toward the bunkhouse just as the supper bell rang. Picking up his pace, he arrived just in time to get at the back of the line. Smelled good, whatever it was. One thing was for sure, no one went hungry or suffered through tasteless food at Colter Ranch. Mrs. Colter and Rosa served up great meals.

Once his plate was full, he took a seat between Jed and Hawk. There never seemed to be much conversation around the table until after everyone finished shoveling their grub down their gullets. Tonight was no different. Only the clank of utensils hitting tin plates echoed in the room.

The gift for Julia was a great idea. Maybe it would help keep him from pining for her as much. He really missed her. He missed her help with the horses. He missed her smile. Dinner this afternoon seemed empty, quiet without her.

"What ya smiling at, Larson?" Owens taunted from his seat on the other side of the table, kicking Adam's foot with his booted toe. "Thinking about your sweetheart?"

Any smile he might have had on his face faded. Owens constantly picked on him about one thing or another. Guess today it was Julia.

"Leave him alone," Jed shot back.

"Let the man defend himself—if he's got any back bone," Owens said, kicking Adam under the table again.

"Excuse me," Adam said, swallowing a bite of food. Leaving his half-eaten meal, he stood and went into the other room, sitting down on his bunk.

Pulling the piece of wood from his pocket, he turned it over in his hands as he heard Owens call him a coward, yet again. He wasn't a coward and he didn't need to throw fists or words at some hot-head to prove it.

Taking his knife from his other pocket, he flipped the blade open. Testing the sharpness with his thumb, he started carving away bits of wood from the block. Feet shuffled from the other room, followed by loud belching—Whitten—and discussions started about how each man might spend his evening.

"I don't get why you don't ever stand up to him," Jed said, flopping down on the edge of his bunk. "Don't you think he'd stop bullying you if you did?"

Adam kept his eyes on the block of wood. "Some people are born bullies. Doesn't matter what I do, he's always going to keep pushing."

"Why's that?" Hawk asked, leaning against the wall.

He thought for a minute. "I'm not sure what I ever did to cause him to hate me. So, how can I fix it? And how will bruising my knuckles on his jaw change it?"

"Guess ya got a point," Jed said.

"What ya workin' on?" Covington asked as he took a seat on the floor. Seemed most nights the four of them hung around each other.

Jed snickered. "Something for Miss Colter?"

Heat singed Adam's checks, but he kept his eyes on the slowly transforming block of wood.

"You guessed it," Hawk answered.

Owens's voice jolted Adam's eyes upward. "What makes you think you might have a chance with her, Larson? You're just a stable boy."

Draining the rest of his coffee from the tin mug in his hand, Owens stood in the doorway. Without warning he hurled the mug at

Adam, hitting him in the gut. Warm liquid ran down his left hand. Looking down, Adam dropped his knife and the wood, grasping his bleeding left thumb.

"Now look what you did," Jed said, standing in front of Owens. "What is wrong with you?"

Adam checked his throbbing thumb. He must have cut it pretty deep, because it was still bleeding. As Jed shoved Owens out of the way, Adam stood and entered the main room.

"Land sakes, boy!" Ben shouted, coming to his side. "Better git on up to the house and have Mrs. Colter take a look at that." Swinging the door open for him, Ben continued. "What happened in there?"

As the door shut behind him, Adam missed the responses. Walking quickly towards the ranch house, his face burned. Nothing like being called a boy by a bully and then by the foreman.

He knocked on the door to the ranch house, thankful that it was still early and he wouldn't be getting Mrs. Colter out of bed.

"Adam," Will greeted. "What brings you—"

Will stopped as his eyes dropped to Adam's hand. "Get in here. Hannah, we've got an injury."

Hannah rushed to the doorway. "What happened?"

"Hand slipped while I was carving." He stretched the truth. "Cut my thumb."

She ushered him to a chair at the table before grabbing some water and bandages. After she cleaned his thumb, she looked at it. "I could stitch it up for you, or you could just keep it bandaged for a few days."

"Bandages will be fine," he answered, growing more embarrassed by the situation.

Quietly, she bandaged his thumb. "There. Try not to bend it or move it around too much. If it starts bleeding again, let me know. Otherwise, come get some fresh bandages in the morning."

"Thank you ma'am," he said, taking his leave.

As he neared the bunkhouse, he looked down at the large bandage that made his thumb look five times its normal size. Should make the next few days interesting.

Chapter 25

Nashville, Tennessee

January 6, 1865

Thomas just finished delivering a dispatch to Major General Smith. Shaking his head, he was surprised by the major general's decision to reassign him to Kansas. It made no sense to him. The war was still heated. Sherman and Grant were planning major campaigns in the south, according to rumors. Why would the major general reassign him—his fasted rider—to the frontier?

Removing the saddle from his mare, Thomas tried to reason through what Smith might have been thinking. Still didn't make sense. He healed quickly from the bullet wound in mid-December. Other than a nasty mark on his right arm and some occasional soreness, he recovered. Within two weeks, he returned to duty, although the major general limited the distance of his dispatch assignments. He had not been assigned any reconnaissance missions either. He tried to remember if he had done anything to warrant the change in assignments but he could think of nothing. The major general commended him for his excellent service, especially during the battle of Nashville.

Perhaps he was just over-thinking the situation.

Regardless of the reasoning behind it all, Thomas knew he had no choice but to follow orders. He hoped the West was not as boring as he feared. Here he was needed. He was valued. He had a purpose. Would he experience the same in the West? Would there be adventure?

He doubted it. None of the western territories were actively involved in the war and what could be more adventurous than the war?

When Thomas finished caring for his horse, he returned to his quarters. He would pack, if he had anything to pack. Having traveled lightly for the last year as a dispatch rider, everything he owned already resided in his saddle bags.

As the hour grew late, Thomas retired for the night. In the morning, he would report to the major general for any final instructions before traveling west with a small contingent—not even a company—just a handful of cavalry men.

Providence, Tommy. Mixford's voice echoed in his head as he fell asleep.

The next morning, Major General Smith handed Thomas a rather large packet of letters and such. He told him that he included an update of the progress of the war for the western forts. He changed Thomas's assignment by requesting he personally ride to all of the forts through Kansas, Colorado, New Mexico, and on to the territorial capital of Arizona. The major general instructed him to deliver the specified packets to the corresponding forts.

Thomas stowed the packet in his saddle bags before mounting his horse. He rendezvoused with the rest of the contingent. This trip would give him more than enough time to ponder the situation. It would take months to cover the distance requested, all the way to the Arizona Territory.

Arizona Territory, Thomas thought. That was where Drew moved. Could this be luck or fate? Or Providence as his friend had suggested months ago. Was this his opportunity to set things right with Drew?

Plodding along the road, he considered this. For months he was haunted by his part in his brother's move. He had thought of heading to the territory on his own once his obligation with the army was finished. He wanted to find Drew. *And what? Ask for his forgiveness?* More like beg.

Why would Drew and Hannah forgive him? Why did he need to be forgiven so badly that it nearly caused him physical pain? Would the guilt finally be assuaged if he pursued this course?

Of course, Thomas had no way of knowing when his obligation with the army would be over. According to the judge and the enlistment papers he carried, he would muster out after three years or the end of the war, whichever came first. Given the major general's actions, and the rumors, Thomas thought the war might be over before the end of this year, perhaps even by the fall. If he were able to delay his time in the Arizona capital, he may be able to muster out while there. That would again require Providence to intervene.

He snorted. *Providence.* He was not sure if he believed in an all-powerful, all-knowing God. If there was a God, why would he allow this war to continue? Why would he sit idly by while tens of thousands of young men died in bloody battlefields?

If there was a God, why would he take Thomas's father from him? The thought brought his mind to full attention. Was God responsible for his father's death? For his mother's?

Growing up, he barely remembered her—his mother. She died when he was five. A cholera epidemic swept through the nearby rural areas. To listen to Drew tell the story, his mother saw it as her Christian duty to go help the sick. Either she never thought she would contract the illness, or she didn't care about her two young sons and her husband, and went anyway.

After she had been gone a month, word came that she became ill and was dying. The messenger carried a letter by her hand to her husband and sons. She apologized over and over that she would not be there to care for them. She said she was being called home. God needed her more.

But that wasn't true. Thomas and Drew needed her more. Their father needed her. How could God just take her away?

Regardless of how much they needed her, she passed on just days later. He had no idea that the morning he kissed his mother goodbye, before she went to tend the sick, would be the last time he would ever see her. Closing his eyes, he tried to conjure the scene in his mind. Only it wasn't his memories. It was the images his father and brother had painted for him.

She was short—probably where he got his lack of height from—and had blue eyes and sandy brown hair. Father said both he and Drew looked so much like her. Father said her smile was so bright you just had to respond with one of your own.

Not having a mother's influence certainly shaped more of his course than Providence, he thought. When Father wasn't looking, it was so much easier to sneak a few pieces of candy from the counter of his store and share them with his friends out back. The lack of nurturing added to his fiercely independent drive. By age ten, he was already bucking his father's discipline. Unlike the obedient Drew, he thought he knew better than his father and constantly broke the rules and bent every boundary set.

Then, at the age of fourteen, the only stable things in his life were ripped away. Father was killed in a freak carriage accident. The horse spooked and ran out of control through the streets, eventually crashing into a building, crushing his father under the overturned carriage. Drew, at eighteen, already had plans to leave for medical school. Suddenly, the responsibility of the store and seeing to Thomas's future rested squarely on his brother's shoulders.

Pursuing his own dreams, Drew sold the store. Then he sent Thomas to live with Uncle Peter before he left for medical school. Thomas hated him for it. Not only had he lost his father, but he lost his brother and his home all in a few short weeks.

The churning emotions he felt from living without a mother only intensified afterwards. Looking back, Thomas did not even think he could say what those emotions were. He only knew those feelings drove him to set his own course in life, even at the young age of fourteen.

Sighing, he turned his thoughts back to his original question. Had God really taken his mother, his father? If that was true, he was even more certain that he could not trust such a being.

Yet, Thomas could not deny the unexplained circumstances in his life these last few years. It was too structured to be mere chance. Was there such a thing as fate or destiny? Was he just following along the path destiny determined for him? If that was true, did he really have any control or say over his own life? If he did not, then what was the meaning of his life? If everything was determined for him, why exist at all?

If it was all about destiny, then was it destiny that he tried to rob that bank? Would destiny seek such sinister purposes? If not destiny, but Providence, would He direct someone to criminal behavior?

Or, was his life truly his own to make?

He had been confused and hurting as a young man. No one pushed him towards drinking and gambling. He made those choices on his own. Yet, not all of his choices were his to make. The judge sent him off to fight in the war. That decision set off a series of events that led to Thomas becoming a dispatch rider, and now being assigned to the frontier. None of those things he chose for himself.

But, he could choose what he did after the army. If he was in the Arizona Territory, he would seek out his brother, if for no other reason than to assure himself that Drew and Hannah were happy. Then, he would need a job. He wasn't sure what sort of job he could do. Other than riding horses fast, he was not good at much else, except gambling and drinking—actions that only brought him, and those he loved, pain.

Knowing he had only more questions and no answers, Thomas tried to push these thoughts from his mind. Things, as he discovered, had a way of working themselves out.

The bell rang from the front lobby just as Julia finished the last bite of her midday meal. Chewing quickly, she swallowed and hurried to greet the waiting customer. The man standing next to the front desk was dressed in dark twill trousers with a very dusty white shirt. Saddle bags lay over his shoulder. A light hat, similar to the one Will always wore, sat back on his head. He looked far different than most of the well-dressed men who stayed at the hotel.

"Good afternoon," she said, drawing his attention. "How may I help you?"

His eyes went wide as she took her place behind the front desk. "Um… Where's Mr. Hamilton?"

"He's busy with other duties. Can I help you?"

Slamming the saddle bags down on the counter, he said, "Here's the mail."

Julia blinked, not understanding.

When she failed to move for another moment, he said, "I'm kinda eager to get home and you're my last stop, so if you don't mind, Miss…"

"Colter. Miss Colter," she stumbled. "Perhaps you could tell me what Mr. Hamilton normally does with the mail, Mr…?"

"Frye. Leland Frye." A big grin stretched across his narrow face. "Mr. Hamilton usually takes the stack," he said as he pulled the mail from the saddle bags, "and places it in those cubbies, right there."

She followed his pointed finger to the cubby holes on the wall behind the desk. Taking the mail from his hand, she wondered what she should do next.

"Pleasure meeting you, Miss Colter," Mr. Frye said as he headed for the door. "I'll be seeing you again in a few days to pick up outgoing mail."

Wishing Mr. Frye farewell, she laid the stack of mail on the counter. Then she went back to Mr. Hamilton's office to find out what she was supposed to do with it. After apologizing for forgetting to show her sooner, he helped her sort the mail into the different cubbies for the businesses and residents in town. Then he showed her where they held the mail for those who lived outside of town, like the ranchers.

"People are still getting used to regular service. Mr. Barnard took over as postmaster back in November when Reverend Read, the former postmaster, left."

Glancing at the last envelope, she noticed it was for Betty Lancaster. "Can I hand deliver this one later?"

"Hmm. Leave it in the cubby for now, just in case someone comes over to check. Then if you want you can take it over to Betty after your shift."

Julia nodded.

The rest of the afternoon went by quickly. Before she realized it, Mr. Hamilton was there to relieve her for the evening. Grabbing the letter for Betty, she headed out the door without eating supper. Deciding to stop by Gray & Company first, she started down the boardwalk.

"Miss Colter!"

Turning, she waited for Mr. Hobbs to catch up.

"Might I escort you," he said, warily eyeing the saloons lining the street. "The sun sets so early these days, I would hate for you to walk the dark streets unescorted."

Looking around, she agreed. Even at six o'clock, the sky already darkened and stars started twinkling. "Thank you," she replied, taking his offered arm.

"Would you feel more comfortable on the other side of the street?" he asked, concern edging his voice.

"I'm going to stop by Gray & Company on this side of the

street."

"Very well," he said, holding her closer.

A man burst out of the doors of the saloon in front of them. Angry curses followed him. Julia stopped, shocked by the display.

"Stay out!" the saloon owner yelled from the other side of the doors.

Mr. Hobbs urged her forward at a fast pace, leaving her almost breathless by the time they arrived at Gray & Company.

"Here you are," he said. "I'll wait here."

"That's quite alright," she answered. "I'm just going over to Lancaster's as soon as I'm done here."

Eyebrows raised, he asked, "Are you certain? It will be no trouble."

"Thanks for your help, Mr. Hobbs, but I don't want to take any more of your time."

"Have a good evening, then." He turned and left.

Mr. Young was just turning the closed sign around when she started toward the open door. She briefly mentioned to him that there was some mail down at the hotel—thus completing the purpose for her visit.

Turning, she cut across the town plaza to Betty's kitchen door. Despite the chill in the air, the door stood slightly propped open. Knocking on the door, she stuck her head in the kitchen.

A Chinese couple laden with plates full of food left the kitchen for the dining hall. Betty stood over the stove dishing up plates as fast as she could.

"Evening," Julia greeted.

"Dear, come on in. Take a seat," Betty said after giving her a big hug. "I'm so glad you stopped by. Have you eaten yet?"

At the shake of Julia's head, Betty thrust an overflowing plate of food towards her on the small kitchen table. "As soon as it slows a bit, I'll sit with you."

Fifteen minutes later, Betty sat down across from her. "How have you been, dear?"

"I've been well. I really like working at the hotel." Sliding the letter across the table, she added, "I brought you something."

"Oh!" Betty exclaimed. Turning the envelope over, she looked closer. "It's from one of my daughters. Bless you for bringing this over. Did it come today?"

Julia nodded.

"I keep forgetting that Mr. Barnard is handling the mail these days."

Setting the letter aside, Betty continued, "Did you know we have a new pastor, Reverend Page? He's holding services here in the dining hall on Sunday mornings."

"Really? For how long?"

"This Sunday will be his first sermon here. I'm so excited," Betty smiled. "His wife is so precious. Pretty little thing. I bet they'll be graced with a few little ones soon. Guess they are newly married."

Julia smiled.

"Anyway, maybe you could join us for services? It'd be a great way to meet more folks from town."

She hesitated. "I work on Sunday mornings at the hotel."

"Nonsense," Betty patted her hand. "Just ask Mr. Barnard for the morning off. It's a day of rest."

As the noise from the dining hall quieted, Betty stood and readied the dish pan. Even though Julia offered to help, Betty refused. Instead, she asked Paul to walk Julia back to the hotel, saying it wasn't safe for a young woman to walk about alone.

Thanking Paul, she entered the hotel. Her new home. It didn't really feel like home. She still didn't know what to do with herself in the evenings. Most of the time, she sat and read a borrowed book from the guest library. Perhaps she would read her Bible this evening, the thought sparked from her conversation with Betty. Maybe it was time to move on.

Chapter 26

Julia smiled and greeted Mr. Hobbs as he entered the hotel. "Good day, Mr. Hobbs. May I assist you with anything today?"

"Miss Colter, your smile brightens my day," he replied with his customary greeting. "I see you made it home safely last night."

Nodding, she wished her cheeks would cool down. Surely her face was bright red.

"I was curious if you might be able to recommend some place for a scenic ride. My associates are interested in exploring more of the area."

Julia, not being familiar with the area other than Colter Ranch, could think of nothing. "Just a moment, Mr. Hobbs. Let me see if Mr. Hamilton might have a good suggestion."

At his nod, she walked down the hallway to Mr. Hamilton's office. She explained Mr. Hobbs's request and Mr. Hamilton followed her back to the front desk. The two men spoke at length about the different possibilities for a short ride. At the end of the discussion, Mr. Hamilton suggested the men hire horses and perhaps a guide from the livery down the street. When Mr. Hamilton returned to his office, Mr. Hobbs remained at the front desk.

"Is there anything else, Mr. Hobbs?" she asked when he made no move to leave.

"I was wondering, Miss Colter, if you liked to ride," he said softly, leaning on the edge of the tall counter side of the front desk.

Nervous, she fidgeted with the corner of the open guest book. "I…uh…"

"Miss Colter," Mr. Hamilton called from his office. "A word with you, please."

Breathing a quiet sigh of relief, Julia left Mr. Hobbs standing there and entered Mr. Hamilton's office. He motioned for her to sit then he stood. "One moment, Miss Colter."

Mr. Hamilton entered the lobby and Julia could hear him

speaking with Mr. Hobbs. "Miss Colter is much too busy with her duties to go on outings with our guests. I do hope you understand and refrain from suggesting such an activity in the future."

Mr. Hobbs acknowledged his request before Mr. Hamilton returned to his office and took a seat on the other side of his desk.

"Miss Colter, I am sorry to see you put into such an awkward situation. Please realize that as an unattached beautiful woman in the middle of the Arizona Territory, men are bound to pay attention to you. It is best if you respond in a manner similar to what I just did on your behalf. They will respect you for it."

She considered his words. She had no desire to go on an outing with any of their guests, knowing deep in her heart none would ever find her acceptable if they knew the truth of her past. She only accepted Mr. Hobbs's offer last night because of the late hour. What Mr. Hamilton suggested made sense. "I understand and I will make my disinterest known."

"Very good, Miss Colter. That will be all," he said, dismissing her with the wave of his hand.

She was somewhat relieved to know she could take a firm stance with anyone who might try to garner her favor.

"Might I ask you a question," she asked as she stood. When he nodded, she continued, "Mrs. Lancaster mentioned to me that Sunday services are being held at the boardinghouse in the dining hall. I was wondering if I might be permitted to attend."

Mr. Hamilton smiled. "Of course. We can adjust your schedule so you may take Sunday mornings off. Be back here by one."

Julia offered her thanks before she returned to the front desk.

On Sunday morning, she donned her navy blue dress and wool coat. The weather turned cold and the skies hinted at a coming storm. Grabbing her Bible, she walked the short distance across the town square to Lancaster's. When Betty first suggested Julia attend the service, she almost said no immediately. But something held back the outright rejection.

Perhaps it was because she remembered what Sunday mornings

used to mean to her. Prior to her father's passing, the morning service was a place to worship her Lord. After his passing, it was a place of comfort. Since leaving Texas, she had not been to a service. In fact the last service she attended was the one where she broke off her farce of an engagement. The beating she suffered under Reuben's hand left her too bruised to appear in public. By the time she healed from those bruises, he inflicted… Well, she had to leave. Then, while living on Colter Ranch, they never made the trip to town, although the services started sometime last fall.

Pushing the more painful thoughts aside, Julia hoped the experience would be one of renewal. Most days, while working at the hotel, she was able to completely forget the incident with Reuben though, there were times his face still haunted her dreams. She wanted to be free from it.

Opening the door to the dining hall, the warmth, not only from the stove, but from Betty's heart-felt smile, engulfed Julia.

Betty took her coat. "So good to see you this morning. Might you have time to join me for tea after the service?"

"It depends on how long the reverend preaches. I must resume my duties at the hotel by one."

"Well," a young man stated, "I'll keep my message brief then."

"Julia, this is Reverend Joseph Page," Betty said motioning to the young man and a young woman standing next to him, "and his wife Rachel. This is Miss Julia Colter."

"Pleased to meet you Reverend and Mrs. Page."

Betty led Julia to a seat next to her. There were no more than twenty or so people in the room. One group of five all looked similar in appearance, perhaps one of the newer families from California.

Mrs. Page led by singing some familiar hymns. Her lovely voice carried the words lightly across the air with such emotion that Julia could not help but be affected. Moisture gathered in the corner of her eyes as they concluded singing. Taking a deep breath, she willed her emotions under control.

Reverend Page stood and read several verses from the gospel of John. When he concluded the scripture reading, he expounded on the meaning.

"Jesus told his disciples they would face trouble. Do you think he was only speaking to them? Or was he speaking to us as well?

"One only has to look around this room to see he was speaking to us. Consider the circumstances that brought many of us here to this territory. One leaves after the death of child, another to escape the war, yet another flees for their life."

Julia swallowed. *Could he know about why I left? That's impossible.*

"Yet, each of these situations that brought us here, to this exact place at this precise time, need not overwhelm us. Jesus told his disciples that he overcame the world and that he came to bring peace. His very presence on earth all those years ago was, in part, to bring us comfort and peace. When we rest in the knowledge that he has overcome the world and all the evil that is within it, we should be encouraged.

"What would happen to us if we let ourselves be encouraged by his peace? What kind of people would we be? How would our lives change?"

Julia did not hear anything further. Her mind spun with many questions. Could Jesus really overcome the evil that was done to her? Could he really bring her peace about that? As the reverend asked, how would her life change if she really felt that peace? Was there really hope she might one day marry? If Jesus overcame the world, could He bring her a husband who would not see her as ruined?

She looked down and studied her hands. She wanted to believe there was hope for her. *How do I let his peace encourage me?*

"All you have to do," the reverend continued almost as if he could read her thoughts. "Is ask him to give you his peace. Pray and keep on praying until you are bolstered by the knowledge that he has overcome the world."

The reverend concluded his remarks and led the small congregation in prayer. Julia bowed her head and spoke to God in her heart. *Lord, I want to know without a doubt that you have overcome the evil in my life. Please help me have the peace that I crave. Please forgive me for blaming you for what happened.*

When she lifted her head, many of the people were standing and gathering their coats. Since she agreed to have tea with Betty following the service, she stayed near the kitchen.

"Miss Colter." The reverend approached. "We are so glad that you were able to join us this morning. We do hope you will join us again."

"I would like that," she said, trying to keep the flood of emotions churning inside from becoming visible.

The reverend and his wife finally left and Betty pointed Julia toward the kitchen. Grabbing two mugs of tea, Betty led Julia into her private quarters to a small sitting area.

"I thought this might give us a little more privacy. Liang and Yu will be preparing dinner for our boarders and it is bound to be noisy in the kitchen."

"So, dear, tell me how have you been?"

The sincerity in Betty's voice undid Julia. All the emotions she felt during the service, all her fears, her pain, her hope, came gushing forth in the form of tears. She sobbed several minutes, feeling a bit self-conscious.

"There, there, dear," Betty said patting her hand. "You just let it all out."

Something about this woman put her at ease. Before she gave it any thought, she told Betty all that happened to bring her to the Arizona Territory. She held nothing back. When she told Betty of the night that haunted her and what Reuben did, she saw only compassion in the older woman's eyes. There was no condemnation, no blame, just compassion and love. Is this how God looked upon her?

Julia concluded, "Now that I am ruined, I fear being alone for the rest of my life, and that no man will want me when he learns the truth."

"Dear, you are not ruined. First, you did not choose for this to happen. Any man of God would surely understand that." Betty patted Julia's cheek, as a mother might to comfort her child.

"Second, God loves you, dear. His heart is breaking that you have suffered so terribly. He wants to give you his peace, just as Reverend Page said. He has not left you. He is right here waiting to wrap you in his arms."

Julia sniffed. "I asked him to bring me his peace this morning. I want to forget this pain. I want to live my life without always being reminded of this."

Betty wrapped her in a warm embrace and she wondered if it wasn't God himself wrapping his arms around her. She felt the beginning of something settling over her heart.

"Well, then dear, we will continue to pray that God will bring you his peace."

Julia dabbed the last of her tears with her handkerchief. She felt embarrassed for having poured out all of her troubles to Betty. "I'm sorry I am so…"

"Dear, there is nothing to be sorry for. We each have our deep secrets and hurt. God puts us with friends so he can help us. I was glad to be here for you today." Betty smiled compassionately and patted her hand one more time.

"Oh, look at the time. You need to be going. Here, wash up," she said handing her a damp cloth from the water on her dresser.

Julia did as instructed then grabbed her things. Rushing across the street, she slowed right before opening the door. A line of men stood at the front desk and another line stretched from the dining hall entrance.

"Oh, Miss Colter, there you are!" a relieved Mr. Hamilton said. "They need your help in the dining room seating guests."

"What happened?" she asked.

"A stage just arrived. I'll take care of checking in the guests. Please, hurry to the dining room."

She did as he asked, glad that she had freshened up at Betty's. Hopefully her eyes were no longer red.

"How many?" she asked, turning towards the first group of men in line.

"Four," Mr. Hobbs replied, lips stretching into a broad smile.

"Right this way," she said, leading them to an open table.

As she turned to leave, Mr. Hobbs touched her arm lightly. In a low voice, he asked, "Are you alright, Miss Colter?"

Forcing a brighter smile and hoping to lighten her tone, she replied, "I'm well. Thank you." Raising her voice, she added, "Someone will be around to take your order shortly."

Without waiting for a response, she returned to the line of patrons waiting to be seated. As quickly as possible she got everyone to tables then made the rounds to take orders. She wondered what happened to the young lady who normally worked the dining room. It seemed Julia was the only one there to serve.

The next hour passed in a blur as she moved from table to table.

At one point, Mr. Hamilton even came back to the dining room to help serve, after he finished checking in all the guests. As the guests finished their meals, most left to explore the town or retire to their rooms. Only Mr. Hobbs, Mr. Franklin, Mr. Hardy, and Mr. Brighton remained.

Breathing a sigh of relief, she grabbed a coffee pot to refill their cups. "Can I get you gentlemen anything else?"

Mr. Hobbs stood. "Miss Colter, might I have a word with you?"

"Certainly."

He led her to an unoccupied area of the dining room. "I was wondering if you were free this evening—if you might like to have supper with me."

"I don't dine with guests, Mr. Hobbs," she answered without hesitation.

"I understand you wouldn't be able to eat here. I thought we could visit the Osborn's restaurant."

Weary from the long day, Julia wanted to make sure Mr. Hobbs clearly understood her position. "I won't be dining with you, sir. Not here. Not at the Osborn's. My duties at the hotel keep me quite busy and I prefer my evenings of solitude."

Before the words finished leaving her tongue, she realized how false they were. She hated the lonely evenings. She wished she had a friend to talk with. But, Mr. Hobbs would not be that friend. She had to keep some distance from the guests.

"I see," he said stiffly, shoulders slumping ever so slightly. "This evening is my last in Prescott for a while. Perhaps on my next visit—"

"Thank you for the offer, Mr. Hobbs. If you'll excuse me, I believe Mr. Hamilton is looking for me."

Darting away before he had a chance to respond, she walked past the front desk and down the hall to her private room. Shutting the door, she sagged against it. Though she wished she could take a nap to recover from the last few hectic hours, six o'clock was still a few hours away.

Letting out a long sigh, she left the solace of her small room to resume her duties at the front desk, hoping Mr. Hobbs would not press the issue further. She could not deal with a handsome young man pursuing her right now, regardless of the new hope she felt from this morning's service.

Well, maybe she could, if it was a certain handsome young horse trainer.

Chapter 27

Prescott

January 12, 1865

As Will helped Hannah down from the wagon, she tried not to sigh. Early this morning he asked her to visit the doctor to make sure the baby was doing well. Ever since Thanksgiving, any time she felt unwell or tired, he became protective. She assured him she was fine, but he insisted.

"Mrs. Colter, how are you feeling?" Dr. Armstrong asked as he led her into the examination room. Will followed.

Will answered for her, his anxiety obvious. "She's been unusually tired and keeps rubbing her back."

Hannah smiled. While she appreciated her husband's concern, his over-protectiveness wore on her. Dr. Armstrong must have sensed her frustration, for he instructed her to change while he showed Will to the waiting area.

A few minutes later, Dr. Armstrong knocked on the door, making sure Hannah was ready. She acknowledged him before he entered the room.

"So, other than an anxious husband," he teased, "how are you feeling?"

"I'm feeling quite well. I've had no further bleeding and I am now several weeks past the time where I lost my first child. Other than feeling a little more tired than normal, I am fine."

"Good. Feeling tired is normal and nothing to be concerned about."

"Tell that to Will."

Dr. Armstrong smiled as he helped her lie down so he could complete the examination. "I will be happy to discuss your husband's concerns once we are done here."

Having completed the examination, he said, "You seem to be

doing well, Mrs. Colter. I would like to see you again in a month or two, sooner if you experience any unusual symptoms."

"Thank you, Dr. Armstrong."

When he left to talk to Will, he closed the door. Hannah could hear their muffled conversation as she dressed.

"I assure you, Mr. Colter, your wife is in excellent health and so is the baby."

When Will started to object, the doctor's voice softened. Hannah hoped he was able to convince him to stop worrying so much.

Tucking a stray strand of hair back, Hannah joined the men in the parlor. Will looked like he had been sufficiently chastised. She smiled at him. After he paid the doctor, he offered her his arm.

"I'm sorry for worrying," he said once they left the doctor's office.

"Everything will be just fine. I don't know how I know it, but I do."

He turned and took her hands in his. Looking down at her, Hannah saw the fear in his eyes. "I just love you so much. If anything happened to you, I don't know what I would do."

She wished she could promise him that nothing would happen, but she knew there were far too many women who died in childbirth for that promise to mean anything. She knew he wanted to keep her from harm, but all of this was out of his control. Likely that was what bothered him. But this was not the place for such a discussion.

Standing on her tip toes, she kissed her husband on the cheek, saying, "Let's not borrow trouble. Be grateful for what we have."

Sighing, he turned and led her toward the hotel.

Adam was nervous as he entered the hotel. Will and Hannah were stopping at the doctor's office first, so he had some time to find Julia before they joined him.

In the weeks since she moved to town, he thought about her often. He missed their conversations. He missed her smile, which he had seen little of since they left Texas. But, he remembered it well.

Most of all, he just missed knowing she was nearby.

He wanted to give her something she would like and remind her of him. The last few nights he stayed up late into the night to finish his gift, making sure every detail was just right. He hoped she would like it.

Mr. Hamilton stood behind the front desk of the lobby. Adam wondered where Julia might be. He thought he'd wait a few minutes to see if she would return, but the man spoke.

"May I help you?"

"Ah…" Adam stammered. "Is Miss Colter around?"

Mr. Hamilton narrowed his eyes. "And you are?"

"Adam Larson. I am a good friend of hers," he said. Mr. Hamilton's scrutiny made him nervous. He hurried to explain, "I have known her since we were children on neighboring ranches in Texas. I work on her brother's ranch."

Mr. Hamilton looked him up and down before responding. "I see. Miss Colter is off for the day. Wait here and I'll see if she is still here."

Relieved to have passed the test, Adam took a seat in one of the chairs in the lobby. He looked up when he heard the soft thud of feminine boots coming towards him.

"Adam!" Julia exclaimed as her lips stretched thin in a smile that lit the whole room. "So good to see you."

His heart leaped at the enthusiasm in her voice. She seemed genuinely pleased to see him. He returned the smile.

"I thought you might care to take a walk with an old friend."

"Just let me get my coat." She turned and walked down the hallway. Reaching just inside a room, she grabbed her coat and was at his side again.

Adam, taking the coat from her hands, helped her into it. Her nearness sent his heart racing. When she started buttoning the coat, he let his hand linger at the small of her back. When she was ready, he reluctantly removed his hand and offered her his arm.

They walked across the street to the town square before he started the conversation.

"Are you warm enough?" he asked noticing the bite to the air and the heavy clouds in the sky.

"Oh yes. How have you been, Adam? How's Percy coming

along? Oh, and Annabel? Has she thrown you? Have you taken her out to the herd yet?" He loved the way she would fire out so many questions when she was excited, as she was doing now.

"So many questions," he smiled stealing a glance at her. "Where should I start?"

"Tell me how you are."

His heart flipped that she would truly want to know. "Just fine. A little tired."

"Is Will working you too hard?" she teased. Oh how he missed this vibrant version of Julia, though he had not realized it until now. Something was definitely changing. She was not as morose as she had been. Perhaps the move had been what she needed after all.

"No. I was working on a special project late into the night," he baited.

"What sort of special project?" She turned to face him as he stopped walking.

Pulling the gift from his jacket pocket, he handed it to her. He was glad that Hannah gave him some brown paper and twine, which served the purpose of prolonging the surprise.

Julia took the gift from him. "What's this?"

"Open it."

As she carefully untied the twine, he stared at her. Her cheeks flushed with pink. Her blue eyes glowed with life. Her full lips twitched with a smile. She looked so beautiful today, so alive.

If only he could tell her just how much he cared for her.

When Julia removed the paper, she gasped and her eyes went wide. She looked up at him and he held his breath. She looked back down at the horse and rider, carefully turning it over in her hands, running slender fingers along the horse's mane.

"Oh, Adam, it's beautiful!"

She jumped into his arms causing his pulse to race. He circled his arms around her waist and kept them there even when she started to pull back, savoring the feel of her in his arms. As Julia's expression went from surprise to embarrassment, he released his hold. Had they not been standing in the middle of the square, he might have kissed her.

He chuckled as he thought how surprised she might look then.

Reeling his thoughts back, he said, "You're welcome, Julia."

Julia was most embarrassed by her impulsive hug. She only meant to thank Adam for the incredible gift. She had not expected him to put his arms around her. While she was surprised by his action, she enjoyed the feel of his embrace, the closeness. And that frightened her.

Stepping back, she looked at the horse and rider carving in her hand. She recognized both—the horse was the chestnut mare, and she was the rider. How much time had he spent working on this? The detail was amazing.

This was the most special gift she had ever received. Her voice came out as a whisper. "Thank you, Adam."

"I'm glad you like it," he said, his voice husky.

Those green eyes locked with hers again. He looked at her differently, intently. He searched her eyes, looking for something. Her throat went dry. What had Will said? That Adam loved her. Could it be true?

Pushing the thought aside, she turned back towards the hotel. She had to move. Adam fell into step beside her, saying nothing more.

Just before they reached the hotel, she spotted Will and Hannah. *They came to town on my birthday.* She smiled and waved in greeting.

"Hannah," Julia said giving her sister a warm hug. Then turning to Will she did the same. "Will, it's so good to see you both."

"We thought we would steal you away for part of the day," Will said.

"Yes, Betty has something planned," Hannah added. "Perhaps we could head over there?"

Julia nodded agreement. "Let me put this inside." Scurrying to her room, she took one last look at the horse and rider before closing the door behind her.

"I'm ready," she said meeting the three out front.

While they walked to Lancaster's, Hannah asked, "How do you like your job?"

Julia explained what her duties were and what her living

quarters were like. She really liked the job and said as much.

When Will opened the door to the dining hall at Lancaster's and motioned for her to enter, she stopped short at the full room. At first she thought it was full of boarders, but as she looked around the room she saw more familiar faces: Reverend and Mrs. Page, Betty, Paul, Chef, Mr. Hamilton, Dr. Armstrong, and some others from the hotel and church. She turned and looked at Will and Hannah with a questioning look.

"Hannah and Betty planned it. Happy birthday little sis," Will said before kissing her on the cheek.

Julia accepted the warm wishes from all her new friends and family, deeply touched that they would do this for her. Adam led her to a seat at one of the tables, adding to her suspicion that he was in on this too. Then he took a seat beside her. Hannah and Will sat across from her. As the rest of her friends took their seats, Liang and Yu began serving them dinner.

As she listened to the conversations around her, she remembered home and the parties her father used to have. She missed him so. Caroline would have been there, too. As a tear slid down her cheek, Adam leaned over and brushed it away.

He whispered, "What's wrong?"

She tried to smile but it felt a little forced. "Just missing my father and Caroline."

He took her hand and gave it a gentle squeeze, sending a tingling sensation up her arm. She was again aware of his closeness as he sat next to her. Glad when he let go of her hand, Julia relaxed.

Chef entered from the kitchen with a big frosted cake. What a special treat! "For you," he said placing the first piece in front of her.

"How did you manage this?"

"Oh, don't tell Mr. Barnard that I used so much sugar, Miss Colter," he teased, giving her a wink. She thought Mr. Barnard might not mind this once.

The cake and frosting melted on her tongue. She closed her eyes and savored each bite. It was positively delightful. When she opened her eyes she caught Adam looking at her. She smiled and he quickly looked away. What was going on between them?

After everyone finished the cake, many of them wished Julia a happy birthday and returned to their day. When she stood and retrieved her coat, Adam helped her put it on again.

"May I walk you home?" he asked.

When she nodded, he held out his arm for her.

"You seem… Different."

You seem different, too.

"How so?"

"Hmm. More like the Julia that I remember growing up."

Intrigued, she asked, "In what way?"

A smiled tilted just one side of his mouth. "Full of life, spirit, impulsive."

Like earlier when I hugged you, I suppose.

"I see."

"Happier," he added.

They were just a step or two from the hotel doors. Adam turned to face her. Julia's breath caught. The way the sunlight filtered through the clouds, his golden hair looked almost as if it glowed. His green eyes sparkled. Her heart beat faster as he looked into her eyes. Her stomach fluttered and she almost wondered if he was going to kiss her.

Finally, Adam broke the spell with a whisper. "Happy birthday."

She swallowed the lump in her throat. "Thank you, Adam."

He continued to stare at her, making no move to leave. Taking her hand in his, he rubbed his thumb over her knuckles, sending waves of warmth up her arm. She tried to tell her feet to move, but they would not listen. Just when she thought she might turn into a statute from his intense gaze, he squeezed her hand and took a step back.

"Take care, Julia. I hope to see you again soon."

"I would like that," she answered. Oh, how she missed him!

As he turned and unhitched his horse from a nearby post, Julia watched him go. Something had most definitely changed between them. And she thought she liked it.

Chapter 28

Colter Ranch

February 27, 1865

How many times had he led Percy around the corral now? Adam lost count. Maybe one more for good measure. Deciding that a ride might suit his mindset better, he returned Percy to his stall and saddled Annabel. Mounting the horse, he pointed her out towards the herd. He would ride close to get her used to the cattle but not too close.

Julia's smile floated across his vision. Blue eyes. Soft dark lashes. Full pink lips. It had been over six weeks since her birthday and he missed her so much it hurt.

Adam remembered his promise to God to be patient and wait for her let go of her past, but it was becoming difficult. He loved Julia Colter. If he had been unsure before her birthday, he was not after. When she impulsively hugged him as a thank you for the gift, he wanted to kiss her and to hold her. He could still smell the light vanilla fragrance he'd come to associate with her. The way her eyes looked, so full of life again, it made him want her even more. There were so many times that day he almost kissed her. He doubted it would be any easier when he went to town tomorrow.

He really wanted to marry her. He was as certain of that as he had been about moving west. But, hearing his mama's voice in his head, he knew Julia deserved to be courted. Give her a chance to make up her mind. See if she felt the same way about him.

Too bad Mama was so far away. He could really use her advice. She would probably be tickled that he'd fallen in love with Julia. Mama always liked her. Caroline—oh, if she had any idea she would be impossible! She would probably try to meddle, but in the end, she'd be happy. Perhaps he should write to his family, let them know what was on his heart. Then again, maybe it was too soon.

Reining in the mare, Adam kept her twenty yards or so away from the herd. He thought Annabel would make a good ranch horse, so trying her out near the herd would help him see if he was right. Unlike the horses for the La Paz Express, where speed and endurance were important, a keen sharp mind and strength were more important in ranching. His father once said that a good ranch horse was smart enough to keep its cowboy out of danger, but dumb enough to want to ride into a herd of longhorns. Adam smiled at the thought.

Skirting the herd and keeping the same distance, he let the mare have her head, testing her. Would she try to move away from the herd? Towards the herd? Or would she keep on the course he already set? The answer would help him determine how much more training she required.

Just as he started the exercise, he spotted a young calf ahead separated from the herd. Annabel saw it too and veered to the outside of the calf. Still allowing the mare to lead, Adam was pleased when she tried to nudge the calf back towards the herd. Taking control again, he helped reinforce the lesson of how to do just that. Still ten yards out from the herd, the calf turned back towards the herd. Adam kept the mare at the now closer distance.

He smiled as he made the connection between the mare and Julia. Like the mare, her working in town was allowing her to have head. Just like with the mare, Adam was waiting to see what direction she would take. Would she make a move in the right direction by letting go of her hurt and pain? Or would she continue to be dragged down by the past? She was strong, just like a good cattle horse, although she might not appreciate what a compliment that was in his eyes.

Hearing the supper bell, he turned the mare towards the ranch. Soon enough he would see for himself how his sweet Julia was faring.

As he brushed Annabel down, the other cowboys came in from the field. Owens seemed in a foul mood, judging by his tone.

"Boss, I don't understand why Larson always gets to go to town," he said. "Ain't fair."

"Has nothing to do with being fair or not," Will answered calmly. "He has different responsibilities. He needs to go in to deliver some horses to the La Paz Express."

"Any one of us could do that," Owens whined.

"But Adam is the only one who has the authority to act on my behalf. He's more than just an employee. He's the manager of the horse business."

"Can't I go in with Whitten? Stay the night? What's the point of makin' money if I can't ever get to town for entertainment?"

A heavy sigh hinted at Will's frustration. "Fine. You and Whitten will go with Adam. Stay the night if you must. But, I expect you back here the next day before dinner."

Owens let out a *whoop* for joy before heading up to the bunkhouse for supper.

Staying the night might not be the worst that could happen, as Adam hoped to spend part of the evening with Julia. Perhaps, she would at least be able to go to supper with him.

The next morning, he put long leads on the two horses for the Express. With leads in hand, he mounted his horse. Whitten took the front and Owens brought up the rear as they started up the road to Prescott.

As soon as they topped the first hill, Owens started shooting off his mouth.

"Larson, you gonna join us for some real entertainment this evening or are you too good for us."

Adam ignored the comment. He had no doubt that the entertainment Owens referred to could only be found at the saloon. Not something he was interested in. He'd much rather spend the time with Julia.

Owens continued, "Maybe your pretty lady friend would want to join us. Bet she ain't too good for us."

Clenching his jaw, he remained silent.

"You kiss her yet, Larson?" Owens taunted.

Adam took a deep breath, trying to keep from showing his rising anger.

"Maybe she'll invite you to that hotel room of hers and you can have yourself a good time—that is if you know how to handle a filly with spirit."

That was it. Adam stopped abruptly, his blood boiling. Turning his horse back toward Owens, he allowed his anger to show. It was one thing to taunt him, it was quite another to suggest Julia's reputation was anything less than virtuous.

Looping the leads around the horn of his saddle, he pulled up directly next to Owens. He grabbed him by his shirt pulling his face to within inches of his own.

"What are you implying?" Adam said between gritted teeth.

By now, Whitten tried unsuccessfully to jockey his horse between the two of theirs. "Come on, Owens, leave him alone," Whitten said. "What you said about the boss's sister ain't right."

Adam, picking up on the connection, used it to his advantage. "Just what do you think Will would do to you if he heard you suggested his sister was the dallying kind?"

Owens glared at him then gave him a shove. Adam released his grip on the man's shirt, but kept eye contact.

"No need to get all riled up, Larson. I was just having a bit of fun with ya."

Adam grunted in disgust. He would rather knock the cocky crass cowboy from his horse than ride the rest of the way to town with him. He had a lot of nerve saying those things about Julia. She was the most respectable, decent woman he knew.

Owens said something else that Adam did not catch before kicking his horse into motion. The rest of the trip passed in tense silence.

Once they arrived, Adam headed straight for the livery. He tied his horse and the two for the Express to the hitching post as Whitten and Owens ambled toward the saloon. It was before noon, but the two would likely gamble and drink the day away.

As Adam walked into the livery, Craig Roundtree greeted him. "Adam, I trust the trip in was uneventful."

Stifling a snort, he said, "I have the two horses we discussed, if you would like to look them over?"

Craig walked out front, with Adam following close behind. Stopping in front of the two geldings, Craig thoroughly inspected both before responding, "Very fine animals. Let's finalize the arrangements."

Adam nodded and followed Craig back inside. Just a few short minutes later, the transaction was complete. Thanking Craig for his business, he left.

Excited by the prospect of having most of the day with Julia, he wasted no time going to the hotel. Entering the hotel, he saw Julia at the front desk, surrounded by a group of four gentlemen. Her hair curled tightly in ringlets, dusting her shoulders as she looked down at the register. Without looking up she called out an impersonal greeting to him and kept her attention on the four guests.

"Mr. Brighton, I have your reservation right here. Here is your key. Mr. Hobbs, here is yours. Mr. Franklin. Mr. Hardy. Will you be dining with us for dinner or supper?" she asked.

"Thank you, Miss Colter," the one named Mr. Hobbs replied. "Would you make us reservations for supper this evening?"

"Certainly. Right this way, gentlemen," she said. Pausing near where Adam stood, she said to him, "I'll be with you in... Oh, Adam!"

She came to an abrupt stop as she faced him. Her smile grew brighter as did her eyes as she finished, "Good to see you. I'll be right back."

Motioning for the four gentlemen to follow her, she showed them to their rooms. Then she came back into the lobby and held up her index finger to indicate one more minute before scurrying off to the dining room. When she returned to the lobby, Adam's heart skipped a beat. She looked lovely.

"I'm sorry I didn't realize it was you," she said, stopping a foot from him. "What brings you to town today?"

You.

"I was delivering some horses to the Express. Owens and Whitten rode in with me and wanted to stay the night."

"I see."

Adam shifted his weight to his other foot. "I don't suppose you could get away for a while?"

She half-smiled half-pouted before replying, "No. I work until six tonight. Normally, I would ask Mr. Hamilton, but with Mr. Barnard out traveling, Mr. Hamilton has extra duties this week."

Hoping for more time, he tried to keep his disappointment from showing. "Would you have supper with me this evening? I could pick you up at six thirty?"

Julia smiled. "I would be delighted to have supper with you. Six-thirty it is."

"I look forward to it," Adam confirmed, as she took her place behind the front desk. Flashing a huge grin, he turned to leave.

"Adam," she called after him. "I've missed… It's good to see you."

His heart soared. She missed him.

Now, how was he going to entertain himself for the rest of the day?

Deciding on dinner at Lancaster's, that is where his feet took him. Following the meal, he made arrangements for him, Owens, and Whitten to bunk there for the night. Then he stopped by the newspaper office to pick up the most recent addition of the *Miner*. While the air was somewhat cool, the bright sun warmed him enough that he chanced finding a sunny spot in the square to sit and read the paper.

When he finished reading the paper, Adam had plenty of time to think. Julia seemed genuinely pleased to see him. Perhaps he would ask her tonight if she would be agreeable to courting. It was risky. She could say no. She might not be ready. She might be holding on to the past. But, on her birthday and today, she seemed to be in much better spirits. Perhaps she was letting go. Then, if she said yes, he would ask Will's permission.

Julia could hardly wait for six-thirty to come. When she first realized Adam was there, her heart started racing. Her happiness at seeing him had not diminished one bit throughout her busy day. She only had another hour until Mr. Hamilton would take over.

I can't believe he's here. I've missed him so much. Julia's thoughts surprised her when she realized just how often she thought of him since her birthday six weeks ago. Every evening when she returned to her small room, she picked up the horse carving. Each time she turned it over in her hands, she noticed some new detail she hadn't seen before. He must have spent hours making it for her.

The next hour flew by in a flurry of requests from guests, with new ones checking in or others checking out or requests for supper reservations. One gentleman even had a complaint about the size of the rooms, as if she could do anything about that. She listened sympathetically and eventually the man accepted the room and went about his business.

Glancing at the clock, she noticed it was nearly a quarter after six. Where was Mr. Hamilton?

A few minutes later he finally appeared. "I'm sorry I was delayed, Miss Colter. Why don't you go ahead and get supper and I'll take over."

She smiled and practically ran down the hall to her room. She only had ten minutes before Adam arrived. Changing out of her worn shirt and skirt, Julia donned her navy blue dress. Checking her appearance in the mirror above her dresser, she snorted in disgust. Her hair would never do—all frizzed from a busy day. Brushing out the mass of light brown curls, she loosely twisted it into a chignon at the base of her neck. Pinching her cheeks for some color, she closed the door behind her and ran down the hall.

Slowing her pace to a more ladylike walk, Julia scanned the lobby. Adam stood, breaking into a broad toothy smile when their eyes met. He covered the distance between them. Taking her hand in his, he placed a gentle kiss on top, sending tingles up her arm.

"You look beautiful," he whispered.

She felt heat rise to her cheeks as she took his offered arm.

Adam led her from the hotel. "I thought if you'd like, we could try the Osborn's restaurant."

Even in the fading light of day, he looked handsome with his golden hair parted to one side.

"That would be wonderful."

As he led her across the square, she asked, "How are things at the ranch?"

"Will is irritating Hannah with his constant worrying. Each day he tries to get her to let Rosa do more of the work and to rest." He chuckled. "At dinner, she wags her finger at him and tells him she can handle things. He leaves it alone until the next day."

Julia giggled. "He does have a way of being a bit overprotective."

He paused, holding the door open. She stepped in and was pleasantly surprised by the restaurant. While nothing compared to some of the finer places to dine in Texas, it was quaint. The tables were placed in an orderly fashion throughout the room, seating two to four people. There were candles in the center of each table, casting a welcoming glow. The delicious smell of some sort of beef cooking wafted through the air. Julia wondered if it was Colter beef.

"Welcome," a middle aged man greeted them warmly. "I'm Mr. Osborn. Will it be just the two of you this evening?"

At Adam's nod, Mr. Osborn led them to a table near the back. When Adam held her chair, she rewarded him with a soft smile, enjoying the special attention he lavished on her this evening.

Once he took his seat, Mr. Osborn outlined the food offerings. Both Adam and Julia selected the beef steaks, fried potatoes, and carrots, with the promise to save room for Mrs. Osborn's peach cobbler.

When Mr. Osborn left, Julia said, "Thank you again, Adam, for the lovely birthday gift. I don't feel quite as homesick when I look at it."

"Do you miss being on the ranch, then?"

She sighed. "Yes. I miss the wide open space, the smell of horses, and the occasional unsanctioned ride." She laughed.

Adam chuckled. "I'm sure your brother doesn't miss that."

"I'm sure you're right."

"Maybe I could come by next week or the week after with Annabel and we could explore the area?" Adam suggested.

Julia's excitement rose. How she would love to ride again. "I would really enjoy that. I usually have Wednesdays off."

"Next Wednesday, then."

Mr. Osborn brought the two plates of very delicious looking food. Once placed in front of the two diners, Adam reached for Julia's hand and said grace. She barely heard the words, as she was so acutely aware of his touch.

"How is Percy coming along?" she asked.

"He is one smart horse. Right now I'm leaning towards training him for ranching, although he is much too young for a final decision. He reminds me of Will's stallion Jackson, when he was two years."

"So my brother picked a few good horses then?"

"More than just a few good ones. I doubt I could have picked better myself—especially in such unsettled territory."

Finishing the last of bite of her beef steak, she swallowed.

Referring to his job at the ranch, she asked, "Is this everything you dreamed it would be?"

He grew pensive. "I'm finding my dreams have changed."

His answer was not what she expected, nor was his intense gaze.

"You don't want to train horses any longer?" she asked, confused.

"Oh, I could never see myself doing anything else. I love training horses. We have the makings of a quality operation out at the ranch."

"Then what did you mean when you said your dreams were changing?"

Adam laid his fork down on the table and clasped her hand. He rubbed his thumb lightly over her knuckles. Julia's heart picked up pace and she very nearly held her breath. When he looked into her eyes, she saw deep emotion there.

His words were soft, like gentle rain, when he spoke, "Would you... Julia, I would like to court you, if the idea pleases you."

She blinked. Was she part of his changing dreams? His hand now covered hers, but she sat motionless. *He wants to court me.* But courtship often leads to marriage. If that was where this was going, she would have to tell him what really happened in Texas. Could she do that? Would she really have to tell him? How would he react if he knew?

Her heart wanted to say yes to Adam, but her mind was warning her it would only end in pain for both of them. *Does it have to?* Her heart cried.

When she saw Adam's expression begin to change from hopeful to disappointment, she finally spoke. "Yes, Adam, the idea pleases me."

"Then I will speak with your brother tomorrow," Adam said, beaming.

I hope you don't regret this, Julia. Please don't let this end in more pain and brokenness.

Chapter 29

At first, when Julia did not respond to his question last night, Adam thought he misread her completely. He thought perhaps she was not interested in him, or that she was still mired in the past. When she finally said yes, he could have danced right there in that restaurant. He hoped she would feel the same when he returned next week.

Again, he almost kissed her when he led her back to the hotel. But, he wanted to get Will's permission to court her first. As much as his heart wanted to rush things, his head reminded him he still needed to tread carefully.

Buckling the saddle on his horse, Adam checked the straps a second time, an old habit. He led the horse from the Lancaster's small stable across the square to the mercantile to pick up a few things.

Mr. Young greeted him as he entered and then continued the conversation he was having with another patron. "Farming, you say. Well, there's lots of good land still available in the area for homesteading."

"I am looking for something with a good water supply, but not too far from town," the farmer said.

"Well, this here might be someone you want to talk to," Mr. Young said pointing to Adam. "Adam Larson, this is Jacob Morgan."

Adam shook his hand. Remembering Will mentioned wanting to bring on a farmer for the horse feed, Adam said, "There is some good farmland near Colter Ranch, where I work. Will Colter, my boss, is looking for someone who might be willing to discuss a deal to provide horse feed for our training business. I'm not sure what terms he would negotiate, but if you are interested, come out to the ranch and speak with him."

Jacob Morgan looked thoughtful, considering the idea. "How far is the ranch from town?"

"Not more than five miles northeast of here," Adam replied.

"Well, I think I might just head out there tomorrow and take a look."

"You are welcome to travel with me today. While we have not run into any trouble with the Apaches for a while, it is always better to travel in larger numbers."

"My wife and daughters would need to come too."

Adam and Jacob agreed to leave for the ranch in an hour, meeting near the town square. Leaving Jacob in the store, Adam walked toward the hotel, hoping to get a few more minutes with Julia. When he entered the building, she looked up from the front desk.

"Adam, good morning." Her smile made her blue eyes sparkle.

"Julia." Moving closer to the desk, he was grateful she was not busy. "I thought I would stop by and say goodbye before heading back to the ranch."

"I'm glad you did. I was wondering if you would take this." She handed him an envelope. "To Will and Hannah for me."

"Of course. You must have been up late writing." Taking her hand in his, he resigned himself to a quick brush of his lips on the back of her hand instead of the kiss he dreamed about. "I'll see you on Wednesday then."

"I'm looking forward to it."

He released her hand then walked to the door. Turning to glance back, she smiled and waved. It warmed his heart to see her so happy.

Having not seen Owens or Whitten this morning, Adam went back to Lancaster's to see if they were done sleeping off all the alcohol they consumed. He was pleased to find them dressing, albeit sluggishly. He told them they would have company on the trip back to the ranch. Owens started to complain, but Adam just walked away, tired of the constant friction. Hopefully, he would tame his tongue in front of the farmer and his family.

At the appointed time, the Morgan family arrived at the square in their beat up wagon. Jacob looked to be close in age to Will and was equally as fit. Lucy Morgan seemed rather outgoing and was a few years younger than her husband. She introduced their two daughters to Adam. Sarah was ten and Becky was eight.

Once introductions were complete, Adam led the way back to

Colter Ranch. The Morgans followed him. Owens and Whitten brought up the rear at a relatively lackadaisical pace.

When they topped the last hill before heading down to the ranch, he heard Lucy's gasp, "Oh my. If that isn't the prettiest piece of land you ever saw, Jacob!"

Adam smiled at her comment. When he first saw the valley below, he knew he would be content to live out his days here. More and more, he didn't want to do that alone. Shaking away the thoughts of Julia, Adam saw movement in front of the ranch house. Likely Will and Hannah heard the unexpected wagon approaching.

The Morgans parked the wagon in front of the ranch house. Adam led his horse to the hitching post and dismounted.

"Will," Adam said. "This is Jacob and Lucy Morgan and their two daughters, Sarah and Becky. Jacob is interested in homesteading somewhere not too far from town. I thought you might like to speak with him."

"Pleased to meet you," Will said extending his hand.

After introductions were made, Adam offered to take care of the Morgans oxen. As he started to unhitch them, he remembered the letter from Julia in his pocket. Turning to catch Hannah before she turned into the ranch house, he handed her the letter.

"It's from Julia."

Hannah, while surprised at the unexpected guests, instantly warmed to Lucy, who was quite excited when she noticed Hannah's bulging belly. Rubbing her lower back, Hannah motioned for the Morgans to follow her and Will inside.

Retrieving a plate of cookies, with milk for the girls, and coffee for the adults, she placed the items on the table.

Will spoke first. "Jacob, tell me what brings you to Colter Ranch?"

"Adam mentioned you might be interested in discussing an arrangement for a farmer to provide feed for your horses. Is that true?"

"Yes, in fact I considered advertising in the mercantile, but had yet to do so. Are you interested in homesteading your own farm, or were you looking to lease land?"

"I'd like to homestead my own farm, but I did have plans for the full one hundred and sixty acres, so I am not sure how it would work to section off an area for horse feed. How many horses do you have?"

"Well over forty at this point. I'm looking to increase that number as Adam and I build up the horse training and breeding business."

"Oh," Jacob said his concern showing. "That is much larger than I expected."

Hannah smiled to herself when she saw how Will tried to quickly assuage Jacob's fears. "I think we could work out some arrangement where I could provide the land necessary for growing the horse feed if you would farm it." Will smiled sheepishly. "While I love working with livestock, I would be terrible at farming."

Jacob and Lucy both chuckled at his comment. "I think that sounds like an excellent arrangement."

Seeing the coffee mugs were empty, Hannah rose to get more coffee. As she refilled the cups, Will and Jacob discussed possible farm sites near the Colter property. Over the last year, Will amassed a rather large track of land as was allowed for cattle ranchers. He spoke of a section on the far eastern edge of the property, where he rarely took the cattle, as the ideal location for the farmland. There were no other settlers nearby, so the Morgans would be able to homestead adjacent to the section.

"Shall we ride out and look at the land?" Will asked.

"Lucy, will you and the girls be fine for an hour or so?" Jacob asked his wife.

Lucy smiled at Hannah. "I'm sure we will be in excellent care."

As Will and Jacob left, Hannah turned to Lucy. "So, what brought you all the way to the Arizona Territory?"

Lucy's laugh had a light airy quality to it. "I think it has more to do with Jacob's sense of adventure than anything else. He has dreamed for years of owning his own land. Back in Indiana, his older brother will inherit the family farm. Unfortunately, there was no land left near his family or mine. So, we decided if we had to make a move, why not find some place where land was plentiful. I don't exactly recall how we found out about the Arizona Territory. I just remember hearing about the milder weather and thinking how nice it must be here. I have to tell you, I am not disappointed so far."

Hannah laughed. "Yes, while we do get snow in the winters, it is nothing like the bitter cold in Ohio."

"Ohio? I thought the lilt to your husband's voice sounded more like Texas."

"Oh, you are absolutely right, Will is from Texas and I am from Ohio. We met here and married last September."

"My, you certainly did not waste any time starting your family," Lucy teased, endearing her more to Hannah.

"No." She chuckled. "We certainly did not."

"How is it that you ended up in Arizona?" Lucy asked. "Because I would not believe it if you told me you came out here on your own."

Hannah told her story about how she and Drew came west and about his death. She sighed. It was not nearly so difficult while living in Will's love to talk about her grief over the loss of Drew.

"I'm sorry," Lucy's sympathy was genuine. "It is difficult to go through such grief."

Hannah waited, sensing the woman experienced some of her own.

"But," Lucy continued, "I see you are very much in love with your husband. Strange how God has a way of turning things around."

"Mama," Becky, the younger of the two girls interrupted. "Can we go play outside?"

Lucy turned to Hannah. "Is it safe?"

"Yes. If they stay near the house they will be fine. If you would like, we can sit on a blanket out near the lake and enjoy the sun."

"That would be lovely. Come on girls," Lucy said, taking each of her daughters by the hand.

As Hannah spread out the blanket in her favorite spot, Sarah and Becky played a game of tag, which was rather interesting with only the two of them. Trying to figure out how to make her way to the ground as large as she felt, she was grateful when Lucy assisted her.

"I remember feeling huge around five months with my son," Lucy said, her voice taking on a faraway quality. "Then I just kept getting bigger." She smiled at Hannah and took a seat next to her on the blanket.

"Your son?"

"Yes. We had a son several years after Becky. He would have been five this summer. He died from measles last year. Both of the girls and Jake got the measles at the same time. The girls bounced back quickly, but Jake did not." A tear trickled down Lucy's check, and she quickly wiped it away.

"I'm so sorry. That must have been painful to watch your son die." Hannah placed her hand over her new friend's hand, giving a soft squeeze.

"It was. Jacob was devastated. He longed to have a son and was thrilled when little Jake arrived. Oh, don't misunderstand—he loves the girls with all of his heart. But, he wanted a son to pass on his heritage, his name. Men are funny about that. They will love and cherish and protect their little girls, but the connection between father and son is sacred." Lucy sniffed. "Forgive me, Hannah. Here we have only just met and I'm pouring out all my sorrows to you."

"Don't think anything of it. We each have our share of sorrows that we carry, right along with the joys. If I learned anything from Drew's passing, it is to trust God and embrace where he has put me."

"Such wisdom from such a young woman."

"Ah, the journey west aged me beyond my twenty three years," Hannah said, knowing it was true.

She watched as Becky squealed trying to out-run her older sister. She hoped her children would be healthy, this baby especially, and that they would live a long, satisfying life. That nagging fear of losing the baby seeped into her heart again. While she lost the first baby much earlier, she sometimes feared losing this one. The way Will fretted about her made the feeling worse. He would be crushed if this child died.

Lucy said something, but Hannah missed it. "Hmm?"

"It looks like our husbands have returned. I certainly hope they have reached an agreement. I would love to be neighbors with you." Lucy stood. Holding her arm out, she helped Hannah to her feet.

A few minutes later, the Morgans oxen were hitched back to their wagon. Will said he would have some papers drawn up, meaning Hannah would write what he still could not, and the two men would review and sign them tomorrow. Then Will and Jacob would ride to town in the next week or so to ask the surveyor to survey the land and finalize Jacob's homestead claim. As the family drove off to the east to their new home, Hannah waved. It would be nice to have a friend nearby.

Looping her arm in Will's, Hannah entered the ranch house with her husband. "Shall I read Julia's letter?"

"I almost forgot about it," Will said.

Taking a seat at the table, Hannah opened the letter and began to read it.

> *Dear Will and Hannah,*
>
> *Thank you again for coming for my birthday all those weeks ago. I was very touched that you remembered.*
>
> *While things are going well here, I must say there are things I miss about being on the ranch. Other than the two of you, I miss riding and working with the horses. Hopefully, Adam has spoken to you before you read this. If not, I am sorry for things being out of order. I am quite excited that he is returning next week to take me riding.*
>
> *Despite missing the ranch, I feel I am where I need to be for now. I hope you will both consider coming to the church that meets at Lancaster's on Sunday mornings. I know life on the ranch can be busy. But, Will, it is truly no farther than what we traveled to attend service back in Texas. Reverend Page is a gifted preacher and we are fortunate he has chosen not to ride a circuit and that we get to share in his wise messages weekly.*
>
> *Well, I suppose that is enough sisterly nagging for now. I miss you both.*
>
> *Julia*

Hannah smiled at the hidden messages. Something was changing in Julia, especially since she acknowledged she missed Will. Perhaps her heart was healing.

"What did she say about Adam?" Will asked, concern wrinkling his forehead.

"That he would be speaking to us. Perhaps you should invite him to have supper with us this evening," Hannah suggested.

Adam nervously walked towards the ranch house for supper, instead of the bunkhouse. He was surprised when Will came to him after the Morgans left and asked him to join them for supper. Other than his first evening on the ranch, he only joined them for the midday meal, so this was very much out of the ordinary.

"Come in, Adam," Hannah said when he knocked on the door.

"Please, sit," Will said motioning to the seat across from Hannah. Then he took his seat at the head of the table and blessed the meal.

Adam shifted uncomfortably in his chair. While he intended to bring up the topic of courting Julia during the meal, he hesitated to start the conversation, deferring to whatever reason Will might have had.

"Adam," Will started after swallowing a bite of butter slathered biscuit. "Thank you for bringing the letter from Julia. I wish to discuss that letter with you."

His heart pounded in his chest. What had Julia said?

"I understand, from her letter that you have something you want to discuss with us. We thought we would give you that opportunity this evening."

Still wondering what Julia said, Adam cleared his throat. "I hoped to discuss this with you when I returned this afternoon."

When he stopped, Hannah encouraged him with a smile. "Go on."

"Will, I would like your permission to court Julia," he blurted out. He bit back a frustrated groan. This was not exactly the way he imagined this conversation.

"You have discussed this with, Julia?" Will asked, smiling.

Relieved that Will was not about to deck him, he answered, "Yes and she agreed. I apologize for speaking with her first, before asking your permission."

Will chuckled and Adam grew confused. "Things are different out west. I'm not offended in the least that you discussed it with Julia first. In fact, I'm pleased you did."

Turning more serious, he continued, "The circumstances

surrounding Julia's departure from Texas concern me enough that I think she should decide for herself if she is ready for courting. If she were still living here at the ranch, I might think differently. But, her months away from here seem to have done her good and I believe she is capable of making that decision."

Adam smiled, glad that Julia already had.

"Though I'm happy she agreed, I will offer some advice. She's been hurt badly, which is for her to speak of." Will shifted his gaze from Adam to Hannah, almost as if he was looking for her permission for something. "When she does tell you, Adam, don't blame her for what she says or how she reacts."

"Will is right. There is more to the situation with Julia than you know. And it may be difficult to hear. We tell you this not to discourage you, but to prepare you."

Adam's smile faded. What could be so terrible that both Will and Hannah would offer such strong warnings? He should be overjoyed at their blessing, but dread took root instead.

Chapter 30

Fort Whipple, Arizona Territory

March 6, 1865

Sergeant Thomas Anderson arrived at Fort Whipple at last. The fort was nothing more than a small outpost, one of the smallest on his westward journey. From Tennessee, he stopped at every fort in Kansas, Colorado, and New Mexico. Each one sent him on to the next with the instruction to report to the major in charge of the fort. He should not have been surprised, as the major general told him he would be going all the way to the Arizona Territory.

As Thomas dismounted his mare, his frustration rose. These small forts were far from the front lines, far from the action. He was a fast rider, so he was able to cover the vast distance in two short months. He had not stayed at any one fort more than overnight. But, would not a fast rider be more valuable on the front lines of the war delivering dispatches than riding from fort to fort in the West?

Handing his mare off to the man at the corral, Thomas asked for directions to the major's quarters. Unlike the general's quarters, there was no guard posted at the entrance to the small cabin structure. Knocking on the door, Thomas opened it when he heard an answer.

"Sergeant Thomas Anderson, reporting, with a dispatch, sir," he said standing straight and tall.

Taking the dispatch from him, the major answered, "Thank you. Take a seat."

He did as instructed while the nameless major read the missive. He experienced something similar at each fort along the way—commanded by a major who failed to introduce himself, less formal than any officer back in the war.

When the major finished reading, he looked up at Thomas. His gaze scrutinizing, he said, "All the way from Major General Smith in Tennessee, huh? Highly unusual."

Those two words could describe so much more than just his present circumstance. Nothing about the last two years of Thomas's life had been usual. *Providence, Tommy, Providence.* He heard Mixford's voice clearly in his head. He resisted the urge to snort. What could Providence possibly want with him?

"It says here that you are to be assigned to run military mail from our fort to Fort Wingate in New Mexico. I am assuming by the bag," he said pointing to Thomas's saddle bag at his feet, "that you are coming most recently from Wingate?"

"Yes, sir."

"Were you aware of these orders?"

"No, sir."

"Please, sergeant, speak your mind. You will find things a bit different here," the major instructed, appearing annoyed by his succinct answers.

Thomas hesitated, not certain what he was expected to say. "Sir, I rode dispatch for much of the last year, first for Colonel Woods, then for Major General Smith. I am capable of riding courier to wherever you see fit to assign me. Sir."

"Indeed, the letter states as much. It also states that there are some unusual circumstances surrounding your enlistment and service, which only recently came to the major general's attention. It says here that those circumstances were what led to his decision to send you west. Would you care to enlighten me, Sergeant?"

Thomas hoped he kept the surprise from his face. He did not know Major General Smith knew of his background. When had he discovered it? Regardless, it seems his past motivated Smith to be done with him. The sting of the truth hurt more than he cared to admit. He had been faithful, loyal, even risking his life for the Union. Had that service meant nothing?

"Sir, what you say is true," he started. "I was young and stupid when I got into trouble with the law. The judge who sentenced me knew men were needed on the front lines. His son, being an officer, agreed to enlist me for service with his regiment until three years transpired or the war ends, whichever comes first. After serving with that regiment for a time, I was transferred to the 89th Indiana Regiment. No explanation was given to me for the transfer.

"Then, while serving on the front lines, a dispatcher was killed before my eyes. With his dying breath, he asked me to carry the message on. I am an excellent rider, so I did as he asked. The dispatch proved to be critical and as a reward for my actions, I was permanently assigned as a dispatcher. That is, until Major General Smith sent me west."

Listening to himself tell the story, Thomas thought it sounded ridiculous. Who would believe such a thing? Yet, it was the truth and it was his life.

"Well, what you say matches the account before me," the major replied, seeming satisfied with his answer. "Sergeant, see the captain for your quarters assignment. Then, tomorrow you will be starting your new job as courier between here and Wingate. You will be expected to ride between the two forts twice per month, one week to get there, one week to return. You will have only one day's rest at Wingate and two or three days here between each run. It is a grueling position, but one in which I am confident you will excel. You are dismissed." He finished with the wave of his hand.

Thomas stood and did as instructed, taking his saddle bags with him. The captain showed him to a tent and pointed out the mess tent and where he should take the military mail. Deciding the mail was most important, he delivered it to another sergeant standing behind the counter of the small supply cabin. Before taking his leave, he asked about mail going to civilian towns throughout the territory. The sergeant told him there was a non-military express rider that came up to the fort every other week to take personal letters heading south or further west.

Walking back to his tent, he tried to keep his discouragement at bay. He could not believe that the major general sent him all the way out here to the middle of nowhere to be a courier across Indian infested desert. He never did anything to warrant a lack of trust from the major general, yet here he was.

Drew. He thought of his brother again. Maybe this would be his opportunity to find Drew without waiting for the end of the war. Taking a sheet of paper from his bag, Thomas sat on the edge of his cot, trying to balance the ink well, quill, and paper on the flat back side of his saddle bag.

Dear Drew,

I am writing to you from Fort Whipple, near Prescott in the Arizona Territory. Odd that I find myself in a situation where I should be stationed in the West.
I have much to discuss with you and hope that you will give me the opportunity to do so, either by coming to the fort if you can, or by letter.
I hope this finds you and Hannah well.

Your humbled brother,

Sergeant Thomas Anderson

He looked the brief note over twice before deciding to seal it. It seemed so inadequate—not expressing his desire for forgiveness and not mentioning any more details of his journey. He did not want to write about these things. Instead, he preferred to speak face to face with Drew. He wanted to look into his eyes and weigh his reaction.

He hoped this letter would be well received. Putting the stopper back on the ink well, he secured his writing supplies. Standing, he made his way back to the sergeant at the supply cabin.

The sergeant said, "This should arrive in the next week, what with the express rider expected tomorrow morning. Good timing."

Or Providence. Thomas chided himself. He did not believe in Providence. It was Mixford's belief not his. At least that is what he tried to convince himself.

Leaving his thoughts and tent behind, he walked to the mess tent. There was a large line out the door, indicating he arrived at the tail end of the meal. Taking a spot in line, the older man in front of him turned to look at him.

"You're new here aren't you?" he asked.

"Sergeant Thomas Anderson."

"Anderson, huh?" the man paused scrutinizing Thomas carefully. "I'm Sergeant Bixley, but most the men just call me Bixley."

Thomas smiled. This Bixley reminded him a bit of Mixford.

"So, Anderson, how'd ya end up stationed all the way out here?" Bixley asked.

"It's a long story. I'll be leaving in the morning to courier mail to Wingate, and then back again."

"Ah, so you're the new courier," Bixley said, all trace of jesting disappeared from his face. "Let's hope you outlast the previous one."

They moved forward in the line, but were still some distance from the grub. "What do you mean outlast?"

"Hate to be the bearer of bad news, Anderson, but this here job ain't exactly one you'll grow old doin'. Last courier was killed on his first ride. One before that lasted a month. If you ain't a prayin' man, you might consider it."

Perhaps the West was not as boring as he thought. Knowledge would keep him alive, so he tried to gain a better understanding of what he would face. "And how did all of these couriers die?"

Bixley looked at him cocking one eyebrow up. "If it ain't the Injuns, which it usually is, then it'll be the cold or the heat or the lack of water. One man died 'cause his horse went lame and he ran outta water."

"Indians, you say?"

"'Round here, it's Johnny Apache you gotta watch out for. Then Navajos as you get closer to New Mexico. They like picking off the couriers because they're an easy target and it irritates the whites."

Thomas rubbed his hand across his chin. He better learn the signs of these Apaches and Navajos quickly, as well as the terrain, if he hoped to survive this job. Holding out his plate to the young Mexican woman serving, he decided to pry as much information from Bixley as possible during the meal. He followed the much older sergeant to a bench and sat next to him.

Throughout the rest of the meal, he learned a great deal about the dangers he would face. He learned where the best and most reliable water sources were. He learned to watch for rattlesnakes. Bixley even gave him tips about one of the cactus that could be found sometimes in the forests called prickly pear. Apparently the pads, once removed of the spurs, were safe to eat. He memorized the description and would write it in his journal once he returned to his tent. Bixley also gave him tips on what route to take and what areas the Indians were known to hide in. By the time the meal concluded, Thomas felt more at ease with the assignment. He wondered if the other couriers had been equally prepared.

Taking his leave, he returned to his tent. He retired, hoping an early start tomorrow would give him more time on the trail.

The next morning, Thomas saddled his mare and left just after sunrise. When he reported to the major for his assignment, the major looked as if he just rolled from bed. He was again struck by Major Willis's lack of military etiquette. He had only learned of the major's name from Bixley the night before.

Mounting his horse, he pointed her in a northerly direction towards Point of Rocks. That was one of the many areas he would need to remain alert, as the large boulders acted like a natural fort. According to Bixley, the Apaches would often hide in between the boulders. From there, he would take Hell's Canyon up to Pishon Road. Pishon Road mostly followed the thirty-fifth parallel across the wide open plains. The first section, when heading east, was covered in thick pine forests and skirted between several mountains. The second two-thirds of the road opened up to flat plains.

Bixley kindly suggested a few campsites along the way. Thomas made notes, figuring he would have to stop for at least three to four nights on the trail each way. He planned to keep an eye out for an alternate campsite as well, since it would be wise to vary his route, especially if he was ever followed.

The first night, he camped on the western edge of the San Francisco Peaks, having made better progress than other couriers before him. Finding a safe place, Thomas cared for his horse then fed himself. The temperature was cool, but he opted against building a fire, just in case any natives watched.

The next day, he made excellent progress again, covering a great deal of the trail over the flatlands. Few landmarks varied the view. As he neared the Little Colorado River to look for a suitable campsite, a movement ahead off to his right caught his attention. Thomas held the reins in one hand and reached for his rifle in the other. There it was again. Even in the fading light, he clearly saw a man covered in tan hide.

His heart pounded rapidly in his chest. Was this one of the Apaches or Navajos Bixley mentioned? As far as he could tell, the man had not seen him. He hoped the man did not smell or hear him either. Thomas sat frozen on his mare until the man disappeared from his sight.

The sun was nearly set, but after seeing the man, he did not feel comfortable making camp here. He pressed on despite the darkening sky. The half-moon gave enough light to see the trail in front of him. After another five miles or so, he stopped, fed the mare and rested until daylight.

The next morning, Thomas woke to the feeling he was being watched. He slowly lifted his head, scanning the empty flatlands around him. Other than a slight dip in the land about twenty yards south, there was nothing but him, his horse, and open flat grasslands. Brushing the dirt from his pants, he stood and mounted his mare.

After riding for several hours, the foreboding feeling would not leave him. He turned around in his saddle to scan the trail behind him. There was a puff of dust, much like what his horse was kicking up, about two or three hundred yards behind him. Looking ahead, he found little cover. It would be near nightfall by the time he left the flatlands.

Not much he could do about that. Perhaps Providence would smile on him again. Shaking his head, Thomas pushed the idea from his mind. Providence didn't control him.

Was it possible the rider did not have sinister intent? Was it an Apache, or could it be someone else? Well, either way, he thought the rider would be on him within an hour of when he stopped for the night.

As the sun hung low in the sky, he came across an area where the ground dipped some. Hopefully it was enough to provide him some cover from the rider, and it would allow him some measure of defense. Leaving his horse loose, Thomas laid flat on his stomach at a vantage point where he could not be seen.

He stared at the approaching rider. The uniformed man was only a corporal. As the rider approached, Thomas carefully rose to his feet, keeping his gun handy. The time he spent in the war made him wary to believe all was as it appeared. Clearing his throat, he got the corporal's attention.

"What are you doing out here?" Thomas asked.

"Sergeant?" the young man asked pulling his horse to a stop. "I've been trying to catch up to you for the past two days. I was supposed to leave with you from the fort."

If he was to have a traveling companion, surely the major would have told him. His hair stood on end on the back of his neck.

As the unmistakable sound of a gun being cocked clicked behind him, Thomas noticed the dried blood and open hole on the corporal's uniform. Adrenaline kicked in as the danger of the situation registered.

The corporal dismounted the horse and stood in front of him. The man behind him shoved the barrel of the gun flush against his back. When the corporal spoke nonsensical words to the man at Thomas's back, he was certain these men were Indians.

He had to get out of here.

Slowly he glanced over his shoulder. Only one man stood behind him.

Thomas brought the butt of his rifle up in a sharp movement, surprising the man behind him. It connected with the man's chin, sending the cocked gun flying. The gun went off as it flew through the air. The corporal scrambled for the gun. Thomas aimed and fired his rifle. The bullet tore through the corporal's chest, shattering the man's rib cage. The victim's eyes were wide with fear as he fell limp toward the ground—the shot fatal.

Heart beating rapidly, Thomas spun around to the other man. The man rose with knife in hand. As he lunged towards him, Thomas fired his pistol. The bullet hit the aggressor right between his eyes. The force knocked him backwards to the ground.

Thomas looked around to make sure he was alone. Only his horse and the dead corporal's horse were standing. He mounted his horse, his blood still fiercely tearing through his veins. With shaky hands, he slid his rifle back in its sheath. That was much too close.

As he approached the corporal's horse, he recognized the Union saddle. Perhaps it belonged to one of the previous couriers. Looping the reins forward, he led the horse behind his own.

Given the unexpected encounter, he decided to ride for two more hours before making camp. And here he thought the West would be unadventurous.

Chapter 31

Prescott

March 8, 1865

"You know, you are going to wear a hole in the floor with all of your pacing, Miss Colter," Mr. Hamilton said.

Julia smiled at his teasing and took a seat in the lobby. Wearing her tan split skirt, a white shirt, and a ribbon holding her hair back, she was eager for Adam to arrive. The last week she thought of this outing daily. She missed the freedom of riding.

The door creaked open and there before her stood a grinning, handsome Adam Larson. Her pulse quickened at the sight of him and she flashed him a big smile.

"I see you're ready to go," he teased her.

Standing she headed straight for the door. He got there just in time to open it for her.

"I guess you're eager to be on the way," he said as he followed behind her.

"Good morning, Adam," she finally greeted him sweetly before mounting her horse without assistance.

He chuckled. "Oh, Julia. If I didn't know better, I might think you missed Annabel more than you missed me."

She felt a little prick at his comment. There might have been some truth to his observation. After he mounted his horse, she stopped the mare beside him. Reaching out her hand to take his, she gave a gentle squeeze. "I won't lie, Adam, I have missed riding a great deal."

At his mock look of hurt, she added, "But, I've missed you more. Where are we headed for the day?"

"I thought we could ride along Granite Creek or up towards the butte."

"Let's ride to the butte," she suggested.

"After you." He motioned for her to take the lead.

She pointed the mare west heading out of town. They rode in silence for some distance, until they came to a small clearing near the base of the butte canopied by several tall pines. Julia stopped, allowing Adam to pull up next to her.

"This looks like a nice place to rest," she said.

He smiled and dismounted his horse. Walking to her, he said, "Please, allow me."

Julia giggled, knowing he was asking her to let him assist her down from her horse—something she rarely accepted assistance with. When he placed his hands on her waist, her breath left in a dizzying rush. She braced her hands on his shoulders as he slowly eased her down. He kept his hands on her waist even after her feet touched the ground.

Her breath caught when she looked into his beautiful green eyes. Deep love and longing shone there, before he drew her closer.

"Oh, Julia," he whispered, pausing just inches from her face. The effect sent her pulse racing with anticipation.

Then he closed the distance, bringing his lips down on hers. She closed her eyes and leaned against his strong frame. His kiss was sweet and gentle, holding a promise of giving, not taking. As she looped her arms around his neck, he pressed closer.

Every sense heightened. The faint smell of horses lingered on his skin. She ran one hand along his jaw line, so smooth to her touch.

The gentleness in his kiss awakened a longing within her. She wanted to be near him, to drink in his love in the safety of his embrace. Her heart opened and she realized she loved him.

As she responded to his kiss, she felt a light tug near her hair before it fell loose. Adam ran his fingers through her hair, the intimate touch sending fire through her veins. His closeness was intoxicating. She wanted to remain here with him all day.

Adam breathed deeply of the light vanilla scent he associated with Julia. When she responded to his kiss it opened the flood of emotion he kept hidden before. He started to deepen his kiss, running his fingers through her soft brown curls. He dreamed of doing this so many times. She tasted so sweet. Even though his mind told him to slow down, he continued to kiss her ardently.

When she leaned back and placed her hand on his chest, he stopped, breathless.

"Julia," he said, his voice husky. Emboldened by the look of love in her eyes, he blurted out, "I love you. I want you to be my wife."

Her eyes went dark with fear and she dropped her arms to her side, stepping away from his embrace. He felt a sinking feeling in his gut as he let her go. She took another step back into the flank of her horse before she stepped sideways.

What had he done?

She began to pace back and forth. That gnawing feeling in his stomach worsened. What kind of fool was he to make such a bold declaration and so soon? While it was true and he meant it from his heart, he knew looking at her agitated state that it had been much too soon for her. Perhaps this was what Will tried to warn him of?

At last, she stopped pacing and turned to face him, keeping her distance. The pain was obvious in her eyes. It pierced him to know he caused it, though he did not understand why.

"Adam… I need to… You should know…" she started to speak several times, each making no sense. Wringing her hands, she looked away.

"Here," he said leading her to a large bolder. "Sit."

When she sat, he released her hand and kneeled on the ground before her.

"You cannot want me to be your wife."

Adam was confused. Isn't that normally where courting led? What was she talking about?

"At least…" Her voice softened, "You will not want to once I tell you what I have to say."

"There is nothing you could say that would change my mind. I may have spoken out of turn, but I meant what I said." He reached for her hand, but she clasped her hands together, resting them on her knees.

"You do not know what you are talking about."

When he started to tell her again that his feelings would not change, she held up a hand to stop him.

"Let me finish. You need to know what happened that night we left Texas."

Adam's heart raced. Swallowing the lump in his throat, he nodded for her to continue.

"That night, Reuben was so angry with me. I refused another lecherous suitor and ruined his greedy plans of using me to further his wealth.

"At first, I thought he would come and beat me, like he did the day you came to get your horse. I waited fearfully, but he never came. Then, after everyone in the house was asleep, he came home."

She looked away, hands trembling. "He was drunk and angry. He burst through the door of my room. Then he…" Her voice broke and her whole body shook.

His heart tore watching her relive this. He tried to take her hand again, to offer some comfort, but she only stiffened at his touch.

"He…forced himself on me. I tried…to fight. But he pinned me down. I was not strong enough."

Julia turned and held his gaze for a minute, tears streaming down her face. "He raped me…"

"I am ruined."

Tears gathered in his eyes as the reality of what she said sank in. Reuben had raped his own sister. Anger rose in him. He wanted to kill that wretched man for what he did. Clenching his fist, he looked at her and realized his anger was frightening her. She needed him.

Exhaling slowly, he calmed his emotions. "This doesn't change how I feel. I love you."

He took both of her hands in his, but she shook them free again.

"Don't you see," she said, her shoulders slumped in defeat. "I am ruined."

She choked on a sob then leaped to her feet.

"You deserve so much better, someone pure and undefiled."

Before he could react, she mounted her horse and rode off toward town.

Still kneeling on the ground in front of the now empty boulder, Adam placed his head in his hands and wept. He wept for Julia and the pain she still carried. He wept that she thought he would love her less. Most of all, he wept because he knew he just destroyed any hope of marrying the woman he loved.

Julia rode Annabel at a hard pace, dodging trees. The mare's heavy breathing mimicked her own. Tears moistened her cheeks, causing her loose hair to stick to her face.

She loved him, she truly loved him. But she could not let Adam think she was untouched. And she could not let him want to marry her. He deserved so much better.

Nearing town, she tried to determine her next steps, but her grief blinded her. Pulling hard on the reins, she stopped the mare in front of Lancaster's.

After dismounting, she burst through the door.

"Betty!" She choked out the name between sobs.

As she entered the kitchen, Betty rose. Ben Shepherd from Colter Ranch sat on the other side of the small kitchen table. Julia started to back away when she realized Betty wasn't alone, but Betty moved to her side.

"Come with me, dear," Betty said, ushering Julia into her private rooms. "Whatever is the matter?"

Sobs wracked her body. She needed to tell Betty what happened. Taking a deep, shuddered breath, Julia said, "Adam kissed me."

Betty smiled. "Dear, I don't think a kiss is what has you so upset."

"I… I told him."

Betty's expression sobered and Julia was certain she understood her meaning. A new round of sobs shook her body.

Forcing words between each sob, she said, "He… wants to… m-m-marry me… but I told him… he deserves… someone… pure." Covering her face with her hands, she let the tears flow freely.

Julia felt Betty's arms wrap around her. She rocked back and forth as Betty stroked her hair and murmured words of comfort. Several minutes later, her crying stopped and she looked up at the motherly woman. She just wanted to curl up and sleep for a week.

Betty must have read the exhaustion in her expression. "Dear, why don't you lie down on my bed and take a nap? I'll wake you for supper after the boarders are gone and we can talk some more if you like."

Julia nodded and did as the older woman suggested.

Adam was not sure how long he kneeled there in the forest after Julia left. His knees ached almost as much as his broken foolish heart. As he started to stand, he noticed the ribbon in his hand. Julia's ribbon. He brought it to his nose and inhaled the scent. Vanilla. *Oh, Julia.* His heart cried, ripped open again.

He urged his legs to move as he tried to stand. He needed to make sure she made it to town safely. He needed to talk to her. To explain that none of what she said mattered to him. He loved her. He could no more stop loving her than he could stop training horses. She was a part of him.

Mounting his horse, Adam stuffed her hair ribbon in his pocket for safe keeping. He pointed the horse back towards town, following the prints from her mare.

Perhaps they would still be enjoying their afternoon together, had he not made his foolish declaration. He should have been more cautious, especially with both Will and Hannah's strong warnings. What had he been thinking?

A frustrated growl escaped his lips, low and anguished. He had not been thinking. That was the problem. He was so enamored with her—and that kiss—that he let his emotions get away from him.

That kiss. She tasted so sweet. When she responded he lost a good bit of his self-control. He wanted to go on. He hated to admit just how far he would have been willing to go. Then guilt stabbed him in the heart. In light of what Julia shared, Adam knew his actions were unforgiveable. He pressed too much even though he knew better.

He forced himself to concentrate as he neared town. He needed to find her. He glanced at the hitching post by the hotel and did not see the palomino mare. Riding around the town square, he finally spotted the horse tied in front of Lancaster's. *Betty.* The woman

276

acted as mother to practically half the territory. Of course Julia would seek solace there.

After tying his horse next to the mare, he entered the quiet dining hall. He heard voices coming from the kitchen. As he entered the small room, he thought he saw Ben Shepherd jump back. Looking down, Adam noticed Ben's hand entwined with Betty's.

"Have you seen Julia?" he asked directing his question toward Betty.

"Adam," Ben answered. "Take a seat." Ben let go of Betty's hand before taking a seat next to him. Both men turned their attention to Betty.

"Adam, she's here."

He started to rise, but Ben's strong grip on his shoulder kept him in his seat.

"She's sleeping right now," Betty continued. "You must understand what she experienced in Texas is not the type of thing that one heals from quickly. She is hurting. And she is scared. But it doesn't mean that she doesn't have feelings for you. Those feelings, while deep, only add to her fear and confusion. She needs time."

Adam stared at his hands trying to accept what Betty was saying about his beloved Julia. It hurt. It hurt to know she was on the other side of that wall and he could not go to her to comfort her, to explain.

"Give her some time, dear. If God has a mind for the two of you to be together, it will happen."

After sitting in silence for several minutes, Adam rose to his feet, numb. "We best head back to the ranch," he said to Ben before walking out to his horse.

When Julia finally woke, there was a sliver of light shining in the window of Betty's room. She wished she could forget where she was, but she could not.

When memories of Adam's kiss invaded her thoughts, she let them come. It was likely the only kiss she would ever receive from the man she loved. Her decision to run, while impulsive, had been the right one. Adam deserved someone who was not ruined.

Sitting upright, she hung her legs over the side of the bed. She pushed herself up, standing. Never before had she been so aware of her own labored movements. One foot stepped forward, followed by the other, again and again until she reached the door separating Betty's private quarters from the kitchen.

Betty looked up from the dishes as she handed Yu another mug to dry. She nodded toward the plate on the table. "I saved you some supper, though it might be cold, dear."

Julia nodded, taking the seat. She moved the food around on her plate. She slowly lifted a spoonful of stew to her lips. Opening her mouth, she pursed her lips together, cleaning the spoon with her upper lip. Chewing slowly and deliberately, she forced herself not to cry. She repeated the motions until the bowl was empty.

She just sat there staring at the table when Betty took the bowl from her. She listened to the soft swish of water as Betty cleaned the dish. Placing her elbows on the table, Julia rubbed her temples. Her head hurt from crying so much. Despite sleeping for hours, all she could think of was her own warm bed.

"I should be going," she said as she rose.

"Just a minute, dear, and I'll walk with you." She dried her hands then opened the back door. They stepped into the fading light of dusk.

"Did Adam find the horse?" Julia asked. He would be long gone by now.

"Yes, dear. He is very concerned for you."

An unbidden tear slid down her cheek.

"Give it some time, dear. Things will work out in the end." Betty patted her check as they stopped in front of the hotel.

Julia nodded and went inside. Not making eye contact with Mr. Hamilton, she marched down the hall straight to her room. Closing the door behind her, she flopped down on her bed face first. Her sobs shook her body as her heart shattered.

The bunkhouse was quiet, well, except for the snores of a few loud sleepers. But Adam could not sleep. His heart was heavily burdened with guilt.

He rolled over on his side facing the wall. Moving one hand under his pillow, he stopped when he felt something silky hidden there. *Oh, Julia, please forgive me.* He ran his thumb over her hair ribbon. *I never meant to hurt you. I love you. Please give me a second chance.*

Chapter 32

For the fourth time, Thomas arrived at Fort Wingate. While the light of day faded rapidly, Thomas was grateful for the safety of the fort. During the last day of his journey, he could not shake the feeling of being watched. He was either truly being watched or becoming quite paranoid crossing the vast open plains between the Little Colorado River and Fort Wingate. Other than the two Indians he encountered on his first trip, he had not seen any natives.

Pulling his mare to a stop, he handed the reins off to another sergeant. Grabbing the saddle bags full of mail, he entered the small supply building. None of the correspondence he carried was of any significance, so there was no need to even report to the fort's major.

Dropping the saddle bags on the counter, he looked around for the supply officer. Not seeing him, he decided to get some grub before getting some shut eye. He would pick up the outbound mail for Whipple tomorrow morning.

As Thomas neared the quaint log structure that served as a mess hall, he heard loud cheering coming from within. When he stepped through the doors, he saw men hugging each other and patting each other on the back. He overhead one man say there was news from the east.

"War's over!" a rough looking man said as he slapped Thomas on the back.

Thomas blinked, not certain he heard correctly. *The war was over? Could it be true?*

He made his way through the crowd to a group of lieutenants huddled together. He stood on the outskirts of the circle and listened to the conversation.

"A rider came in about an hour ago."

"Said he got the word via telegraph to Santa Fe. Then he rode here with the news."

"Only word was that it was a Union victory and that cagey ol' Lee finally surrendered. Happened early in the month."

"There was a second rider who confirmed the news, so the major thinks it is reliable. He's gonna include it in the dispatch to the other forts in the southwest territories."

"War is over."

Thomas barely kept his jaw from slacking open. He never expected he would muster out in the Arizona Territory—where his brother now lived. With the war over, he would not have to finish out his three year commitment. He could leave once he got back to Fort Whipple. The strange circumstances of his life were getting more bizarre. He never thought, not for one minute, that he would serve anything less than the three years. Oh, he hoped for the war to end and for his freedom, but never really believed it would happen.

Providence. Mixford's voice floated around in Thomas's head. If it really was Providence, why pick now? Why drag him to the Arizona Territory to let him be free? Was it possible he was meant to find Drew?

He shook his head. Now he was starting to sound like Mixford, wondering what he was supposed to do. A man makes his own choices and his own way. There's no preplanned path for his life. Wasn't his life a fine example of that?

Then again, when Thomas really thought about his life, his argument came up lacking. There were many things he had not chosen. He did not choose for his father to die. He did not choose for Drew to leave. He did not even really choose to serve in the Union or become a dispatch rider. These things happened around him or to him.

Picking up a plate from the stack, Thomas held it out to receive a healthy portion of food. While it looked like the same simple fare they served at Whipple, it smelled delicious to his growling stomach. After eating jerky and bread on the ride between the forts, he looked forward to the more substantial meals.

The possibilities of what his future held rose to his mind between every bite. He considered what he would do once he returned to Fort Whipple in a few days. After resting tonight, he would make the return journey to the fort tomorrow morning. It was a grueling journey, but this time it would be worth it to gain his freedom at the end.

Riding defined him and he was not sure what he might do if he wasn't riding. Perhaps he could learn the skills of a cowboy and get a job on one of the ranches in the area. Or he could work at the saw mill. Of course, he may have to take whatever he could get, if there weren't many jobs available. Although, he was certain the growing territorial capital of Prescott would have jobs in abundance. He would really just have to wait and see what was available.

Then there was his search for Drew. He still had no answer from his letter to his brother. Thomas thought about searching for him, but he could not do so if he was tied down to a job in town. Perhaps he should go to La Paz first. If need be, he could always take a few short term jobs until he found Drew and Hannah.

As he swallowed his last bite of food, he knew he was no closer to having an answer than when he started the meal. Any plan would be meaningless until he mustered out and he could not do that until he made it back to Whipple safely.

Five days later, Thomas pulled his horse to a stop in front of Major Willis's quarters at Fort Whipple. He carried a dispatch from the major at Wingate specifically for Major Willis. Tying his horse to the post outside, he knocked on the door. When the major bade him enter, he walked straight to his desk with the missive.

"Sir, a message from Wingate," Thomas said.

The major quickly scanned the message. "Sergeant, is this true? Is the war over?"

"Yes, sir. The report has been confirmed."

"That's good news. Now maybe we can get some decent supplies around here," Major Willis muttered under his breath.

"Was there something else?" the major asked, clearly expecting Thomas to dismiss himself.

"Yes, sir. It is just that… My papers, sir, say I can muster out at the end of the war."

"And I suppose that is what you would like to do now having heard the war is over?"

"Yes, sir."

The major tapped his finger against his chin. "Very well, Sergeant. You may have someone take you to town. Leave all of your army supplied items behind—tent, guns, horse, extra uniforms."

His horse. Thomas had not considered he would be left without the horse. That would impact his ability to search for Drew. But, he really had no say in the matter. It was not as if he brought the horse in with him, as many dispatchers did. He inherited it along with the copper tube when he picked up his first dispatch on the battlefield. None of what he had was his own, not even the paper and ink well in his saddle bags. Not even the saddle bags were his.

"You may pick up your final pay from the supply officer and make arrangements with him for transportation to town."

Thomas Anderson—no longer a sergeant—nodded and left to make the arrangements for his new life.

The next morning, he rode in the back of a military wagon into town. He still wore a uniform, but would need to replace it with other clothes. The precious little money he received as his military pay would hopefully cover purchasing some clothes and give him shelter for a while. He would have to secure a job as soon as possible.

Jumping down off the back of the wagon as it pulled to a stop in front of the livery building, Thomas surveyed the town. While he had been at Fort Whipple for nearly two months, he had no reason to go to town. This was the first time he visited Prescott.

The rutted streets, if one could call them such, were wide enough to pass two wagons. There were several structures in town. From what he could tell, there were two boardinghouses, a hotel, a restaurant, the livery, two different stores, a newspaper office, and a few saloons, among several other buildings. For such a young town, it seemed rather large.

Keying in on the saloons, Thomas had an idea. He had always been a good poker player. Perhaps he could supplement his meager funds by winning a few hands. There would be no harm in that and he would be able to get a better start, maybe even win enough to purchase a horse.

Starting toward the saloons, the excitement for the game sent blood coursing through his veins in anticipation. Then a large sign posted on the side of one of the buildings caught his attention. "Help Wanted" it said. He dropped his head back to look up at the sign above the building. "Livery and La Paz Express – mail delivery service to La Paz." Impossible.

Thomas patted the letter in his pocket as he stared at the sign. Before he left Fort Whipple he checked one last time for any letters from Drew. The only letter waiting for him was the one he had sent to Drew. It was returned to Fort Whipple with a note in choppy letters saying no one heard of him. Confused by the message, he wanted to travel to La Paz to see what he could learn for himself. And now, here he stood before a sign looking for help for a mail route to La Paz. This was so ludicrous he just had to ask.

Opening the door, Thomas was immediately greeted by a man behind a desk.

"Good morning. What can I do for you?" He looked Thomas over. A wrinkle formed on his brow. "In from the fort?"

"Name is Thomas Anderson. I just mustered out and I saw the sign out front saying you were looking for help. What kind of help?"

The man introduced himself as Craig Roundtree. "We are looking for an experienced rider to run the mail route between Prescott and La Paz. Our current rider, Leland Frye, is getting too old to be running the route every two weeks. Got any experience riding?"

"Yes, sir," Thomas said. "Most recently I have been riding the military mail between Fort Whipple and Fort Wingate. Prior to that I was a dispatcher for Major General Smith in the XVI Corps."

"Hmm," Craig said rubbing his hand over his chin. "And you're looking for a job now, are ya?"

"Yes, sir."

"Well, it pays pretty good, mostly 'cause it is pretty dangerous. Though it sounds like you are used to that."

Thomas smiled. If he only knew. "Yes, sir. Been shot at, chased down by rebels and Indians, run out of rations, ridden through the night in the pouring rain, just to name a few of the situations I've been in."

"Well, Anderson, I think you'll do. We'll start you out on a trial basis. See how you do on the first run. If you can keep to the tough timetables and make it back alive, the job is yours."

"Thank you, sir."

"Oh, and Anderson, you can just call me Craig. No need for the 'sir'."

Thomas chuckled. "Yes, Craig."

"Come back here for a horse first thing tomorrow morning. You'll make your first run then. Frye will run with you this time, sorta show you the ropes. You might want to pack a bag with some food, for you'll need to supply your own on the trail, and get some new clothes. The uniform is bound to confuse the stations along the way."

Thomas thanked him again and left. He had a lot to accomplish for the day if he was going to be ready to leave in the morning. Craig suggested that he could find everything he needed to purchase at Gray & Company across the square, so he stopped there first. Looking around the small store, at least small compared to his father's store, he found some cotton shirts and trousers. Setting aside two pair each, he looked around for some food supplies. There was not much in the way of food he could readily prepare on the trail. He would have to find food another way. Looking around the store, he found a decent blanket, pistol, and rifle. He carried his purchases to the counter and was relieved to have just enough money left for the boardinghouse and hopefully some food.

Stuffing his belongings into a burlap sack, Thomas swung it over his shoulder and walked across the square to the building labeled "Lancaster's Boardinghouse." Not certain which of the three larger buildings he should enter he followed the delicious aroma of food. He missed the midday meal, but it would still be a few hours until supper.

Pushing the door open to the dining hall, he walked in. Muffled sounds were coming from the back, presumably the kitchen. When he stuck his head in the kitchen, a small Chinese man and woman moved items around on the stove.

"Excuse me," Thomas said.

The woman jumped and gave a little squeal. The man rushed over to Thomas.

"No eat," he kept saying waving his hands for Thomas to leave.

"I came to see about a place to stay," he replied not budging from his place in the doorway.

The man paused for a moment then let out a big, "Oh!" Opening the back door, he scurried off. In a few seconds he led an older white woman by the arm into the kitchen. "Stay," he said pointing between the older woman and Thomas.

"Alright, Liang, I'll see what this gentleman wants." The woman appeared rather kind and had a way about her that instantly put him at ease.

"Good afternoon, dear," she said. "I'm Mrs. Betty Lancaster, one of the owners of this establishment. What can I do for you?"

"Ma'am. Thomas Anderson." He thought for a moment the woman gave him a funny look, but when she quickly smiled he decided he imagined it. "I'm looking for a place for the night."

"Just one night, dear?"

"Yes. I ride out with Leland Frye in the morning. I'm trying to get the job on their express line."

"Oh, that's wonderful! I know that Mr. Frye is getting tired of making the long trip so often. It'll be good for him to have your help. Let me think. Yes, I believe I can put you in the Mother Lode, the bunkhouse to the south. Follow me."

Thomas followed Betty to the bunkhouse. She assigned him a bunk and explained the fees.

When she mentioned three meals were included in the higher than expected price, he tried to negotiate. "I won't be staying after breakfast tomorrow. We'll be leaving first thing."

"Dear, it doesn't seem to me that you got much in the way of belongings. Now, I know there are some stations along the way, but you'll be lucky to get one meal out of them per day. Do you have food for the trip?"

"Well, I was hoping to find some jerky, bread, and cheese to purchase, but have come up empty so far."

"Say no more. I'll fix up a small supply for you, no extra charge. I think you'll find the jerky mighty good. It comes from a local ranch up the way, Colter Ranch. Anyway, I'll have something ready for you in the morning, dear."

As Betty turned to leave, she paused. "Have we met before, Mr. Anderson? You look awful familiar to me."

"I don't think so ma'am. This is my first day in Prescott," he answered, not wanting to divulge too much about his past.

The older stout woman shrugged her shoulders, apparently giving up on trying to place him. "Well, then, welcome to Prescott, Mr. Anderson. Supper service starts at six."

Thomas watched as she closed the door behind her. He was positive he never met the woman before. Waiting another minute to make sure he was alone, he changed from his uniform into one of the cotton shirts and trousers. It felt so good to wear something other than the scratchy wool.

Chapter 33

True to her word, Betty had food packed for Thomas, ready to go the next morning. After devouring a savory breakfast in the dining hall, he grabbed his things and met Leland Frye at the livery. The man was shorter than he expected—for once Thomas was the tall one.

Leland showed him their horses boarded at the livery. He let Thomas choose his horse. Carefully looking over the options, he picked a chestnut mare. The horse looked strong, and he suspected she was fast.

"Nice choice, Anderson. That's one of our fastest horses. Let's get her saddled up."

As Thomas went about the task, Leland explained how they ran the express. "You might find how we do things a mite different than the army. We typically change out horses at stations along the way, roughly every fifteen miles. Then about a third of the way there, in Wickenburg, we'll stop for the night. The next day we'll go through a similar change of horses until we reach Fredrick's station. The third day, we should reach La Paz towards the end of the day. Most the stages take twice as long to cover the distance, but we set a fast pace so we can make the circuit twice a month. Once we get to La Paz, we'll stay for a day or two then head back. When we get back to Prescott, I usually take three days off to rest up for the next run."

Leland was right. It was a bit different in that he would have a fresh horse every fifteen miles and would be able to cover greater distances. That was not possible when couriering the military mail. He looked forward to having a bed to sleep in most nights.

When they finished saddling the horses, they stopped at the Juniper House and then Fort Whipple to pick up the mail before heading southwest on the rough road. Leland told tales similar to what Bixley told him at the fort. They would have to keep a sharp eye out for Apaches and robbers. Since the mail route was the same as the stage route, Leland said they were more likely to run into robbers.

Following a series of switchbacks, they wove between tall pines perched on the edge of the Bradshaw Mountains. Several times they traveled so close to the edge, they had a clear view of the valley stretching miles below. A hazy purplish blue in the distance hinted that there were more mountains to be crossed on this journey, though Leland said they would not reach those until the third day.

At the base of the mountain, they stopped off for their first change of horses. They picked up the pace, riding at a slow gallop, across the open valley floor. Within an hour and a half they arrived at the next station. Both men refilled their canteens, transferred the mail to the fresh horse, and took off at a fast pace. The routine repeated several more times throughout the day.

Around noon, when they stopped for another change of horses, Leland pulled out some of his bread and jerky, suggesting Thomas do the same. They slowed to a trot while eating, then pushed forward at a faster pace veering slightly east along the trail towards Wickenburg. Sometime around three in the afternoon, they arrived in the small town.

Dismounting his horse, Thomas threw the reins over the hitching post. Grabbing his saddle bags, which contained all of his belongings, he followed Leland into the station house.

"Drop your bag in one of the rooms. Then come out back. There's cool fresh water to wash up," the station owner said.

Eager for cool water to splash on his face, Thomas did as instructed. He wanted to dump the entire bucket over his head but settled for splashing some of the refreshing liquid on his face. The temperature increased steadily since they reached the valley floor— and it was only the end of April. He wondered just how hot it would be in the height of summer.

Pacing back and forth, he worked out the kinks in his sore legs. It was different riding all day at a gallop as opposed to the gentle walk he used on his military runs. The constant jarring movements required him to use different muscles to remain in control while in the saddle. He was glad the day was done so early. Thinking of the bed waiting for him this evening, he nearly gave in to the temptation to take a nap. Not the best way to make a good impression on

Leland.

Leland and a few of the station hands sat at the table with a deck of cards. The soft *whoosh* of shuffling cards set Thomas's heart to pounding. It brought back memories of sitting around the poker tables at the old saloons. Fingers itching in excitement, he took a seat and asked to be dealt in, even when they said the game was just for sport.

After a few rounds of poker, with Thomas thoroughly trouncing the other men, supper was served. The hearty fare of desert quail, biscuits and gravy, and fried potatoes, satisfied his hunger. The apple pie for dessert was a treasured bonus. He could not remember the last time he had apple pie. Was it when he lived with Drew and Hannah? Her apple pie was one of the sweetest and best he ever tasted. The one before him did not quite compare, but it came close.

When it came time to retire for the night, images from his days at Drew and Hannah's house floated through his mind. They had been so kind to him, even when he was rebellious and angry. Guilt flooded him nearly to the point of drowning when he thought of how horrible he must have been to live with. He had to find them and make amends.

Thomas's dreams were fitful as he imagined every sort of reaction when he arrived in La Paz. There was compassion and excitement for being reunited with his long lost brother. There was joy that he had settled into a fine man. There was anger for ruining Drew's business. There was resentment for causing them such a long strenuous journey. By the time he woke the next morning, he felt wearier. The anger and resentment he felt in his dreams stayed with him throughout the day.

The first station he and Leland arrived at on the second day was not much more than a watering hole, a shack, and a small corral with two horses. Obviously the two they were leaving behind would be the ones they picked up on the way back. The day before Thomas wondered why they stopped so early with so much daylight left. Seeing the poor condition of this station he understood why.

After leaving Wickenburg, there was not much to look at except desert brush. They followed the open valleys most of the day. Towards the end of the afternoon, they skirted to the north of another mountain range, before stopping at a station in a place called Desert

Wells, which was nothing more than a few buildings and deep water well. While not as nice as the station in Wickenburg, the men were provided a place to sleep and hearty food to fill their stomachs.

By the middle of the third day, when Thomas and Leland started weaving through mountain passes, he was more than ready to arrive in La Paz. Even though he spent the majority of the past two years of his life on the back of a horse, this type of riding was far more strenuous than he imagined. He hoped he would toughen up by the time they returned to Prescott.

When he spotted buildings dotting the horizon around five in the afternoon, he could barely contain his excitement. Surely that was La Paz. As they neared the town, his suspicions proved true. The town of La Paz was situated on the eastern bank of the Colorado River. It was more than twenty times the size of Prescott and seemed to have most every of type of business you would expect for a bustling western city.

Pulling to a stop in front of the post office, his jaw slacked in awe. They actually had a dedicated post office building. After dropping off the mail sacks, Leland led his horse back to the eastern edge of the city to the station where they would stay.

Too exhausted to start his search for Drew tonight, Thomas resigned himself to starting early the next day. By the time they dropped off their horses and washed up, supper was on the table. Propping his head on one hand, Thomas slowly brought a forkful of steak to his mouth. Each bite seemed to take more energy than he had.

Leland slapped him on the back, nearly causing him to drop his fork. "You did real good Anderson. Best first run I ever saw. Most other riders would have me camped somewhere in the desert tonight, not even making it to town."

Thomas smiled at the compliment. Sounded like, unless he made some major blunder on the trip back, he would have this job. Although, right now he could see why Leland wanted to get out of riding.

After supper, Thomas headed straight for bed. Within seconds, he was fast asleep.

The next morning, breakfast aromas already filled the building. Thomas shot upright. He had overslept. As he entered the dining room, he saw Leland just now sitting down at the table.

"Don't look so surprised," Leland said. "It's my day off. Believe me when I say you will come to enjoy those days you can sleep in without fear of missing the next station."

"What do you usually do when you're here in La Paz?" Thomas asked as he dug into his plate of food. Scrambled eggs never tasted so good.

"Explore town. Hang out at the saloon. Visit the mercantile. You know, get caught up on the latest news of the area."

Thomas nodded. He knew what he planned to do for the day. He was going to every doctor's office in town until he found Drew. He learned last night at supper that there were two doctors in town, one dentist, and many other professionals. Surely someone would know his brother.

Once breakfast was over, Thomas borrowed a horse from the station and rode to the post office to speak with the postmaster. The thin gangly looking man turned from sorting the mail when Thomas entered.

"I was wondering if you might know Andrew Anderson, goes by Drew? He's a doctor and his wife's name is Hannah," Thomas asked.

"Never heard of no Anderson. There's Doc Henry and Doc Nick, the only two doctors in town. Then a dentist, Doc Johnson. No Anderson though," the postmaster replied.

"How long you been in these parts?" Thomas asked, hoping the man was new and just never met Drew.

"Oh, been here for three years now. Know pretty much everyone in town."

Dejected, Thomas left the building. Not much point in visiting either doctor, if the postmaster was so familiar with everyone. Drew and Hannah only left Ohio less than two years ago. They should have been in La Paz for at least a year, maybe more.

By the time supper rolled around, Thomas was utterly discouraged. He went to each mercantile, two churches, and five saloons. No one had ever heard of Drew. The next day he broadened his search, speaking with the livery owner, the two doctors, the dentist, the land agent, and anyone who would give him time. It was clear that Drew and Hannah never resided in La Paz.

At the end of his second day in La Paz, Thomas was glad they would be returning to Prescott the following morning. The only useful piece of information he uncovered was that several wagon trains followed the stage route into La Paz for settlement. On the way back to Prescott, Thomas would ask more questions at each of the stations.

Four days later, Thomas pulled his horse to a stop in front of the livery in Prescott. No one along the route had ever heard of Dr. Anderson. He even told Leland about his search on the first day back from La Paz. He never heard anything either.

Where could Drew and Hannah be? Was it possible they settled somewhere along the way? Thomas had not considered that possibility before. But, if they found a place they liked and that needed a doctor it made sense. Did one or both of them die? Is that why no one seemed to know who they were? That possibility was too horrible for Thomas to consider. For if it was true, he would have been responsible for their deaths, since it was his actions that caused them to leave.

He tried to shake such morbid thoughts from his mind as he followed Leland into the livery. Leland nodded for Craig to follow him back to the other room. The two spoke in hushed tones for several minutes before both men returned to the main office.

Craig held out his hand to Thomas. "Congratulations, Anderson. Leland here says you were an excellent rider. The job is yours if you still want it."

Thomas smiled and shook both men's hands. "Be glad to have it, sir…um, Craig."

Craig reached into his desk drawer and counted out Thomas's pay for the first run. Once they agreed on his wage, Thomas picked up his saddle bag and left.

As he neared Lancaster's Boardinghouse, he spotted Betty behind one of the bunkhouses. She waved as he approached.

"Mr. Anderson, back from the express run, I see."

"Yes, ma'am. I am officially the new rider for the La Paz Express."

"That's wonderful, dear. Will you be staying here when you aren't riding?"

"Well, I was hoping we could work out something." He

explained his anticipated schedule and Betty agreed she would keep a bunk for him when he would be in Prescott. The days he was gone, if needed, she would rent his bunk to someone else. He would only have to pay for the days he was in town. The rest of the time, she told him he could store any personal items in a crate under his bunk. He doubted he would be leaving anything behind.

The next two days were uneventful, even boring. While the first morning he enjoyed sleeping in, the other days seemed too long. Thomas thought when he returned from the next trip he would see if Craig needed some help at the livery on his days off. At least then his hands would not be idle.

Entering the dining hall for supper, he took his usual seat. Again, when Betty poured him a cup of coffee she gave him a strange look. He smiled and thanked her for the drink. She smiled back. When her son, Paul, set a plate of food before him, he thought the man looked at him odd as well. Thomas was usually pretty observant, so he trusted he was not seeing something that was not there.

After he finished his meal, he remained seated until all of the other boarders left. He did not really have a plan for broaching the subject, so he hesitated when Betty stopped by with the coffee pot again.

"Can I get you something else, Mr. Anderson?" Betty asked.

"No, no. And please, call me Thomas."

She nodded and started to leave.

"Betty," Thomas started. "You know a lot of folks in the area, right?" At her nod, he proceeded with the question he intended to ask several days ago. "I've been looking for my brother and his wife. Thought they were going to settle in La Paz, but no one there knows them. I just thought you might be able to ask around to see if anyone has ever run into Drew and Hannah. He's a doctor, so I figure he would be more memorable than most."

Betty's face went pale and she slid onto the bench opposite from him. "Paul!" she yelled.

"What is it Ma?" Paul asked running into the room.

Thomas was confused by Betty's reaction. What did he say that had her so upset?

"He's looking for his brother, Drew Anderson," she whispered to her son.

Paul's eyes grew round and he sank onto the bench next to his mother, placing an arm around her protectively.

Betty sat up straighter. "Dear," she said locking gazes with Thomas. "We traveled west with Drew and Hannah Anderson."

Thomas's palms grew sweaty. What was she saying? She knew his brother? He wiped his hands on his pants.

"Where are they?" he asked, frantically.

Betty looked at Paul. When he nodded, she continued, "Well, I'm sorry to tell you this, but Drew is gone. He died in an avalanche in the San Francisco Mountains just a few short weeks before we arrived here."

She reached out to take his hand, but Thomas recoiled. They were dead. It was his fault that they were dead. Standing abruptly, he tripped over the bench. He had to get out of here. He could not breathe. He burst through the front door and made his way straight for the saloon. A strong drink should numb the pain.

He wasn't sure how long he sat in the saloon. No matter how much he drank, nothing numbed the realization that he killed his own family. The only family he had left and his actions killed them. Glancing up at the window, he saw the darkened street through blurry eyes. He had to ride out in the morning.

Standing, he knocked over his chair and stumbled towards the door. When he went to step off the side walk, he landed face down in the dirt. His arms felt limp, but he forced himself to stand. The distance to the boardinghouse seemed like miles.

"I killed them," he moaned, leaning against the door frame of the bunkhouse.

Someone stirred and shushed him. Then a man grabbed his arm and led him to a bench outside. Thomas half sat on the bench, barely able to keep from sliding off.

"You did not kill them, Thomas," a familiar voice said.

Thomas searched his foggy brain. "Paulie, is that you."

"Yes. Look, Hannah is not dead. You ran out before we could finish explaining."

Thomas sat up. Hannah was still alive? But Drew wasn't. "I killed him," he slurred. "I killed my brother."

"No you did not. The avalanche was an accident and had

nothing to do with you."

Thomas tried to let the words sink in. "Where's Hannah?"

"She is married to a rancher, Will Colter, northeast of town. She's safe and happy."

"I have to see her," he said trying to stand. A hand clamped down on his shoulder and he lamely tried to wiggle free. "I haft apologize. I haft..."

His limbs were getting heavier, harder to move. But he had to ask Hannah's forgiveness.

"Come on," Paul said, helping him up. Stumbling into the bunkhouse, Paul deposited him on his bunk. "Get some rest."

Chapter 34

Prescott

May 12, 1865

Julia sighed heavily, staring at the guest book in front of her. Mr. Hobbs and Mr. Franklin were scheduled to check in today. They made numerous visits to Prescott over the last several months. Mr. Hardy contracted a group of men to help build his toll road between Prescott and Hardyville, the most northern port along the Colorado River. Rumors circulated that Hardy, Hobbs, Franklin, and Brighton were funding the road. She also heard that Hardy planned to open a store in the growing town.

Maybe she would see if Mr. Hamilton could check them in. Certainly she could come up with some errand elsewhere in the hotel needing her attention. It's not that she didn't like Mr. Hobbs and Mr. Franklin—they were both fine gentlemen. She just wearied of Mr. Hobbs's repeated attempts to get her to dine with him.

The only gentleman she cared to dine with was Adam. But, since their outing—the one where she told him the awful truth—he hadn't been around. It had been almost two months since she'd seen him. If he came to town at all during that time, he avoided her completely. She had no word from anyone at the ranch since then, so she couldn't even find out how he was doing. And she desperately wanted to know.

Rubbing her fingers on her temple, she sat on the small stool behind the counter. Was his silence an indication of his disinterest? Did he hate her now? Or was this her fault for assuming he wouldn't love her anymore if he found out?

Then, Reverend Page's message yesterday had been about forgiveness—not a subject she wanted to hear, especially in conjunction with Reuben. Reverend Page said she should forgive those who wronged her, even if they didn't deserve it. He said the act of forgiving was for her benefit—which was why Jesus told his disciples to forgive seventy times seven. Reverend Page said it was because the one doing the forgiving sometimes needed to forgive that many times.

Oh, he had not been talking specifically to her. It just felt like it. As soon as he said "forgiveness" she knew the one person she needed to forgive was the one person she would never forgive. Never. It took the entire night arguing with God to come to that conclusion.

Forgive anyone who wrongs you, no matter how deep the offense.

Were those words from Reverend Page or from God? It didn't matter. She could not forgive Reuben. She would not forgive him. He ruined her. He destroyed her chance of having a happy marriage with the man she loved. She would never be Adam's wife. She would never have his children. All because of Reuben's heinous act.

The lobby door opened and Julia struggled to rein in her churning emotions. Stretching her lips in an insincere smile, she looked up.

"Good afternoon, Mr. Hobbs, Mr. Franklin," she greeted, wishing she paid more attention to the arriving stage. So much for ducking out before it arrived.

"It most certainly is, now that we've been graced with one of your beautiful smiles," Mr. Hobbs replied, leaning against the counter, gold eyes sparkling.

Resisting the urge to roll her eyes, she grabbed two room keys. "Right this way, gentlemen."

Without another word, she escorted them to their rooms. She handed Mr. Hobbs his key and turned to go back to the front lobby. He lightly touched her arm.

"Miss Colter," he said his voice low. "It's good to see you again."

Stiffly, she replied, "Likewise."

A brief frown flitted across his forehead. Raising his voice, he said, "Perhaps you could make early dinner reservations for Mr. Franklin and me. We'll be ready for a good meal in about an hour."

Nodding, she took her leave.

The day could not pass fast enough for Julia. Other than Mr. Hobbs and Mr. Franklin, only a handful of guests stayed at the hotel.

For the three days since Sunday, things had been slow at the hotel. If only her mind found such a pace. She had too much time to think about Reverend Page's message. She wanted to forget about Reuben and not constantly battle with the idea of forgiving him.

During the day, and more so in the quiet evenings at night, she waged a war in her mind. She imagined screaming at him to even shooting him in revenge. Then she calmed and felt remorse for her hateful thoughts. Maybe she should just forgive him.

If she did forgive him, maybe she would finally have true peace in her heart. Maybe she would be able to move on with her life.

Thankfully, a stage arrived with half a dozen guests. Setting her thoughts aside, she focused on getting them situated.

An hour later with stomach growling, Julia entered the kitchen, long overdue for her midday break. Sitting at the small table near the back door, she stretched the sore muscles in her neck. She needed a good night's sleep soon.

"Miss Julia," Chef greeted. "I have just the thing for you today."

Ten minutes later, he set a delicious plate of food before her, remembering the smaller portions she always requested. Taking a bite, she let the venison melt on her tongue. She didn't know how he did it, but Chef could make anything drab taste amazing.

As she finished the last bite, a knock at the door startled her. Chef hurried over to open the door.

"Ah!" he exclaimed. "You've brought me more Colter beef."

Julia turned to see who came from the ranch. For a brief second she held out hope that Adam might be here. Ben and Snake each carried a crate into the room, setting them down on the counter where Chef pointed.

"Miss Julia," Ben smiled when he spotted her. "How ya doing?"

"Fine," she lied.

"Snake, why don't you head on over to our next stop. I'd like to catch up with Miss Julia for a minute," Ben said.

Why did she suddenly have the feeling that she was in trouble?

"Take a walk with me," he said, leading her out the back door, around the building to the town square.

She followed silently beside this bear of a man she'd known all her life. In her father's absence, he filled in nicely.

"Will is real worried about ya."

"If Will is worried, why hasn't he been in to visit?"

"Couple of reasons. He's worried sick 'bout Hannah and doesn't want to get too far from the house. And he's tryin' to respect your space."

"Hmm," she responded, not really sure what to say.

"And Adam—he ain't been himself since... Well, since his last day to town."

"Ben—"

"Hear me out. It's plain as day that the two of ya fancy each other. I don't know what all happened that day between ya, but ya both need to let it go. What you got is special, little Jewel."

She smiled at the nickname her father often used. How she missed him.

"Don't let what happened with Reuben keep ya from happiness with Adam. That young man loves ya more'n his horses. And ya know how much he loves them horses."

Her stomach tightened and her mouth went dry. "How did you know about Reuben?"

"Little Jewel, I don't know. Not exactly. But, I've heard enough of pieces of conversations and I've known ya since ya was a baby. And I know all 'bout what kind of man Reuben is. Somethin' bad drove ya here. I know it's got to hurt. I know it's tough to forgive."

Nervous, Julia wrung her hands together, taking in what he said, even if she didn't want to hear it. He saw things that others didn't always see. He had always watched out for her when he was the foreman at the Star C. She trusted him.

Ben turned and looked down at her, "Yer papa would want to see ya move on. He'd want to see ya happy. And if it's Adam that makes ya happy, he would've been downright joyful."

Tears sprung at the mention of her father. "I miss him," she croaked. "None of this would have happened if he wouldn't have died."

Adam's apple bobbing, Ben struggled to say, "I know. None of us were ready for him to leave."

Burying her head against this fatherly man's chest, she cried, her heart broken over all she lost.

"Aw, little Jewel," Ben said, patting her head. "I didn't mean to get ya all upset."

Swiping at the moisture on her face, she stepped back. "I know. I better get back. Mr. Hamilton must be wondering what's keeping me."

"Take care, Miss Julia. Think about what I said."

As Ben left for Lancaster's, Julia squared her shoulders and walked towards Juniper House. She wouldn't be able to stop herself from thinking about what he said.

Chapter 35

Prescott

May 22, 1865

Prescott. At last. Having started his second run to La Paz with a terrible hangover, the trip seemed to drag endlessly. Accompanied by memories of his brother, guilt hounded Thomas. If only he had not tried to rob that bank, his brother would still be alive.

He would not have spent the better part of the last two days rehearsing what he would say to his sister-in-law tomorrow. He didn't want to do it—was afraid to do it. But he had to. He felt compelled to ask her forgiveness. He needed to end this turmoil chewing up his soul.

Sliding off his horse, too tired to dismount with any dignity, he led the chestnut mare into the livery. Craig offered to care for the horse. Taking the saddle bags and mail bags from the horse, Thomas slung both over his shoulders.

"You look beat, Anderson," Craig said. "Didn't run into any trouble did ya?"

"No, no trouble. Just have a bit of a headache." He lied. The last thing he needed was his new employer to think he did not have the stamina for this job.

"Alright. See you in a few days."

Walking towards the Juniper House, he tried to shake some of his weariness away. Stepping inside, he felt awkward, suddenly aware of his bedraggled appearance and how poorly it fit with the elegance of the hotel.

A young woman behind the counter greeted him, before saying, "Mr. Frye hasn't been by in a while. Please tell me he is well."

"Ma'am. He's fine. Just tired of this grueling job. I'm his replacement, Thomas Anderson." He tried to force a smile from his lips.

"Miss Colter," she introduced herself. "Pleased to meet you, Mr. Anderson."

Colter. Wasn't that Hannah's new husband's name?

"Any relation to the Colter who owns the ranch?"

"My older brother. Have you met him?"

"Just heard of him."

Taking the mail from his extended hand, she thanked him and wished him a good day. Turning, he left the hotel musing at the strange coincidence of Colter's sister working there. *Providence, Tommy.*

Shut up, he thought. He was tired of it.

Thomas shuffled his feet across the square to Lancaster's. He walked into the Mother Lode, found his bunk, and tossed his stuff underneath. Then he left to find Betty. After letting her know he returned, he went back and stretched out on his bunk.

Later he woke to noise in the bunkhouse, likely many of the boarders returning from a day's work. He considered rising to join them for supper, but rolled over instead, sleep still unsatisfied.

The next morning, he woke before dawn. Quietly moving about the bunkhouse, he washed up and donned the fresh change of clothes that Betty washed while he was gone. Dousing his hair with some water, he toweled it partly dry. While he was ready earlier than Betty normally served breakfast, he decided to sit in the dining hall anyway.

Betty must have heard him enter, for she brought two steaming cups of coffee. Taking a seat across from him, she asked, "How are you doing, dear?"

He smiled at her fond overuse of the word "dear." "Okay, I guess."

"You know what happened to Drew was not your fault," she said, patting his hand.

How he wished he could believe it—to be fully absolved of his responsibility. He avoided her gaze. "Yeah, I know."

He took a swig of coffee. "I'm going out to see Hannah today."

"I think that's good for you both, dear. I'll be prayin' for you."

Thomas snorted. No amount of prayer would help him. It certainly would not bring Drew back.

Betty rose and wagged a finger at him. "Don't you be underestimating the power of talking to the good Lord. I'd wager you've already seen his hand in your life, but you just aren't ready to let him take charge quite yet."

When she walked back to the kitchen, Thomas stared behind her. Did she know about his past? That was impossible. No one here knew about all of his past. Why would she say that he'd seen the Lord's hand in his life? All he saw was his own mistakes and failures.

After breakfast, he briefly spoke with Paul to get directions to Colter Ranch. Then he hired a horse from the livery and set off going northeast out of town.

Hannah rose after a fitful night of sleep. Besides the baby being very active, she dreamed about Drew. She was confused why memories of him would haunt her now, especially since she was so happy with Will. She splashed water on her face then patted it dry. Brushing her hair out, she tried to make sense of the emotions warring inside.

Will rolled over and groaned as he stretched out tired muscles. As she watched his movements, she wondered again why she would have thought of Drew this morning. While she loved him with all of her heart, after he died she let go. When she fell in love with Will, she dreamed anew of having a family and growing old with her second husband.

She frowned, still bothered by the images from the night as she donned her light blue calico dress.

"Grumpy this morning?" Will teased as he stood and wrapped her in his arms.

"I didn't sleep well. And I feel as large as one of your cattle."

"You are the most beautiful woman in all of the Arizona Territory."

Hannah frowned at Will's teasing. "I'm not so sure your eyesight isn't going bad."

"Maybe I should take a closer look," he said, moving until his nose touched hers.

Goofy expressions crossed his face, looking sillier up close. She smiled at his antics.

"Ah, there's that smile," he said, pulling away. "Now go make me breakfast, woman." Pointing towards the kitchen, he chuckled and tried to swat her.

Scooting away just before he caught her, she left the room to start breakfast with Rosa.

With branding several days underway, Will left before breakfast to start the branding fire. The calves were weaned and old enough to receive the "CR" brand of Colter Ranch. She quickly learned that branding days were longer than most, starting before breakfast and going well into the evening.

As she finished cooking the last of the eggs, Rosa rang the dinner bell.

When Will entered the ranch house, he paused, concern wrinkling his forehead. "You look really tired, Hannah. Maybe you should let Rosa handle things today and rest."

This conversation was getting old. They had the same discussion almost daily for two months. Unfortunately there was far too much work for Rosa to handle by herself. When she mentioned as much yesterday, Will suggested bringing Julia back to the ranch. But Hannah wanted her to come back on her own, not out of obligation, and certainly not because of her. Hoping to avoid tension between her and Will, she nodded in agreement. Maybe she would take it easier today.

Once Will left for the day, she laid down again, letting Rosa take care of the dishes. Sometime later, she woke to the distant sound of hoof beats coming down the road and not from the pastures.

Hannah went to the front door and peered out. The man did not look familiar from afar. Knowing Will and all of the men, including Adam, were on the far side of the lake, she checked the rifle to make sure it was loaded. Then she set it within reach of the doorway just to be safe. Closing the door, she waited for the man to dismount and approach the house.

When he knocked, she opened the door, never expecting the man before her.

"Thomas." Her breath caught in her throat. Feeling all the color drain from her face, she stumbled toward one of the chairs to sit down, leaving her brother-in-law standing at the door.

Anger and disappointment warred within her breast. She never expected to see him again so she never really considered what her reaction might be. A flash of a memory from over a year ago floated before her eyes. She and Drew were talking, discussing that they would have to move—because of *him*.

"What are you doing here?"

More images floated in her mind. The trail to Arizona. The avalanche. Her husband's death. Anger started to bubble up and she didn't try to conceal it. He deserved to see it—the destruction he caused.

"I...um... Hannah," Thomas stammered, crunching his felt hat in his hands nervously.

Good, let him squirm, she thought, her old friend bitterness returning.

"It's a long story. Hannah, I came to apologize to you. To ask your forgiveness." He stepped closer to where she sat at the table.

"Forgiveness?! You do not deserve forgiveness!" *Neither do you, Hannah.* A voice reminded her of her own unworthiness for her Lord's forgiveness. But, did she have to forgive him? It was his actions that led to Drew's death.

"I have been searching for Drew and you for some time. It was not until recently that—" He looked away and his voice cracked. "—that I learned of Drew's passing. I'm so sorry that I'm too late to seek his forgiveness."

Hannah sat there silent. Not wanting to forgive, but knowing she should. But she was not ready. This man's actions turned her life upside down.

Will hesitated as he put the branding iron back in the fire. All morning he had an uneasy feeling. When Hannah agreed to rest this morning after breakfast, he grew more concerned. It was the first time she hadn't argued with him. Her quietness when she woke this morning made him wonder if something wrong with the baby. Did she sense it?

He looked toward the ranch house, although the view was somewhat obscured by the trees surrounding part of the lake. Rosa was hanging laundry on the line, but Hannah was not with her. Maybe she really was resting.

A woman's scream pierced the air. Will looked at Adam who was standing next to him. He heard the noise too. Taking off on foot, Will sprinted the distance to the ranch house as another scream echoed through the air, Adam following closely behind. His heart lodged in his throat as he covered the distance quickly.

"Hannah!" he yelled as he burst through the door.

There was a man he had never seen before standing there, but not anywhere close to his wife. Hannah doubled over on a chair clutching her stomach in pain. Oh, God, no. Not the baby.

"Will, the ba…" she managed before being hit with another pain. She was going into labor.

Will gathered his wife into his arms frightened for both her and the baby. *Lord please!*

"Adam!" he yelled as he deposited her on the bed. "Saddle a horse and ride for the doctor!"

The stranger replied, before Adam could, "I'll go."

Will caught his arm. "Who are you?"

"Thomas Anderson. Drew's brother."

Will frowned. "The bank robber."

The man looked down. "I see Hannah has told you about me. I was here seeking forgiveness for the pain I have caused her. Please, let me ride for the doctor. I work at the La Paz Express and have one of our fastest horses."

Will was hesitant to trust him, given what Hannah told him, but he knew it would take Adam several minutes to saddle a horse. "Go."

Thomas ran out of the building and almost instantly Will heard hoof beats thundering up the road.

Will looked at the gathering crowd. Adam and Ben, as well as several other cowboys had followed him to the house. "Adam, can you ride for Julia? We're going to need her help."

As Adam ran from the house, Will returned to Hannah's side. The pains kept coming. He prayed the doctor would hurry.

Saddling a horse, Adam mounted the gray gelding. Pressing for a hard gallop, he made his way to town to fetch Julia. His stomach lurched and flopped with the horse's fast pace—not because of his mission. He was nervous about seeing her again. Considering they hadn't spoken since the kiss, he had no idea what her reaction might be.

That kiss. He thought of it and that day often, replaying his role a hundred times. He should have done things so differently. He should have held back. He should not have asked her to be his wife. Not yet. Especially in light of what she told him.

Ducking to avoid a low hanging branch, he prayed for Hannah, for the baby, for Will. And for Julia. About a mile before he reached town he saw Thomas and the doctor riding back towards the ranch. They would have help soon.

Reining in his horse in front of the Juniper House, he still felt unprepared to see Julia again. No matter. It was Will calling her home, so he hoped she would not raise any objections. When he opened the lobby doors and saw her, a lump formed in his throat. When she looked up and her smile faded, that lump became a boulder.

Clearing his throat, he said, "Will needs you to come home. It's Hannah."

Fear clouded her eyes. "What's wrong with her?"

"The baby. We think it is coming."

"But, it's too soon. She's only seven and a half months," Julia said.

"We need to go," he said impatiently, wanting to tell her he still loved her, but knowing now was not the time.

Finally, she moved into action. "Let me get my things."

Two minutes later, she wished Mr. Hamilton farewell and handed her carpet bag to Adam.

As they stood before the one and only horse he saddled, he counted himself a fool again. He hadn't thought far enough ahead to saddle a second horse for Julia. He climbed up then reached down to help her up behind him. As soon as her hand brushed his, fire shot

311

through his arm. He handed her carpet bag back, asking her to loop her arm through it then around his waist. Once she was settled, he clucked the horse into motion.

The ride back, while short, seemed to stretch on for Adam. He was very aware of her body pressed against his. At first her grip around his torso had been light, but as soon as the horse got up to full speed, she leaned into him and kept a firm hold. Is this what it would be like when she was his wife?

He mentally kicked himself. She would not be his wife. She had made that abundantly clear the day she left him standing there in the forest. The day he wished he could change.

When he pulled the horse to a stop in front of the ranch house, Julia did not even wait for him to help her down. She dropped the carpet bag on the porch and ran inside, leaving him to miss her nearness.

Julia, shaking from Adam's nearness, hoped others would think it nerves. He smelled awful—like he'd been working the branding pit. But, she was so desperate to see him, to be near to him again that she didn't let it bother her.

Pushing those painful thoughts aside, she stopped short when Hannah screamed. It was a howling wail, different from the normal sounds of child birthing. Julia knocked on the door before entering.

Hannah was writhing in the bed, still in her dress. The doctor kneeled over her on one side trying to get her to lie still so he could examine her, while a frantic Will stood on the other side. The express rider, Thomas Anderson, hung back near the door. Confused by his presence, she coaxed him from the room, thinking she would find out more later. Right now Hannah needed her.

"Can I help?" Julia asked.

"Miss Colter," Dr. Armstrong said, his relief obvious. "Would you be able to help Mrs. Colter into a nightdress? It would make the examination easier."

"It's too soon," Hannah cried, her fear evident. "I can't lose the baby. I can't!"

Julia nodded to the doctor and shooed him and Will from the room. She whispered words of comfort to Hannah between the pains as she slipped the loose nightdress over her head. Helping her lie back down, she paused and said a quick prayer.

"Lord, please help Hannah to calm down. Fill her with your peace. Let her know your hand is on this baby."

"Th-thank you." Hannah sniffed.

Julia let the doctor and Will back in the room. Will took a seat on the side of the bed, intertwining his fingers with his wife's. The tender action prompted a longing in Julia's heart. Would Adam react in such a way?

Dr. Armstrong instructed Hannah to take several deep breaths and release them slowly. She did as he asked. When he listened to the baby's heartbeat, he said it was strong and healthy. He asked Hannah to describe what happened when the pain started and she relayed the events that took place with Thomas's arrival.

Julia listened, shocked that the express rider was Hannah's brother-in-law. Strange that he ended up out here.

Finally, the pains lessened and subsided altogether. Hannah appeared to be calming down. The doctor explained that sometimes emotional stress could cause the onset of pains similar to labor.

Dr. Armstrong said, "I think that it would be best for you to remain in bed until the baby comes. I'm concerned that any undue exertion or emotion may cause the baby to come early."

Julia glanced over at Will. His gaze remained fixed on Hannah as he stroked her hair. Tears pooled in the corners of his eyes. She'd only seen him cry once before—the day he brought their father back to the ranch battered and dying after having been trampled in a stampede.

Wiping away her own tears, she said, "I'll stay, Hannah, and help you with whatever you need. Whether it's helping Rosa with cleaning and cooking or if you need me to sit with you. Whatever you need."

Hannah stretched out her hand towards Julia. Moving closer, she grasped the outstretched hand. "Thank you, dear sister. Thank you."

Julia squeezed her hand before Dr. Armstrong ushered everyone from the room insisting that Hannah needed her rest.

As soon as they were in the living room, Will headed directly for Thomas with fists clenched at his sides. "What are you still doing here?"

The young man lowered his head. "I wanted to make sure Hannah was alright."

She saw the twitch in her brother's jaw and knew there would be trouble if he did not get himself under control. Will took a step and pointed to the front door. "Get out!"

Thomas stood there for a second and Julia hoped he would heed Will's instructions. To her relief, the young man went to the door. Stopping in the doorway, he said, "Please tell her I'm sorry for everything." Then he shut the door. Hoof beats pounded up the lane confirming he was gone.

Julia took a deep breath trying to recover from the strange events that brought her back to the ranch. Looking around the room, her gaze connected with Adam's. His look was still intense and sent pleasant tingles up her arms. Fulfilling the promise she just made to Hannah was going to be harder than she thought.

Chapter 36

Two weeks into her bed rest, Hannah grew restless. She wanted to be up and around. Bored, she spent much time reading her Bible. The more she read through the gospels the more convicted she felt about her anger and bitterness towards Thomas. She knew that it truly was not his fault that Drew died. But, seeing him so unexpectedly brought those unresolved feelings to the forefront. When he asked for her forgiveness she contemplated giving him a piece of her mind. However, the labor pains stopped her short. Perhaps, God was granting her the time she needed to think. The Thomas who asked for her forgiveness was definitely a different man than the one they left behind in Ohio.

Sighing, she reached for the cowbell on the stand next to the bed. She smiled every time she rang it. Will said it was the only bell he could find at the mercantile. Giving the bell a good shake, she set it back down.

"How can I help you?" Julia said, peering in from the doorway to her room.

Patting the edge of the bed next to her, she motioned for Julia to sit. "I would like some company for a few minutes."

Crossing the room, her sister sat with one leg tucked underneath her, allowing Hannah to easily make eye contact.

"I've been thinking about what happened with Thomas. I know I haven't heard his full story, but I would like to talk to him."

"But, why would you want to do that? Hasn't he caused you enough pain?"

"I need to forgive him and to let go of the past."

A frown settled on Julia's face and her back stiffened. "Why do you need to forgive him? What does it benefit you?"

"These past weeks reading through the gospels have given me new insight into forgiveness. I know that I need to forgive Thomas— not because he asked it of me, and not because he deserves it—but because I need to forgive him and let go of the bitterness and anger I've carried with me. I need this even more than he does."

Julia crossed her arms, a flood of emotions crossing her face. Anger. Pain. Fear. Remorse. Hannah wondered if she might need to forgive someone too.

"Perhaps the time has come for you to forgive Reuben," she ventured.

Julia bolted upright and began pacing back and forth. "How could you suggest such a thing?" She turned wide fear-filled eyes towards Hannah.

"Because, I see the way you look at Adam and the way he looks at you. You both love each other, yet there is something holding you back. I don't know all the details of what happened the day you went riding with him, but I do know what I see now. I see a beautiful young woman, loved by God and by a wonderful young man. I see your bitterness and anger building a wall between you, God, and Adam. Don't you see, Julia, you need to forgive Reuben. Not because he deserves it, for he does not, but because you need to let it all go."

Foot tapping a rapid beat on the floor, Julia glared at her. "Is there anything else you need?" she asked between clenched teeth as she walked closer to the door.

"Yes, I have a favor to ask," Hannah said, deciding not to press the issue further. "I would like you to have Adam ride to town and ask Thomas to come visit me when he can. I want to hear what he has to say."

"Anything else?"

Hannah shook her head.

Julia was barely able to keep herself from slamming the bedroom door shut behind her. *Dear sweet Hannah has sharp teeth when she chooses to use them. How could she possibly suggest she forgive that vile Reuben? She knows what he did to me!* There was no forgiving such monstrous wrongs. Let him rot in hell.

Torn between taking a brisk walk to calm her nerves and

fulfilling Hannah's request to speak to Adam, Julia chose the former. She could not deal with talking to Adam while she was so angry. Stomping forcefully, she headed towards the lake.

Tears began rolling down her cheeks. Why did Hannah say those things? Why couldn't she just let Julia forget? She spent the last months leaning on God to take away the pain and give her strength to face her trials. Now, her sister was asking her to forgive her wretched brother.

Not Hannah. I am asking you to forgive.

But you ask too much! Lord, you know what Reuben did to me. How can you ask this of me?

Dropping to her knees on the shore of the lake, she rested her head in her hands. As much as she tried to run from forgiving Reuben, God seemed intent on hounding her about it.

Her tears rolled from her cheeks making ripples in the water below. Mesmerized, she watched the water. One little teardrop's splash sent the ripples dancing far out into the lake until the depth of the water swallowed them up. Placing her fingers in the lake, she watched as the next teardrop did not ripple as far when the waves crashed into her hand.

Sitting there for several minutes, Julia pondered the ripples. Was her bitterness and hatred towards Reuben like those ripples that crashed into her hand? Was she unable to see beyond the barrier caused by her lack of forgiveness? Is that why she was running from a possible future with Adam? What if she did forgive? Would she be like those far reaching ripples, swallowed up in the embrace of something larger than herself?

Lord, I am not strong enough to forgive such evil.

But, I am child. I am.

She held her breath. *Lord, help me forgive. Help me truly let this go. I don't want to carry it any more.* Sobs shook her body as she freely forgave Reuben.

As her crying subsided, she wiped her eyes on the sleeve of her dress. She splashed some of the cool lake water on her face, mimicking the renewing taking place in her heart. She slowly stood and lifted her arms over her head. Spinning in a circle, she let the last of the bitterness and anger float heavenward. Breathing deeply of the crisp clean air, she smiled. She was truly free.

Not wanting to leave the gentle Spirit of God, she walked the rest of the way around the lake, letting His peace settle around her healing heart.

By the time she finished the walk, she was ready to speak to Adam about Hannah's request. Cutting across the yard, she walked towards the corral with renewed purpose. She smiled at Adam when he looked up from the horse he was training. As she leaned against the rails, he removed the bridle from the young filly and let her skip around the ring.

"You look like a woman on a mission."

His teasing was refreshing. Since she came back to the ranch, all of their encounters were tense or awkward. This was the first glimpse of something normal between them and she cherished it.

"I am on a mission. For Hannah. She asked me to see if you could ride to town to fetch Thomas Anderson, the young man that works at the La Paz Express. She wants to hear his whole story. I think she realizes he may not be in town, so you may need to leave a message for when he returns."

"Does Will know she wants to speak with Mr. Anderson?"

"She didn't say and I didn't ask."

Adam rubbed his hand across his chin. "I best go put the filly away if I'm to make it back before dark then."

As he turned to call the horse to him, she started to speak, "Adam..."

When he glanced back over his shoulder, she changed her mind. She wanted to smooth things over, but the words would not come. Instead, she said, "Thank you."

Adam tried to calm the butterflies in his stomach as he led the filly back into the stables. When he saw Julia approaching the corral he had not expected her to stop, much less to talk to him. Things had been strange. He had been avoiding her as much as she was avoiding him, until she leaned up against the fence. Although her eyes were red-rimmed and puffy, when she smiled they lit up. Oh, how he missed seeing her really smile.

Then, she asked him to run this errand for Hannah. A scowl formed on his forehead as he saddled a horse. Any hopefulness he had vanished at the end of her request. Worse yet, Hannah was asking him to do something that would most likely upset Will. He did not really understand who this Thomas Anderson was or why he came here. Will said nothing about him. The only thing Adam was able to glean was that he was somehow related to Hannah or her first husband.

Mounting the horse, against his better judgment, Adam rode to town. Just under an hour later, he dismounted in front of the livery, having been in no particular hurry.

Peeking inside, he was greeted by Craig. "Adam, what brings you here today?"

"I was looking for Thomas Anderson."

"He's not due back for a few days. Can I give him a message?"

He thought carefully. It might appear unseemly if he mentioned Hannah was looking for him. "Please tell him the Colter's request his presence when he can make his way out there."

Craig looked confused, but did not ask any questions. "I'll pass along the message," he said as he jotted a note on his desk.

Adam nodded, walked out the door, and mounted his horse. He had no other business in town and did not wish to draw Will's attention by being gone too long.

His thoughts went back to the conversation with Julia. She looked different. Could it be possible she was changing? Might she be receptive to his attention?

He was twisted in knots—had been since she returned—over what, if anything, he should do to repair their broken relationship. He contemplated apologizing to her, but he was not sorry for kissing her. He was not sorry for courting her. The only thing he was sorry for was her refusal to give him a chance. And he could not apologize for her actions.

Lord, I know I have asked this a thousand times, so what is one more time? Please, find a way to bring Julia back to me. I need her.

Three days later, Thomas reined in his horse in front of the livery. Handing the lathered horse off to the livery owner, he retrieved his things and the mail bags.

As he turned to leave, Craig called after him. "Anderson! One of Colter's men came by and asked if you could head out to his ranch when you can."

Thomas nodded, acknowledging he heard the message. His heart sank to his stomach. Mr. Colter and he had not parted on the best of terms. Odd that he should ask him back to the ranch. The hidden message behind his final words left Thomas believing there would be no chance to reconcile with Hannah. In fact, he got the distinct impression that he might get himself shot if he showed up there again. No matter, he was too tired from the run to worry about it now.

The next morning, Thomas dressed in one of his nicer shirts and trousers. He rented a horse from the livery then set out down the road to Colter Ranch. Regardless of what Mr. Colter wanted to discuss with him, he hoped to get an opportunity to finish the conversation he started with Hannah. He needed to have some peace about Drew's death.

As he reined in the horse by the hitching post, Mr. Colter covered the distance from the barn quickly.

"What are you doing here?" he thundered.

Confused, Thomas started to respond but another man, one he recognized from when he was there last, said, "Hannah asked him to come back. She wants to speak with him."

Will pushed past Thomas into the house shouting over his shoulder, "Wait here!"

Thomas kicked at the dirt feeling uncertain about the whole situation.

"I don't think we met earlier," the other man said. "I'm Adam Larson, the horse trainer."

"Thomas Anderson, Drew's brother." At Adam's raised eyebrow, Thomas explained, "Hannah's first husband was my brother."

"Ah."

The silence stretched and Thomas could hear a muffled discussion inside the house. Looks like Craig misunderstood who it

320

was that wanted to speak with him. A few minutes later a rather cross looking Will emerged from the house.

"Hannah will see you now. But," he said stepping closer to Thomas, towering over him. "Do not do anything to upset her."

He nodded. Entering the house, he waited a second for his eyes to adjust. Julia motioned him forward to Hannah's bedroom.

"Thomas, welcome," Hannah smiled at him and pointed to the chair near the bed—a far different reaction than their last encounter.

"Hannah," he greeted hesitantly. As Julia closed the door all but a crack, Thomas sensed this would be a very private discussion.

"Forgive my husband. He is very protective and I confess, I didn't tell him I invited you here."

"He has every right to be protective."

Hannah waved her hand in the air dismissing the topic. "First, I want to tell you that I forgive you. I did several days ago. I no longer hold anything against you."

That was it? No further explanation needed? She just forgave him?

"However, I would like to hear what you came to tell me the other day. I just wanted you to know before the telling that there is no need to beg forgiveness, for it is given freely."

This was not the same docile domestic woman he remembered. Hannah had a strength and grace about her, which put him at ease. Taking a deep breath, Thomas plunged forward. "I came to apologize to you and Drew, only I'm too late. I know that my actions back in Ohio forever changed your lives—even took Drew's life." His voice broke.

He struggled to go on. "I'm not the same man I was then. I know what I did was wrong. Since then I have tried to live a good life, one that Drew would be proud of."

Hannah smiled. "Tell me how you ended up here, of all places."

Thomas recounted the story, starting with the trial in Ohio. He told her of the judge's strange sentence and his service in the Union, how he seemed to be in the right place at the right time. He told her how he tried to find her and Drew in La Paz. Then he told her the bizarre story of Betty Lancaster being the boardinghouse owner, probably one of the strangest parts of his tale yet.

"Betty and her son, Paul, told me they traveled with you. Said

Drew died in an avalanche, but you were safe. They told me you were here."

Pausing for a moment, he gathered his courage. "Hannah, I wish I could take back all that I did to cause you and Drew harm, but I can't." Tears trickled down his face. He ran the back of his hand over his eyes.

"Thomas," she said, reaching for his hand. He scooted closer so she could reach. "All these things happening in your life—it's astonishing. God has blessed you with great opportunities. He brought you here, so both you and I could have some peace about the past. I'm glad that you found me."

Thomas looked at her hand cupped over his. He still did not believe God would grace him with even the tiniest thought. But he was finding peace in just pouring out to his sister. Even though his brother was gone, Hannah would always be his sister.

"I wonder if I might ask you a favor."

The debt he owed her was so great. He would do anything for her. But the emotion choked the words from forming. He simply nodded instead.

"Would you be an uncle to my child? I know he or she will not be related to you by blood, but it would mean so much to me for you to be a part of my family."

Thomas barely got the words out in a whisper. "I would be honored."

Then they talked for hours, until it was supper time. Hannah told him about Drew on the trip west, how proud she was of him when he tried so hard to handle the team even though he did not know what he was doing. She told him of Drew's child that did not survive. She told him about how she met Will and how blessed she was to have loved two such wonderful men. Through the conversation, Thomas began to feel the heavy burden start to lift.

When Julia knocked on the door to invite him to join them for supper, Hannah said, "Thomas, Drew would have been very proud of the man you've become."

As he leaned over to kiss her cheek, he held back the rush of emotions. Thomas's only regret was that he would never be able to hear those words from Drew's lips.

Chapter 37

Colter Ranch

June 26, 1865

"Julia, wake up," Will's panicked voice pulled her from a sweet dream.

She sat up in her bed waiting for the fog to clear. Before she could ask Will what was wrong, she heard Hannah's screams from the next room. The baby was coming!

She dropped her feet to the floor trying to think. "Go fetch some water and start a fire in the stove," she told Will. Keeping him busy would hopefully get him to calm down.

Poking her head in to check on Hannah, she said, "I'll send someone for the doctor. Then I'll be right back."

Hannah panted. "We have some time yet."

While Hannah had coached Julia on what to expect, she was still nervous and would much rather have the doctor here to deliver the baby. After lighting a lamp in the kitchen, she ran across the yard to the bunkhouse barefoot. As she knocked on the door, she was suddenly aware she forgot to grab her robe. Even though it was dark out, the moon shone rather brightly.

The door opened before her and Adam stood there bare-chested. The sight caused her heart to leap and her memory to flee. What was she doing here again?

"Julia," he whispered. He partially closed the door and blocked any view with his body.

"The baby." She managed to gather her wits. "It's on the way. We need someone to ride for the doctor. And someone to get Lucy Morgan, just in case."

"I'll ride," Covington said from somewhere in the shadows.

Adam said, "I'll go get Mrs. Morgan. Everyone else, back to sleep."

He stood there for a few seconds longer, a strange smirk on his face. Then he closed the door.

Julia, now embarrassed, ran back to the ranch house. After a quick check on Hannah and Will, she ran to her room to dress. No need for further embarrassment once the doctor arrived. Securing her hair into a loose braid, she heard rapid hoof beats sounding up the lane. With the way Covington rode, he should get back with the doctor in an hour.

Gathering some rags set aside for this purpose, Julia checked to make sure everything was ready in the kitchen. Pouring some cool water into a pitcher, she went in to help Hannah. She soaked a small cloth in the cool water and began mopping her forehead. The night seemed rather hot, even for late June.

When Hannah cried out with the next pain, Will's face went white. Julia wondered if she should make him wait outside. Then again, he would probably put up too much of a fuss.

A half hour later, Adam showed Lucy into the room. Julia was thankful for the woman's experience. Then nearly another hour ticked by before the doctor arrived.

Julia took a quick break while Lucy helped Dr. Armstrong as he examined Hannah. Stepping outside for some fresh air, she nearly collided with Adam. Dark blue and purple tinged the sky signaling dawn was upon them.

"Everything, okay?" Adam asked, as he steadied her.

"Yes. From what Hannah told me, these things take time. I'm just glad she told me what to expect. Being the youngest, I've never been around the birthing of a baby."

"You'll do fine." Adam put his arm around her shoulders and rubbed his hand up and down her arm. The movement was soothing. "Besides, Hannah is the one that has to do all the work."

"I'm just not sure if Will is going to make it or not."

"I imagine it is difficult to watch someone you love go through so much pain," he said, placing a soft kiss on the top of her head. Then he released her. "Well, sun's coming up and the cows are going to start crying soon. Suppose I could help the antsy soon-to-be-father by seeing to his chores."

He flashed a grin before bounding across the yard towards the barn.

Julia sighed as she reflected on his words. Somehow she got the feeling he was not really talking about Will watching Hannah in pain. Seeing Rosa heading up the path from her shack, Julia turned and went back inside.

"Will." His sister's voice sounded far away. Somewhere in the background he thought he heard a baby crying.

"William!" Julia's voice was clearer this time. The hard pat to his face now had his attention.

Did I black out? He hoped not, but suspected that was the case, especially now that a baby's cry filled the room. Hopefully no one would mention this to his men.

Baby. He turned to look at Hannah. A tiny little bundle lay in her arms. His wife and child. Her eyes glistened with moisture.

"Will, come see your son," she whispered.

"Son?" he asked as he scooted onto the bed to get a closer look.

"Do you want to hold him?" She didn't wait for his answer before she placed his son in his arms.

Instantly his heart connected with the small child. "James William Colter," he whispered, marveling at how tiny he was. Pride welled within his chest. This was his son, James.

"After Father's middle name?" Julia asked from the corner.

Will nodded, too choked up to answer. He placed a big kiss on Hannah's lips.

"He's perfect," she said as the door clicked shut. Julia and the doctor were both gone from the room.

"He's so tiny."

"No he's not!" Hannah exclaimed. "He's actually rather large for a newborn."

"Must come from my side of the family."

"Yeah, I bet he's going to be as tall as you." She smiled up at him. "But, hopefully he won't swoon when his wife bears his first child."

Will gave her a sheepish look. "Let's not get him all married off already. I'm kinda looking forward to watching him grow."

As James started to squirm, Will handed him back to his mother. He did not think he could possibly love anyone more than he did his wife and his son.

Two weeks later, Julia just finished setting the table when their guests began arriving. Will and Hannah invited Betty, Paul, Thomas, the Morgan family, Dr. Armstrong, and Reverend and Mrs. Page for Sunday dinner. Of course, Julia was sure it had more to do with everyone wanting to meet baby James, but she was sure Hannah's secret was safe.

As the Morgan family entered the ranch house, James started to fuss.

"I'll take him," Julia said, knowing Hannah just fed him a little while ago. Sure enough, he needed a fresh diaper. She took him into Hannah's room and cleaned him up, dropping the dirty diaper in a pail to soak. Kissing him on top of his cute little forehead, she cradled him in her arms and returned to the gathering crowd.

When Adam entered the doorway, their eyes locked. My, he was looking fine today. An odd look passed over his face, one she had seen another time when she was holding James.

She smiled at him and he smiled back. She scolded herself for not making time before today to talk with him. Since James's birth, she intended to speak with Adam to apologize for her reaction on their first and only outing. If she was reading his looks correctly, he still very much loved her. She loved him and wanted to mend their relationship.

But, Hannah needed all the help she could get caring for James and keeping up with household chores. When either of them had a free moment, it was usually spent napping, since James kept them up frequently throughout the night.

"Let me see the little man!" Lucy Morgan exclaimed rushing to make silly noises to James.

Handing James over, Julia went to the door just as Betty, Paul, and Thomas pulled up. Thomas jumped down from the wagon and then helped Betty down as Paul climbed down the other side.

"Let me look at you, dear," Betty squealed in delight as she wrapped Julia in a hug. "You look lovely, dear. Tell me," she asked seeing Adam standing nearby, "are there wedding bells on the horizon?"

Leave it to Betty to be so direct.

"Ma," Paul chastised with one syllable before ushering her inside.

Thomas nodded a greeting as he carried in one of the crates from the back of the wagon. Julia and Adam started towards the wagon at the same time, bumping into each other.

"Sorry," Julia said, as heat rose to her cheeks.

Adam continued forward. One brow arched, he curiously looked at the remaining items in the wagon. "What do we have here?"

Julia leaned over the side. "Oh! Hannah will just love it!" she exclaimed, speaking of the little baby quilt. How did Betty find time to work on such a lovely piece while running the boardinghouse? She picked it up as Adam lifted the other crate. If they did not have a house full of guests, she would try to talk to him now. But, it would have to wait.

Adam carried the crate into the kitchen while she deposited the quilt on a stack of gifts by the fireplace. The rest of the guests arrived, so she helped Rosa set out the food. Setting the last item on the table, she took James from Hannah so she could enjoy the meal. Once grace was offered, Julia stood off to the side, bouncing baby James on her hip, cooing at him. When she looked up, she saw that strange look from Adam again.

The sight of Julia holding baby James stirred Adam. How he wished she was his wife and that was his child she was holding. Ever since the night James was born, he had longed to talk to her, to convince her to let him court her again. When she stood there that night, her brown curls loose and framing her face, he wanted to take her in his arms and never let go. The image played over and over in his mind.

"So when are you two going to start courting?" Hannah asked

looking directly at him.

Adam glanced at Julia as her face flushed. She met his gaze and smiled. Maybe it was time.

"I thought they already were," Thomas said, looking confused. Despite the strange circumstances that brought him into the family, Thomas seemed to belong there.

"What made you think that?" Rachel Page asked.

"I guess it's just the way they keep looking at each other."

"How do they keep looking at each other?" Jacob Morgan asked.

Little Sarah Morgan piped up, "Like they're in loooove." She emphasized the word by clasping her hands together and smiling sweetly while batting her eyes.

That brought a round of laughter from the entire table, except from Adam. When he looked over at Julia, she was not laughing either, though the look in her eyes told him they needed to talk.

"Here, Julia, let me see my grandson!" Betty exclaimed to another round of laughter.

"Ma," Paul said. "He is not your grandson."

Betty swatted at her son with her free hand as Julia took a seat across from Adam. "I can adopt whomever I want as a grandson. And since I adopted little James's parents, it's only fitting that I adopt him. Isn't that right?" Betty said nuzzling her nose against the baby's belly. He squealed in delight.

Ben sat next to Betty, one arm slung over the back of her chair. He leaned forward to tickle the baby's belly, sending more happy coos to fill the air.

The conversation continued around them, but all Adam could think of was finding a minute alone with Julia. Now that others brought up their obvious attraction, he wanted to talk to her.

When Julia finished her last bite of food, she asked, "Shall we see what lovely items everyone brought for James?"

"Can I hold my nephew?" Thomas asked tentatively.

Betty quickly handed the baby off. "Little one, you will

certainly not want for being loved."

Leading the way, Hannah took a seat by the fireplace and stack of gifts as the rest of the women followed. Most of the men hung back at the table, except for Will who stood behind his wife, placing a hand on her shoulder.

Julia smiled at the tenderness her brother showed his wife. He was so different from the young man who left Texas almost two years ago. Then again, Julia was equally changed. She was stronger, happier. She loved this family, whether they all were related by blood or not.

When the gifts were all opened and passed from giddy woman to giddy woman, Julia stood and began clearing the table, carrying several plates to the wash basin. Ladling some hot water from the reservoir into the basin, she shaved a few pieces of soap into the water and then let the dishes sit. When she turned around, there was Adam with another stack of dishes in his hands. She jumped, not having heard him.

"Oh, thank you," she stammered. When she reached out to take the dishes from him, her hand brushed his. Lightning shot through her arm and she almost dropped the stack. Thankfully she managed to get them in the dish pan without dropping any.

"Julia," Adam started. Taking her hands in his, he gazed into her eyes. "I—"

"Oh!" a startled Lucy Morgan exclaimed as she brought the remaining dishes to the wash basin.

Adam quickly dropped Julia's hands and walked out of the kitchen, following the men outside when someone suggested a game of horseshoes.

"Sorry, Julia." Lucy tried to apologize, but she waved it off.

Baby James started fussing, so Hannah excused herself to feed him at the table. Betty followed her and started washing the dishes, so Julia stayed to dry them. Soon the kitchen and dining area filled with the women, chatting away.

She did not pay much attention to the conversation as her thoughts were on Adam, wondering what he had been trying to tell her.

"Julia?" Hannah asked.

"What? I'm sorry, my mind was elsewhere."

"Did Adam ask you if he could court you? Was that what he was doing earlier?" Lucy Morgan asked.

Julia's face flushed. Obviously only Hannah and Betty knew the whole story, but Lucy and Rachel seemed particularly interested in her future.

"He was just helping me bring in the dishes."

Rachel spoke with a dreamy quality to her voice. "He is so perfect for you."

"If he knows what is good for him, that Adam will clear this up by the end of the day," Betty said. "And if he doesn't soon, he may have some competition."

Julia grew uncomfortable with all of the attention. When Hannah finished burping baby James, she reached out to take him.

"Let's go outside for some sunshine," she whispered to her sweet nephew.

She could still hear the conversation of the ladies as she sat on the porch in the rocking chair. Gently rocking back and forth, Julia hummed a lullaby.

Will sauntered over. Nodding at his son, he teased, "Now how is he supposed to learn the game if you lull him to sleep?"

"I thought you'd be thanking me, either that or finding a shady tree to catch a nap under."

Will chuckled. "Well, when our guests leave, I may do just that." He reached out his arms for his son.

Julia's heart melted every time she saw her big brother with his fragile little son in his arms.

"You know, Julia, despite all of the joking about you and Adam, don't you think you should give him a second chance?"

She sighed. "I've been meaning to talk to him for days now. I'm just not even sure how to begin the conversation. My unwillingness to forgive Reuben is what drove me from him. How do I explain that to him?"

Will smiled and shrugged his shoulders. "Just like you did to me?"

Leave it to Will to state the obvious, she thought with a half-smile on her lips.

"Why don't the two of you take a nice walk around the lake? No reason why you can't talk now."

She stood, taking his suggestion to heart.

"Julia," Will added with a wink, "just don't be gone too long. Some of us will want to have dessert soon."

She swatted at his arm before walking toward the horseshoe game.

When Adam saw Julia approaching, he bowed out of the game. Will already told him when he left to talk to her that he would try to convince her to take a walk around the lake with Adam. Apparently, Will had been successful. As he neared Julia he offered her his arm.

"Care for a stroll?"

Julia took his offered arm and nodded. He steered her towards the lake, away from prying eyes and ears.

As they arrived at the shore of the lake, she said, "I'm sorry I let my anger towards Reuben turn to bitterness and hurt you in the process. It was not until I could forgive him that I could really let myself love you."

He stopped and turned to look at her. His heart beat fast. He would take her hands, but he felt his palms getting sweaty. "What are you saying?"

"I love you, Adam Larson. I have for some time. When I... The day I ran away, I was not running from you—not really. I was running from myself. I was afraid to love you. I was afraid you would reject me because of what Reuben did to me, so I ran. But, you didn't reject me. You pursued me. You came to find me."

"How did you know?" he asked, surprised. He thought she had been sleeping.

"Betty told me you came looking for me. She said you looked wounded, defeated. For days I was angry with myself for hurting you so badly. But, I was still hurting myself so I didn't know what to do. Then, shortly before James was born, I came to realize that I needed to forgive Reuben in order to be truly free. And I had to forgive him several times before I was really sure I could move on."

Adam soaked up all that she said, but especially that she loved him.

Julia gazed into his eyes. She saw no judgment from Adam, but needed to hear his answer to her question, "Do you still want me, even though I'm not pure?"

His face blurred before her.

Please, Adam, I want you to still want me.

He drew her into a warm embrace. With his lips near her ear, he whispered, "You are pure, Julia. Our Lord has made you pure. That is not something that can ever be taken from you."

She sobbed, letting the truth settle into her heart. As her sobs subsided, he kept her firmly in the safety of his arms.

"And yes, I still want you. I want you to be my wife, to share my life. But, I also want you to have as much time as you need to be ready for our life together. So, right now, Julia Colter, I'm asking if you will allow me the honor of courting you, until such a time as you are ready to become my wife." With the last words, he pulled away.

She looked into those wonderful green eyes. So full of love—for her. "Yes, Adam Larson, I would be delighted for you to court me," she answered. "Until such a time as when you are ready to be my husband."

He leaned forward towards her and her breath caught. Just inches from her lips, he asked, "My dear sweet, Julia, might there be kissing involved in our courtship?" The roguish grin he gave her sent pleasant shivers through her body.

She closed the distance to press her lips against his, hoping that would be answer enough. Adam parted his lips and kissed her sweetly. When she put her arms around his neck, he stopped.

"Ah, Julia," he said, his voice husky. "I love you so."

"I love you, Adam."

Reaching behind his neck, he unclasped her hands. Holding out his arm, he said, "I think there is a house full of people who would like to hear our news."

Julia took his arm and followed where he led.

"And," Adam said smirking, "I think they are ready for some dessert."

Julia giggled as joy bubbled up within her. She was with the man she loved, finally free from her past, her heart renewed.

Author's Note

It is always a challenge when writing about a difficult subject like what Julia experienced. It breaks my heart to know that this sort of thing happens today—within the borders of the United States and around the world. I chose to write about this because I wanted to share the message that there is still hope after abuse. Jesus really does love you and his heart breaks when his children suffer.

In my dedication, I mentioned the women of Homes of Hope. This organization is dedicated to rescuing young women from the sex slave trade in Fiji. The stories of these rescued women are inspirational. Some of their stories are similar to Julia's. Some are far darker. Yet, these women are rescued—by people who care enough to help and by a Savior that sees them as precious beautiful pure women. My prayer is that organizations like Homes of Hope will grow and thrive in the coming years increasing their ability to rescue more girls around the world.

On another note, like in my previous book, there are several real historical details included. The Juniper House was a real hotel owned by George Barnard and is cited as being one of the first hotels in Prescott. George Barnard also became the postmaster general following the departure of Reverend Read.

Communication within the Arizona Territory and to points outside of the territory was sporadic, at best, for more than a decade after the territory was formed. Numerous express lines, pony express, and stages won contracts to carry the mail. Some, like Robertson & Parish, only lasted a few months. Others lasted several years. While the La Paz Express is fictional, it is loosely based on the La Paz Express & Saddle Train, among other several other express lines.

The governor's ball mentioned early in the book did occur on the date cited. Many area citizens were invited to attend the ball in the 2,000 square foot mansion which was four times larger than the average pioneer's home. The accounts of the first ball mentioned only a handful of women in attendance. Those that were there danced their feet off!

William Hardy was really involved in building a toll road from Hardyville (yes he owned a good bit of that town) to Prescott. While he initially acted as the manager, he eventually owned shares in the toll road company. His associates, Mr. Hobbs, Mr. Franklin, and Mr. Brighton are inventions of my imagination and represent the investors Hardy worked with to build the road. Hardy did end up building a store in Prescott as well.

While Thomas's character is purely fictional, the places he saw and battles he participated in while a part of the XVI Corps were true. For the Battle of Nashville, I found a few good eye witness accounts that described the slow start of the battle due to heavy fog. The colonels and major generals mentioned by name were real commanders that participated in the events as mentioned in the story.

Much of the information about dispatch riding came from a wonderful firsthand account I found from a young man who served as one in the Civil War. Many of the dispatchers really did bring their own horses with them. They also were often lackadaisical with using the appropriate passcodes and hand signals, according to the firsthand account.

I did take some liberty with the timing of when Thomas found out that the war was over. Most likely, the western territories would not have heard the news for several months. In fact, there were battles fought after Lee's surrender in April of 1865, most notably the battle of Mobile which happened in May, I think. Anyway, in order for Thomas to have time to search for Drew and then find Hannah prior to the baby's birth, I took the liberty of allowing the western territories to discover the news only weeks after the end of the war.

I hope you enjoyed Julia and Adam's story. Thomas's story does not end here. This is only the beginning.

No book would be possible without the effort and prayers of many individuals. I'd like to thank:

My editors – Arlene and De. Thanks for all of your help with rewording and editing.

My critique group – Fae, Karen, and Tami. Thanks for your encouragement and feedback.

My prayer group – Thank you for always lifting me and this book up in your prayers.

My husband, Jim, for always supporting my writing and listening to all of the highs and lows that come with it.

My Lord and Savior, Jesus Christ. I pray that this book honors you and helps others know you more.

Book Club Questions

1. How could Will and Hannah handled Julia's situation differently?

2. Like Julia and Hannah, do you have someone in your life that you need to forgive?

3. Thomas was confused by the strange events in his life. Has there been a time when you looked back on your life and could see certain things falling into place? How did that make you feel?

4. Have you experienced pain from lack of patience, like Adam did when he tried to rush things with Julia?

5. What was your favorite part of the novel?

KAREN BANEY, in addition to writing Christian historical and contemporary fiction novels, works as a Software Engineer. Spending over twenty years as an avid fan of the genre, Karen loves writing about territorial Arizona.

Her faith plays an important role both in her life and in her writing. She is active in various Bible studies throughout the year. Karen and her husband make their home in Gilbert, Arizona, with their two dogs. She also holds a Masters of Business Administration from Arizona State University.

To find out how Caroline Larson handles the separation from her brother and her best friend, look for Prescott Pioneers 3: *A Life Restored*.

Making mistakes is a part of life...

Social butterfly, Caroline Larson, longs for adventure. Since her best friend left Texas, she grows dissatisfied with her life. A little lie to her parents sends her on the journey of her life. Stranded in the Arizona desert, far from her final destination, she must rely on a stranger who gets under her skin.

Thomas Anderson has always struggled with making good decisions. A twist of fate, or Providence, leads him to Arizona to take a job as an express rider. Dealing with the ghosts of his past threatens to overshadow his future—until he meets a woman needing his help. Sparks fly as she grates on his nerves.

As they both struggle to move beyond their past mistakes, will they find their lives restored?

For more information about Karen Baney, the history behind the books, or other books written by her, please visit www.karenbaney.com.

Other books by Karen Baney:

Prescott Pioneers Series
A Dream Unfolding
A Heart Renewed
A Life Restored
A Hope Revealed

Contemporary Novels
Nickels